INCEPTIONS:

The Kate and Robert Chronicles

Inceptions:

The Kate and Robert Chronicles

Suzanne Eglington

Library of Congress Control Number: 2013905596

ISBN:	Hardcover	978-1-4836-1722-0
	Softcover	978-1-4836-1721-3
	Ebook	978-1-4836-1723-7

This is a work of fiction. Names, characters, places and incidents either are the product of the author's imagination or are used fictitiously, and any resemblance to any actual persons, living or dead, events, or locales is entirely coincidental.

Print information available on the last page.

Rev. date: 02/01/2016

To order additional copies of this book, contact:
Xlibris Corporation
1-888-795-4274
www.Xlibris.com
Orders@Xlibris.com
126230

Acknowledgments

First, I want to thank the police officers, firemen, soldiers, and guards who keep themselves in athletic shape to make a stand and command a presence. You are the guardians of our country, and your appearance carries great significance. Thank you.

My greatest appreciation goes to my friends who read my book page by page, unedited, and suffered through all my grammar mistakes before they were fixed. Their patience and overwhelmingly positive feedback on this story line meant the world to me to forge ahead. Thank you, Kim Buckler, Colleen Anderson, Kim Yablonski, Lisa Barry, Amy Bradbury, Melisha O'Quinn, Kristy Cool, and my one token male friend that made it through the book, Mr. Scott Beddia. You all rock! I can't thank you enough! I would also like to thank Xlibris publishing house, especially Christian Bailey and Herbert Perez. You guys are the best leading men holding my hand through this whole process.

I have to also acknowledge Fitness Concepts, the supreme exercise facility in Massachusetts. Anthony, Joyce, Joel, Marianne, Becky, Lauren, Diane, Katie, Alissa, Vicki, Kristen, Kim, Julie, Matt, and Kate—you all kick my butt and work me hard in every class, making me forget everything else that goes on in my life for the time I am with you. Thank you, thank you, thank you. You keep me sane!

And last, I would like to thank my family for eating suppers in a can and ordering out at times. You have been patient and supportive. I vow to make it up to you. I love you.

To all my future readers, I hope to give you a story you will fall in love with, which will give you the escape from reality you may need. Happy reading.

Chapter 1

I came to consciousness, my brain now registering that first, it was still dark out. That was a good sign. It meant I at least had time for a shower. Check that off the list of potential fuckups. Second, I was warm and covered. Bravely and slowly, I forced the heaviness from my lids and opened my eyes wider.

It was a miracle knowing I was in my own bed. I felt around under my covers and let out a cautious sigh. I was alone as well. Lifting ever so gingerly, I leaned over to my mini refrigerator and inhaled the cool air as I grabbed for a water bottle.

This cube has become my most cherished asset. Left over from my college days, Fridgie and I have had a fond relationship. She is cold, solid, supports all my valuables (clock, jewelry, gum, phone, keys), holds my bottles, and is always turned on. My kind of appliance.

I twisted the cap off to take a slow savoring sip then drew out a longer one. The slow ache of my head was apparent and making my consciousness fully aware of last night's shenanigans. I retrieved my cell phone. The time read 3:21, and I expelled another heavy sigh, checking to see that there were four text messages and two voice mails. The conflict started whirling around my misfiring brain. Sleep/respond? Sleep/respond?

I reached for the Advil and emptied half the water bottle down my throat. Gripping my cell, I hit the text icon. I responded to Pepper: "Made it home and I am alone, have a splitting headache, thanks for threatening to neuter him. Call you on my way to work :(." I hit SEND and dropped my phone back on the bed. Twisting my water cap back on, I flopped to my spot, which was still indented.

"Crap!" I reached for my phone alarm. *Why does two hours feel like ten minutes?* I picked up the cell just to double-check. Three additional voice messages. I dropped it back on the bed. Getting up, I swung my legs over and grabbed the bottle to drink the remainder of my water. I mentally ticked off the time for when I could take more Advil.

Rising to my feet, I stretched tall and snapped into work mode. Stepping over my outfit from last night, I headed to my closet. I gave myself a mental pat: there were two clean uniforms to choose from.

"I think today is a blue day." I reached up and pulled my blue nurse's uniform from the hangers and headed for the door. I stopped to faintly hear voices upstairs.

"Shit!" I backtracked to Fridgie and pulled out more water, chugged another half bottle, and headed to the stairs.

"Is that you, sweetheart?" my mother's singsong voice called out to me. *Aargh!*

"Hey, Mom."

"Had a late night, dear?"

"Uh-huh." I cringed.

"Come say good morning to your grandmother."

Oh shit, she is up too! I took the last step and walked across to the kitchen then put on my sweetest smile. "Morning, Grams. Morning, Mom."

Grandma looked sourly at me. "Don't you 'good-morning' me, young lady. I heard you come in after one o'clock, and on a Wednesday! What were you doing out until one o'clock!"

I sighed and I lied, "Working, Grams."

"Working? Is that what you call it? What respectable woman works those hours?"

I looked at Mom, who was trying to cover up a smile. "Grams, I'm a nurse, you know that."

"Oh, you think so?"

I have to say that line floors me every time she says it, and she does say it a lot. I shook my head and turned for the shower. "Last I checked, at least that's what my degree says."

"Kaaate." My mother's drawn-out breath was my warning.

"Showering now!" I sang back.

The heated spray was rejuvenating to my soul as I had a sudden premonition. Another thirty years and I'd be taking care of my mother in this house that I grew up in. I will be alone because I'm apparently too stuck up on my high horse to attract a decent man.

"Fuck you, Scott!" *Decent man? Hah! You mean working-class asshole.* "I should have stuck to my standards instead of wasting seven years on a stupid mechanic!" I rinsed out my hair and shut the water off.

"There! A little verbal sparring cleanses the conscience." I grabbed my towel and dried myself briskly. Now clean and feeling more awake, I slipped into my uniform then wrapped my wet hair up in the towel and opened the bathroom door.

My father was just walking toward me from their bedroom. He looked so handsome in his suit. He is the anchor of our family—the rock that is a constant support of love, good advice, and a touch of bone-chilling, utter fear.

During our teenage years, we were very unpopular here once they knew who Dad was. Stacey still has not forgiven him. She brought home Charlie Reed, her prom date, to meet them. Dad, being a top lawyer and ex-military man, sat him down on the couch. (I mean physically laid his hands on poor Charlie's shoulders and guided him to the couch and, without losing contact, sat across from him on the coffee table.) He looked straight into Charlie's eyes and said, "Anything you do to my daughter, I'm going to do to you." That got around the school quicker than wildfire, so the Quinn girls were off-limits.

No wonder I clung to the first guy to actively pursue me. *Again, fuck you, Scott!*

"Good morning, baby," Dad said as he kissed my forehead. He still called me baby even though I was twenty-six years old, two years out of college but still living on the ground floor of my parents' (huge) home.

I followed Dad into the kitchen, and as he greeted his mother good morning, he pulled Mom into an embrace, kissing her. I tried to ignore them and poured myself some coffee. Mom leaned out from around him. (Yuck! Thirty-three years and he is nuzzling her neck. At least we are at home.)

"Honey, will you be joining us for dinner tonight? We're eating at the club, give Olive a change of scenery."

Oh my god, he just slapped her ass! Mom swatted at his hand. *Lord, take me now!*

"I'm not going out tonight!" Grams barked her protests.

I interrupted so I could get the hell out of Dodge. "I was planning on going out with Pepper."

Mom smiled as Dad moved to pour his coffee. “She can come.”

“What time?”

“Seven.”

Grams pipes in, “I’m not eating at seven. I’ll miss my shows.”

“I will tape them for you, Olive. You won’t miss anything.”

Grams pressed her lips to a frown. “Oh, you think so?”

Ha! Take that, Mom! My smile betrayed me. “Yes, I think I will meet you for dinner. I’ll call Pepper. This could be fun.”

Dad gave me the look. I smiled sweetly, cupping my coffee as I headed for the stairs.

Grams picked up where she left off. No wonder Dad is a good lawyer. He learned to argue from the best. Too bad Mom was better.

I finished styling my hair only to pull it up in a ponytail. At least, I will be able to do something with it later.

I put on my minimal makeup and scooted back to my bedroom. Grabbing my phone off the bed, I kicked my pile of clothes to discover my purse buried under my discarded outfit. I dragged it out and fished for my keys.

Relief! I kissed them and turned with a snap to stride out the door. I pulled open my car door, mentally berating myself for how my car was parked. Maybe I shouldn’t have driven home. I pulled out my sunglasses and squinted at the beautiful morning. It’s a top-down day. I hit the button and flashed back to my graduation. My parents bought me a Mercedes convertible for my graduation (spoiled, spoiled me). Yeah!

I pulled out my CD case and fished for an oldie-but-goodie: Aerosmith. I popped it into the stereo and immediately started dancing in my seat. Oh! Almost forgot. “Fuck you, Scott!”

I looked behind me and backed up. OK, so I was too in the moment, stepping on the gas a little too hard as I peeled out. Oh man, I knew I’d hear about that later, but it felt so good! (Waa haa haa.)

“Steven, sing it to me, baby!” I lost myself in the song and forgot my troubles for another thirty seconds until I saw a drive-through up ahead. “Good, drive-through coffee.”

I pulled down on my turn signal and pulled up to the speaker. *Oh jeez, she is slow.* “Hello?” I was tapping on the steering wheel when a voice finally came over the speaker. Placing my order, I said, “Medium coffee, milk only.”

I ended up with a coffee regular. Maybe the universe was telling me I could be a little sweeter today? Damn you, karma! Again I peeled out and headed for my victim.

I arrived at work and Jess pulled the door open. "You know we worship the ground you walk on, right?"

I laugh.

"It's only a uniform thing." She gave a full-teeth, gleaming smile. "No, it's you!"

I grab my computer and my essentials bag from the back. "How was he last night?"

"Asking where his angel was? I'm so glad you're here. At least he will rest."

Jess put her arm around me as we walked the hall. "You think he is close?" She exhaled.

"Yeah, I called Maggie to get her ass up here just in case."

"When does she arrive?"

"This afternoon."

"Good! This will be good for Frank."

"Yup, and then the shit will hit the fan." I looked at her, but I knew that look all too well. The settling of the estate. I drew my lips in a grim line; but being my father's daughter, I play Switzerland.

"Good morning, Frank." I leaned over him and kissed his forehead. He had that faraway look. The look of death. "Please don't die on my shift," I muttered quietly and petted his cheek with my knuckles ever so softly.

Karen emerged from the bathroom. "Jesus, I'm so glad you're here. I thought he was a goner during the night. I will never accept this part of the job. Freaks me out all the time."

"I know how you feel."

"Well, I'm outta here. Good luck, Kate." Karen gathered her bag and computer as fast as she could and scrambled to the front door, shouting a good-bye to Jess.

I sat next to Frank and held his hand, rubbing the back of it tenderly with my thumb. I've had him for a client for the past four months and had gotten to know this wonderful man/father/husband. The stories he shared about his life were extraordinary, and I've come to love and respect this man. A tear escaped from the right corner of my eye, and I blinked rapidly to wipe it away with my left hand.

Jess entered the room with two coffee mugs, and I turned and smiled. One look at my face and the reality overcame her. She burst into tears as I shot up to take the cups from her hands.

"Oh no you don't," I chastised her. "I have to make it through the next eight hours, and I can't afford to break down right now. I have too much shit going on in my life that I refuse to deal with at the moment. So if I lose it here, right now, you're gonna be all alone for the rest of the day, and I don't think you are prepared for that!"

Jess wiped her tears away and grabbed a tissue to blow her nose. She let out a nervous laugh. "Back under control now, so did you break up with him?" She reached for the coffee in my left hand.

"Sort of."

She raised an eyebrow. "Sort of? How is it a sort of?"

I walked over to the desk and took my computer out and grabbed the logbook. "Well, this is part of the crap I'm not dealing with, I guess. We all went out last night, right? And I had this feeling for some time that Scott has been cheating on me. Remember I mentioned it last week?"

"I remember—and?"

"So Scott and Pepper hadn't shown up yet, and we were all drinking. Robert was paying extra attention to me, and I know he has liked me for some time."

"Is he the cop?"

"Yeah, he's good-lookin' and all, but I just . . . I don't know. He's Scott's friend. I never have looked at him in any other way."

"So what happened with Scott?"

"Well, like I said, Robert was acting like my date last night. He wouldn't leave my side until Pepper showed up."

"And?"

"Robert started telling me Scott wasn't worth it, that I could do much better. And then I asked right out if he knew that Scott was cheating on me."

"And?"

"He said it was not up to him to say."

"So he confirmed it?"

"Basically."

"Then what did you do?"

"Scott had picked up Pepper because he was fixing her car, and she came in before him. Like a whole ten minutes. I kept my cool, but then this blonde arrived shortly after, and Robert noticed her too. He shook his head and let out a sigh as she smiled at him. I glanced at Scott, who was taking a long drink from his beer. Then he walked over to me and put his arm around my waist."

I fired up my computer and looked over the logbook.

"So you knew right then, and the blonde was the one? What a set she must have to show up at a club, checking out the competition."

"Trust me, there is no competition," I added sourly. I walked over to the meds and started pulling out Frank's morning doses.

"Did you tell Pepper what was going on?"

"Been telling her the past few weeks, that's why she got her car in. Knows we won't have a mechanic in the family much longer." I let out a sarcastic laugh.

"I miss being young." Jess smiled.

I pushed the button on Frank's hospital bed and gave him his meds. He mumbled something and shakily held the cup. In a moment of awareness, he clasped my hand and gave a ghost of a smile. He looked tired—must have been up all night. I shook the nutritional drink and popped a straw in it. "Not last-meal worthy, is it?"

He smiled a little brighter.

"There's my angel." I caressed his cheek again and announced, "Maggie's coming today."

Jess whirled her finger in the air out of sarcasm. "It's about time."

He pushed the nasty drink away and closed his eyes. "That's enough, I'm tired."

"OK, Frank, just rest. I'm right here."

I picked up my coffee and took a long swallow. "Damn, I'm gonna miss your coffee, Jess."

"I'm going to miss your love life. Who else am I going to live through?"

"Your gorgeous husband."

"He's boring. If he wasn't so good in bed, he would not have survived this long."

I smiled. "Yup, poor baby."

Jess laughed. "Want some breakfast? I want to hear the rest of your story."

"I'm good, but go ahead. I have to log some stuff in."

Jess came back with two muffins.

"Are you trying to make me fat?" I cursed her.

She smirked. "Oh, that's right. You're back on the market again."

I grabbed the muffin before she could take it away. "So Scott had his arm around you, and his blonde was roaming the club?"

"I know. Dirtbag, right?"

"What did you do?"

"Two thoughts came real quick. Either I let him stay there and piss her off, or I save my dignity and tell him to fuck off and make her night."

"I know I'm going to love what is next."

I smiled. "As much as I wanted to piss her off, I just couldn't act like nothing was happening. Pepper was looking from me to him. Robert turned to the other guys and was giving me some privacy. So I turned in to Scott's arms and wrapped my arms around his neck for a seductive embrace. His breathing quickened as I ground my pelvis into his groin."

"I'm sure that threw him off the loop."

"Oh yeah. I could feel him against me, so I moved from side to side. And just as he moved his hands up my back, I leaned in and panted against his lips, making sure it was me he was thinking about. I opened my mouth, and he smiled, leaning in for a kiss when I so softly turned my cheek to whisper, 'Is that the blonde you are fucking over there?' It took a second for him to realize as he pulled back. Pepper answered for him. 'Yup, that's the one. Good going, Scott, at least she's not a total sled dog.' He looked at Pepper and dropped his arms to his side while not spilling his beer. I have to say I was a little happy about that because, most likely, it would have ended up on me."

Jess grinned. "Oh, this is good."

"So I took a step towards Pepper, and Robert turned around. That's when Pepper threatened to neuter him."

"What did yours truly have to say about that?"

"You mean dickhead? He was stunned momentarily then tried to deny it."

"You're kidding!"

"That's when he looked at Robert, and I have to give him credit because Robert just said, 'I didn't tell her, but I won't cover for you anymore.' The coward just turned and walked out."

"Really?"

"Yes, I switched over to whiskey then. Blondie raced out after him. I suppose he needed a ride home since he drove in with Pepper."

"Oh, that's right. He didn't have a car there."

"I couldn't help but feel really betrayed. I mean, why not just break up with me if you want to move on and then date all you want? But to sneak around and fuck someone while he's still having sex with me? Gross! Now whatever dirtbag she has been with is now my problem too.

I guess that's what really sucks. I grilled Robert as much as I could about this slut, but he didn't know too much about her."

"Another point for my man-toy husband. He always used a condom. As a matter of fact, right up until we decided to have the kids."

"Good advice. I'll remember that for the future. Scott is the only guy I have been with. I never thought about any dangers like that. But I guess I have to now."

"Did he try and contact you?"

"Yes. I have two voice messages from him and six from Robert."

"And?"

"I haven't listened to them yet."

"Ooh, this could be good!"

"I'm not ready. I read the text from Robert, and he wanted to make sure I got home safely. And another said if I need to talk, he is there for me—blah, blah, blah."

"Sounds like you have an admirer."

"I don't know. He is Scott's friend. I never saw him that way."

"Well, can you see him like that now?"

"Oh, don't get me wrong. He is tall, dark, and handsome and is in super shape. He's a cop."

"Well then, I'm sure he is very good with his nightstick."

I laughed. "You know, anyone listening to our conversation would have me fired. This is totally inappropriate for work."

"Well, it's a good thing you are in our private home. Now tell me about tall, dark, and handsome."

I laughed again. "I'm really going to miss you."

"Me too, now spill the beans. We don't have much time before the witch gets here, and this is going to have to carry me over the next few days."

"Let's see . . . what can I say about Robert?" I thought carefully and smiled. "He has that clean-cut look about him—you know, military. He is muscular, works out a lot. He has to be over six feet. He makes a presence when he walks in a room. He is nice, can hold a conversation easy enough. Only known him to bring a girl around once or twice a while back."

"Well, sounds like you have paid attention."

"I guess, but I just don't have 'that chemistry' with him."

"If he asks you out—and it sounds like he is going to—will you go?"

"I don't know, too soon to tell. I've just caught Scott cheating. I haven't properly ended our relationship yet. I'm not doing anything for a while. I need to let it all sink in and make sense of it all."

"Life is too short, sweetie. Strike while the iron is hot."

"Well, I'm certainly steaming." I smiled.

"Take an experienced woman's advice. If he asks, go. Put your lips all over him and see if you still feel the same way."

"You're shameless!"

"Never claimed anything otherwise."

I finished my muffin and took my last swig of cold coffee. My phone vibrated, and Jess smiled. "Is that the cop?"

"Yup."

"Answer it and tell him you would like to see what he is packin'."

I blushed and snorted as she encouraged me. Against my better judgment, I answered the phone. His voice was full of concern. "Kate . . ." he sighed.

"Hey, Robert, sorry, I didn't get back to you. I'm at work at the moment."

"I just want to make sure you are all right. I can't believe he had the whore come to the bar."

I pulled the phone from my ear and stared down at it. Whore. Did he just call her that?

"Now, now, Robert. I'm sure she has lovely qualities."

"No, she is a whore."

"I thought you didn't know much about her?"

"I found out more today."

"Oh, that's not good."

"She is known around the station by a few of the guys."

I let out a disappointing breath. "Great."

"Hey, I'm sorry I didn't say something sooner. I didn't know much about their relationship. She's just been hanging around the shop a bit. I thought it was just a flirting thing."

"It's OK. I don't hold you accountable."

"Have you talked to him yet?"

"No! And I really have nothing to say to the bastard!"

"He called me. He said things were going really smooth between you two. Doesn't understand why he did it. He says you're the girl. Wants to marry you."

"What the fuck! That is so not happening."

Robert exhaled. "I knew you were a smart girl."

Anger swept over me in a flash from that information, and revenge grabbed a hold of my wounded soul. I could not have predicted what came out of my mouth next. "So, Robert, are you doing anything tomorrow night?"

"I'm working a double tonight. I might be pretty wasted, but if you just want to hang out . . ."

"Sounds good to me. I'll get a movie, and we can just hang out together." There was a long pause. "Robert? You still there?"

"Kate, as much as I would love it, I just want to make sure you know that I won't be your revenge fuck."

I was stunned and a little mortified. "Because you have feelings for me?"

"Yes, because I have been waiting for that ass to screw up for years."

I smiled like a schoolgirl. "Well then, it's a good thing he finally got around to it."

"What are you doing tonight?"

"Having dinner with my folks and Pepper."

"Good, so you won't be alone."

"Nope. Hey, tell me. Why did you never hook up with Pepper?"

"Too strong a personality. Don't get me wrong, she is hot. I mean smoking hot. But then she opens her mouth, and that mind-to-mouth filter is just nonexistent. That, to me, is a turnoff."

"She does give her opinion freely." I laugh.

Pepper was raised—with her younger sister, Dallas—in the Deep South by very strong-willed, gun-toting, equal-rights, tell-them-that-you-mean-it, earthy-crunchy-type parents. They would shoot first and then ask questions while they bury you in that biodegradable gauze, lay a bunch of fish over you, then plant the veggie crop on top.

"Where are you going to dinner?"

Jess peeked back in with her two thumbs up. I looked at Frank, who was still sleeping. "Oh, the country club."

"Are you meeting Pepper?"

"Not sure yet, why?"

"Well, I can meet you for a coffee if you drive her home."

Hadn't thought about that possibility. "That might be a tempting offer, Officer Beckham."

I could hear his smile. "Text me when you know."

"I will."

Another long pause. I wanted to snicker. He drew in a breath.

"All right, look forward to hearing from you. Bye, Kate."

"See you soon, Robert."

"A man can hope."

"Bye, Robert," I said and hung up.

All I could do was stare at the phone for a minute. Jess came barreling back in. "I heard every word. So are you going to see him tonight?"

"Yes. You are definitely shameless!"

"And? Don't keep me waiting. The suspense is killing me!"

"Yes. I will meet him for coffee and take a really good look at him. I think he has a crush on me."

"Duh? Who wouldn't? You're beautiful, Kate."

"I don't know how I didn't notice him before."

"Oh, that's easy. It's called *integrity*! Yup, you're cursed with good morals and manners."

"Damn those sticking qualities!"

"Sounds as if the cop shares those too."

"He was on to my intentions. What the hell made me sound desperate?"

"Something he said in the beginning?"

"Oh yeah, Scott has apparently realized that I am the girl of his dreams and wants me back."

"Oh, those voice messages should be interesting."

I smiled up at her. "Shall we listen?"

Jess waved me out to the kitchen. "Just in case I scream. Don't want to startle Daddy. I need you back for a few more days."

"Shameless."

I checked on Frank before leaving the room. I straightened his pillow and pulled his blanket up higher.

I walked over to the kitchen table and placed my phone down on it and called my voice-message center. I punched in my code and put the speaker on.

First one was from Robert. He sounded very concerned if I made it home. I hit DELETE. Next one was again from Robert, telling me if I did not ring him back, that he was going to drive by to make sure my car was in the driveway. I smiled as Jess said "potential stalker." I deleted that one.

Next message. Again it was Robert, confirming that my car was in the driveway; and if I needed to talk or a shoulder to cry on, that he was there for me. I was now wearing a stupid grin on my face. This message I saved.

Next message: dickhead! "Kate, I'm so sorry. I really don't know what to say to you, but I know if I just keep talking, it will all get out and you might just understand. Please call me back, let me explain. I love you, honey, please call me." I hit DELETE.

Jess did not speak, and I could not lift my head to look at her. *Do not cry! Do not cry!* I said over and over in my head.

Next message: Robert. "Hey, Kate, I know you are working tomorrow, but maybe we can meet for some coffee later. I am on a double, but if you're in town, I can meet you somewhere. Hang in there, kid, he's not the only fish in the sea." I hit SAVE for that one too.

Next message: dickhead. "Katie, please talk to me. I know I really fucked this up. But you see, I have been thinking about us a lot lately, and I went ring-shopping a few weeks ago. I was getting up the nerve to pop the question when the guys started ragging on me and telling me that my life was going to be over and then you would stop having sex with me—not that there has been much of that lately. But it got me thinking and scared. Then this girl came into the shop and came on to me. I have to tell you it just . . . it got me thinking, and then I really fucked up. I liked the attention. It made me feel good. But when I saw you last night and you were rubbing up against me, I felt ashamed, and I realized that it is you. You are the girl for me. Please let me prove to you that you are my life. You are who I want to be with. Please, Kate, I am so, so sorry. Just give me a chance. I love you, Katie. It's all up to you, sweetheart. I don't want to lose you."

There goes the waterworks. Tears streamed down my face. I was mortified. I hit DELETE and got out of the voice message.

How could I look up to Jess's face? I know I was blushing; tear puddles started accumulating on the table. And how the fuck was I going to get out of this? I could hear Jess's chair move, could hear her walk across the kitchen, could hear her place the tissue box on the table, could hear her blow her nose.

She leaned down and put her arm over my shoulder. "I'm crying too, but if you go back to that two-timing piece of shit, you will get what is coming to you, and that will be years of disappointment. He will do it again. That I am sure of. Now I'm going upstairs so you can pull yourself together. Thank you for sharing that with me. I may just give it up for my gorgeous husband simply because he is a good man."

She walked out just as promised, and I grabbed a handful of tissues and began wiping up my mess. I blew my nose and wiped my eye, then my phone vibrated.

Pepper. I answered in a feeble voice.

"Oh, for Christ sakes! Are you crying? Tell me you stubbed your toe or something that physically does hurt and it's not emotions for that loser! He is a fucking idiot! How long have you been questioning where this has been going? It was simply convenient. You're too goddamn lazy to date anyone with quality. I'm so happy he finally fucked up. Don't you dare shed another tear over him! Hell, I want to go shake his hand. The fucker finally did something right. He lost the best thing that could have ever happened to him. And I do mean lost as an underlying threat. If you think of going back to him, I will physically hurt you, understand?"

I laughed. "I'm thinking of having sex with Robert tomorrow night."

Then there was silence.

"Oh, I'm sorry. Can you put Kate back on the phone?"

I laughed again. "It's me."

"You didn't kill yourself last night and come back as a creature from beyond, did you? I mean, this is my Kate, right?"

"Yes, your Kate who is in desperate need of being bad."

"Well, that's the spirit. Can I watch just to make sure you do it right?"

"No!"

"Can I peek through the window and just get a frontal of Robert? I always wondered how big a club he was carrying."

"Jeez! What is it with the cop innuendos?"

"He is fine on the eyes, girlie. How did this come about? I mean, I know he had a thing for you."

"What thing? He had a thing about me?"

"Kate, it doesn't take a rocket scientist to know that. Why do you think he hasn't really dated over the past two years?"

"I don't know, I haven't thought about it."

"Well then, I will tell you. It's because you came back to town. You graduating and moving back home gave him hope."

"No."

"Yes"

"No way."

"Yes way. So he's going to be your mercy fuck, huh? I'm sure he's offering himself for the sacrifice as we speak."

"Well, he actually told me I can't do that to him."

"What?"

"Talked to him a little while ago and told me—in not so many words—that he's gonna be around for a while. If I have sex with him, he does not want a 'wham-bam thank-you' quickie."

"Great. From the pot into the frying pan. At least this one has a hotter job, and he owns his house. Super fine to look at too. I sooo will not let up on demanding every detail. God, I bet he is sexy hot in bed. He dances really well, so that has to be a prelude to the bedroom. I dance amazing, and I'm really good in the sack."

"Too much information, buddy. Anyways, before we go too much in the gutter, wanna grab dinner with my family at the club tonight?"

"Stacey going to be there?"

"I don't think so, but I'm not sure. Why does it matter?"

"I like your sister, but I don't think I can shut my mouth if she says something tacky about you right now."

"I never realized you actually have that ability. To shut your mouth?"

"Now, now, now, little friend, don't make me prove it can't be done."

"Only kidding, cookie. No, I don't think I could take it either, and she would say something shitty just because."

"Want me to meet you?"

"How about I pick you up? Will you be done by five thirty?"

"Should be. I will bring extra clothes with me. I can change in the bathroom."

"You'll be in the gym, right?"

"Yup."

"Bye, Pepper, and thank you."

"See you in a bit, buddy."

I pressed END and suddenly realized I was still at work. Shit! I jumped up and ran into Frank's room. Still breathing and still sleeping. "Oh, thank God." I kissed his forehead. I was dealing with my fucked-up relationships in front of a man who was departing this world much too soon for my liking.

Jess came down about an hour later. "The witch should be here in an hour," she announced as I smiled at her. "You, though your morning was bad—just wait till you see what I have to endure the next few days." She smiled, making sure I was better.

"It's all good, don't worry about me. I'm meeting Robert tonight, and then we will see what happens."

"Make it good. I need you, kid." She kissed her dad as she caressed his face. "Maggie's coming, Daddy."

He opened his eyes and smiled. "OK."

She turned and made a sour face at me. "God give me strength." Then she left.

Four hours and counting. I gave Frank a sponge bath and shaved him as he was in and out of sleep. We changed his clothes. At least he would be fresh and clean for his other daughter. After lunch, he took another nap. He hadn't been asleep for more than fifteen minutes and the tornado arrived. Maggie Fuller entered the house.

"Where is he? Where's my daddy!"

"Oh please," Jess commented.

"Don't keep me away one spare moment from him."

"Fuck off, Maggie. He's in the spare bedroom. I suppose the past two weeks were too taxing for you to spend with him?"

"How dare you make such an accusation? I didn't know he was on his deathbed."

"Yes, you did."

"I must go and see him."

Jess led the way. As they entered, Maggie screamed, "He's dead already, isn't he?" She began crying.

"Oh, for fuck's sakes! He's sleeping, asshole."

"Don't you talk to me like that!"

"I'll talk to you anyway I like, jerk!"

"And in front of his staff. You stop it right now." Maggie turned to me and started apologizing for her sister's rude and inappropriate behavior.

I got up to check on Frank. I turned to her and calmly asked her not to scream again and that her dad would love it if she sat next to him and held his hand.

She look a little appalled and then collected herself and asked if I could pull over a chair.

"Of course." I put it next to his bed, and she proceeded to dust off his hand with her handkerchief and was examining how to grip it.

My eyebrows shot up as I turned to Jess and mouthed "What the fuck?"

"Oh, sweetie, now you see why I want to escape to your world."

Maggie cleared her throat. "Um, so what, I won't catch anything, right?"

"Unless old age is a disease," Jess shot back.

She opted to just lean in and talk to him. "Daddy, I'm here. It's me, Maggie."

He opened his eye. "Maggie, my little girl, is it you? Are you here?"

"Yes, Daddy, I'm here."

"Good, good girl. Now I want you to listen to your old daddy."

"Yes, Daddy, I'm listening."

"I need you to promise me something."

"Oh, Daddy, anything. You're breaking my heart. What is it that you want?"

Jess muttered over to me, "Drama queen." I fought a smile.

"Now swear to it. I want you to respect a dying man's last wish."

"What is it, Daddy? I'll do anything for you."

"I signed over the house to your sister—and only to your sister. I want her and her family to have it. They have taken care of me for many years, and this is their payment for their good deed."

"But . . . but . . . but—"

"I don't want to hear none of it, child. Jessica did right by me while you were too busy doing whatever it is you do. You married well and have enough to keep you happy."

"But, Daddy, this is my home too."

"Not for the past twenty years it hasn't been. I've gotten nice letters from you telling me what you have been doing, all the pretty places you visited. But if you plan on fighting your sister, you will get nothing."

"Daddy!"

"Don't 'Daddy' me, Maggie. In five years, if you behave, you will inherit about twenty-five thousand dollars coming to you. It will be well past the time you can fight my decision. But if you do, Jess has permission to start with that money to fight you. Do you understand, child?"

"Oh, Daddy, you are not in your right mind. You don't know what you are saying."

"Child, I know exactly what I am saying. And so does my nurse, Kate, and Jess, who is listening to every word I say."

Oh crap, I am being set up. Naughty, naughty Frank. Men! Maggie shot me a look that could kill.

"I believe Frank to be of sound mind," I said. "He's dying, but not on any medication that would alter his decision making."

Jess smiled at Maggie. "Oh, and, little sister, if you have any questions on what Daddy has said, I have it all right here on video." She held up her smartphone.

Maggie looked into her father's eyes. "Of course, Daddy, anything for your dying wish."

I could hear the undertone of *Die now, mister.*

"Excuse me, Daddy, I have to freshen up."

"Of course, baby. I don't plan on going anywhere today."

Jess leaned down and muttered in my ear, "And the blows just keep coming."

I coughed to cover up a laugh.

Maggie excused herself and told Jess she would be back this evening. She had to check in to her hotel and rest from her long journey. Turned out to be a whole three-hour plane ride that was probably first class.

My breakup was officially dust mites compared to Hurricane Maggie. I went to Frank. "Can I make you something to eat?"

He reached for my hand and took it. "Scrambled eggs?" he said with a smile.

Jess took over. "Coming right up, sir."

He held my hand for a few minutes more. I sat him up in his bed and adjusted his pillows.

"Kate, getting old is overrated."

"Oh, I don't know, sir. It's better than the alternative."

He laughed. Good. That was my intention.

I checked my phone: an hour and a half to go. I could see the light. Frank ate better than I expected. He may have a few days left after all. *Keep it up there, buddy,* I mentally cheered him on.

I was finishing up my day in the logbook, registering everything that happened in case Jess needed it in court.

After shutting my computer off, I sat on the edge of the bed, stroking Frank's hand. He smiled with his eyes closed.

Beth arrived twenty minutes early. "Hi, good-looking," she announced as she entered the room.

Frank smiled again, opening his eyes. "My next date is here."

"Yup, but I don't have to go right away. She's early."

"Two beautiful women at once. I don't know if my heart could take it."

"Flirt!" Jess called from the kitchen.

Beth and I smiled at the same time. She said, "Honey, I've got this, you can go. Kids are at my mother's, and I was actually bored. Can you believe it? I couldn't wait to get to Frank. I'm lonely."

I laughed. "You just forgot how to have fun."

Jess gave an "Amen" from the kitchen.

"I know. I am pathetic."

Just then, John came through the door.

Beth smiled. "Yeah, eye candy."

I chastised her with a glare. "You are so bad."

"Yes, bad. I admit it. I wish Eric looked that good."

"Looks aren't everything."

"OK, we will have this conversation again in twenty years, and you can give me your opinion then."

"I give up."

"Yes, that's what I thought."

John went straight to his wife. He leaned into her for a soft kiss but got back a full-on attack. His day was getting better and better. Jess took his hand and dragged him toward the stairs as she shouted good-bye to me.

My day was looking up as well. I was leaving early, and what better way to dump the blues than to hit the mall. New clothes were in order. I kept thinking good thoughts about Robert. I texted him and confirmed that I would meet him after our dinner. He responded right away that he was looking forward to it.

Out with the old, in with the new. Wow, even the dress selection seemed better. I ended up with two. I couldn't decide. Next were the shoes. Holy shit, the shoes were super cute as well! I bought three pairs of them. New panties also, wow! What have I been missing? New bras and a couple pairs of sportswear. Hell, I was going to be looking good. Really good! How was he going to be able to say no to me now? I almost felt bad for the guy. Almost.

I was grinning like an idiot when I pulled into my driveway.

I was struggling to open the front door when my mom called down to me. "Kate, is that you?"

"Yes, Mom."

"Come up here a minute."

"Be right up. I just got a couple of new outfits I gotta put away."

"OK, dear."

I changed into comfortable sweats as I gazed at my new collection. "Score!" I pumped my fist. Then I headed for the stairs.

As I reached the top step, I froze in my tracks. The smell hit me first, followed by only a nanosecond of the sea of red. "What the fuck!" was all I could manage. The house was filled with dozens of red roses.

"You were lucky you did some shopping after work. Scott was here, hoping to catch you."

Again, as I gazed around, there must have been twenty dozen roses. *What the fuck!*

"He told me everything. I think. Two sides to every story anyways. Want to clue your old mom in before I feel sorry for the bastard?"

"Mom . . ." I just stared, stunned. I started to gain my train of thought again. "He cheated on me. His excuse was he was thinking of asking me to marry him, and his buddies were giving him the old ball-and-chain speech, telling him he was whipped and stuff. So he did something stupid and fucked someone else."

"Well now, dear, don't sugarcoat it on my behalf. After all, I am your mother, and you can give it to me straight."

"Sorry, Mom. I didn't mean to blurt it out like that."

"Well, his version was less graphic but had the same meaning. So what are you going to do now?"

"I'm going to take two dozen of these flowers and put them in Grams's room."

"Already beat you to it."

"Oh crap! How many are there?"

"Twenty-six dozens, dear. I must say, I'm glad you are not a year older."

"What the . . ." I was stunned. "Who delivered them?"

"The florist down on Main Street. Here's a card." She handed me a card, and I opened it.

It read: "Kate, I am so sorry. Please forgive me, honey. Hugs and kisses, Scott."

Yuck!

I dialed the florist's phone number. "Um? Hi, this is Kate Quinn. Your delivery man just delivered a whole bunch of roses here."

"Oh yes, Kate Quinn, you are a very lucky lady. You're all we have been talking about this afternoon."

I cringed.

"Well, Mr. Lawton is very smitten with you. You're a very lucky lady."

"He cheated on me."

There was silence on the other end.

"Hello? Are you still there?"

"I'm very sorry, miss."

"Don't be. Anyways, could you guys come back here and pick these back up for me? All but two dozen. I gave those to my grandmother."

"Oh . . . ah . . . sure."

"I'll pay you, of course, but can you deliver them to the maternity ward at the hospital on Chase? I'll call ahead so they can expect them."

"Of course, Ms. Quinn, and we would be happy to do that. No charge."

"Well, thank you. That's very kind of you."

"I will send the driver out immediately."

"OK, thanks again." And I hung up.

I called the hospital next. My mother had the phone number ready and waiting. They sounded delighted and thanked me several times before I hung up.

"Now what?" my mother asked, looking for an opportunity to give me advice.

"So after dinner, I am meeting Robert for a sort of pre-date."

"The police officer?"

"Yes."

"Well, looks like you have everything under control."

"A little bit of shopping therapy does wonders."

"How much did you spend?"

"About four hundred dollars."

Mom turned on her heels and told me to wait right there. When she came back, she handed me the four hundred dollars. "That's for not marrying the mechanic. Thank you."

I doubled over, laughing. Hysterical tears, can't-catch-your-breath laughing.

When I got a hold of myself again, she still had the money held in my direction. "Am I going to have to give you the Heimlich maneuver?"

"No, that was just so unexpected." I took the money from her.

"Look real cute tonight. He is a catch. I know he has liked you for some time too."

"How does everyone know that but me?"

"You're young and naïve."

"Gee, thanks."

"It's a very good quality, Katherine. Don't lose it too quickly."

The florist came and took all the flowers away. I gave the driver a forty-dollar tip that he accepted with a smile. Then I got myself ready for my evening. I went with my plaid schoolgirl skirt and a plain white collared top with white lacey wedges. All I needed were pigtails, and I would be the cause of men excusing themselves to the bathroom.

Yeah, not a look I was quite going for, so I settled for the sophisticated updo. I pulled a couple of tendrils out on either side by my temples. Yes, this is sexy sophisticated.

I went up for my mother's approval. She smiled, and I kissed her cheek. "I'm going to pick up Pepper. I'll see you guys at the restaurant." Then off I went.

My cell phone rang. Scott. I let it go to voice mail. I'll have to text him later so he will stop calling.

I pulled into the school and headed for the gym. Pepper was screaming at the exhausted dance team. "Now why is it that I seem to be the only one who wants to show up here and work! You girls have signed up for this. You told me you want this, but here you are, pretending. I don't think you want this. I think you are just trying to learn some new moves for out at the clubs. Thus wasting my time and the few girls who actually showed up here wanting to compete. You have five minutes to figure out if I am coming back tomorrow. Now talk amongst yourselves and come back either ready to dance or hit the road!"

Pepper walked over to me. "Oh, you are so not playing fair."

"Whatever do you mean?"

"You're seeing him tonight, right?"

"After I drop you off."

"Jesus, he's gonna come in his pants."

"Shhh . . . stop that."

"Hell, I want you."

"That just might be a possibility."

We giggled.

"I just want them to go through the number two more times. Hopefully, they will get it right once."

"That's if any of them stay."

"Oh, they will stay. They want the glory, they just don't want to put in the work. Fifteen minutes."

She smiled at me, and I took a seat on the bleachers.

"OK, ladies, everyone who wants this, it's time to show me. Line up! And five, six, seven, eight!"

Chapter 2

We pulled into the country club, and it was packed—it being a typical Thursday night. The jumpstart to a much-needed weekend. Pepper sported a sapphire-blue short-sleeved silk shirt with black dress pants that made her dancer's butt look amazing. I caught several men enjoying the view.

We were half an hour early, and that meant Mom, Dad, and Grams were in the bar for at least twenty minutes.

Pepper smiled. "Righto, ole gal." She took my hand and dragged me in the direction of my parents.

"There you two are." Mom greeted Pepper with a genuine kiss on her cheek and embraced her. Next was my turn. "Wine, darlings?"

"Yes, thank you, Helen," Pepper answered and then turned her attention to Grams. "So, Grams, are they keeping you from your shows?"

Grams scowled and then smiled. "Yes, I'm here against my will."

"Pepper Harris! Don't you wind her up."

Pepper laughed and took the wineglass my mother handed her. Pepper put her hand on Grams's shoulder. "What's going on in the land of game shows, Grams?"

That opened her up. She explained about the different hosts and how they did, what they looked like, and how smart she thought they were. Fifteen minutes of nothing and Pepper was glued to every opinion Grams had. It was actually cute to watch.

Dad made his way over with an admirer in tow. "You made it. Girls, this is Mark Dow." He turned to Mark and started introducing him to Grams, Mom, Pepper, and myself.

Mark had trouble letting go of Pepper's hand. I smiled.

Dad continued his presentation of how Mark was showing great talent in the courtroom, and he was expecting a successful career for his future. He must have heard about the breakup.

Mark clearly had his sights on Pepper. She took over interrogating him when Dad was finished with his introduction. He smiled, showing a cute set of dimples.

Pepper was a goner. That's all it took. She blushed and took a quick sip of her wine. Speechless? Wow! I jumped into the questioning while Little Miss Infatuated regained control. She squared her shoulders and was back in the game.

Mark handled us with everything my father promised, and he took his eyes off Pepper only when spoken to by another member of our party. Had she met her match—a man that may actually be a worthy player? Oh, the possibilities. I realized I must have had a stupid grin on my face and took a large gulp from my wine. I received a disapproving look from Mom.

"Sorry," I mouthed to her. She shook her head but continued to show interest in Pepper and Mark.

When our table was ready, Mother asked Mark if he would like to join us. He accepted immediately, making Pepper grin. She corrected our seating arrangement with the waiter as they asked us to wait a moment longer. Then we were finally escorted into the dining room.

The lighting was low, and it had a nice feel to it with all the candles burning on the tables. We had a beautiful view of the sunset, and I took the seat next to Grams, allowing Pepper to sit next to Mark. She shot me a look that she knew what I was up to. My phone vibrated, so I took a quick peek.

Text from Robert: "I'm on the west side tonight, so I won't be far from Pepper's. Let me know when you leave the club."

I texted him back: "Just sitting down to dinner. I think Pepper may have a date. Call you when we are done."

"Kate, is everything all right?" My mother hated cell phones. (Unless she was on one.)

"Fine, Mom. Just work."

Nope, she did not buy it. I stuffed it back in my purse.

My parents and the happy new couple monopolized the evening's conversation. Grams and I followed along. Except I think Grams snuck a nap before dessert. I must learn that trick! I opted for another glass of wine instead of the final coffee. My stomach was starting to get butterflies. It was almost half past eight, and Granny was getting restless.

"Well, we had a lovely evening. Thank you all for sharing it with us, Mark. It was a pleasure to meet you." My mother extended her hand. "Pepper, it's always a pleasure to spend time with you. Make sure you bring Dallas by when she arrives."

"I sure will, Helen. She really enjoys your company."

My mother flashed her movie-star smile. Points for Pepper!

"Don't be too late, love." She leaned in and kissed me.

"I won't. I have an interesting day tomorrow."

"More so than today?"

"Oh yes."

She winked at me and took Grams's wheelchair.

Dad was behind her in a flash. He leaned in and kissed my cheek. "Be safe."

He scooted my mother's butt to the side of the wheelchair. *Uugh!* Pepper caught that too and wiggled her eyebrows.

Picking up my glass, I finished my wine. As the three of us were left at the table, Mark took control. "So how did you ladies arrive?"

I grinned. "I drove us."

He bashfully smiled.

I searched Pepper's face for a signal, and she gave it to me. The hussy! "I do have a long day tomorrow, and Pepper lives on the west side—"

He cut me off. "I live in the city. I could drive you home. If you would like?"

She looked to me then to him. "Are you sure it's no problem?"

"My pleasure, really."

"Well, all right then. Now you're sure you're sure?"

"Very." His smile was genuine.

We all stood together, and he pulled her chair away, offering his arm as she stepped away from the table. Very gentlemanly. Nice touch, I thought.

She grinned and rested her hand on his arm. He didn't drop it when she was safely away. She kept the contact as well.

"Well, I'll be damned," I muttered as she gave me the fastest covert kick to the ankle.

"Ouch!"

"Are you all right, Kate?" Mark asked.

Pepper answered for me, "She's fine."

We arrived at the parking lot, and Mark gave the valet his ticket and turned to me. "Do you have your ticket, Kate?"

"Ah, no. I just parked in the lot over there." I pointed to my right. You could hear the engine approach, and a sleek black convertible stopped in front of him.

"Wow!" was all I could come up with. I saw Pepper was doing cartwheels in her mind.

"Let me just get Pepper settled, and I will walk you to your car."

"What kind of car is this?" I asked, knowing before Pepper probably already knew. She loved flashy cars.

She smiled and silently mimicked Marks words, "Jaguar XK."

"I wouldn't leave the keys with her alone in there."

He chuckled and turned to her. "Well, it's a good thing you met me before I introduced you to my car." He opened the door for Pepper.

"Don't mind her. I'm leaving with the hot guy in the hot car. She's just cranky. Night, sweets, talk to you later." She blew me a kiss, and I snorted.

Oh jeez! Did I just do that!

Mark walked me to my car and commented, "Not too shabby yourself, Ms. Quinn."

I smiled. "Take care of my girl or Daddy will be the least of your problems."

I got the dimples again. "Sure thing, Ms. Quinn. I promise."

I climbed in my car, and he shut the door, making sure I was safely inside.

"Nice touch there, Mr. Dow," I mumbled as I pulled out my cell and called Robert.

Right then, the butterflies started again. Robert answered on the first ring. "You on your way?"

"Yes, but I'm not going to Pepper's."

"Oh?"

"Yep, some hotshot lawyer that my dad introduced to us tonight is bringing her back."

"Really?"

"Yes, it was so weird. The chemistry between the two of them was pulsating. Like if you got too close, you would blow up."

"Well, I'm glad you didn't get too close."

I stifled a giggle. "So where am I going to?"

"How about I meet you at Ray's Diner?"

"Oh, I know where that is. I love that place."

"Good. See you soon. Be careful."

"Yes, sir." I hung up.

Half an hour later, I pulled into an almost empty parking lot. A cruiser was parked out front, and my mouth went dry. "Shit!" I grabbed my bag and quickly applied some lip gloss. I parked next to the cruiser, and there he was. He turned and smiled. I opened my door and swung my legs around. He was adjusting his hat and opened my door wider.

He offered me his hand, and I mentally smirked. *See, my new guy is just as chivalrous!*

I took his hand, and he pulled me effortlessly to my feet then to him as he closed my door. I was about six inches from being against him, and my pulse went off the charts.

Damn, I shouldn't have had that last glass of wine. I think he can hear my heart beat. I knew I could.

"Wow!" He took a step back to check out my outfit. "I may have to take you out tomorrow night."

My pulse started to slow, but I was too nervous to smile.

"Why is it so empty here?" I went for taking the attention off me.

"My cruiser keeps all the drunks out. I've been here for an hour. I pulled in, and they all scattered."

"Oh, they are going to love you in there. Hope they don't spit in my coffee too."

He laughed and spun me slightly from my hip and kept his hand on the small of my back as we entered the diner. Robert guided me to a booth on the far left. He sat me on the left while he slid in on the right with his back to the wall.

Our waitress came over and was not happy. I could tell she was going to get us out of here as quick as she could.

Robert could have cared less. He was like a predator studying his prey (me). He ordered both of us coffee with milk on the side. I think she actually stomped away.

Takes away their business and only orders coffee—they are going to poison us. I could feel the ex-lax being dropped in as we spoke. *At least I'll shed a few more pounds from this.*

Robert leaned in and took one of my hands in his. "You look beautiful, by the way. How was dinner?"

"You mean the Pepper-and-Mark love-match dinner? Food was awesome, Granny fell asleep. Pepper was speechless for about a minute!"

"Wow, no way!"

"Yes way. I know. Can you believe it? And she blushed!"

"Get out. Now you're lying."

"No. Cross my heart." I made an *x* over my chest.

"Wow, didn't think she was capable of that innocent girlie stuff."

"I know. Just think how shocked I was, and I have known her for four years. 'Ms. I Have a Set of Brass Balls, Want to See Them?'"

He let out a low velvety laugh and started stroking the back of my hand with his thumb.

OK, this is a little weird. Nice, but weird.

Our coffee came, and he reluctantly released me. She didn't even ask if we changed our minds, just slapped the bill down at the end of the table.

Oh god, I think I'll leave her a twenty under my cup.

He took a sip and asked how I was doing. I ratted Scott out and told him about the roses and what I did with them. I left out the part about Mom paying for my shopping spree and thanking me for not marrying him.

"So you gonna talk to him?"

"Not too soon. But yes, I am eventually going to talk to him. I'm done, moving on, and I guess I've known that for a while deep down inside. So maybe he did me a favor."

"He certainly did me one."

That got me to smile, and I looked at him through my lashes. Boy, Robert was attractive!

We finished our coffee, and he put a few dollars down. I slipped my twenty under my mug. It at least made me feel better.

Robert stood, adjusted his hat, and held his hand out. I slid out of the booth and adjusted my skirt, and he guided me toward the door.

He was like walking with a tiger on a leash. The energy that was coming from him—jeez, I felt like a conductor tonight.

He held the door for me, and I slipped through. I think the wait staff applauded.

Robert guided me between our cars and stopped me at my door. I turned to him, and he rested an extended arm on my roof.

Oh god, is he going to kiss me? Am I ready for this? Would I be disappointed if he didn't? Am I going to faint? I think those were huge possibilities!

He caressed my cheek with his free hand. "Would you mind if I took you out to dinner tomorrow night?"

Yes, I was hyperventilating. "I thought you wanted to take it easy tomorrow?" Jesus, was that my voice?

"I think it would be safer if we stayed out in public."

"Ah, OK, sure. Can I meet you at your house? Park there?"

"Absolutely." He leaned in closer and tilted my chin up, planting a soft kiss on my lips. I don't know what the hell happened next, but my body had its own mission. Instead of fainting, like it was supposed to, my hands shot up and cupped his hairline below his hat, and my mouth seized his, shoving my tongue into his now-open mouth.

We were rolling along the side of my car as his arms encircled my body, and his hand was cupping my ass, pulling me against him. Oh god, he was a good kisser! I could feel my pelvis against his erection. Shit! I hope that's what it was, though he was wearing this goddamn belt, and it could have been something else stabbing into me.

Ouch, crap! What the hell was that digging into me!

He pulled us apart and held me at arm's length. "Oh Christ! I want you!"

I was panting and glad he was holding me up. My legs were jelly, so the only place I could go was down, and that would have been embarrassing. "I know how you feel."

We—well, he stood there (I was just posing where he was holding me). Forever it felt like. The feeling started coming back in my legs.

A car pulled in and took one look at us and spun around, hightailing it out of there. All the waitresses ran to the windows. I definitely heard a "What the fuck!"

"OK, lover boy, time to go before you have to arrest the mob that is building in there."

He straightened up and laughed. "Yeah, that car probably thought I was searching you."

"You were."

"Can't wait to do that again." He came at me, and I held my hand up.

"Oh no, you don't. I know exactly how those lips feel now, and unless you want to go the distance, I advise you to back off."

He again enclosed the space between us. I looked down at his belt.

"What the hell was pressing against the left side of my pelvis bone?" I examined the area more carefully.

"Taser."

"Of course, how could I have not known that?"

He laughed again. "You better open your door before I go the distance this time."

I fumbled for my keys and unlocked the door. Robert reached over and opened it for me. He grabbed my wrist as I was about to duck in, which got me to turn toward him again. He kissed me softly once more. Just our lips, no tongue, and my heart leaped into my throat.

"See you tomorrow." He turned me and helped me in the car. "I'll follow you to the city limits."

I nodded my head. It was the only thing I could do. I was having a panic attack. I could not swallow; I lost my heart somewhere in my body. I had no feeling in my arms, and I had to drive normally while the super-hot cop followed me in his cruiser.

My phone rang. I looked down. It was Pepper. Oh, no way, not now. I can just imagine this phone conversation. My hotness in his high-tech machine probably had one of those scanners that could pick up cell phone conversations. Nice try, sexy. She will just have to wait. He signaled me to back out, and I obeyed.

Music. That will distract me. OK, right! Like the cruiser behind me was so easy to ignore. Twenty agonizing minutes later, and he turned on the lights and siren. I made it, and he pulled a U-turn.

I let out a breath I hadn't realized I was holding. Wow, what the hell did I get myself into? And how the hell hadn't I noticed him? He's yummy, and he wants me! Adrenaline kicked in, and I was home in fifteen minutes. There was a missed text from Robert: "Just text me when you get home. I need to know you made it safely."

Awww! I liked that he's checking up on me. I texted him back: "Just parked the car, sliding into bed in five minutes." Sent. I smiled.

Robert replied: "Sweet dreams, baby."

I looked at the text again. "Baby?" Is it too weird to have my dad and a potential boyfriend using the same term of endearment? I'll have to think about that.

I texted him back: "Keep us safe tonight. And by the way, you are a really good kisser. Lucky me J" Sent.

Robert replied: "I'm really good at many things. Get some rest, plan on keeping you out late tomorrow."

I was grinning like a fool at that. I replied: "Yes, sir!" Sent.

Then I climbed into my bed and fell into a deep sleep.

The five-thirty alarm woke me with a start. I grabbed it and shut it off.

Slipping back to my pillow, a grin made its way across my face. I think this is where the birds are supposed to start singing and small animals are helping me get out of bed and fetching my clothes while, in some parallel universe, I can actually carry a tune.

My phone vibrated, pulling me out of my Snow White fantasy.

Five text messages from Pepper:

"Where R U?"

"I know U R holding out on me!"

"Spill the beans, Quinn."

"Has he taken you hostage?"

"Do I need to track your cell!"

Oh shit! I texted back: "Had the best night sleep ever. He is a really good kisser. Who knew? Taking me out to dinner tonight. Call you later J." Sent.

My phone vibrated immediately. It was Robert texting. "Good morning, beautiful. Be at my house at five. Reservations for six at The Loft."

I was giddy. I returned his message: "Looking forward to it." Sent.

That's strange, I thought as I pulled into the Fields' driveway. *John's car is still here.*

A flash of panic hit me, and I grabbed my bag and rushed toward the door. I heard Jess shouting, "That you, Kate?"

I'm like a beacon to her voice. "Everything OK here?"

John stepped away from her, smiling as he acknowledged me.

She gave me a wicked smile. "Never better."

I sighed with relief and greeted Bev, who was finishing her entries. Frank was clean, changed, and awake.

"Well, what have we here? Hello, handsome."

He smiled.

Bev filled me in on his night. "So all you have to worry about is meds and breakfast." She leaned in and kissed Frank on his forehead. "Goodbye, handsome. I'll see you again tonight."

He patted her hand. "Thank you."

"See ya, Kate." She winked.

Jess strolled in. "So, had a good evening?"

"Tell you in a bit. I can see you did."

She glanced over her shoulder. "That's always a sure bet."

"Yes, I feel your pain. Hot, talented husband who adores you. Poor thing."

She laughed. "Want some coffee?"

"Is the pope Catholic?"

"You're feisty this morning."

I grinned back at her as I prepared Frank's meds.

"Want some breakfast, Frank?"

"Not yet, angel, just let me rest a bit."

"OK, whatever you want, handsome."

Jess gave John a travel mug and slapped his butt toward the door. He leaned in and kissed her. They exchanged "I love you's," and he was out the door.

I leaned against the doorframe, and she started right in on me. "Did you meet up with the cop last night?"

"Yup."

"So?"

"He kissed me."

"And?"

"It was good."

"Good?"

"Outstanding good."

"That's better. Kissing is an art. If you don't have that down—well, you're screwed."

"He has that down."

She handed me my coffee. I proceeded to tell her everything with a big grin on my face. I had decided Jess was my very own life coach. When I was done, she gave out a heavy sigh. "It's going to kill me to wait until Monday."

"Well, sorry, but you'll just have to get over that one."

She grinned. "Oh, by the way, the witch is coming around noon."

"Thanks for the warning."

"And I'm going out to lunch with the girls."

"Deserter."

"You bet."

"Don't worry. I'll keep everything under control here."

"Good, I need all my wagons in a circle."

"You can count on me."

Jess headed out at ten thirty. I was just finishing up with Frank and settling him back down to rest when my phone vibrated.

I answered it and walked out to the kitchen. "Hey, Pepper."

"Don't you 'Hey, Pepper' me. Start talking!"

I gave her all the details, and she sounded very pleased. She then told me about Mark and that they made a date for tonight. I said it before I thought about it and revealed where Robert was taking me as well as the time. Oh crap. Pepper suggested we do a double date.

Robert was probably asleep for the next five hours, and I didn't want to disturb him. I knew what it was like to come off a double, but she kept at me until I broke. She informed me that she would take care of the reservation and that she would see us at six. I hung up.

"Shit!" I stared at my phone for a minute. "Better get this over with."

I texted Robert: "Do you mind if there is a slight change of numbers for our dinner party? Sorry. I blurted out to Pepper where you were taking me tonight, and she suggested—no, that's not right, insisted—on a double date. She is changing the reservations as of now. I will make this up to you. I promise." Sent.

Nope, those were definitely not butterflies in my stomach. I think it's an ulcer acting up. The witch arrived, and thank the Lord, she only stayed half an hour. Told her daddy the time difference was affecting her. I mentally laughed a whole one hour.

My phone made a jump. It was Robert texting me. "All right, you will be safer in a crowd anyways."

I was beaming. I replied: "You, sir, should be asleep." Sent.

Robert replied: "I'm too busy thinking of the ways you're going to make it up to me."

Naughty! And everything south of my belly button jumped to attention. I thought for a moment then replied: "Me too." Sent.

Robert replied: "Definitely fearing for your safety."

I blushed. *Oh shit!* I didn't respond.

My shift couldn't end quickly enough. God, I want out of here and at Robert's door right now!

Beth arrived half an hour early, and I just finished my notes. "I know I'm pathetic."

"You rock! I have a hot date tonight."

"Good, get out of here then."

"Don't have to ask me twice." I grabbed my bag and kissed Frank. "See you Monday."

"OK, angel."

I ran out the door.

Straight to my house, I rushed in and started getting ready. I grabbed my robe and headed up the stairs.

Mom met me halfway down the hall. "Had a good date last night?"

I burst into a grin. "Yes."

"Why, Kate, do tell."

"OK, he is cute—really, really cute. How did I not see it?"

"Integrity. All of us have it except you, sister."

"Mom!"

"She's my child, I can say that. Must be a defect on your father's side."

"We're meeting Pepper and Mark for a double date."

"That's wonderful. Mark is such a nice man and full of promise. He will go far."

"I might crash at Pepper's tonight if it's too late, so don't worry if I don't make it home."

"All right, just text me so I know. Have fun, sweetie, and maybe you can bring Robert by sometime. I am sure your father would like to meet him."

"Let me snag him first. I don't want him running for the hills just yet."

"I'm sure that young man can hold his own."

I smiled and kissed Mom's cheek. "See ya."

"Have fun tonight and be safe."

"I will."

I closed the bathroom door. I washed every nook and cranny and shaved twice, grabbed some perfumed body lotion, and zipped down the stairs.

My new black halter dress was hanging on the door. I smiled. "Oh, he is going to love this." I pulled out my garter and black silk stockings. "Been a long time, girls, but I'm back."

I dropped my robe and slathered the lotion all over. I pulled my black lace panties on and my garter belt with the stockings next, and I hooked them securely. I shimmied over my new dress, and because of the way it crossed in the back, I went braless. I adjusted my breast in the front panels and opened the middle a little wider, giving a perfect cleavage display.

Yeah! I mentally cheered. Over to my vanity, I decided with eyeliner, shadow, mascara, a little blush, and tinted lip gloss. Perfect! I was happy and feeling pretty.

I started blow-drying my hair, and I went with the straight look. A little spray to hold it all in place, but not too sticky just in case hottie wanted to run his fingers through it. My hormones awakened at the thought, followed by a flash of panic. I had only been with Scott. *Oh crap! Can I do this?*

I took three deep breaths and looked at my reflection in the mirror. "Well, Kate, let's find out, shall we?"

My reflection approved.

"Showtime!"

Moving off the chair, I flipped the lid off and pull my new black platform-heeled sandals out. The platform part is a black background with white polka dots. Super sexy. I strapped them on. I looked at myself in my full-length mirror. "Hell, even I want me." I twirled around to see how high the dress revealed. *Oh yeah, just a hint of Pandora's secret. Perfect!*

I looked over at the clock, and I had a few minutes to spare. Looking around, I spotted my gym bag. I packed my new sexy gym outfit into it with clean underwear and my toothbrush. And I threw in some beauty essentials—just in case—and headed for the door. I yelled good-bye to my mother and headed for my car.

My butterflies were back, but I put my gym bag in the back storage area and climbed in. Picking my cell out from my purse, I checked to see if any plans had changed. Just a text from dickhead: "Can I meet you tonight?"

Tapping on it, I hit his whole file and deleted everything.

There, that gave me a little satisfaction. I started my car and headed to the hot cop's house. It took me half an hour, and I was ten minutes early. I pulled into his driveway and parked. Grabbing my purse, I applied extra gloss just to look perfect. Then I headed for the door. Taking a settling breath, I knocked instead of pressing the doorbell. My ears picked up his footsteps coming toward the door. I watched the handle turning, and everything was in slow motion from there.

The door opened, and I got an eyeful of pure and utter carnal appreciation.

Holy crap, he is stunning! I heard a low growl, or it could have been a purr. I couldn't tell right now, but he was smiling.

He pulled me in and said something that was just not registering right at the moment. I just stared at his lips that were moving: ". . . ful. Just beautiful."

There was a slight pause, and my brain snapped back. "You look . . . wow, Robert . . . this look . . . suits you. I may have to slap someone tonight."

He was in a gray-sheen short-sleeved shirt with the top three buttons undone! He wore gray pants with sort of the same sheen on them, but not as much as the shirt. They fit him *sooooo gooood!* Black belt and black dress shoes.

He laughed. "Well, it's a good thing I have my very own Nikita here. The dress I highly approve of. Makes me want to strap my .45 to you just to complete it."

"You better not. I might use it."

He closed the distance between us.

Oh no, danger, danger!

He leaned in and kissed me. Fifteen seconds. I stopped counting as I panted into his chin. "Come on, let's get this over with so I can have you all to myself."

"OK," I agreed.

He stepped back and looked into my eyes. Oh Christ, what the hell was my soul revealing to him? He stroked my cheek and asked if I was ready to go. I nodded. It was all I could do. He turned and headed up the stairs to grab his wallet, keys, and a sport coat.

Getting myself back under control, I smoothed my dress and remembered to breathe. He strode down the stairs and flipped a couple of switches. Opening the door for me, he placed his hand just above my buttocks but below my waist, and I could feel that he felt my garter belt. He took in a sharp breath. I mentally patted myself.

Looking at my car, I wasn't sure whose car we were taking, so I offered to drive.

He hit the garage door open and muttered, “Not a chance.” That’s when I realized I didn’t know what he drove. The door slowly pulled its way to the top, and oh my, there waiting was a new Ford Shelby GT500.

“This is what you drive?” I stopped moving.

“Yes. I like a good ole American muscle car.”

“Wow.” He could have me right, here right now. I was helpless. *That’s it! Game over! He wins!*

I could feel his grin as he guided me over to the passenger seat and settled me in. Was I that dumbfounded? Because he buckled my seat belt for me.

He walked behind the car, and I pulled it together and adjusted the strap between my breasts. He slid in with ease and pulled his belt over, and the car roared to life. Picking up my hand, he kissed the back of it. “Ready?” he asked, locking eyes with me.

“Ready!” I grinned like a teenager. I knew this ride was going to be fun. As he was backing out, I asked about what vehicle was under the tarp.

His grin was full of promise. “My project” was all he said. I glanced over at him several times. My god, he looked so hot behind the wheel of this super car. He was the poster model for masturbation. I could make a million with one photo of him right here, right at this moment. Maybe just loosen his belt and undo the button and zip down his fly just an inch or so. I shuddered.

“You all right?” he purred.

“Oh yeah.” I adjusted in my seat.

He tilted his head and flashed a grin. I was going to combust.

We arrived, and there was a line outside. He parked right out in front—not sure that was even a spot.

He walked around and opened my door. “Nikita,” he called me and gave me his hand. With his right hand gripping my waist, he pulled me close to him, and we walked toward the crowd.

Using my dress, his finger slipped under the front garter strap and glided down to the top of my stocking. He leaned into my ear. “Is this for me?”

I tilted my head to the side and down. “Yes.”

I felt his grin against my ear. “Thank you.”

Chapter 3

We walked right up the stairs past the waiting line while several women checked out the hot cop. *He's with me, girls,* I cheered to myself inside.

"Seems I'm not the only one who appreciates the dress," he whispered in my ear.

I turned my head around to look at the crowd. I received a smile and a nod from an attractive middle-aged man then turned back to hottie. "He's got nothing on you. By the way, you have your own fan club."

His laugh was velvety and sexy. "You're the only one I'm trying to impress."

"Mission accomplished."

He held me tighter against him. "And the night has just begun. What am I going to do now?"

"I can think of a few things."

He stopped our forward motion. As if we were the only ones around, he turned me to him and planted a kiss right on my lips. I heard a "damn!" from a woman a few feet away. Then we were back moving again, except now he had his arm around my shoulder.

Going through the door, we went right to the podium, and he stopped us at the greeter, who was very busy looking over her chart. Robert cleared his throat, and she annoyingly glanced up and froze, taking in Mr. Hot Cop. I could actually see her brain misfiring as she tried to speak and nothing came out. Robert announced his reservation, and she cleared her throat. "Oh yes, sorry. Your other party is waiting in the bar. We will have you seated in a moment."

"Should I go get—" I hadn't finished the sentence when Pepper and Mark approached us.

She hugged me, and Robert took a step back. That's when she got an eyeful of him. She released me and whistled, "Boy, you sure clean up well."

He broke a ghost of a smile but stayed impassive.

Then she spun me around. "Did I miss the memo for the modeling shoot?"

I blushed and greeted Mark then introduced him to my date.

Mark wore a clean navy pin-striped suit with a crisp white shirt, and Pepper was in a matching white tailored shirt with a plain navy miniskirt that showed off her bare tanned dancer's legs in five-inch killer heels. They matched; it was cute. The greeter looked at the four of us and muttered something under her breath then grabbed the menus and waved for us to follow her.

"Come on, Barbie and Ken, our table awaits."

"Robert said I was Nikita."

The grin from Mark was like he finally placed my dress.

That got my date's possessive arm back around me. Pepper laughed as she said, "Nikita! Can you picture this one as an assassin?" She glanced back again. "Though you do have the body for it."

I shot her a look to zip it.

Mark led the way and pulled out a chair for Pepper. Robert's glare warned him not to even try, and he held my shoulder and pulled mine out with ease and then scooted it forward so I was at the correct distance from the table. Then he moved and angled his chair toward me. Pepper studied him for a moment.

I started the conversation by thanking Mark for taking Pepper home, and his face lit up as he answered it was his pleasure. I presented to my hottie all that I knew about Mark as a general conversation piece on the table then asked Mark how he liked working at my father's firm. He answered very politely, and Pepper shared more information about him. When he was done, he asked Robert about his job, and Robert simply stated, "I'm a cop." That was it.

There was a five-second silence, and Mark broke out in a smile. "We make a good team then. You arrest them, I convict them."

Robert didn't reply. I hope he didn't take it as "You're the muscle, I'm the brains." But Pepper was already filling the silence.

I turned my head to Robert and winked at him, and that got me a grin. He looked so friggin' hot in that shirt, I wanted to lean over and lick his biceps.

Pepper asked me again. "What are you having, Kate?"

"Hun?" I glanced over to her.

"Besides a fantasy right now? What do you want to drink?"

"Oh, oh, ummmm?" I looked back to Robert, and he ordered us a bottle of sauvignon blanc.

Pepper glanced at Mark, and he nodded. "Sounds good. Make that two please," she added.

"So, Rob, you know about wine?"

"I know what I like."

"Apparently." She looked right at me.

I changed the subject. "When is Dallas coming?"

"In a week."

"She is staying a month, right?"

"Yes."

"She's on school break?" Mark piped in. "How old is your sister?"

Pepper gave her full attention to Mark and filled him in on her family tree. The wine came, and Robert poured my glass then his. I took a sip. "Hmmm, this is really good ho . . . honey."

Oh shit! I almost said hottie, but I think *honey* is just as bad at this stage.

"Well, thank you, baby," he answered with amusement.

I think he liked me calling him *honey*. I took another sip and put it down.

Two police officers approached the table, and Robert was grinning like the Cheshire Cat. They stopped in front of me and looked at him. "We were wondering who the asshole was who parked the Shelby in a no-parking zone."

Robert laughed, and Pepper blurted out, "Shelby? You have a Shelby?"

The other cop looked at me. "Well, you must be Kate?"

I nodded.

Robert introduced me to his cousins. "This one is Liam, and he's Sean."

They nodded at me.

"Hi." I gave a small wave. This was so embarrassing. Everyone is staring, for god's sakes! I introduce our guests, trying to take the attention off me.

Liam asked Robert about coming over on Sunday. He answered, staring straight at me.

"Depends?" Liam chuckled and patted Robert on the shoulder. "OK, folks, I heard the food here is pretty good. Have a good meal. See ya, Rob."

"Bye."

Pepper leaned in, smiling. "They came here to check you out."

I was mortified, but Robert still held on to his grin.

Then Pepper turned to him, "What kind of Shelby?"

"GT500 anniversary edition."

"Color?"

"Black with gold strip."

She sucked in a breath, "Rob, I never took you for a muscle-car guy."

"No?"

"Definitely no! I pictured you for the undercover sedan type."

He laughed.

I jumped in. "He has another car under a big tarp."

Pepper looked intrigued. "What's going on under the covers, Mr. Beckham?"

"Project." He gave me a look. Oops, should have kept my mouth shut.

"What kind of project?"

"My kind of project." He glared at Pepper.

Mark rescued her. "Nice wheels, Robert."

Robert just nodded.

"Mark drives an XK Jag." I leaned over closer to Robert. That made him happy.

He turned to Mark. "Nice ride yourself."

"Thank you."

The waiter came over and took our order. The food was good, but I had to leave half of mine on the plate. The portions were just too big. Robert poured me my third glass of wine.

"You trying to get me drunk?"

"Maybe?"

I snorted, and he laughed.

Pepper butted in, "What are you two laughing about?"

"He's trying to get me drunk."

"Good luck with that. We're going dancing after, wanna come with us?"

"Where?" Hottie and I asked at the same time, making me giggle this time.

"The Boulevard."

He looked at me. I nodded, and he answered, "Sure."

Pepper replied, "Great, let's get out of here."

The men split the bill, and I finished my wine. I had a warm feeling inside me, and I was a little tipsy. Robert put his arm around me again as we were walking toward the door, and I became brave and wrapped my arm around his waist. He grinned and tucked me against him tightly. I fit perfectly. *Yeah!*

Mark held Pepper's hand, and we had an audience watching us leave. Robert whispered something I didn't quite catch. I lost my balance on the last step and started to trip when he scooped me up in his arms. I shrieked and laughed out loud as he carried me to the car. Placing me on my feet in front of my car door, I held on to his shoulder for balance and to get control of my laughter. His hands held me around the waist. He was even yummier.

Pepper and Mark followed behind us, and she checked out Robert's car. "Very sleek, Rob, we'll meet you there. We're parked over in the nosebleed section."

I snorted again.

"See, it's all about whom you know!" I bragged as Robert opened my door and ushered me in. I waved like an idiot to Pepper.

Robert slid in. "Ready to dance off that dinner?"

"I don't know if you call shaking my ass to the music is dancing—but hey, any opportunity to burn off some calories, I'm all for."

"Good to know, Nikita."

Then I burst out laughing again at what I just implied.

He started the car and peeled away from the curb, making me squeal again with laughter. We pulled right up to the front again. I flipped the vanity down and applied more lip gloss. I was feeling confident. He opened my door—"my door!" I was taking claim. He held out his hand again, and I grabbed it this time and yanked myself toward him.

He pulled me right in and planted those beautiful lips right on me. He kicked the door closed and pinned me to the car. My arms were around his back, holding on for dear life. His tongue was in my mouth, swirling around and caressing mine. He cupped my buttocks again and had me against his groin.

Oh god, I could feel him. I wanted to grab the front of his pants and squeeze to get a better idea of what I was dealing with. Right then, I heard a familiar voice yelling at us, "Get a room!" And we broke free of each other.

I was panting.

He growled, "She's really getting on my nerves."

I smiled and rubbed my nose to his then clasped our hands. He straightened and caressed my chin.

"Come on, kids, let's take it to the dance floor."

Pepper and Mark walked by us.

Mr. Hottie pulled me to his side again, with our hands linked, and gave me a quick kiss. "Come on, baby, let's go sweat."

I wanted to skip to the door, do cartwheels—something. I had so much nervous energy, and I couldn't get this stupid grin off my face. *Blah!*

Pepper grinned at me.

The techno beat was booming. Robert paid the admission, and I started swinging my hips slightly to the beat. He grabbed my hand and twirled me to him. I squealed again, giggling. As he dipped me, I held on to his biceps. He kissed my neck several times before letting me back up.

"Come on, you two!" Pepper yelled.

He stopped us at the bar and ordered two more glasses of wine. I took the one he handed me and clinked our glasses. "To black dresses and hot cops."

"Definitely to the black dresses," he replied.

We drank, and he held my hand again, leading us to where Pepper and Mark where.

She leaned into me. "Looks like you two are getting along pretty good."

"He's so yummy."

"I agree. He is really into you."

"Not yet, but soon I hope."

"Why, Kate, are you horny?"

"I'm going to combust. Is it just me or can you feel his sexual presence?"

"Every woman he passed tonight and every woman in this bar can feel his sexual presence."

"What?"

I looked around. Yup! They were checking out my date.

"I'll give them something to look at."

I put my glass down and took a few steps to him. He automatically put his arm around me, and I asked him if he wanted to dance. He smiled and put his glass down and led me to the floor. I covered my hand over my mouth, glancing back at Pepper. She grabbed Mark and led him out as well.

Robert dragged us to the middle of the floor. Then he pulled me into him and started to move. Really move.

Holy crap, can he dance!

He was moving both of us, and it was so hot.

The space around us started to widen as people made room, and he spun me left and back to him then again, and I laughed as he caught me back in his chest. Gyrating our hips in a circle together, he placed my arm seductively behind his head. I lifted my right leg around his waist, while he supported my thigh to him and arched my back to the floor.

I lifted up, and we locked eyes. I wanted him. Right here, right now. I was panting and wound too tight.

Pepper's arm touched us, and he was back in the beat. I released my leg from him. I needed a minute to regroup. He was pulsating to the beat as I stepped away, and he started to follow, but I encouraged him to stay.

Pepper started right in dancing with him. Man, could she dance too. This is what she did for a living, and it showed. Robert was keeping up move to move with her, and then he spun and flipped her. The crowd cleared another eight feet around them, and they were putting on quite a show. I danced with Mark on the outside circle. He was much more tame, and my sex drive was back under control. The song finished and faded into another. From behind me, Robert's hands were back on me. He turned me around away from Mark and into him.

He was not even sweaty. But boy did he smell divine.

"Stay or go?" he asked me.

I pulled back and looked into his eyes. "Stay just a little bit longer."

"OK, baby."

"I need a drink."

"Coming right up, beautiful."

He led us off the dance floor and to our table. He had wrapped around me with his hand pressed into my belly, his middle and ring finger playing with the strap on my garter.

I drank my wine and slowly wiggled my butt into his crotch. He let out a sexual moan in my ear. My vagina was screaming! *She is so mad at me right now.*

I drained my glass, and he put his in front of me. I let my head fall back onto his shoulder. He kissed my hair, and I melted in that moment. I felt cherished.

Pepper and Mark made their way back, and I lifted my head back upright.

Mark said, "Wow, that was some show, you two. I think they ought to give you back your cover charge."

Pepper praised him. "Yes, Rob, you're a good dancer."

He just smiled and cuddled into me.

"Looks like I'm going to need lessons," admitted Mark.

"You're fine, Mark, he's just a freak of nature," Pepper offered to soothe his ego.

Robert started to trail kisses down my neck. I giggled and squirmed because it tickled. He whispered in my ear, "Time to go?"

I turned in toward him ever so slightly and nodded yes.

He picked me up, and my elbows shot to his shoulders. I was suddenly aware my breasts were in his face. I collapsed my upper body over and laughed out loud. He spun me around and placed me back on the floor.

"We're leaving," he announced to Pepper and Mark.

Before I could say good-bye at a respectable distance, I'm yelling it and laughing as he was dragging me toward the door.

Outside, he was all hands and mouth. He pinned me against the wall, and his hands went up my dress to explore my lingerie.

"Holy shit, just knowing you have this on is making me crazy. Can I see it?"

I gasped, "Not here!" I pushed his hands back down.

He looked around and let out a growl. He clenched his teeth. "You're so fucking sexy!" And his mouth was back on mine. Ten seconds that time. He straightened my dress and picked me up over his shoulder. I squealed and laughed again as he carried me to the car.

There were several admirers gawking at his car. One guy tried to initiate a conversation, and Robert just told him to fuck off while I was still hanging over his shoulder. Awkward!

He opened my door and let me down. The crowd scattered. He moved with purpose to his side and slid in, taking my face with both his hands. He asked, "Ready?"

"Yes." I put my hands over his.

He kissed me softly then gave me a mischievous smile. Turning the keys, he fishtailed away from the curb.

I laughed again. "Slow down! You're gonna get a ticket."

His smile widened as he put more pressure on the gas. This car just sounded awesome, and we made it back to his place in no time.

He parked in the garage and jumped out to get my door. I waited to let him open it. Instead of offering his hand, he just scooped me up and carried me in, kicking my door shut once again. I took this opportunity to wrap my arms around his neck. He stopped halfway to the house and kissed me with no intention of putting me down. He started walking again.

"I can walk if I'm too heavy."

"You're not heavy at all. I could run a marathon with you in my arms." He proved it by doing a curl with my body, and I squirmed and laughed again as he nuzzled into my tummy.

"Stop that!" I protested, trying to catch my breath. My sides were aching from laughing so much.

Walking up the stairs, he still had me trapped in his grasp. He pulled out his keys, opening the front door. Without missing a beat, he kicked it shut.

Again, he glided up the stairs with me still in his arms. Walking into the great room, he released my legs and slowly let them touch the floor. I was smiling as he brushed my hair back from my shoulder.

"Can I get you anything?"

I felt my heart rate picking up. "Water?"

"Sure." He stepped away, and I just watched, enjoying the view.

Oh my gosh! Am I ready for this? Can I do this so soon?

He came back in from the kitchen. Oh, he looked so friggin' sexy.

"Nice house," I commented. I had never been inside—just outside to pick up dickhead.

"Thanks."

"How long have you been here?"
"Two years."

He led me over to the couch, and I took a seat on the edge. I took another sip of water. My mouth was going dry. He sat next to me but relaxed back against the cushions.

Turning toward his direction, I was building up my nerve. "So how do you feel about monogamy?"

He chased the smile away that I knew he wanted to show. "All for it."

"Sooo?"

Not sure what to say next. I was so new at this, and he helped me out. "So you think you're ready to start another relationship?"

I cleared my throat and looked into his eyes. "Yes. I'd like to try."

He scooted forward. "Good answer."

He was so close again. His hand moved to my hair, and my breath quickened. "How about one with me?"

"Yes," I answered, almost breathless, and he tackled me backward.

His hands went everywhere trying to touch me all at once, and he broke off the kiss briefly. "Me too. I want you so badly."

I was looking into his soul. "Take me. I want to be all yours."

He growled/purred again. Pulling back the material from my dress, he revealed one of my breasts and gently sucked on my nipple as he manipulated the other between his thumb and index finger. They popped out to attention, and an ache was clenching in my groin.

He lifted his head. "You're so fucking delicious."

I smiled at him.

"But not here. I want you in my bed. That's where you belong."

I melted as he lifted me again and carried me down the hall. His bedroom was huge, and I notice a master bathroom attached.

He laid me down softly and put one knee next to my hip and the other leg on the floor. He began kissing me again with a soft passion, like I was breakable. Right then, I realized this was not going to be the hot, "let's get this over with" sex—but he was going to make love to me.

His lips brushed back and forth over mine, and then he moved to my chin and placed a soft kiss right at the tip. His hand glided up my stockings to the top, where there was bare skin. Letting the tips of his fingers glide across the skin a few times, he slowly continued his journey, tracing the garter line to my panties. He was now trailing kisses down my neck.

His fingers slid across my hot sex, and just the feel of them through my panties was so, so good. He traced the shape of my clit over and over, and his tongue was mimicking the exact moves on my right breast.

Oh god, too many sensations. I'm going to come.

Catching my breath, I found my voice. "Keep that up and I will come. Soon."

I felt his smile, and then that was it. He sucked a little harder and rubbed a little stronger. I gasped and mumbled, "Oh, Robert! Oh god! Oh my god! Oh my god! Ahh, ahh, ahh!" And my chest was heaving.

He released my nipple but continued circling my clit again. His other hand pushed up my dress so he could see what I was wearing.

I opened my eyes and looked up. He approved and started to unsnap the garter to my stocking. One, two, three, four. They were all released while he still was building my tension back slowly.

He's going to kill me; death by orgasm. I didn't even think it was possible to have another one at that point.

He reached down, slipping my shoes off one at time, then he stuck a finger between the skin and stocking and slid it down slowly. God, he was so friggin' hot. Then he repeated on the other one with his other fingers still working on my clitoris. Directing my body weight to the left, he turned me slightly, unhooking the garter belt and removing it from my body. He brought it up to his lips and kissed it.

Oh crap! I was going to orgasm again.

He placed it on his nightstand and stopped the assault on my clit.

No no no! Don't stop.

He hooked a finger on each side of my panties and slowly pulled them off as well.

I arched my hip to help him, and there was that wicked grin again as he dropped them to the floor. He pulled me up and started with the dress. Again with fingers staying in contact with my body, he guided my dress above my head. I was naked now, and he was still dressed, looking so damn hot!

I rose off the bed. It was my turn.

My left hand went straight for his crotch. I felt the outline of him. "Mmmm." It just came out; I had no control. I stretched up to plant a soft kiss on his mouth. He leaned down to accommodate me.

My right hand pressed against his shirt. I started at his abs, feeling the ripples. I slowly moved toward his chest and then to the buttons. I unfastened them carefully with one hand, trailing my fingers on his skin.

On the last button, I placed my hand flat on his chest and explored. My god, he was magnificent, and he was mine.

He shrugged out of his shirt, and I got the whole effect. I wanted to pump my fist. This was like winning a jackpot. I leaned forward and kissed his nipples. My girls puckered as his did. Still stroking him through his pants, I undid his belt; but he pulled it off, dropping it to the floor.

I stopped with my assault, and he drew in a sharp breath. With both hands, I unfastened his button and pulled down his zipper. Tucking my thumbs inside his pants, I guided them down, and I went with them. I put my mouth on his boxer briefs where he was protruding. I mouthed the material as he flicked off his shoes and pants. He groaned and held my head to him.

Oh, he was definitely bigger than Scott.

Scott! Shit! I stopped and shot up in panic. It just all fell out.

"Shit! I slept with him about twelve days ago!" I blurted and started shaking.

Robert held me up. "What, baby? What are you talking about? Come on, here, sit." He sat me on the bed and wrapped a blanket around me. I had my head in my hands and was about to cry. "What's going on, babe? Talk to me."

Great! Tears!

"I slept with Scott about ten—no, twelve days ago. And he was with that whore. I don't know if he used protection."

He handed me a tissue and rubbed my back. I could see he was doing the math. "You're safe, baby, you're safe. He didn't sleep with her until a week ago."

"How do you know this?"

"He bragged."

"Fuckhead!" I was so pissed, and then I wiped my eyes.

"It's OK, you're safe. Nothing to worry about." He embraced me.

I calmed down. There he was, stripped down to his underwear, consoling me from my jilted relationship. *Screw this!* I straightened up and looked right at him. "I need to be fucked! I am assuming you are my boyfriend now. That's what we agreed earlier, right?"

"Yes, right."

"Well, boyfriend, make me forget that asshole. That's your job from now on."

The wicked grin was back. "Yes, my queen. Your wish is my command."

He pulled the blanket off and picked me up, throwing me farther on the bed. Just as I landed, he pulled my legs down and apart, and now I know the visuals to muff diving. He was on me like I was his last meal. Oh god, he knew how to work that tongue. This man had talent, and he was mine! Just like his finger, his tongue circled around and around my clit, pausing to suck so effectively.

"Ahh!" I was squirming.

He held me in place with a little more force. His mouth licked, sucked, circled, and broke the pattern to torture me all over again. Then out from nowhere, I came and I screamed, and I climaxed some more, muttering his name and cursing while gasping from pleasure.

He opened the nightstand drawer and ripped open a new box of condoms. Tearing one open, he rolled it on and positioned himself on top of me.

"Ready, baby?"

I opened my eyes and nodded as he thrust into me. I gasped again! He was much bigger than the other guy and a little thicker.

He stopped when he was all the way in. "Are you OK, baby?"

"Yes."

"You want me to continue?"

"Yes." I was still panting.

"Good girl." And then he slowed it down to build a rhythm. He filled me up completely. I didn't think I could take another millimeter. He was hitting areas that I hadn't known existed.

Impossible! I was building again, and I think he could feel it too because he groaned with pleasure. He sounded so sexy, and my hands were all over him, feeling his everything; and then he stopped.

"What? No!" I actually said that out loud.

He pulled out and flipped me over and sank back inside me. Oh my god, this was a whole new feeling. He gripped both hips and started gently at first, pulling me into him, and I started to build. By the tenth thrust, he was ramming himself into me.

Oh jeez! I was gonna go again. One, two, three—I screamed his name and moaned and cried out and panted. And one more thrust and he was growling my name and cursing as he milked his orgasm into the condom inside of me.

Gently he was pulling me toward him and away. I needed to lie down and pass out. This was it. I was leaving this earth well fucked and happy. Robert pulled out of me then slapped my ass as I fell over.

He pulled off the condom and wiped himself. Then he reached between my legs and gave me a quick wipe. That was a little intimate, but I couldn't move. He pulled the blankets over and climbed in behind me. He wrapped his arm over me and pulled me tight against him.

"Did I make you forget?" he whispered in my ear.

"Forget who?" I muttered. "Can I stay tonight?" I asked. I didn't feel like sneaking out in the middle of the night.

He replied, "Stay forever."

I smiled and kissed his arm. He tightened his grip, and that's all I remembered.

I woke up with a pressing urge to pee. Robert was still holding me, and he was hot. I moved slightly and pulled the covers down.

He whispered, "Are you all right?"

Busted! Well, I was going to have to wake him anyways. I didn't know his house, so I told him I needed to use the bathroom.

He rolled over and turned on the light. Then he pointed to the left corner of the room. I was still naked but nature called, and I had no time to be shy. I made my way over to the bathroom and closed the door.

Oh my god, this felt so good. When I finished, I spotted a T-shirt in the hamper. I grabbed it and smelled it. I inhaled a deep breath, and it smelled like him. Divine! I put it on and grabbed a cloth to do a little wash between my legs. I was sore. My vagina had not seen that much action ever!

I flushed the toilet, put the cloth in the hamper, and washed my hand again. I turned out the light. As I opened the door, there was Robert, all nude and gladiator-like, grinning at me. "It suits you, but do you want a clean one?"

"No thanks, this one smells like you. I like your scent on me." I climbed back in bed and moved back to my spot.

"I like my scent being on you" was his answer, and he turned out the light and pulled me back into him again. I could get used to this.

I felt his erection sliding back and forth in between my legs, against my sex. He knew I was awake now because I started breathing heavily. He was masturbating me with his cock. *Holy jeez!*

I lifted my leg slightly so he could get a better angle, and that was his green light. His hand reached down to my clit and started with the rubbing again. My body took over and had a mind of its own and just started following his rhythm.

"That's my girl," he whispered in my ear and began kissing my shoulder. "Are you on the pill?" He sounded so friggin' sexy.

"Yes," I replied, panting.

Then he continued. "I'm clean, baby. Would you mind if I enter you without a condom?" he asked in a sexy purr.

"Please do." I just about begged, and then I didn't know if I should turn or stay where I was, but he decided and stuck the head of his cock right inside me.

Oh my god! I was going to come.

He traveled deeper in. I was panting harder. He sort of guided me onto my stomach and slid all the way into me. Skin on skin, he felt amazing as he straddled my legs so they were nearly closed. Then he quickened the pace.

He was so deep in me. *Oh jeez!* I was not going to last long. He thrust into me harder. I was coming! I was screaming into the pillow, and he kept going until I stopped my orgasm.

He pulled out and flipped me onto my back. "Wrap your legs around me, baby."

I did as I was told, and he was filling me again. He kissed my mouth, my nose, my forehead, my chin. "I am so happy you're here," he proclaimed.

"Me too" was all I could get out. This man was a fucking machine. I'm gonna need a cold compress on my vagina after he was done. But right now, I don't want him to stop.

There, right there—he was nailing a spot that was very happy it could be reached by his longer, thicker length. And I gasped. I was building again.

Oh shit! I grabbed at his arms—his beautiful muscular arms–and I cried out, "Yes, right there, Robert! Oh jeez! Rub me right there!" And his thrusts were slamming me now while I was about to climax again. I could feel he was getting larger and closer. I couldn't hold back, and I screamed his name. He growled out mine with several f-bombs in between as he emptied himself into me; and this time, he was rubbing his orgasm out skin on skin.

He looked even more handsome between my legs with his five o'clock shadow. I stared up at him . . . yum!

He grinned down at me. "Good morning beautiful."

"It's certainly turning out that way."

Instead of pulling out of me, because he was still hard, he rolled me on top of him. I didn't bother holding myself up. I just straddled my legs and plopped my head on his shoulder. My hair covered most of his face and chest. He laughed and pulled it to one side.

I muttered, "I can't believe you're still hard."

"Baby, I can't believe you are here and all mine! I've been waiting a long time for this."

Great, here comes that ridiculous grin on my face. "How long?" I held my breath.

"The first moment I laid eyes on you."

I thought back to when that might have been. "Six years ago?"

"Yup, six years ago."

I sat myself up on him. "Was it worth the wait?"

"Absolutely!"

I blushed. Then I put my hands on his chest and started to move around him.

"Yes please," he begged, and that was my inspiration. I rode him until he came.

I woke up again in the same position we started out in. We were on our side, and I was tucked into him, with his arm securely around me. I moved slightly, and he kissed my shoulder. I turned toward him, and he kissed my nose and then my forehead.

"I'm starving," I announced.

He laughed. "Want me to cook, or do you want to go out?"

"You cook?"

"Yes."

"Let's eat here. We can cook together."

"Deal!" He kissed my forehead again then released me.

I watched him get out of bed and stretch. I can't believe he was all mine. He opened a drawer and pulled out a black T-shirt. Next drawer down, he pulled out flannel pants with a drawstring tie.

Oh no! No underwear. And I realized that I wouldn't be able to walk on Sunday!

"You want a pair, baby?"

I remembered my gym bag. "I have a change of clothes in my car. I was going to go to the gym today, but it looks like I already had my workout."

He grinned. "I'll go get them for you."

"OK." I stretched out in his bed and cuddled into his spot. "Keys are in my bag."

"Got it," he called back to me.

Chapter 4

Closing my eyes again, I heard him leave and took a deep breath in. His scent was so good, so masculine. It was just plain delicious! I smiled into his pillow at the thought that he had wanted me for the past six years. I let out a little giggle into his pillow and wrapped my arms around it. I began fantasizing on what it would have been like if I was with him then.

I quickly snapped out from dreamland as I heard the front door close and he was coming toward the bedroom. I released the pillow and watched him carry my bag to the bed.

"Don't shower yet. I want to do that with you," he ordered.

I smiled. "OK."

He stepped over and leaned down to kiss me.

I automatically wrapped my arms around his neck, and he removed the blankets off me. Then he dragged me toward him. He lifted me effortlessly up and wrapped my legs around his waist. Man, was he strong. He then rubbed and tapped my butt, supporting an arm underneath me. All that without losing contact with my mouth. Then he finally released his kiss. He carried me down the hall to the kitchen.

He explained, "I need to feed you so you don't pass out on me."

I could only smile. He placed me on top of the breakfast bar in the center of the kitchen. I was still clinging to him, and he was rubbing my back. I could feel his grin.

"What do you want to eat?"

I drew back with my arms only, and suddenly, I felt playful. "You."

And there was that wicked grin.

"Oh, that can be arranged," he purred, and I felt his aura wrapping around me. My god, he had a presence about him. Then I felt his length growing against me. My body ignited, and then my stomach let out a growl.

"Let me cook something for you first, baby."

I laughed.

He was stroking my cheek and searching my eyes. Then he asked so thoughtfully, yet with complete seduction, "What does my queen desire?" He put on a fine English accent.

"You if you keep talking like that."

"Does my lady prefer the tongue from a foreign land?"

"I, sir, have nothing to compare. I have never had such a tongue."

"My queen is mistaken, she already has." He was trailing kisses down my neck.

"Surely I would know of such a man?"

"Ah! But he is standing before you, my queen."

I was stunned. "You're English? I mean from England?"

"Born and partly raised," he whispered in my ear.

"Really?"

"Yes, my mother is from Ireland. Father lives in England."

"How come you sound so American?"

"Moved here when I was five. My father had a job over here. My parents divorced when I was in my late teens. Mom moved back to Ireland, but I was already established here, so I stayed with my father for another year."

"So where are they now?"

"My father is back in England, and my mother is in Dublin. I spent my final teen years with my cousins. You met Liam last night. Then I applied for my American citizenship when I was eighteen and went to college."

It occurred to me that I didn't know this man at all.

"Does my queen disapprove?" He sounded so friggin' sexy.

"Ah, no! Your stock just shot through the roof." I was cheering inside. Hot Cop was sexy, strong, educated, and foreign! Bingo! And best of all, he's all mine! Yes, that ridiculous grin was on my face again.

He swept my hair back. "Good to know." And he leaned in for another kiss.

Bang! Bang! Bang!

I jumped back on the island, panicked. It was two seconds, but in those two drawn-out flashes in time, he had released me, grabbed a book on top of the refrigerator, and pulled a gun out from the middle.

He was no longer sexy, seductive, purr-in-my-ear Robert. He was dangerous.

And then someone shouted "Kate!"

Oh shit! It was Scott!

"That fucker!" Robert growled.

I panicked. Holy Christ, there was a gun. "Robert, Robert, please put the gun away. He's not worth it, please, please, please. Put it down."

"Kate!" Scott started banging on the door again. Robert took in what was happening and put the gun in his pocket.

Shit! No underwear and a loaded gun.

He looked to the door and then at me. "I'll feel better if you talk to him while you are with me. I can protect you if something happens."

"It's fucking Scott, seriously?"

"He is not in his right frame of mind if he has shown up here to confront you. Anything can happen."

"OK, let's get this over with." I jumped off the counter. "Pants would probably be a good idea."

"I don't know. I kinda like you like that."

I muttered to him, "Troublemaker."

There was a trace of a smile on his face. "I'll go calm him down."

"Just don't shoot him."

"I make no promises."

Crap! I ran down the hall and grabbed my yoga pants and sweatshirt. Didn't want to rub it in with wearing Robert's shirt. *Wait a minute,* I thought real quick. *Yes, I do.* I threw the sweatshirt back on the bed.

I could hear Robert being all authoritative, telling Scott to calm down while Scott kept asking him if he'd fucked me. I showed up at the door, and Robert positioned himself between us.

That dangerous aura wrapped around me again. I knew Robert was in protective mode. I stayed calm for his sake.

Scott took one look at me and saw I was wearing Robert's shirt. *Take that, you loser!*

"What! So you're fucking him now?"

"Calm down, Scott. I'm warning you," Robert let out.

I stayed calm. "As a matter of fact, yes! Since you're so eager to know, and we are now dating as well. I have you to thank for that."

His face fell. "But, Kate, we have been together seven years. I said I was sorry."

"I heard it, and thank you for apologizing. The flowers were beautiful too. I'm sure they made a lot of women happy."

"Women?"

"I sent them over to the hospital."

"Oh."

Robert stood in a slight crouch, like a tiger ready to strike his prey.

"But I want you back, Kate."

"You don't get to make that decision. I don't want you back. I'm moving on. I suggest you do the same."

I was shaking from the confrontation, and Robert was still in high gear. His energy felt unsettling.

I slowly and carefully reached out and touched his shoulder, hoping this was over. His stance changed, and he clasped my hand in his.

"Go home, Scott," Robert straightened and commanded.

"This isn't over, Beckham!"

I answered for him. "Yes it is, Scott. It's over. Leave us alone." I could see he was seething.

"I'll fucking get you for this, Beckham!"

"I'll be ready and waiting."

I started to pull Robert back in, but it was like pulling on a marble statue. I stopped pulling and tried a new approach. I tucked myself under his arm at his side. That worked. His whole body relaxed.

"It's over. Let's go back in," I said as I looked into his green eyes. Wow, they were stunning in this light.

He searched my face for a moment. "No one will ever hurt you while I'm around."

I smiled at him. "I know."

My stomach growled again as Scott peeled away.

"Come on, let's go feed you."

We walked back into the house with me still tucked under his arm. He shut the door behind him, and I waited on the landing. Robert assaulted me with his mouth as he pinned me against the wall. I wrapped one leg around his waist and he guided the other so I was once again wrapped around him like earlier. He had one hand under my butt and the other around my back, pressing me to him. Without breaking the kiss, he carried me up the stairs. I drew back first, needing to breathe, and he deposited me back on the island.

"Now let's try this again." He stepped away and put the gun back in the book and returned it to where it originally was.

I hopped off and wrapped my arms around him. "Thank you."

"You are entirely welcome, my lady." Again, his accent. *Yum!*

I made the coffee while he cooked us bacon and eggs. I made the toast then we sat and ate.

I remembered my phone. "Shit, I forgot to text my mother." I jumped up and checked. Whoa, there were a lot of messages.

"Oh crap!"

"What is it?"

"I have to enter back into reality."

He laughed and glanced over my shoulder as I showed him all my messages. One by one, I started answering.

Ten minutes later, Robert had the kitchen cleaned up. He approached me and brushed my hair off my shoulder, which sent tingles down my back as I finished typing.

"There, sent! That's it. I'm all yours. But I have to stop over at my house sometime soon."

"I'll go with you."

"Um? My parents think I'm staying with Pepper for the weekend."

"You can drop me down the street. I'll go for a run."

"Really?"

"Yes, if that's all right with you?"

"That's fine with me."

"Good, let's go have a shower now."

He grabbed my hand and dragged me back to the bedroom. He stripped off first and then turned the water on. I stared with my mouth slightly open. Swaggering over to me, he tilted my chin up to look at him. "Like what you see?"

"Yes." I answered shyly.

"Good." And he leaned in for a soft lip-touching kiss.

I melted. He lifted his T-shirt off me and again kissed me so, so softly. He lowered himself on his knees and kissed each one of my nipples. They reacted instantly. Again, he inserted his thumbs on each side of my pants and pushed down gently. I stepped out of them.

His hand was now exploring my sex again, and his other hand was around my butt, slightly pushing me toward him. He looked up at me, and our eyes were searching each other. His sexual aura was wrapping around me again, and he inserted two fingers into my now-needy sex and had his thumb on my clit, rubbing.

Holy shit, what the hell is this! I have never felt anything like this before.

He gently rocked my behind toward him with slow pulses, and his fingers were easing in and out of me with a slightly faster rhythm.

Oh shit, I'm gonna come.

No, I stand corrected. *I was coming.*

My orgasm ripped through my body, making me grab a hold of his shoulders for support. He didn't let up, and I want to stop him. He was dragging the feeling out so long.

"Oh no, stop, please stop! I can't take any more! Oh god! Oh, Robert! Ah! Jeez! It's so good . . . oh, Robert! Please! Ah . . .!"

Then he slowed down and released his thumb first and then stopped the rocking of my behind. He then stood with his fingers still inside me, slowly stroking.

The room was full of steam.

"You are so beautiful when you let go." And then there was one more soft, soft kiss on my lips. He pulled his fingers out slowly and took my hand, leading me to the shower.

His bathroom had a walk-in shower big enough for the both of us plus one. He had a separate bath and whirlpool tub big enough for three as well. It was all tiled in rich brown-colored stone and copper. Very appealing. He placed me under the spray first then began to wash me from head to toe. Who knew I liked someone washing my hair? He was fantastic at it. I enjoyed the pampering, but it was his turn, and I returned the favor. After washing every sexy inch, I put more gel in my hands to let him know I was not done.

I started to massage his balls slowly but firmly. He responded just how I wanted him to. First with a groan then with a growl, and he put one hand out to steady himself. I pulled one hand from his testicles and took a hold of his hard length. I stroked him firmly and with rhythm, just as he did with his fingers in me. Then I squatted in front of him, licking and sucking his beautiful head first. I looked up after a few seconds to see how he was reacting.

He had both hands out, supporting himself, and he was breathing heavily. With my eyes on his, I pulled him deeper into my mouth. I was taking him in halfway and coming back to tease his head while still massaging his balls.

"Jaysis, Kate! That's so fucking good, baby."

I was beaming inside. He liked what I could do to him. Not that I ever experimented this passionately—but it was him. He was making me explore the possibilities.

I turned my gaze back down, and I took him nearly to the end, rubbing the back of my throat. *I can do this!* I mentally cheered. Again,

I took his full length, tracing my tongue on a vein. I did this two more times and then sucked his head some more and went back to taking him most of the way in. His hands came off the wall and grabbed my hair, holding my head as he took over.

"Baby, I'm so close. Do you want me to come in your mouth or pull out?"

I wrapped a hand around his ass, keeping him in my mouth.

"That's right, baby. Work that tongue." He was fucking my mouth, and it was sexy hot.

I released my teeth behind my lips, and that was his undoing. He growled my name and spurted hot salty fluid into my mouth. I swallowed and sucked his head to get another mouthful. He even tasted delicious.

That's it! I decided. *He is a god.* A sexy, dangerous, yummy god. And he has claimed me! I licked him a few more times with both my hands holding him.

He pulled me up and wrapped his arms around me, sealing his lips over mine. He shoved his tongue into my mouth. Breaking off the kiss, he simply stated, "I am definitely keeping you."

I laughed. "Good because I'm definitely keeping you."

"When do you go back to work?"

"Monday morning."

"Stay with me until then?"

Stupid grin back on my face! "Yes."

"Good." Reaching back, he turned off the shower. "Come on, let's dry off and go to your parents." He wrapped a towel around me—not one of those regular economy bath towels but a huge, plush "I'll just wear this for the day" towel. For a young single guy, he sure had expensive and fine taste.

I turned to him. "How old are you?"

"Twenty-nine."

"When's your birthday?"

"August 15."

"You have a thirtieth birthday coming up?"

"Yup."

I smiled. "Do you know how old I am?"

Uh-oh! There was that wicked grin again.

"Yes."

I was surprised. "Do you know when my birthday is?"

His grin widened. "Yes."

I became a little irritated. "Do you know my bra and shoe size?"

"I do now."

"Robert!"

He swaggered over again and put his hands on my shoulders. "You have to remember, I've had my eye on you for six years. I paid attention to detail."

I looked around the room. "I'm not going to find some blow-up doll with my picture on it, am I?"

He chuckled. "No, I got rid of that."

I swatted at him, and my god/man—who had excellent reflexes—diverted my hand with ease. He then turned while swatting my butt with his towel. "You're so in for it."

Rubbing my behind, I charged him.

He stepped—and I mean simply stepped—out of the way like I was Toro. Then he spun around and scooped me up, launching me onto the bed. He leaped on top of me, tickling and kissing me everywhere. I was laughing and screaming, begging him to stop. He put his lips to mine, and I returned his kiss with passion.

We finally got out of the house an hour later. I let him drive my car. I was just too worn out from all the sex while Mr. Hot Cop was going to go for an hour's run. I gotta get in better shape. There he was, looking all sexy again in his running gear.

He looked over at me. "I am taking you out tonight, OK?"

"Dinner and a movie?"

"Dinner at a pub. I want you to meet some people."

"People?"

"Yes, cousins and colleagues. I want to take you to a family cookout tomorrow. So pack something comfortable for that too. And whatever you wear to work. I want to wake up with you Monday morning."

That got a smile from me. "Why don't I just move in?"

"All right."

"I meant that as a joke."

"I didn't."

"Robert!"

"Six years I've been waiting. I want every minute, every possible second with you."

"Let's start with this weekend. It's a lot to take in, and I barely know you."

He didn't say anything, just lifted my hand and kissed it.

About half a mile from my parents' house, he pulled over. "I'm going to run straight for half an hour down this way, and then I'll turn around and run back. I'll meet you here. Can you bring me some water and a towel?"

"Sure thing, stud."

He got out and came around to my door. Offering his hand, he walked me to the driver's side and gave me a parting kiss.

Well, OK, we were making out. He looked so good.

"See you in a bit."

I slapped his butt, and off he went. He will probably have every female walker and jogger following him back.

I pulled away from the curb and headed to my house. Thank goodness it was quiet. Everyone was out, so I got busy with packing. I grabbed my pills and popped one in my mouth and then stuck them in my bag. I also grabbed some makeup, nightshirts, and a couple of outfits.

Shit! All I have are dirty uniforms. So I'll do some laundry at Mr. Hottie's house. His hamper looked almost full.

I pulled out the other dress I bought. It might be too much for tonight, but what the hell. He's taking me out.

Then I grabbed some shorts, my sexy blue jeans, a few T-shirts, and a matching sweatshirt for the cookout. I knew these shorts would make him lose his mind. I grabbed my shoes, sandals, and an extra outfit just in case.

I carried my bag out to the car and called Pepper.

She picked up on the first ring. "Details! I want details!"

"Well, hello to you too."

"Jesus, he couldn't keep his hands off you, and he had this protective force field around you all evening."

"Until he danced with you."

"Fucking hell he can dance! So tell me. I know you were over there last night. Spill the beans, Quinn. How is he?"

"A freak of nature."

"Oh, Jesus, he's that good?"

"Better."

"You lucky bitch! I hate you."

"What about Mark?"

"I haven't slept with him yet."

"What! You're kidding?"

"He makes me nervous. I feel like I'm back in high school, and he's the one I want."

"You're screwed."

"I know. I think it's going to be the L thing."

"I can't get past infatuation at the moment, let alone love."

"If this was it and you couldn't see him ever again, how would you feel?"

"At this moment, I would feel empty and sad. Knowing it would not ever get any better than him. He is the friggin' jackpot."

"Let's face it. You already fucking love him, sweetie."

"I think I'm in shock."

"No, it's 'blindsided kick you in the gut' love!"

I laughed. "I'm spending the weekend with him."

"Oh really?"

"Yes, he's taking me out tonight to meet family and guys from work. Then tomorrow we are going to a cookout at a relative's house."

"He's bringing you to meet the family?"

"I think, or relatives. His dad lives in England, and his mother lives in Ireland."

"He's European?"

"Yup."

"I so fucking hate you!"

"Hey, Scott showed up at his house this morning."

"What the fuck!"

"We were about to cook breakfast, and he was banging on the door."

"What did you do?"

"Well, Robert grabbed some kind of handgun that he had hidden in a book."

"Did I mention I hate you? He is like James Bond."

"No, more like scary, dangerous dude. Anyways, all's I was wearing was his T-shirt, and I told him I needed pants on."

"Why?"

I laughed. "That's what he said. So I slipped into my yoga pants and went down to confront Scott. Robert was already there, all Mr. Cop, telling him to calm down. And Scott took one look at me and realized Robert and I were together."

"Hey, can't say he's a dummy."

I snorted into the phone. "Anyways, I told him I was with Robert now, and he needed to move on."

"I'm so glad I got my car fixed before you broke it off. How did he take it?"

"He threatened Robert."

"And how did Mr. Universe take that?"

"Basically with a challenge."

"What kind of gun was it?"

"I don't know."

"Revolver or pistol?"

"Revolver."

"Size of your hand extended, or smaller or larger?"

"Size of my hand."

"It's a .38 special. He's getting better and better in my eyes."

"Mine too." I giggle.

"You doing anything Sunday night?"

"Yes, sleeping with Robert. He wants to wake up with me before work."

"I really, really fucking hate you."

"I gotta go pick him up."

"Where is he?"

"Running. I dropped him off on Elm and came home to grab some clothes and essentials."

"Well, go catch your guy. Call me to let me know when you can come out and play again."

"I'll call you on Monday. Bye."

"Be safe. Bye-bye, girlfriend."

I hung up.

I had grabbed two waters from my fridge and a towel that I put on the passenger seat when my sister pulled into the driveway.

"Heard you finally broke up with that loser."

"Yup."

"It's about time."

"Yup."

"Don't worry, someone will scoop you up."

"Yup."

"Where are you going?"

"Over to Pepper's for the weekend."

"Tell her I said hi."

"Sure thing, sis. Bye."

"Bye, Kate. Let me know if you want to go out, OK?"

I smiled and waved.

I jumped into my car and headed down to our rendezvous spot. After parking on the side of the road, I exited out of my vehicle and I saw him in the distance. With his towel and water in hand, I watched him in motion. I could just picture him in a chase. The bastard never had a chance.

He slowed about two hundred feet from me and walked. He was glistening. Then I walked to meet him halfway and handed him the water. He snapped it open and downed half the bottle. Then I handed him the towel and took the water bottle. He wiped off his face and neck and pulled me in for a kiss. He looked even stronger after a workout! *Drool!*

"You all set?" he asked.

"Yup, got my bag packed."

"Good, let's go home."

He took my keys from me and led me to the passenger side.

"You do know this is my car?"

"You wouldn't let me take mine."

I smiled and let him drive. "Did you know I have a sister?"

He grinned. "Yes."

"Did you know my favorite teacher was in fourth grade—Mrs. King?"

He was giving me a low velvety laugh. "I do now."

"You're rotten."

"You're beautiful." He picked up my hand, kissing the back of it again.

I couldn't help but join in his grin. "So what was your major in college?"

"I had a double major. Criminal Justice and Economics."

"Wow, that's quite a spread."

"I became very focused. And when I made money, I wanted to know what to do with it."

"Why a cop?"

"It satisfies my dark side."

I didn't know what to ask next. That was a powerful response, and I felt that dangerous aura that I felt this morning.

"Do you have a lot of student loans?"

He kissed my hand again then went back to stroking the back of it. "Not a one."

"So did your parents help you out?"

"They paid for my education, but I had to pay all my living expenses."

"How did you pay for that? Living at college can be just as expensive."

"I worked my way through college."

"Double major and working? Wow, you must have been ambitious."

"Absolutely."

"What did you do for work?"

"Stripped."

"What?"

"Male stripper."

"No way!"

He raised his eyebrows to me as if he didn't like being questioned. Then all the dancing visualized in my brain. Man could he dance.

"Holy cow, you were a stripper!"

"Paid for my college, helped pay for my house, and gave me investment money."

"You don't have a mortgage?"

"Nope. Paid in full."

"Car?"

"Paid for."

"Holy crap! How wealthy are you?"

I was mortified that I just asked that, but he laughed.

"Comfortable, not wealthy."

"Well, that explains your dancing abilities."

He grinned and kissed the back of my hand again.

"What were you on stage?"

"Cop."

I snorted. "I bet. You might have to perform for me one night."

"Gladly." And he rubbed his lips back and forth over my hand.

We arrived back to his house shortly after. He came around and opened my door then went to the back of the car and retrieved my bag. Walking toward the door, he interlinked our hands together. I could feel his sexual energy beginning to envelope me again.

"How was your run?"

"Not long enough. I want you again."

Everything south of my belly button ignited. "Only if you wear your hat."

"Oh, baby, that can be arranged." He actually scooped me up onto his hip, like how a mother carries a two-year-old. I giggled and nuzzled into his neck.

He couldn't get that door open fast enough. He just left my suitcase on the landing and positioned me in front of him again and took the stairs two at a time. We didn't make it to the bedroom. The couch was an acceptable alternative. He ripped my yoga pants off this time. No fingers were used to glide them down, and my top was history. Then that two-second rule popped into my head. I was noticing exactly what my new boyfriend could accomplish in only two seconds. I added "stripping his clothes off."

Oh my gosh! He's a stripper. My new boyfriend was a stripper!

My libido just shot off the Richter scale. Then he couldn't be in me quick enough. No foreplay. Just hard-core fucking, and I wanted this. I wanted him slamming into me.

Right away, he assaulted that new spot in my body I hadn't known was there; and with every thrust, it became hungrier. I started to meet him thrust for thrust. Then he grabbed my hips to assert his dominance, and I came. One more full-length pump and he emptied himself inside me, letting go, growling out my full name with curses.

It was like I ran for an hour. I was heaving and trying to catch my breath.

"You're. Going. To. Kill. Me," I managed to get out.

"Not a chance, baby. I'm counting on you being around for a long, long time."

Ridiculous smile, I really hate you right now!

He gave me a couple of more pumps and leaned over to kiss me.

"Yeah, yeah, yeah. OK, OK, I need a nap," I muttered.

He laughed and scooped me up over his shoulder and carried me to the bedroom. Placing me in bed, he climbed in behind me and pulled me to him.

I really did fall asleep. I woke up starving. Stripper boy was still hugging me, and I had to pee. I think I moved a fraction of an inch, and he was awake. He was kissing my shoulder when I blurted out, "Honey, I gotta pee." And he released me.

I ran to the bathroom. *Oh no! Did I call him honey again? Hot cop, tiger, stripper deserves a more worthy endearment than that. I'll have to think about that one.*

I grabbed another cloth and gave myself a quick wash. There, ready for the fifth round.

I wondered, how many times could I have sex with this man in twenty-four hours? I looked at the clock. *Crap! It's only one o'clock.* I did the math to about what time we started last night. Nine more hours! I pushed the thought out of my head and opened the door. He was sitting up in bed, and he pulled the covers for me.

"No, get up. I'm hungry."

He failed at hiding his amusement.

I strolled over to his T-shirt drawer and pulled one out and slipped it on. *See, I'm getting to know him.* He rose out of the bed and came up behind me. I pulled out a shirt for him too and just handed it to him over my shoulder. He was definitely amused and ran his hand up the T-shirt that I had on to my bare butt and rubbed.

"Oh no, you don't. I require food, and for the next nine hours, you have one more shot at it. So pick your chance wisely."

He nuzzled my neck. "I have a limit?"

"Yes, until I get used to you. I think five times in twenty-four hours is more than fair."

He was rubbing my clit again.

"You can use it now if you want, but just once. You will have to wait for the next eight hours and whatever minutes to have me again."

He growled in protest. Definitely part-tiger.

I handed him some pants, and he yanked them away from me. I really tried not to smile but failed miserably as well.

"Can I kiss you?" He sulked.

"Absolutely, as much as you want."

He brightened up at that. "I'll get your bag. We'll go out for lunch. You'll be safer in public."

I freshened up in the bathroom. When I came out, he had on black jeans and a classic black short-sleeved collared shirt, a belt, and boots!

"That's not fair!" I protested.

"All's fair in love and war, baby." There was that wicked, wicked grin.

I'm toast! He's swaggering toward me. *Oh shit! Hold your ground! Hold your ground, woman! Give in now, and I will lose all credibility!*

He kissed me and kissed me and kissed me. I was panting, but I was still upright and still dressed. *Yes!* I wanted to pump my fist in the air.

"Hang on, I want to change."

"Why? You look beautiful."

"Because I am a woman, and after seeing you, I'm not happy with my choice."

He shook his head. "I'll be in the living room."

I reach up and kissed his cheek. "I'll just be a minute."

He slapped my butt and strutted out of the room.

I unzipped my bag and grabbed that spare outfit and darted into the bathroom. Red tartan miniskirt, white knee-highs, heeled Mary Jane with a collared white shirt. I rolled up my sleeves and unbuttoned the bottom three buttons then tied it in the front to show off my midriff a little. I checked out my new look, and inspiration hit me. Low ponytails!

Finishing my hair, I looked very pleased with myself and headed to the living room. I heard the television click off, and he stood as I came down the hall.

"Oh. Fuck. Me!" He bit out.

I stopped about ten feet from him. "You like?"

"You're wearing that . . . out? In the middle of the day?"

I twirl for him.

He growled. "I better bring a gun." And he moved past me to the bedroom.

I looked around for my purse and spotted it on the coffee table. I walked over and picked it up. Robert was heading back toward me. His look was stern, and he reached for my hand.

"Let's go." He pulled me toward the door.

I caught up to him and snuggled to his side.

The garage door was already up. "I like your car, by the way. It really suits you."

"You better be wearing underwear," he stated through clenched teeth.

"Of course." And I lifted up my skirt to reveal my red boy shorts.

If he had less control, I would have been up against the car and he would be slamming me right then. But Robert took a step back, adjusted himself, and then opened my door.

His energy was dangerous, and I was playing with dynamite. He slid in on his side, gripped the wheel, and started the engine. I kept my hands on my lap and waited. It took five minutes for him to settle, and then I relaxed. With his right hand, he lifted my skirt again and peeked under.

"This outfit is staying at my house." This was a command.

"Do I get visitation rights?"

"And you can only wear it in my presence."

I grinned. "If you like this one, you're gonna love a few of my others."

He simply took the wheel with both hands and accelerated.

We arrived at a pub in the south end. O'Connor's was the name on the outside. I waited until Robert came around to my side and opened the door.

He pulled me out and into him. "You are a handful of trouble."

"Too much?"

His sexual energy was back. "I don't like the new rule."

I was breathing heavier as his energy wrapped itself around me.

I caved. "All right, no rules this weekend, but I'm going to need to be able to walk on Monday."

He scooped me up, and my legs wrapped around his waist. Both his hands slid right to my butt. He was holding a cheek in each one. There was that wicked grin back again. He kissed me and bumped the car door closed. I moved my hands from his biceps to wrap my arms around his neck. He carried me all the way to the entrance before reluctantly releasing me. I tucked myself back under his arm again with my arm around his waist. He was much more relaxed.

We were seated right away, and the greeter gave him a wink. What the fuck was that!

"You know her?" I tried to sound even, but his smile gave me away.

"Yes" was all he said.

Shit! Do I want to know?

"Where is he!" was all I heard from the front of the room. Then this older, very attractive woman approached our table. "Ah, there's himself, and he's brought his daughter." She looked down at me.

OK, *mortified.* Maybe not the right choice in outfits.

"Where ya been, child? Are we getting too dull for ya?"

He let out a low velvety laugh, and everything south of my belly button reacted. My mouth was dry, and I needed water.

"Busy working. This is my girlfriend, Kate." He introduced me, but I had no idea who she was.

"Kate?" she questioned as he nodded and was smiling at me sprawled out in his booth. "Kate?" she questioned again, and then something snapped in place for her. "This is *theeee* Kate?" She said it as though it was a question that you didn't want to really know the answer to.

I stared at my tiger who was basking in pride.

"Well, come here, child, and let me get a good look at you," she ordered me out of the booth.

I quickly smoothed the naughty skirt down, and she turned me all the way around as I entered degradation. I glanced over to lover boy who just looked smug!

"How old is she?"

Oh my god! She was directing the questioning to him.

"Twenty-six," he answered.

"My god, child! You don't look a day over sixteen." She directed me back to the booth. "Pretty little thing you are."

I wanted to kick him.

He tried to lose the smirk then grabbed both my hands and brought them to his lips.

"Now what can I get for ya?" she asked the both of us.

He was still hiding his smile in my hands, and I just looked at her. "Whiskey please."

"This time of day, love?"

"Yes, please."

She disapproved but turned to him.

"Usual," he muttered into my hands.

"Coming right up." She turned and headed for the bar, shouting our orders to the barman.

Robert kept running his mouth back and forth over the back of my hands, holding them firmly while searching my eyes for my next reaction.

The drinks came, and she asked him if we knew what we wanted to eat.

"Give us a minute" was all he said, and she headed back to the bar, shouting out orders to the employees. I pulled my hand slightly, and he released them but still searched my eyes.

I broke the staring contest and picked up my whiskey and knocked it back then pulled his beer over to my side.

"Oh, baby, don't be like that." He sprawled out again in the booth.

"Who is she?"

"My aunt." There was a hint of amusement in his voice.

I took two big swallows of his beer. "And what did she mean by '*theeeee* Kate'?" OK, I was getting sarcastic.

He reached for my free hand, and I quickly pulled it into my lap. He leaned forward. "They all know I fancied you."

"What does that mean?"

"I really liked you."

OK, either the shot calmed me down or that was really sweet. I lightened up a little. "Liked, huh? So you like me?"

"Oh no, baby, this is way beyond like now."

Cha-ching! The smile was working its way back.

"Yeah, more like possess."

"That's about in the ballpark."

I took another sip of his beer then slid it back to him. He turned the glass to where my lips were and took a long swig himself.

Oh jeez! I'm not going to be walking right on Monday.

"Keep staring at me that way, and I'll drag you downstairs to the bathroom" was his velvety warning.

I snapped out of it and picked up the menu. He took another drink off his beer.

I went straight for the meat choices. I needed protein to be able to survive him this weekend.

"Anything strike your fancy, love?" He was playing with me now.

"The stew sounds really good."

"It's the best around."

"Do you have any suggestions?"

"You on a plate."

A younger waitress came over. "Rob!" she sort of squealed. I studied her reaction. He gave her a bright megawatt smile. I turned back to her. I hated her immediately and pulled his beer back over.

"And who's this?" she inquired.

"Nathalie, this is my girlfriend, Kate." He then returned the introduction for me, but more personally. "Baby, this is Nathalie, a friend of the family."

Crap! They are not related.

She nodded to me. "Nice to meet you, Kate."

I was feeling the whiskey right about now. I gave her just as dazzling a smile as he did. "Likewise, Nathalie."

She studied me for a moment then turned her attention back to my hottie.

"Did you two decide what you want?"

He looked right at me. "I know what I want. How about you, baby?"

I was sure of two things right now. I was starving, and I was going to get fucked downstairs in the bathroom. I just secretly wished Nathalie would be listening.

I cleared my throat. "I'll have the beef stew."

"Good choice."

"And how about you, Rob?"

"I'll have the same. Can I get another beer and Kate a whiskey and soda?"

She looked at the beer in front of me. "Is that the usual?"

Damn she knew what he drank!

"Yes," I chimed in before she left. "Could we get a couple of waters as well?"

"Sure thing, Kate."

I think there was a slight displeasure in her tone. I slid his beer back to him and scooted out from my seat. I was staking my claim.

He straightened up and moved in. "You're barely safe across from me, and now you want to test my limits without anything to stop me?"

I looked into his eyes and put my hand on his thigh. That got me another low growl. I thought, *Now, now, now. Be a nice kitty.* Now where did I put that whip and chair? My kitty! I grinned as I caressed him higher.

His arm went around my shoulder, and he reached across with his other hand and put it over mine, softly stroking it.

Nathalie came back to the table with a disapproving look. Yup, I knew it! She had the hots for him. Then I looked around, but who wouldn't?

Oh yeah, me? I didn't even pay attention to him for six years. I'll be making up for that now.

She placed our drinks on the table. I wondered for a split second if mine would end up all over me.

Bring it on, bitch. Honeybunch here would be all too eager to lap it all up.

I squeezed him in my hand, and he cleared his throat. I realized my little fantasy had brought my hand to his growing cock.

He leaned into my ear. "I have no problem ripping those panties off you right here and sitting you on my lap."

I stopped with the gripping and picked up my drink with both hands. He started playing with my ponytail.

Nathalie came back with fresh rolls and butter.

"Food!" I picked one up and split it open and buttered it. I fed it to Tiger first, which brought an approving grin as he took a bite from my hand. I took the next bite then fed him the rest.

He kept playing with my ponytail as I did the same to the next roll.

Nathalie came back over and cleared her throat as I was feeding the last piece to him. We both looked up at the same time.

She had a fake smile on. "How is everything?"

"Delicious," I answered her.

"Can I get either of you anything else?"

I shook my head, and Robert answered, "No, we're good. Thanks."

"Food will be out in a few minutes."

I took another sip of my drink then offered Robert some.

"I don't drink whiskey."

"Why?"

"Brings on a different personality."

"Oh."

"Yes, I can become . . . unreasonable."

"Good to know. No whiskey for hubby."

Oh shit, that was a Freudian slip. He stopped twirling my hair. "Honey—I meant honey," I sputtered.

"I kinda like the sound of that."

What! We've only been dating a few hours and he is thinking marriage? I didn't know what to say.

Here comes Nathalie. Suddenly, I'm like, *Yeah, Nathalie!*

She placed the plate before him first and then mine.

"Looks fantastic!" I cheered.

"Rob, you need another?"

"No, I'm good."

My drink was half gone.

"How about you?"

Where's the love, Nathalie? Now it's "you." Kate, I'm Kate. Theeeee *Kate.* "I'm good. Thank you, Nathalie." *See, I remembered your name.*

Robert pulled his arm out from around my shoulder, and right then, I should have shot back to the other side. But no, I stayed next to him, and his hand encircled the top of my knee then slowly drew up and under my skirt. He stopped at my boy shorts, slipping his pinkie up under them. I mixed my stew around, trying not to react, and blew on it. Now his ring finger was in there. I blew again, but with more gusto. And there was his middle finger. He glided them down between my legs and rubbed. I clamped them together, trapping his fingers still. I reached down and tugged his hand out.

"Weak and starving here." I put his hand on the table next to his plate.

Nathalie came back over. "How is everything?"

He brought his left fingers to his mouth and licked them. "Finger-licking good."

I choked as I started to swallow. He thumped on my back a few times, and I coughed. It was out of my throat and back in my mouth. I grabbed my napkin and spit the piece into it then finished off my whiskey.

"You OK, baby?" He rubbed circles on my back.

"Fine!"

Nathalie was just standing there, watching. "Do you want another drink?"

"No, I'll stick with the water."

She directed the next question back to the sex fiend I was sitting next to. "Rob, you just let me know if there is anything else I can tempt you with."

Seriously? I mean, why not just say, "If you want to fuck me, I'm right over there." I hated her again!

"No I have everything I want right here."

There—take that, bitch! Good, good kitty. I almost wanted to scratch under his chin.

I finished my stew and felt much better. Then a revelation came to me. I can have dessert! I have burned so many calories in the last (I did the math) twenty-two hours, and there was a promise of many more in the future. I want my cake!

Nathalie returned. "You all set?"

"Can I see the dessert menu?"

"Sure, I'll go get one."

Robert smiled. "Room for more?"

"Are you kidding? I'll have this burned off before supper."

There's that wicked grin.

"Exactly." He nuzzled into my ear.

Nathalie handed me the menu.

"I'll have the cheesecake."

"And you, Rob?"

"I'll just have some of her."

I think he meant to say "*hers.*" *Some of hers.* I turned to him shocked and smiling, with my hand over my mouth. Nathalie was gone.

"Did you really just say that?"

He winked at me and took my hand away from my mouth and put it to his.

Anyways, she came back with two forks. We had just finished the cheesecake, and that awful woman came back over to our table. "So, lovebirds, how was your meal?"

"It was delicious, Louise, thank you."

She turned to me.

"I really enjoyed it, thank you." *Take the high road, Kate.*

"Well, you come back real soon. Nice to finally meet you, dear. You take good care of our Robert."

"I'll do my best."

That got his arm around me and a kiss to my temple. I came to realize I learned another fact about my new beau. He didn't give a crap about public displays of affection. If he wanted to kiss me, he was going to kiss me. No matter who was around. Add *bold* to my list to describe him.

He threw seventy dollars on the table without even looking at our bill. I said nothing, and he signaled for us to leave. I slid out and smoothed my skirt.

"Need to use the bathroom?" he asked as I smirked at him.

"No."

His hand was tracing the lace to my panties under my skirt. I batted him away, playfully stepping back. He did this thing that I did not see coming. He jolted forward and scooped me to him. My legs automatically wrapped around him, and he had my crotch pressed against his.

I wiggled to get free. "Oh my gosh. Not here, not here. Put me down," I pleaded in a whisper.

"For a kiss," he purred.

I gave him a quick kiss on the lips. His eyes narrowed. I kissed him again, a little longer, and he released me. Good! Feet back on the ground. I tucked myself back under his arm because I knew he liked this, and we headed for the door.

"See ya, Rob," Nathalie called to him.

"Thanks, Nat," he answered.

Nat? He has a nickname for her? Nat I liked it. It's a small bug, very annoying. Suits her.

As soon as we were past the doors, three things happened at once. Robert was falling to the ground, Scott was pointing a gun at me, and blood splattered my white blouse. Time slowed to a frame-by-frame picture. I looked down at the blood then kept looking down to the ground at Robert, who was on his back, holding a gun and emptying it into the man who shot him. I then became aware I was screaming something.

"Stop! Stop! Please, Robert, stop!"

Scott was no longer holding the gun but was being jolted back by each bullet. I knelt down next to him with tears streaming down my face. I reached out and touched his shoulder, and he stopped firing. He saw that Scott was going down to the ground and then made eye contact with me. The look in his eyes was pure and utter hatred.

He took one look at the blood on me, and the darkness faded to fear. He leaped up off the ground and grabbed me, holding me at a distance to examine every inch. I was sobbing, and people started pouring out of the restaurant, and everything sounded so muffled.

When Robert was satisfied with what he saw, he crushed me to his chest. Then I cried and cried, wrapping my arms around him. It sounded like everyone was talking underwater. Then not so much underwater, but it changed to a constant high-pitched tone that would not let up. I stopped crying, but Robert did not let up pinning me to him. There were cops everywhere. Someone approached us with some blankets, and Robert took one and swaddled me in it then put me back to his chest. I wrapped my arms back around him, hanging on for dear life.

They covered Scott's body, and it registered that he was dead. I turned my forehead toward Tiger's chest, and he cupped a hand behind my head.

An EMT was trying to pull me away from Robert, and I held on tighter, and there was a lot of yelling. Robert kept telling them I was not harmed, and then he just told them to fuck off.

There was arguing around us, and then Robert was talking to two cops. I peeked up, and it was the two that came to the restaurant last night. Liam and Sean. Yes, those were their names. I could hear Robert through his chest.

"No, she's not leaving my side. No! I fucking said no!"

Liam ran his fingers through his hair, frustrated.

Louise approached us with two drinks in plastic cups and held them out to Robert. He asked what was in them, and she said it was water.

He took one and rubbed his chin on my forehead. "Baby, here, take a few sips of this. It's water." He held the straw up to my mouth. "That's a good girl. Drink for me, baby." His arm was still wrapped tight around me and my blanket.

I took the straw between my lips and sucked. It was only water, but it tasted so good.

He brushed his lips back and forth over my forehead again. "That's it, good girl," he praised me and pressed a kiss in the middle as he stopped.

I took another sip then released the straw. He moved it to his mouth and took two big swallows. I could hear it moving down inside his body. My hearing was coming back, and it was really loud around us.

He made me sip again, but this time, I was very willing. Louise just hung out by Robert's side to exchange the empty cup for a full one. I started to relax slightly and loosened my death grip on Robert.

"That's it, baby, come back to me."

Some man in a suit approached us. "We'll need a statement. We have to go back to the station. I need the girl, Robert."

"You need a statement from me as well. We'll go together."

"Robert!" he started to say something but stopped. "Well hell! Come on, you can both sit in the back."

"Liam!" yelled Robert.

Liam quickly came over.

"We're going down to the station. Here, take my keys. When they're done with my car, bring it down for us, OK!" It was more a command than a request.

"Sure thing." He took the keys from him. "It will be all right, Kate." He touched my shoulder, and I thought Robert was going to snap. I felt every muscle tighten, and he turned me slightly to the right, breaking the contact from Liam's hand.

Liam slowly pulled his hand away and apologized to Robert. In the new angle, I peeked over my left shoulder and saw all the ambulances, police cars, vans, and news trucks. *Oh fuck! News trucks!*

I looked up at Robert. "My bag! Where's my purse?"

"Right here." He had it on his forearm that was wrapped around me.

Robert was wearing my purse. The more I thought about it, the more I giggled. My giggle turned into a laugh. Robert rubbed my back and shushed me until I stopped.

OK, back under control.

He explained everything that was happening. That we needed to walk about fifty feet to a cruiser and that he was going to put me in then slide in next to me.

Everything was exact, so there were no surprises. He kept talking and making sure I was aware of everything that was happening.

After walking fifty feet, we were at the police car.

"Pulling the door open." He pulled the door open. "Releasing you." He released.

I felt a little anxiety.

He turned me and kissed me. "It's OK, baby, I'm right here. I'm putting you in the car." He put me in the car, sliding right in behind me. "I'm closing the car door now." He closed the car door.

I jumped a little, and he pulled me up on his lap and rested my head back on his shoulder and wrapped his arms around me. I relaxed. I was safe.

The guy in the suit opened his door, and Robert ran through him: "Sliding in, closing the door, starting the car, and driving away." Every motion had a name, and Robert was reinforcing all of them.

I felt so safe and cherished by him. I curled up in his lap and extended my right arm around his chest. He kissed me again, but I was so tired, I just wanted to go to sleep. Then I did. I fell asleep in the arms of a man who completely possessed me.

Walsh was trying to reason with Robert, and Robert was growling low, telling him to fuck off and give him twenty more minutes. Then I heard him whisper, "Her parents are here, and they are worried."

That snapped my eyes open. "Oh shit!" I sat up, startled.

"Shh, baby it's OK. We are at the station. They want a statement."

I was awake and alert now.

I looked at Walsh. "Could you give us a minute please?"

"I'm not supposed to let you talk to anyone until they get a statement."

Robert shot him a look.

"Please, I won't say anything about what happened today. I just need to talk to Robert about something else."

"You have two minutes."

"Thank you."

He left and shut the door.

"What is it, baby?"

"My parents. I lied to them about being at your house last night. I told them I was staying with Pepper."

"It's OK, baby, we can handle that small detail."

"Oh god! You don't know my father. He's going to find out Scott came to the house in the morning and we had a confrontation then.

He's going to be *real mad.* My dad is an ex-SEAL and a ball-busting attorney."

"We will get along just fine. And it looks like we are going to need a good attorney right about now, so stop worrying." He kissed my nose.

"Robert!"

"It's all right, baby."

Walsh rapped on the window to let us know the time was up. He opened the door and extended a hand to me. Robert would not let me take it. He moved me to the opposite side of the car and got out first. Then he helped me out.

Chapter 5

He clasped my hand and held it firmly as we walked into the station. I stayed close by his side. Walsh led us down the hall to the waiting area.

There they were, James and Helen Quinn. They rushed me, and Robert put me behind him and went into a slight crouch. My dad recognized exactly what was happening and stopped my mother's forward motion.

"What are you doing?" she pleaded.

There was a five-second silence. I put my hand on Robert's shoulder and told him it was all right. My parents relaxed their stance as well. Robert stood up straight, and I went around him, never leaving contact with him.

"It's all right." I smiled to him.

There he stood, more relaxed.

My father let my mother's arm go, and she walked calmly toward me, gently lifting her arms to wrap around me. I hugged her back. No tears. I didn't even want to cry.

My father walked right to Robert and extended his hand. "Thank you. I owe you for keeping my daughter safe."

Robert shook my father's hand. "You owe me nothing."

See, that statement right there would have been perfect. "Blah, blah, blah, great, let's move on." But no! My super new, possessive, overprotective boyfriend just had to stake his claim. To *my parents*!

"I will protect her for as long as she will allow me."

Now both my parents were staring at him.

My dad just nodded, and my mother let me go and walked over to him. "Robert, I am Helen Quinn. We met a few times in more casual settings."

He took her extended hand.

"I just want to thank you as well. From what I understand, your quick actions saved my daughter's life."

"She is worth every breath."

My mind was willing him to shut up! *Shh! Bad kitty!*

Walsh came in again. "They're ready for your statement, Kate."

Robert took a step toward me so he was between Walsh and myself.

My father spoke calmly and directly to Robert. "Robert. I will be acting as Kate's and your attorney. I will not leave her side for a moment just as I will not leave yours during questioning."

"Fine, but she will have to be with us when they question me."

"That can be arranged," my father promised.

I think Walsh rolled his eyes.

Robert pulled me into him.

No no no! Not in front of my parents!

He kissed my temple and released me to my father.

"Come over here, Robert." My mother extended her hand. "Let's talk."

Oh god. Panic crept into my body. He's not safe with her. I needed to save him. I turned my head in their direction, but Daddy kept moving me forward.

I was in there for one hour. I told them every detail, from my first breakup with Scott to my first hookup with Robert and him coming to the house . . . yada yada yada. I was a slut! And all in front of Daddy! *Lord, take me now.*

We walked back to where Mom and Robert were sitting. They were laughing about something. *What the hell is going on!* I wanted to scream. The universe was fucking with me. Then I looked down, and I looked like a bloody teenage sex kitten. *Oh my god, I still have ponytails!* I ripped the elastic bands out of my hair and saw that Robert was staring at me, puzzled.

Bad! Bad kitty! I screamed at him from the inside. He should have at least taken those out to save my dignity!

They came for Robert, who got up and took my hand as I growled at him. "You should have at least taken the ponytails out!"

He, in turn, let out a laugh.

I wanted to stomp my foot. "I have to use the ladies' room."

He stopped the entourage. They all looked at each other.

"Kate needs to use the ladies' room," he said.

Mom scrambled up and spoke to Robert. "I'll go with her. She will be safe, I promise."

Why was everyone sucking up to Hot Cop?

The bathroom turned out to be a few feet away, and Mom came in with me. Robert could see the door. Everyone was happy.

Man, I needed to pee. While I was in the bathroom, I suddenly felt empowered! I was at the sink, and I turned to my mother. "I'm staying at Robert's tonight, just so you know. And tomorrow as well."

Hey, why not go down swinging?

"All right, honey, just make sure we have his phone number and address."

Not the answer I was expecting. *Ever!* I almost felt dizzy. Yes, the universe was fucking with me.

I grabbed the sink and cupped some water to splash on my face. My mom handed me a towel to wipe with. Unbelievable! Shoot-out at the OK Corral and Kate gets whatever she wants.

I opened the door and saw that Robert was intense. My tiger was pacing, and he looked toward me. He relaxed.

Calm down, sexy. Momma is back.

I walked right up to his side and took his hand. How's that for bold in front of my parents?

We continued to the questioning room. Oh, sorry. "Statement/ interrogation room." Robert led me in first, and I took a seat in the corner. Great! Super-hot new boyfriend confirming to my dad and everyone he worked with that I am a slut. *Record his statement. Let's get this over with.*

It happened that his version and my version were exactly the same. I mean exactly! I wanted to jump up and give him a high-five. That means we won't have to come back for more questioning. Even I knew that. When they were satisfied, they released us.

It was about seven o'clock now. Mom hugged me and leaned into Robert for a hug. What the hell! Dad shook his hand and kissed my forehead. Then they left. Liam had put Robert's car in the underground garage.

He met us in the waiting area. "You guys coming tomorrow?"

Robert looked over to me for an answer. I nodded my head.

"Looks like it," he answered. "But we'll see what tomorrow brings."

Liam cupped Robert's shoulder. "Ah, it will do you both a world of good."

I know from training that when trauma strikes, it's best to take basic baby steps of what is familiar. As far as our relationship went, so far, we had basic baby steps or full-open throttle. Go! Go! Go!

I went for the first thing I learned with Robert. I tucked myself under his arm, and I felt his whole body relax. It got me a kiss on the forehead. We walked down to the car, and he opened the door for me.

I was a dirty, bloodstained mess. I did not want Scott's blood on me a second longer, and I reached for Robert's arm. "I can't wear this any longer. I don't want this blood in your house."

He untied the knot in front then pulled each button free. He slid my shirt off my shoulders and down my arms. This would have been super hot if it wasn't totally horrifying. He folded it up and walked back to the "boot," as he called it, and pulled out a T-shirt. It was plain white, and he dressed me in it.

Pulling my hair out, he said, "There, baby, it's all gone. Let's go home."

He buckled me in. The roar of the engine made me think of pre–shoot-out times, and I put my head back and closed my eyes. When I opened my eyes again, I was horizontal, tucked into a familiar mass, with his arm secure around me. I was safe, cherished, and desired by this man. And I knew he knew I was awake.

"Don't let me lose our passion. Make me want to make love again." I said it out loud, and that was all it took.

His lips were on mine, and his hand was on my crotch. I had not realized I was no longer wearing panties. He had already stripped me down to only the T-shirt. *Pervert!*

His mouth left mine and trailed kisses down my neck and to my breasts. God, they ached for him. He fondled, caressed, and sucked, and I even held his head to each of them. I wanted him; I needed him.

We spent the first fifteen hours of our relationship licking, sucking, and fucking—and I was missing it. I missed that intensity. I missed his aura wrapping around me, and I wanted it back!

He was kissing and sucking my inner thigh when I realized I momentarily lost my train of thought. Then he was on my clitoris again, having his last meal. *Oh my god!* I wasn't going to last long. *Oh no, not long at all.*

That last tongue flick and suck was the end of me. I grabbed the sheets with both hands and grunted primal sounds that came from my chest. I screamed out Robert's name several times. And that was his cue; he moved over my body with ease and drove his cock right to that spot that loved him dearly. It missed him and wanted him home.

Too quickly, I was building again. Or maybe my last orgasm never stopped. All I remembered was I was going to let go again very soon. I felt him thicken inside me, and that did me in. I was in full-blown orgasm again, but so was he. He pumped me for a few more strokes, and that was it. He wrapped himself around me and turned us over so I was on his chest.

My hand was resting over his pectoral muscle, and I slightly stroked back and forth. He felt so good. I cleared my throat. "I know it's a little too soon, but I just want to say I love you."

He stilled. Then he pulled me up to his mouth and turned us both to the side. "I've been waiting a long time to hear those words come from you."

"Was it worth it?"

"Completely," he purred. "I love you too," he added, and that sealed my fate to him.

Then I felt him growing again, and I knew I was going to be fucked this time. I was wide awake, tucked into the man I now loved and who loved me back, his arm securely around me. I knew the instant I moved, he was going to wake up, but nature was calling. I brought his hand to my lips and kissed each finger. He kissed my shoulder and pressed me to the bed with his weight.

"I gotta pee," I warned him, and he released me. I jumped up and ran to the bathroom.

As I was washing my hands, I spotted his huge bathtub. I turned around and went over to explore. Time to christen the tub! I turned it on and rinsed out any dust. Then I put the stopper in, and it began to fill.

"Tiger needs a bath," I muttered to myself. I bounced over to him. "Wanna christen the tub?"

There! There was that wicked grin.

"Absolutely!" And he pulled me on top of him to the other side.

I was wrapped in Robert, and he was kissing and tickling me. I squealed and laughed. It felt so good to laugh.

He finally let me up. I stressed he let me up! I pulled off the covers. It looked like he was ready. His length was hard and ready. I examined it closely. He was two and a half handfuls, and I could not enclose my one hand fully around him.

I looked up at him, and he was sharing that megawatt smile with me. He knew exactly what I was doing, but I didn't care. Where the hell did all this confidence come from? I took him in my mouth to see if I could go all the way down his length. Almost. There was a small space between me and him. Maybe it's that half hand.

I withdrew from his penis and heard the tub was still filling. I looked at him again, and the smile was gone. His lips were separated, and his breathing was heavy. His body radiated with that sexual energy. I felt it! He was wrapping me in that aura. *Welcome back, feeling.* I embraced the sensation.

Come on, kitty, bath time! I pulled him—well, more like motivated him—toward the bathroom. I stood in front of the tub all perky to let him undress me, which he did on command. I have to remember this stuff. He's doing exactly what I wanted. *Go Team Kate! Catch that tiger by the tail.*

Then I let him trail the back of his fingers down my body. He was so hard. The bath was filling nicely, so I wrapped my hands around his length and massaged it; he purred. I just now realized he was giving me all the control. I forged ahead, thinking only about him and how he felt to me. I kept stroking him, and everything south of my belly button wanted him inside. I reached up on my tiptoes and placed one hand around the back of his neck and guided him into my kiss. Our tongues touched and circled.

Oh jeez, this is what he does against my sex. My vagina clenched; it had need of him right now. I pulled back from his gorgeous mouth.

"Take me from behind," I seductively commanded, and he moaned loudly.

Yes, I can do this. I turned and leaned down, grabbing the side of the tub, and parted my legs a little wider. He was feeling my butt with his greedy hands. I felt his cock masturbating my clitoris, slowly rubbing up and down on it. I spread my legs slightly wider. I wanted him in me. I wanted him in me now!

"Robert, I want you in me, please," I begged.

"Sshh, baby." His voice was so fucking sexy. "I'll take care of you."

Only he was still rubbing me with it. I wanted release, but he was just moving too slow for it to happen. Another few frustrating moments, and he guided his cock to my opening, only sinking a few inches in. I wanted to push back and take all of him, but the way he had me positioned, I couldn't.

"Robert, please! I am so close."

"I know, baby, I've got you."

I wanted to scream in frustration. He reached around and began to rub my clit.

Oh god, there is that slow ache again. I couldn't take it, so I rubbed myself into his fingers, and right there, I was feeling his hot breath against my neck as he moaned. My excitement built, and right when I was about to release, he grabbed my hips and shoved his cock up in me, pumping into my vagina.

I exploded! It was an out-of-body experience. I think I actually blacked out for a few seconds. I was incoherent, trying to say his name, trying to say anything, but it was all jumbled. A moan I've never heard came from deep in my throat. And I was still coming.

"That's right, baby, you're squeezing my dick so fucking good . . . ahhh fuck . . . Kate!" he yelled out.

And there he found his release. I felt him spilling into me, and I felt my insides gripping his length. Wow, these were completely new sensations for me, and I liked it.

He pumped a few more times in me and rubbed my ass again with his hand. "You're so fucking beautiful, baby. I can't get enough of you." His voice was velvet hot.

I was toast, so all I could come back with was "I love you." That was all I needed.

He slapped my butt. "I love you too." Then he pulled out.

I had to turn and sit on the tub for a moment. He reached over and shut off the tap. Placing one foot in, he lifted me and guided me in too. He lowered himself in first and then positioned his back against the wall and spread his legs for me to lie up against him. My head was back against that rock-hard chest, and he slowly poured water all over me. It felt so good.

We had a whole ten minutes of utter bliss, just the two of us lost in this small luxury. Then the phone started ringing and ringing and ringing. Our bubble burst, and we were back in reality.

I began to move, but he held me against him. "One more minute" was all he said. I knew his head was back, and he was still totally relaxed.

I turned and wrapped my arms around him. He smiled and caressed my back, still with his eyes closed.

The phone stopped only for a few seconds and then started ringing again. I grinned into his chest and trailed kisses down the middle. "Time to pay the piper," I stated.

He lifted his head. "What do you want to do today, baby?"

That came out of nowhere.

"I didn't know there were options."

"We hold all the cards."

Huh, I never thought about it like that. "So give me the options," I said.

I sat up, as did he. I still had my hand on his chest, so I rubbed my finger lightly back and forth. He put his hand over mine and rubbed the back of my hand.

"We are invited to my cousin's cookout. We can go there."

I tried to keep the horror out of my face, but I think I failed because he just grinned.

"We can stay locked up in here all day, or we can just go drive somewhere and get away." He tucked a piece of hair behind my ear. "Or we could check into a hotel, and I can lose myself in you all afternoon."

I smirked at that.

"What do you want to do?"

Yup, the phone was still ringing and getting on my nerves.

"Well, I personally like the hotel idea."

He raised my hand to his lips. "But we can't ignore the elephant in the room forever, and the sooner we deal with everyone, the quicker it will be behind us."

Damn it, he was right.

I took a deep breath and let it out sharply. "You're right. The quicker we expose ourselves to everyone, the sooner it will be over, and we can move on. Damn you for being so logical."

The phone was totally annoying, but it sealed my decision. "Let's go party. With your relatives."

"Trust me, baby, I don't want to go either. But we'll get our life back sooner and put this in the past." He caressed my cheek.

"Well, it looks like I'll be able to walk tomorrow after all. Work is going to be so boring."

"Work?"

"Yeah, I still have to go in tomorrow. By the way, can I do some laundry today? I need a clean uniform."

He looked at me in amusement. "Baby, you are not going to work tomorrow."

"What do you mean? I have to."

I thought this was his possessive protective mode talking, but he continued, "We have just been in a highly stressful circumstance. Neither your employer nor the department will allow us back on the job without being cleared through a psychiatric evaluation first."

"What?"

"Post-traumatic stress disorder. We'll get at least a week off." He smiled.

"No fucking way!"

"Oh yes, baby."

My brain started working again. He was right. I remember I was trained in this as well. In school, we had a half of a semester in PTSD.

His smile was infectious. "I've got you for a whole week."

I muttered, "I think you've got me for a whole life."

Oh no. I said that out loud.

"Even better." His megawatt grin was plastered on his face.

I wanted to splash him. "Get the phone. It's making me crazy."

He stood up and stepped out. Drying off, he wrapped a towel around his waist. I watched him walk out of the bathroom and called after him, "Hey, honey, what time is it anyways?"

The bedroom phone stopped ringing.

"Six fifty," he called back, and the phone in the kitchen went silent. He swaggered back in and picked up a towel for me. "Come on, baby, back to reality. They will be knocking at the door next."

"What did you do to the phones?"

"Pulled the plugs out."

He was so sexy and smart. Wrapping me in my towel, he moved over to the sink to brush his teeth. I went to the bedroom and opened my suitcase. No clothes. *Where the heck were my clothes?*

"Hey, honey?"

"Yeah, babe?" I heard him spit.

"What happened to my clothes?"

"They're hanging up in the closet."

What? I headed over to his walk-in, and there were my weekend outfits on hangers next to his.

I yelled, "If I'm staying the week, I'm going to need a few more things." I was smiling as I pulled down my sundress.

I turned, and he was leaning against the doorframe. "I'll help you pack."

"You'll move me in."

He strutted toward me. "What a delicious idea."

"You do realize we have only been dating like three days."

"The best three days of my life." He leaned in for a kiss.

I was aware of my breath and gave him a peck. Then I dodged around his mass, and I dashed into the bathroom. When I emerged all fresh as a daisy, I smelled food. Just then, my stomach let out a growl. I followed my nose to the kitchen and froze.

Bare feet, faded blue jeans, white T-shirt that clung to every bulge. He looked up with the same appreciation I apparently shared. He liked the dress.

He flipped the pancake and wiped his hand on the towel then closed the distance between us. He lifted my dress and admired my little white lace panties. Clenching his teeth together, he bit out, "Those don't have a chance in the world. They will be shredded by noon."

I brought him back to the task at hand. "Pancakes?"

That was it. He moved back to the stove—growling I think.

"Need any help?"

"No. Get your lovely ass up on that chair," he commanded.

I walked over to the place setting, and he placed a stack of pancakes in front of me. He then poured my coffee and placed that in front of me as well.

"Thank you."

He quickly kissed me. "You're entirely welcome, my queen."

I grinned; my Englishman was back.

He turned off the stove, put the pan in the sink, and filled it with water. Then he wiped the counter a little and came over with his own stack of cakes and his coffee.

I started eating. "These are really good. Box or scratch?"

"You wound me, my queen. For you, only the best. They are my own family's recipe."

I smiled up at him. "Really, really good. Thank you."

"You are welcome, my pet."

Pet? It is you who is my pet. My very own grrr grrr.

"How long do you—"

Bang! Bang! Bang! That was a trigger for me. I dropped my fork and shuddered.

"Kate! Robert! You guys in there?" It was Pepper.

I didn't even see Robert stand up. His hands were on me, turning me to him. "It's OK, baby. It's OK. It can't happen again. It's all over."

I was now standing and in his arm, with my arms locked in a death grip around him.

"Ssh, baby, it's only Pepper. You're OK." He soothed me so well.

I was coming out of it. I relaxed against him, and he explained the next few steps carefully to me while there was still knocking and the doorbell was still ringing. Robert's frustration reached his limit, and he forgot to mention he was going to yell. "For fuck's sakes! We'll be there in a minute!"

I began to cry; the noise stopped. He tightened his grip on me as I did the same. He repeated the soothing process all over. It took five minutes for me to let go, and when I did, he scooped me up and wrapped my legs around him.

"I was wrong. These panties will be shredded as soon as she leaves." He was trying to lighten my mood, and he succeeded.

I laughed and wiped my nose with the tissue he gave me.

"Are you ready for this? I'll send her away if you're not. Remember, we hold *all* the cards."

"No, I'm OK. That just freaked me out a little."

"PTSD. We might get two weeks out of this. Looks like you're moving in, baby." He kissed me, and I was completely back in the light. He carried me down the stairs still in his arms, mine wrapped around his neck, and he opened the door.

"Oh, for god's sakes! Get a room, you two."

"We have one, but you kept banging," Robert retaliated.

Pepper handed Robert the Sunday paper and marched ahead, dragging Mark along. "So what's been happening, Bonnie and Clyde? Last we seen, you were tearing up the dance floor. Now you're making national headlines."

Robert carried me up the stairs, reading the paper over my shoulder. Pepper gave him a disapproving stare.

He turned to my ear; we were in the living room now. "You OK, baby?" He kissed my ear and rubbed my back. I brought my legs to the ground and tucked myself under his arm.

Pepper just stared. "What's with the two of you?"

I answered, "PTSD."

"What the fuck is that?"

Mark answered her, "Post-traumatic stress disorder."

"Again? What the fuck is that?"

Mark continued, "It's a type of anxiety disorder. It can occur after you've seen or experienced a traumatic event that involved the threat of injury or death."

She softened. "Oh!" She took a seat next to Mark.

"So that's why it took us so long to get to the door," I confessed.

"The feckin' banging triggered her, eejit," Robert scolded Pepper.

"Sorry" was her apology; then she became too quiet.

Mark, being an up-and-coming lawyer, went right for the elephant in the room. "What happened?"

I looked up at Robert, and he looked down at me. He moved us to the oversized chair across from them and sat down first then pulled me on his lap. I curled up in it. Pepper kept quiet. I nodded for him to tell the story, and I put my arm around his shoulders.

Robert went through the story better than I could have. I would have mentioned a lot of unnecessary facts. I looked at the awful photo on the front page.

Then we heard a truck pull up, and Pepper leaned back to look out the window. In a flash, she blurted, "Shit! News team."

Robert shook his head.

Mark announced, "I can handle this."

Then Robert and I spoke together. "Thank you."

I grinned at Tiger. "Jinx." And he lurched forward to attack my neck. I squealed and giggled.

Pepper just stared. "So one minute you're fine, and the next you're rocking back and forth sucking your thumb?"

I laughed harder. Mark had to close the door behind him so they wouldn't hear us.

"Shh . . ." Robert grinned in my ear.

"So this BDSM thing—will it go away?"

Robert's face altered, and there was that wicked, wicked grin creeping across. He purred, "Well, that one I would like to keep around for a while."

I was really trying very hard not to laugh. But I failed, and Robert was suddenly crouched over on top of me like I was his prey.

"Would you two quit it!" Pepper protested. "You're in front of company!"

Mental Note: Confess to Pepper that Robert has no boundaries on public displays of affection with me. Oh yeah, and that he was a stripper.

I scolded him with my finger. *Bad kitty, bad kitty, down.*

He scooped me up again and sat me back on his lap.

"Jesus! No wonder Scott jumped off the deep end. Watching the both of you is like looking at porn."

Not far off there, buddy, I thought.

She added, "I'm surprised he didn't just shoot himself."

"That would have been a lot easier," replied Robert.

"Oh, and by the way, Robert, thanks for saving her."

"Trust me, my motives were strictly selfish." My Englishman took my hand and kissed it.

Mark rejoined us and went over what he said. I was feeling playful again, and I told Mark about Pepper's faux pas on my BDSM disorder, and that got those dimples showing. She didn't understand what was so funny and what she actually had said.

"What?" she asked, irritated.

He cleared his throat. "It's PTSD."

"Well, I got two letters right."

"BDSM is bondage, discipline, submission, and masochism."

She laughed.

"Well, that one seems like more fun. Can you switch?" Robert squeezed me to him and begged, "Please? Pretty please with sugar on it?"

I just narrowed my eyes at him.

"So did you shut your phone off?"

I shook my head. "No, why?"

"Because it's very quiet here."

"I pulled the plugs out."

"Did you check your cell? Oh no, wait a minute. If you did, you would have returned one of my hundred messages!"

"You called me a hundred times?" I started to get up, but Robert pulled me back to him. I swatted at him, and he restrained my hands and manipulated my position so he had my neck exposed to him, and he assaulted me with kisses. I was squealing and giggling again. Just as I was going to scream, he let me go and lifted both of us off the chair and set me down. Man, was he strong!

I went to my purse and pulled out my cell, and then he was right behind me.

"Baby, when was the last time you checked your phone?"

I turned my head to look at him. "Yesterday with you in the morning. Why?"

"Can I see it for a minute?"

"Why?"

"Just in case Scott left you a message. We should have checked it down at the station."

I handed it to him. That was the last thing I needed. He kissed me for reassurance and took it in the kitchen.

"Mark!" Robert called.

Mark stood up and went to him. I blinked, and Pepper stood up and guided me back to the couch. "I would turn the television on, but your story is probably plastered all over it," she said.

"I'm good." I smiled, but I was getting anxious. Robert was too far away from me.

He came back in without Mark and brought me a cup of coffee. "You want a cup, Pepper?" He was playing respectful host.

"Sure, thank you."

He turned and yelled to Mark, "Mark, get your woman a cup of coffee." He stroked my face. "It's all good, baby. We just found a text from him, and I want to know if it's going to be a big deal if we deleted it."

"OK."

"I love you, baby. I'll be right back in. Drink some coffee. You're going to need the caffeine in a bit." He winked at me and strutted back into the kitchen.

Pepper's mouth hung open as she leaned into me. "Did he just tell you he loved you?"

I giggled and nodded.

"Whoa! Is that because of the incident? You're not moving in here, are you?"

"For the next week at least."

"Are you sure you want to leap right in like this? I mean you have just ended a long-term relationship, hooked up with a guy who has been obsessed and maybe even stalking you. Don't get me wrong, he is totally into you. Maybe even a little too scary into you. You don't really know him. You just made national headlines. Maybe you should take a step back and breathe."

I had to distract her. She was bringing me down to a bad place. "I do know a little about him. He used to be a stripper." I giggled again.

"What did you just say?" Mark came in and put coffee in front of Pepper.

"Thank you," she said as he smiled and walked back into the kitchen.

"Robert. He was a stripper in college. It's how he paid for his living expenses—even paid for this house, I think." I looked around, so proud of my man.

"What the fuck?"

"You have to admit he is a very good dancer."

She laughed and laughed as Robert strutted back in to check on me. "You girls having a good time?"

"Yes, honey." I pulled him down for a kiss to distract him. It worked.

"I'll just be another minute."

"Take your time, hot stuff." He knew I was up to something but turned back to the kitchen.

"Holy shit! I can just see it. He must have made a friggin' fortune!"

"He promised to dance for me some time."

"Demand it tonight!"

We both laughed.

The men joined us at last, and there was another knock at the door. Robert was irritated because he was looking over my shoulder as I checked my messages.

Pepper jumped up. "I'll get it."

We were on the couch—Robert on the end with his feet on the coffee table and me pulled up into his side. Mark was sitting at the opposite end, holding his mug.

Pepper opened the door the width of her body. Whoever it was didn't expect to deal with my little force of nature. "Wait!" she barked at them. "There is a Liam, and the other ass just gave me his last name. Walsh."

"Let them in," commanded Robert.

Pepper opened the door all the way, but they had to walk past her. I knew she was armed.

Liam took in the scene. He greeted me first, "Hi, Kate, how are you holding up?"

I looked up from my phone. "It's a little overwhelming at the moment."

"I bet," he reassured me.

Robert's hand tightened around my waist, and he planted a kiss in my hair. It was becoming automatic, all these kisses of affection. I turned and tilted my head up for him to really give me a proper kiss. This made Robert very pleased. He was very soft with the brief kiss on my lips, and I went back to my phone.

Right there, I hadn't realized I claimed him in front of our company. But apparently, I did. He stretched out like the big cat and turned to our guests. Pepper stood behind them, and Robert took notice.

"Everything all right, boys?" he asked.

"Yes, we are just checking on you. Chief wants you to come in tomorrow morning. You're on leave until further notice. PTSD evaluation."

I looked up at him, and he winked at me.

Liam spoke to me then. "Just standard protocol, Kate. You'll be required to go through the procedures as well."

Walsh cleared his throat. "You have something for me, Rob?"

I could tell he did not want to get up. My kitty was relaxed, happy, and had his little woman by his side. But all good things must come to an end.

"I gotta get up, baby. I'll only be a minute." He moved me slightly and motioned to Mark.

I think Pepper was making them nervous. I looked up to her. I motioned her to the couch. She narrowed her eyes at me.

"Liam, thank you for bringing Robert's car back for us. That was a huge relief to be able to drive home ourselves. Thank you."

He sat in the chair next to me. "Oh, that was nothing. Hey, I'm real sorry all that shit went down at my mother's restaurant."

I put my phone on the table. "Your mother is Louise?"

"Yes, she is really worried about you. She knows Rob is tough as nails, but . . . you know . . . Anyways, how are you holding up?"

"Please tell her I'm freaked out but good. I'll get through this. I have Robert and a large support group to help me. Thank you, Liam, for your concern. It makes me feel good to know I have Robert's side of the family to lean on as well."

"They are all eager to meet you, Kate. Are you guys still coming this afternoon?"

Pepper gave me "the look." (Going to meet the family? You're screwed.)

I turned my attention back to Liam. "As far as I know. Hey, Liam, can you just give me a hint on the number of people who are going to be there? I'm just a little fragile right now, and I think it will help to know basic facts."

"Oh sure, Kate. Let's see . . ." He did a mental calculation. "I would say no more than seventy-five."

"That's not a family gathering, that's a wedding!" I gasped.

"Time to get used to it, Kate. It's the family and the force. We are all one."

I turned to Pepper. "Great!"

Robert, Mark, and Walsh walked back in to join us, and a call came in over Liam's handheld device. "Gotta go. See you two in a few hours." Walsh followed.

Mark reached for Pepper's hand. "Come on, Pepper, let me take you to breakfast."

I knew she did not want to leave me and that Robert wanted her gone. I waved my hands for her to go. She slowly got off the couch and made her way toward the door. I followed her.

On the entrance landing in front of the door, she gripped my sides, sending Robert pacing.

Oh shit! My eyes widened. I was his trigger!

I placed my hands on Pepper, speaking directly and as quietly as I could so only she could hear me. I told her, "Let go of me right now. It's very important. I will explain this to you later."

She dropped her grip and hugged me instead.

Robert flew down the stairs and was by my side, taking my hand to pull us apart. I released her first and wiggled slightly for her to release her hold on me, and she did. Robert pulled me into his front, and I was feeling the tension radiating off him. I acted as if nothing was happening. "Thank you two for coming over. I'll call you later, Pepper."

"You better. I know where to find you now if you don't." She leaned in to hug Robert.

He didn't know what to do, so he put his arms tighter around me. *Oh, good Lord!* Robert shook Mark's hand. It seemed he was much more comfortable doing that.

The door closed, and he did exactly what he promised. My panties were shredded on the floor!

We didn't even make it a few feet—well, he didn't make it a few feet. His pants were unzipped, his cock out, and my shoulders and head were against the wall. He was thrusting himself into me, and the feeling was sexual and dangerous all at the same time. I think that was pretty close to a rape if my body hadn't craved him just as much right at that moment.

He pushed like he couldn't get deep enough into me, even though he was at my breaking point for filling me. He wrapped my legs around his waist and was supporting my whole body with his arms and hands on my lower back. About thirty seconds of him just pushing himself up into me, I felt that danger fade, and carnal craving took over completely. He stopped trying to force himself and started a sexual rhythm that had my body wanting that dangerous intensity back.

"I'm sorry, baby, for being so rough. I just need you badly right now."

I cupped his head in my hands. "I need you too. Take me!"

I assaulted his mouth as he pulled me off the wall and moved me up the stairs. Crouching down, he laid me on the floor at the top of the stairs, breaking our kiss and taking me. He was breeding me.

That need, that desire to exist—it was all there in how he was seizing me. It was so sexy that I was building—ah, no . . . I was coming. I threw my chest up and my head back and let out some primal moan that sent him into an orgasm as well. His was a low growl. Then the doorbell rang as he was still pumping his orgasm into me. It rang again.

He turned his head toward the door. "Fuck off!" he simply called back.

"Robert?" I shot up, and he grabbed my waist, pinning me to the ground with his cock still in me.

"It's my mother!" I was desperately trying to get out from under him; he just used his weight and kept me almost immobile. "Let me up, let me up!" I tried to keep quiet, but the panic was wrapping around me.

He was grinning, and he was still inside me. "Shh, baby, it's OK. Door's locked, she can't get in."

I wanted to knee him—anything to just get out from beneath him. I stopped thrashing and caught my breath. What was the use? I couldn't move. He was calling all the shots. So I narrowed my eyes at him and bit out. "Let. Me. Up. Please!"

He let out a low laugh and pumped himself one more time inside me and pulled out. "Be right there, Helen." Then he released his weight, and I shot out from beneath him and ran down the hall to the bedroom. I heard him fix his pants, and I ran back to him as he was descending the stairs.

I banged on the handrail to get his attention and pointed to the scrap of white material on the floor. Great! His wicked grin was plastered to his face, and he scooped them up and brought them to his nose and inhaled before tucking them into his pocket. I know my mouth dropped open because I slammed it shut and heard my teeth smack against each other. I just pointed sharply at him twice as a mother does to a child in a silent warning. *Bad kitty! Bad, bad, bad, bad, bad kitty!*

He started to open the door, and I bolted down the hall again. *Oh shit! Oh shit!* I ran into the bathroom and brushed my hair and put it up in a ponytail, straightening myself out, and gave myself an exam in the mirror.

Underwear! Shit!

I scampered around for my suitcase and nearly fell over trying to get the damn things on. I checked myself again. With deep breaths, I stood straight and peeked around the corner from the doorframe. I heard Robert with my mother in the kitchen. I stepped toward the kitchen and turned back to the bedroom. *Jesus, get a grip!* I let out a breath again and slowly inhaled and made my way to the kitchen.

Mom was leaning against the island with a coffee in her hand, talking with Robert who was across from her, up against the counter. She turned and smiled at me, making no move toward me. Instead, she took a sip from her mug. That was strange.

Robert held out a mug for me, and I gave him a disapproving look. It made him grin.

"How are you doing, honey?" Mom asked.

I took the cup from Robert and decided standing next to him was better than across from him. "I'm good, Mom."

"Robert told me what happened this morning when Pepper showed up."

Oh did he! I sipped my coffee.

"And about the message on your phone."

Did he tell you about the fucking session we were having while you were waiting at the door! I grumbled inside.

"Helen, can I get you anything to nibble on?"

Nibble on? I gave him a questioning look. Who says *nibble*? Oh yeah—my hot, dangerous, gun-toting, sex-fiend Englishman cop!

My mother smiled. "No, dear, I'm quite all set. I just wanted to come by and check on you two. See how you are holding up."

"Pepper brought us the Sunday paper."

"They are making quite a big deal of this. I'm surprised there is not a news team parked out front. They were at home until your father talked to them."

"They were here also. Mark dealt with them."

"That is very good to know. I will inform your father." She looked around and noticed the phone plug down on the floor. "Well, that explains why I couldn't get through."

Robert answered, "The calls started about quarter to seven, and we have the cell phones silenced."

"I figured. That's why I am here to check up on you. I know if Kate listened to my message, she would have contacted me." There was that disapproving tone.

Robert continued to answer. "Sorry about that, Helen. We just needed time to sort this all out."

Sort this out. Is that what he calls what we were doing?

He grinned down at me. I wanted to smack him.

My mother turned her attention to me. "The agency called. They could not get a hold of you, so I filled them in. They are insisting on a one-month paid leave."

Robert's smile grew. Yeah, looks like I'm moving in. Bastard! Well, sexy, strong, gorgeous bastard. *I hate him!*

He adjusted his stance to that sprawled-out relaxed look that I noticed was a bit closer to me.

Mother continued, "They also faxed over some paperwork for you to fill out when you are ready and they have made an appointment with . . ." She pulled the papers out from her purse and removed the second one. "Dr. Green."

She held the papers in my direction, but Robert intercepted them with grace then started looking over everything. Both my hands were still wrapped around my mug. I knew he would do that.

My mother smiled as I answered. "I know of him. He is really good. I've heard nothing but positive feedback about him."

"That's what Jill said. She is worried about you. They all love you over there and want what is best for you."

I brightened. It's good to be appreciated. Well, time to get this over with. "Hey, Mom, I'm coming by later to pick up a few things. I'm gonna be staying here for a while." *There, I can pass out now!*

Robert was just prideful. It was just oozing out of him.

"I understand, sweetheart. We want what is best for you. And if staying here is what you need, then that is what you do."

Who is this woman? And what has she done with my mother?

She continued, "Your father and I would like to have you two over for dinner one night."

I looked at Robert.

"Apparently, we are free all week. Seems our schedules have been cleared," he answered.

That got us all to chuckle.

"I'll talk to your father and call you with the details," Mom said.

The doorbell rang, and Robert straightened up. "I'll get it."

Yeah, it's your house, I thought.

My mother took a few steps toward me. "He is much more handsome than I remembered. How are you really doing?"

"I'm happy, Mom, really happy. He is . . . everything. Is that too weird? I mean, it's still so new."

"When you know, you know. And it looks like Cupid blindsided you this time. You two make a very handsome couple."

I was grinning like a fool. Mom approved. I wanted to clap my hands and jump up and down.

"I know he is going to take good care of you. Your father was very impressed at how he demonstrated his protection for you. It had him talking for about an hour last night. Brought him back to his military days. What time will you be over?"

I tuned her out for a moment to hear the commotion going on outside. Robert had shut the door behind him when he answered it.

"Sorry, what did you ask, Mom?"

"What time are you coming home to pick up your things?"

"Oh, we have a family gathering this afternoon. I think late afternoon, so probably in about two hours."

"You're going somewhere this afternoon?"

"Robert's cousins. He thinks it's a good idea to get this behind us and deal with all the questions now rather than put it off. Says we will get our lives back to normal sooner rather than later."

"I think your man is very wise." She kissed my forehead. "I'm going now. Turn your phone on so I can reach you. I will see you soon." She looked around. "He has a very nice home."

"Yeah, and no mortgage." *Oops! I said that out loud.*

"Must be very good with his money. Your father will approve."

We headed for the door, and as I opened it, Robert turned to me with a smile. There were about seven women of all ages crowded around him. *Great, a fan club.* They all stopped talking to check me out.

My mother extended her hand to him, and he took it, wrapping both his around hers. I heard that sharp intake of her breath and looked at her, shocked. She was smiling at him and saying something that I could not register at this moment. He was guiding her around the women, quickly introducing each of them to her; but he positioned himself so I was once again safely behind him, away from everyone. He let go of my mother's hand, and she brought it right to her body and continued with the smile.

What the hell!

She turned and walked to her car, waved to us, and drove away.

The women were still checking me out, glaring around Robert for a better glance. He reached back and grabbed my hand then pulled me under his arm to his side. He started to introduce us. They were cousins, of course—except there was Nat. *The annoying little bug!*

A few of them gave me an approving smile. Then they all started talking at once. None of them were American. All had a thick brogue. I was just trying to listen carefully so I could understand what they were saying. They were talking so fast. Then Robert was answering in the same kind of accent. Oh my god, he sounded so sexy.

I was just watching his mouth and taking in how he could transform so easily. *Yummy.* I made a mental note for him to use that on me often.

He glanced down at me and saw that I was staring with carnal appreciation. He grinned and planted a big kiss on my lips. Nope, no boundaries. Didn't give a crap who was around.

Nathalie scowled. All the other women smiled like that was the dearest display of affection one could give. Jesus, they're all exhibitionists!

"Ah, that's right, love, you two will be fine, just fine. Are ya comin' over this afternoon, love?" asked his cousin Laura.

Silence. Oh, that was my question! "Yes, as far as I know."

"Good, good, love. We can't wait to see you there. Everyone is eager to meet the one and only 'Kate.' You'll have a grand time, I promise."

I wanted to crawl under his shirt and hide. One and only "Kate." *Oh god! Dog–and-pony show coming right up!*

Robert was shameless. "We just have to go over to Kate's parents' house and pick up her stuff. She's living here now!"

Argh! Bad kitty!

"Are ya now? Well, you two make a fine, fine-looking couple. Welcome to the family, love. Now we have real cause to celebrate."

My arrogant, preening, inappropriate boyfriend was basking in his pride again! He even moved me out from under the safety of his arm and placed me right in front of him, swaddling his arms around me and collapsing his upper body to mine while gently rocking me from side to side. They were all beaming at his display of affection toward me. Now I wanted to crawl under a rock!

Hey, if I grabbed his crotch, they would probably all cheer. *Uugh!* They're all shameless. Except Natalie. She looked mortified. I have some respect back for her.

"Well, love, we just wanted to make sure you were all OK. We'll be going now. You two get going with your business." Laura winked at me. "See you soon, love." Then she touched Robert's arm. "She's lovely, Robert. Worth waiting for, I can see. Congratulations to ya. You take care of her now."

Hello? I'm still here. Trapped in a Robert cage, but I can still hear every word!

He kissed my cheek and released me enough for him to wave to everyone. They all piled into the SUV and waved as they backed out.

I could feel his grin.

"You're shameless," I muttered.

He purred. "Let's go get your stuff. We're taking my car. It will fit more."

"Oh, you think so?" *Now I get it, Grams. You go, girl!*

He released me and smacked my butt, sending me forward. I no sooner put my hand to block another than he scooped me up like a bride and did this bicep curl toward his head so his face was shaking in my belly and his teeth were nipping at me. I was giggling and screaming again! He put me down in the kitchen and pulled out a bowl of cut-up fruit and yogurt.

"Here, baby, you didn't get much for breakfast. Eat something. You're gonna need energy later."

"I bet." I just took the bowl from him. Why argue?

"What do you want to drink?"

He looked so happy it was hard to stay irritated. "Water, please."

He turned and pulled two bottles from the fridge. "Want a glass, baby?"

"Nope, bottle's fine," I answered with a mouthful of fruit. I didn't care at this point.

He peeled the yogurt lid back and scooped out a spoonful and raised it to my mouth. I just looked suspiciously at him then opened my mouth. He fed me then himself, just as I had with him at the restaurant. I smiled, and he kissed me.

"Can you get my phone? I promised my mother I would turn the sound back on. Oh, and grab the charger. It probably is low on its battery."

"Sure thing, babe."

"Hey, hon, why don't you put it on speaker and let's listen to the messages so I can get rid of them."

"Will do, love." He was coming toward me with everything I asked for, and he plugged it in on the kitchen counter.

I started to clean up after the little brunch. "I can do that, baby," he said, glancing over his shoulder as he was preparing my phone.

"If I'm going to be living here for a bit, I don't want to feel like a guest. I'll do it."

He smiled.

"I need to do some laundry, so you'll have to show me where that is too."

"I'll give you the tour after this. Oh, and count on more than just a bit."

Don't smile, don't smile. My face betrayed me. I wrapped my arm around from behind him and peeked around his arm.

He was grinning. "Ready, baby?"

He turned to me and handed me the phone. He pulled me against him, and I hit the first message. It was on speaker. Pepper. Erased it without listening; she warned me she called a lot.

"How do you know Scott didn't leave a voice message?"

"I checked all the phone numbers. None were his."

"What if he used someone else's phone?"

"All the phone numbers were consistent except for one, and I did a trace to a John Field."

"Oh, that's my current client. Where is that one?" I handed him my phone back.

"You want me to just delete all of Pepper's messages?"

"Yeah, go ahead." I leaned against him, stroking his arm. It took less time than I thought, and he handed me back my phone.

"Jeez, that was quick. What did you do?"

"I'll show you after."

I pressed PLAY. "Hi, Kate, it's Jess. Jesus, I was just watching the television, and there you are! Are you all right? What's going on? Did you score with the hot—"

Embarrassed, I switched it off the speaker and held it to my ear. He tightened his arms around me, kissing my head as he rocked me again. I knew he was grinning.

I cleared the message.

"Definitely . . . I would say, hot cop, aye?"

"Yes. Hot cop . . . are you happy!"

"Very!"

I kept my eyes down and returned the phone to speaker. "Who else is on this?" I asked, not wanting to make eye contact with him. It would only feed that ego.

"Parents, work, sister."

"Here, erase them all but Jess's number."

I think he hit four buttons. "Done. How about your texts?"

"Same phone numbers?"

"Yes."

"Delete them all and put the sound back on please."

"OK."

He was still grinning when the doorbell rang. "Since you're living here now, love, do you want to answer it?" He kissed the tip of my nose.

"Not that comfortable yet. You get it. But I'll go look out the window."

He put my phone down.

"Cruiser!" I called to him.

My phone rang when he was about to answer the door, and he panicked.

"I'll just look at the number. I will only answer it if it's my mother or Pepper."

He relaxed and answered the door. I darted over to the phone. I didn't know the number. I let it go to voice mail. Then I heard another female's voice.

Walking around, I noticed Robert had the door wide open. I looked to see whom he was talking to and . . . *holy fuck! Who was that!* Her face was stern as she just looked over his shoulder at me.

That made Robert turn. "Baby, come here." He motioned me over.

As his body turned, I got a better look at her. A supermodel in a uniform. *Oh shit!* And she didn't like me one bit!

He held his hand out toward me. I could feel her willing me not to take it. He didn't quite pull me in like all the other times, but he did settle me to his side. *Who the fuck is she?*

He made the introductions. "Baby, this is a colleague of mine, Chris Foss. Chris, this is my Kate."

Oh, good kitty! Good, good, good kitty! She kept her hard line. *What, no handshake?* She would have probably crushed my hand anyways. I started the conversation, empowered by my boyfriend's introduction.

"Hi, Chris, nice to meet you."

"Yes, I was checking to see if Robert was all right."

Well, that was blunt.

"That's very kind of you. Everyone has been so concerned. It's good to know so many people care about us."

Take that, bitch.

"I tried calling, but you didn't pick up."

Robert answered, "We unplugged the phones and turned the volume off the cells." He raised his arm to pull me in.

Yes! Ggrr, ggrr's gonna get a kitty treat!

"Well, I'm glad you weren't hurt. I'll see you at the station."

"Thanks for stopping by," I commented.

See, I can be cocky too.

I could feel his aura wrapping around me. Me staking my claim was exciting him. He closed the door.

I turned to face him, and I wrapped my arms around his neck. "What would you like to do now, my darling?"

He widened his stance and settled into my embrace. "Move you in." Then he kissed me.

Chapter 6

Robert brought me upstairs and led me down the hall. We walked into the room that was all the way down on the right (a new room). It was his office. The colors were very soothing—salmon, sage, and white, with dark furniture to bring that wow factor to the setting. This was where all his uniforms were kept along with his police gear. There was a gun safe, a desk, and a computer station (which looked like command central). And there was a seating area with two comfortable chairs, an end table between them, standing lamps and recessed lighting, bookshelves, and a huge case of trophies that was chockablock full. There was also a wall of weapons—I think I could identify three—and a walk-in closet. He went to the walk-in, and I went to the trophy case.

Holy smokes, all martial arts and shooting medals and trophies! Whatever these were, it showed he was really good. Some were even dated this year.

I felt him behind me, and he put down a bag and snaked his arms around my waist.

"Boy, whatever these are, you sure are good at it."

He pointed to the top shelf: "Shooting." Second shelf: "Jujitsu and judo." Bottom shelf: "Grappling."

I giggled. "No wonder I couldn't get out from under you earlier."

He purred, "Not a chance, baby."

I turned in his arms and brought mine around his neck. "You're pretty dangerous."

"You have no idea, love." Then he kissed me.

Twelve seconds (I counted) and I was feeling lightheaded. It was either from my libido kicking in or simply his presence.

He squeezed my butt and straightened up. "Come on, we have a mission to accomplish."

"Really? What?"

"Emptying the room at your parents'."

"Oh, that." I looked down and saw that he had a rather large black duffel bag. "What's the bag for?"

"Bags. And they are for your clothes and stuff."

"Good idea. How many do you have?"

"Three."

"All that size?"

"Yup."

"You better not get sick of me in a week. This is a lot of work, you know. Not to mention I'm a little scared. I've never lived with a guy before."

"I am very happy to hear that."

"But you probably already knew that."

He just gave me a smirk and did not respond. "Don't be scared, I'm the happiest man alive. You're lucky I'm not dragging you on a plane right now to Vegas for you to marry me."

Whaaat! That ridiculous grin was plastered across my face. *No! No! It should be a shocked look. Go for shocked! Freaked out would even be more appropriate! Don't encourage him! He's insane!*

He kissed my forehead. "It's coming, baby. So you've been warned." And he kissed me again.

Faint! Faint, damnit! Now is the time to faint. The appropriate response is to pass out and shut down! Why are you not listening to me, body! Drop, woman! And lose that smile!

Nope. Instead, I was floating by his side effortlessly, heading down the hall. *Oh look, the birds are singing so sweetly.*

He grabbed my phone off the counter, and we floated down the stairs to his car. He put the duffel bags in the back and opened my door. There, in I went. I heard his door close, and the roar of the engine snapped me out of it.

Holy crap, he wants to marry me!

My head was arguing back and forth.

You only just started dating—

But it feels so right.

You don't even know him—

He's honest, hardworking, strong, and sexy.

He's overprotective—

He's overprotective.

OK, both sides agreed on that one.

He's dangerous—

He's dangerous yum, yum, yum.

Back, back, back, you naughty thoughts!

I turned and stared at him. He glanced over at me and took my hand, bringing it to his mouth.

I found my voice and spoke. "You're overwhelming."

He just smiled. "You're mine!" And he kissed my knuckles.

I kept studying him. "I wonder what it would have been like if I dated you six years ago."

Oh no, there was his wicked grin. "I'm glad we didn't."

"Really? Why?"

"You would have been a total distraction."

"Distraction?"

"Yes."

"Do you want kids?"

What the hell was I asking him that for? *Everyone, back in their corners!* I chastised my brain.

"Absolutely," he replied.

"How many?"

"As many as you will let me have."

Stupid grin, go away! I put my head back against the seat, and he accelerated to my parents' house.

There was another television news truck outside the gate. Robert slowed then drove past the house. He pulled his phone out then hit a button. "Hey, we're at Kate's house to pick up a few things. Channel 7 is parked outside. Send someone down."

He gave the address and drove around the block.

"Baby, call your mother and let her know there is another news truck parked out front. Tell her I just called for a cruiser to remove them."

Oooh, he was sexy powerful. Yes, I will marry you! Ask me right now! Yes! Yes! Yes! The answer is yes!

"Oh, honey, there is that message on my phone we forgot to check out. I didn't recognize the number."

"Let me see that, kitten. Call her on mine."

Kitten? I liked that since he was my tiger. I handed him my phone, and I took his. *Wow, how does this thing work?* I was studying it. I typed in the number and hit SEND. *Oh, that worked, yeah!*

"Hey, Mom, we're here, but there is a news truck out front. Robert has sent for a cruiser to remove them. As soon as they are gone, we'll pull in."

"All right, Kate. I didn't see that van. I will let your father know. See you in a few minutes."

"Bye." And I ended the call.

Robert looked distraught.

"You OK?" I asked.

"I need to see your father when we get inside."

"Oh-kay. Is everything all right?"

"Just a minor technicality."

"Is it whoever called?"

"Yes."

"Are you going to tell me who it was?"

"Adam."

"Adam Briggs? Scott's best friend?"

"Yes."

"I never gave him my cell number."

"It would be easy to obtain."

"This is a new phone and new number. I haven't even had it a year. You only had my number because you lost your cell that time we were all at the park playing football, and you had to call your cell—" I stopped, realizing it was all a ploy.

He grinned and took my hand again.

I narrowed my eyes at him. "Stalker!"

He shrugged.

His phone vibrated and made me jump. I looked down at it but didn't recognize the number. "Here, it's for you."

He put it on speaker. "Yes," he commanded.

"Elvis has left the building."

"Thanks, Cahill."

"Any time, brother. How are you doing?"

"Never better."

"How's the little lady?"

"Perfect! And right next to me."

"See you tonight."

"Bye." He hung up.

Oh, it's going to take more than that, buddy!

He started the car again and headed down the road, pulling into my driveway.

I was having one of those strange "rites of passage" moments. I knew all my things were inside and that I had lived there for the past sixteen years, but it felt like I didn't live here anymore. Kind of like I was just visiting, which was all exactly true. But I didn't expect it to feel like that right away.

Robert was already around, opening my door, and he pulled me into a long kiss. And suddenly, everything just fit. I was supposed to be with him, and this was the right thing to do.

Jeez, I loved this man.

"I just gotta see your da for a bit, pet. Show me the room and I'll leave the bags in there, and you start packing. OK, baby? I won't be long, and then I can help."

"Hey." I stopped him before he released me. "What time is this thing today?"

"Four o'clock, but we will show up when we want."

"What should I wear?"

"Depends on how big a gun you want me to carry. I kinda fancy this sundress. Easy access."

"You're naughty."

"You're luscious."

He kissed me again, and the front door opened. Did he let me go? No, of course not! He kept talking to me in his embrace as if we were the only two people there. Awkward!

"Ready, pet?"

I gave him the thumbs-up. "Ready." It got me another quick kiss. *Oh jeez!* My parents were just watching and *waiting*!

Robert took the bags out of the back and grabbed my hand with his other. He greeted my parents and talked to my dad a moment. Yup, I was still holding on to his other hand.

He turned to me. "Where's the room, baby?"

The room—not *your* room.

I led him to it. He took a quick look around, checked my closet, and seemed to be satisfied.

Oh, those faded jeans on him were delicious.

My mother walked in behind us, and Robert gave me another quick kiss on the lips—of course, in front of my mother! Then he headed back out to my father with my phone.

My mother came over to me. "Why does it feel like this is permanent?"

"Because stupid Cupid blindsided me."

My mother looked into my eyes. "I get it. Believe me, I get it."

"Then explain it to me."

"You two just have that unbreakable bond now, and it's coming at you like wildfire."

I thought about that. "Exactly."

"Well then, let's get you packed. It's time for you to grow."

"At least he is really good-looking."

"You two are going to make beautiful babies."

Whoa! Hang on, where did that come from, Mom!

"Don't hold your breath, Mom. I'm not planning on kids anytime soon."

"Just saying, Kate. Look how beautiful you and your sister are. Your father and I have been known to turn a few heads."

Please stop now, I beg of you!

I emptied my whole dresser and filled one bag. My mother managed to fit a few pairs of shoes in there as well.

"I took all the little memorabilia that Scott gave you and threw them away," she said.

"I hadn't even thought about that, Mom, thanks. That is where it was going anyways."

"I destroyed all the photos as well."

"Dad's rubbing way too much off on you."

"On the contrary, he doesn't rub enough."

Mother! Do not want to talk sex with Mother! Repeat: do not want to talk sex with Mother!

"Too much information, Mom," I said.

She laughed. She knew she was messing with me. "Dinner Thursday? At the club, just the four of us?"

"I think that's all right. Just let me pass it by Robert."

She smiled. We went to work on the closet.

Robert came strolling in with my father in tow. "We need to go down to the courthouse in the morning, baby. Right after the station. Your da will meet us. We need to call him when I'm done with the chief."

"OK, why?"

Robert was very good at organizing events, taking and explaining step-by-step how and when things happen. But I'm noticing he leaves out the "why the fuck do we need to do that in the first place?" He is definitely an "only as you need to know basis" type of guy.

Hmmm, who else do I know like that? My father! But if you asked Robert enough questions, he would follow through whether you wanted to know or not.

"Adam threatened your life," he explained. "We need a restraining order on him."

Great! Good luck getting past my tiger, Adam. They won't know where to look for the body. If there is even one left.

I knew this was where I should shudder at the thought, but look who's in the room with me? *Go ahead, Adam, I dare you. Ha!*

I think my mother was questioning my lack of reaction, so I shrugged my shoulders. "Okeydoke."

In hindsight, maybe that was not the best response to show. Robert chuckled, my mother gasped, and my father was quiet.

Robert came toward me to examine the bag that was already zipped. "You're taking this a little lightly, Kate."

"Seriously, Mom? Do you not see the man I am with? He's friggin' Rambo. Anyone who even looks at me funny, Robert will eat for breakfast and use their bones as toothpicks. I kinda want to dare the asshole just to make my point."

Oh crap! I fed the prideful ego, and there he was, scooping me up and kissing me in front of my parents! *Down, kitty. Not here. Shoo.*

I whispered in his kiss, "Put me down."

He pulled back and grinned then kissed me again.

Argh!

My mother ignored us and went back to packing. My father smiled.

What the hell! Why was he smiling?

Robert released me, and I went back to packing as well. *I want outta here sooner rather than later.*

Robert unzipped the already completed bag. "You got loads of room in here, baby. Give me some more clothes. Who taught you how to pack?"

My father was not taking blame for that job. "Certainly was not me. I have been telling her that for years. You should have seen it when she left for college. Way too much wasted space."

I just gasped at him. *Seriously?* They're discussing my packing ability. *Hey, Mom and Dad, remember, daughter leaving to move in with her hot new boyfriend of, what, a couple of days now?*

Robert grabbed the clothes I was holding. "Get me a few more things, love."

What the fuck? I turned and pulled a few more dresses from the hangers and handed them to him. Yup, another kiss!

He zipped the bag back up. "There! That one's much better. Now what's going on with this one?" He took control of the next one.

"Hey, is Grams upstairs?"

"Yes, watching her shows."

"I'm just going to run up and say hi. Do you guys mind?"

"That's a fetching idea, baby. We'll do better without you here."

"Hey!"

"Sorry, love, you suck at packing."

That did it. My father was gut-shaking laughing. My mother was biting her lip, trying to keep it in. I wanted to kick him again!

"Fine!" I think I actually stomped my foot. I'm not sure though.

Robert reached for me, but I moved just in time. *Ha! You didn't get me.*

Then he lunged, and there I was in his arms. "But you are an expert at many other things," he said. Then he kissed me.

Ground? If you can hear me? Swallow me up now! Please!

He must have been satisfied that I didn't struggle because he released me after just the one kiss then turned me toward the door and smacked my butt. All in *front of my parents*! Then he went right back to packing my clothes.

I was upstairs with Grams in her room for about twenty minutes when my mother peeked in. "He's just finishing up, Kate."

I nodded to her.

She proceeded to walk toward me. "That fellow of yours is something." There was an appreciation in her tone.

"It's so strange, Mom. I know our relationship is new—I mean brand-new. What's a whole three days? But it feels like these are the first three days to the rest of my life."

"I know what you mean because your father was the exact same feeling."

"So is that why you're not freaking out about this?"

"What's meant to be is meant to be. Who am I to stop fate? You're a grown woman. I have raised you to be strong and independent. You know what's right for you."

I heard doors close and open. I heard the car's trunk closing. I heard my tiger bounding up the stairs.

"I mentioned Thursday night to Robert. I will set the reservations for six."

"Sounds good."

And there he was, my kitty, heading right for me. He scooped me up like a bride (again) in front of my *grandmother*! He said his farewells while I just said bye-bye and that I would call them. My mother was smiling, and Grams was asking who the nice young man was.

What the hell? Who are these people!

Robert shook my father's hand with me in his arms then reiterated Monday's schedule, and off we went.

He started his car and pulled me in for a long kiss. Fifteen seconds, I counted. He was grinning like the Cheshire Cat.

"What?" I asked.

"You're all mine."

"Seems to be that way now. Where are we going to put all my clothes?"

"I have a matching dresser in one of the spare bedrooms. I'll move it into the bedroom tomorrow, and the walk-in has plenty of room for what you are bringing."

"I can help you move the dresser."

"Oh no, baby. Murphy will come and help me with that."

"I'm not fragile, you know."

"I am fully aware of that, love. If you were, I would have snapped you by now. I need you to save your energy for other physical exertions."

I narrowed my eyes at him. He lifted my hand and rubbed his stubble gently against the back of it. My eyes went right to the stubble. *Yum, hot cop with day-old growth.*

I sat back against the seat and kicked my shoes off. I leaned over for the button that adjusted the seat. I could feel Robert's tension adjusting. I pulled the knob up, and my seat slowly reclined. I stopped it halfway and lay back against it, bringing my right foot up to rest against the dash, and I heard his low growl. That sexual aura slowly wrapped itself around me, and he put his foot down on the accelerator. I let my right leg fall open, and he muttered a curse. His right hand was suddenly in my crotch, slowly stroking my clitoris through my panties. This felt so good; he did this so well.

He was deliberate with his strokes, which were just enough not to make me climax. This was torture, but I knew the release would be earth-shattering. I was willing to let his fingers continue their assault to get me to a place I knew he wanted me to experience. I trusted this man to take command of my body.

The next thing I heard was the breaks locking up and the car skidding to an abrupt stop. His door slammed while my eyes were searching what had happened. Then my door flew open, and I was in the air with my legs wrapped around . . . *his neck!* I was on his shoulders, my ass against the roof of his car, and then there was a loud rip.

There went another pair of panties. His mouth was on me. Hungry—very, very hungry. I had nothing to grab on to, so I just balanced back with my arms splayed on the roof. He circled and flicked his tongue against my clit.

Oh god, here it comes! No wait! I was falling.

He had released his mouth and pulled me down straight onto his cock, and he rammed inside me. All these movements and sensations had me confused; and then I really, really felt his length pushing into me.

"Baby, put your arms around me!" he demanded.

So I did. His hands were gripping my waist, lifting and lowering me with his pace. And there, right there—he was nailing that new spot in my vagina that loved him! And then I was coming and coming and screaming and coming!

Right when I was getting back under control, I felt his release, and my tiger roared. My back was against the car, helping to support me. His hands were holding me up by my ass and waist. He leaned in to rest his forehead against mine. He pumped into me a few more times and moaned with a velvety pleasure. He rubbed his forehead against mine, and I started stroking my thumbs along his cheeks where I could reach.

"I love you, baby," was all he said.

That was enough to start the waterworks. Tears began to run down my cheeks.

He looked into my eyes. "Shh, baby, no tears. It's gonna be good, so very good."

"I love you too. I have no idea why I'm crying."

"Because you haven't embraced the total feeling yet. You're still fighting it."

"You're right. I'll work on that." Then we kissed and kissed and kissed. I pulled back first. "You know you are rapidly decimating my panty supply."

There was a purr. "I know. That's the idea."

"Well, I can't wait to see the look on your face when one of your cousins accidentally gets a free glimpse because I don't have any more."

A growl! Oh, kitty hadn't thought about that. He started pumping me again. "Mine!" And that got me a fucking from behind. Robert carried me because I simply could not walk.

"Bed," I ordered him.

He smirked and placed me under the covers. "I'm going to go bring your stuff up here."

"OK." I closed my eyes and fell asleep.

It was only an hour later when I felt his hand caressing up and down my side. He was naked and sealed against the length of my body. I turned toward him, and he adjusted to my new position.

"How are you feeling, kitten?"

I thought for a second. "Refreshed."

"You are so beautiful. I am one lucky man."

"I am a very lucky woman to have such an admirer as yourself, sir."

His serious expression smoothed out to a beautiful smile. "Are you ready to go and meet the family? Because I am very ready to show you off."

Right there went my moment of bliss. I let out an exasperated sigh. "Let's get this over with."

Then his mouth sealed over mine, and he dragged me out of bed. "Come on, Sleeping Beauty. Time to get up or the villagers will come to us. If they come to us, we will never get them out of here."

"Good point, Prince Philip. What are you wearing, by the way? It will help me to know what I will choose. Hey, where are the bags?"

"Everything is hanging in the closet."

"You hung up all my clothes? In an hour?"

"Had to do something while you were sleeping. Besides, it let me censor your outfits."

"You're censoring my clothes?"

"Yes. Especially after you paraded out in that mind-fucking school uniform yesterday."

I went to say something, but the more those words sunk in, I knew he was right. *Damn him!*

"OK, show me."

He went in the closet with me; he was still naked. "All these you can wear anytime, any place. Those!"—he pointed to the ones in the corner between his suits and shirts—"are only allowed out at night with me!"

I should have been mad, but I couldn't help but smile. I walked up to the red dress and pulled it out, holding it against me. "You like?"

His energy darkened. "Oh, baby, just put it on and see what happens."

I was tingling inside, and an electrical storm was brewing in those piercing green eyes.

"I think I will save this one for your birthday."

Uh-oh, I was going to get pounced on. *Put the dress away! Put the dress away! Danger! Danger!*

I hung it back on the rod next to his navy pin-striped suit. "If you fuck me again, I'm going back to bed for the night!" I said with a foot stomp for special effect.

There! He scooped me up over his shoulder and slapped my ass once. "Little girls who play with fire get burned."

"Yeah, well, the only burning I'll get is from a yeast infection from too much semen and all the friction. You're going to drown my vagina from taking in too much sperm."

He released me slowly down the length of his body. When my feet touched the ground, he tucked a strand of hair behind my ear.

"Well then, it's a good thing I am trained in mouth-to-mouth."

I couldn't give him a comeback to that one. I was trying not to laugh. "Where did you store my panties?"

"With mine." He opened his underwear drawer.

"Are you trying to breed them to make me new underwear?"

"Do you think it could work?"

I smacked him and pulled out a thong. "Bras?"

"Hanging in the closet."

He followed me back in. I pulled off my new hot pink sequined bra that matched the thong I was holding.

"T-shirts?"

"With mine."

I walked back to his dresser and opened it. All of mine were on the left; his were on the right.

I grabbed my scuba-blue V-neck. "Jeans?"

"Closet. In the basket on the floor."

"You did all this in an hour?"

"I had a system."

"You're a freak."

Ah, there they are. I reached down and grabbed my thin light blue ones. He was still following me and still naked.

"Do I have time for a quick shower?" I asked.

"Only if I don't join you. But I can't see how you are going to stop me."

"Well"—I cuddled right up to his chest—"I've always been told, if you can't beat them, join them."

He carried me and all my apparel to the bathroom. He was very tender and sweet washing me. When it was my turn to wash him, I ended it with a blow job, giving back my appreciation for packing and unpacking for me.

He shaved as I dried my hair. I made no attempt to dress while he was with me, and I could see he was stalling just to watch me. When I knew there was nothing else for him to do in there, I ordered him out and shut the door.

I think he sulked. I brushed it off, knowing he would forget as soon as he got an eyeful of me in these jeans. My ass looked superb in them. I fixed my hair smooth, my makeup for the sultry look, and gave one last approving look.

Sitting on the bed, he was pulling his jeans leg over the gun attached at his ankle. He was wearing a crisp white collared short-sleeved shirt that fit his arms almost snugly. I think if he flexed, it would tear. His shirt was hanging loose over his belt. His pants were the same kind of blue that my jeans were, but his were thicker, and he had Doc Martens on. *Drool!* He was leaning over, resting his forearm on his knee.

"Damn, woman, turn around! Now!"

I gave him a twirl. "Those jeans are going back to the restricted section after tonight. Understand?"

I was beaming. "How do I look?"

"Very fuckable." He was coming toward me. "I can't get to you as easily, so it brings on a whole new challenge." His hand squeezed and cupped my breast then pulled the V-neck down to expose my bra and cleavage. "Damn, I'm going to get into a fight tonight."

"It's your family."

"They're men with dicks."

"I won't leave your side."

"Oh, baby, that's a given." He turned me one more time. "Come on, sexy, let's go."

"What did you do with my bag, dear?"

That made him grin. "I put it in the kitchen, and your cell is on the charger."

"Can I use my phone, or is it off-limits?"

"You can use it, just don't erase any messages."

I reached up and kissed him on the lips. "You're the best."

"You got that right, baby."

I smirked at the skid marks leading into the garage.

He opened my door then settled me in my seat and planted another tender kiss on my lips. I looked over to the car under the tarp. He slid in.

"Hey, honey?"

"Yeah, babe?"

"What's under the tarp?"

"I am rebuilding a '71 Mustang Mach 1."

"Wow, you can do that kind of stuff?"

"Had to keep myself busy somehow while waiting for your lovely ass to arrive."

"So now that I am here, that's it? The car retires?"

"Oh no, kitten. Now you're going to finish it with me."

"What? I can't do mechanical things like that."

"I am a very good teacher."

He took my hand, and this time, he sucked my index finger.

Oh jeez! That went right to my vagina. He was tonguing my finger, and holy crap! Who would have known that would be such a turn-on!

Oh yeah. My hot cop, stripper, Rambo boyfriend from England! I knew if I showed him too much pleasure in what he was doing right now, we would be parked on the side of the road with me spread-eagle hanging out of his mouth. I traveled deep down to my inner soul and prayed we wouldn't make too much of a show of it.

He stopped; I was panting. He grinned and was purring.

"I want to actually make it to this party so we can leave at a reasonable time," I said.

"We hold all the cards, baby. That means we come and go as we please. Never forget that."

I grinned at him. He was just such a force of nature, and he's all mine! "How long until we get there?"

"About fifteen more minutes."

"After your work and after the courthouse, can we go and stop in at my client's house? I want you to meet Jess. Her father is my client, and he's just hanging on. Any day could be his last."

"Baby, that rule applies to each of us."

"I know. I just don't like to think that way. And now, since I am with you, I hope there is a lot of time left."

He swerved the car to the breakdown lane.

Oh shit, he's going to fuck me on the side of the road!

He took my face between his hands and kissed me. "Me too, baby. Me too." He pulled back out into traffic, and I was left breathless.

"Yes, but tell her early afternoon."

What was the original question? *I'm thinking, I'm thinking.*

"Where does Jess live?"

Bingo! Jess—visit Jess.

"Just outside the city, Well's Park area."

"Forty minutes from the courthouse."

"Yes, about that."

He gave me a look. Oh, that wasn't a guess; he actually knew the answer.

"Do I want to know how you know that?"

"We did a sting operation in the park. Cleaned up an upper-class drug ring."

Yum. That's my super hot cop.

"Make the call, kitten, we're getting close."

I found my cell, and there were only two numbers displayed. I hit Jess's. John answered. I'm not quite sure what happened next. I think Robert thought I hit Adam's number, and my phone was snatched out of my hand quicker than my next breath.

"Who is this!" Robert demanded.

John was completely caught off guard, and he told him, "John Field."

Mr. Dangerous just simply handed me back the phone.

I was stunned and John was talking. "Hello? Hello?"

I put the phone back up to my ear. "Aaahh . . . H-hi, J-john?"

"Yes?"

"It's Kate. Kate Quinn."

"Oh, Kate, I'm so glad you called. Jessica has been worried."

"I'm fine, really. How is Frank?"

"Hanging in there."

Then I heard Jess demanding the phone from her husband. "Kate! Kate! Are you OK?"

"Yes. As a matter of fact, I was wondering if Robert and I could stop by and visit for a bit tomorrow?"

"That would be fantastic. What time?"

"Early afternoon? I can't give you a more specific time than that right now, but I can call you when we are done with a few errands."

"So it's working out between you two?"

I was fully aware he was listening to my conversation, so I just stared at him. "Yes."

"Is his nightstick everything you were hoping for?"

Oh no! No! No! No! He is going to preen.

I studied his face as I answered, "And more."

His grin was fighting itself not to erupt, but he just couldn't hold back. I'm creating a monster!

"Call you tomorrow, Jess."

"Bye, Kate. Can't wait to meet the hottie."

He heard. Before I could end the call. He heard.

He pulled the car over. I thought he would jump me, but we were here.

"You ready, baby?"

I looked ahead at all the cars up and down the street. We were parked right in front, blocking a driveway.

"Ready as I'll ever be."

"You look like sex on a stick."

"Come on, stud, open my door."

He leaned over to kiss me and hopped out. Was that a swagger? Yes, he was swaggering. This meant I was going to get the Robert cage.

He pulled me out and scooped me up in front of him, wrapping my legs around his waist. He closed my door and slid his hand under my butt.

I leaned back, not fighting him but suggesting, "I would really like to be walking on my own feet upon meeting your family."

He just smiled and kissed me, continuing to move forward, not making any motion to release me.

"Hey, Robert!" I heard from all directions.

I wanted to bury my face. I was mortified.

He swung me around, still wrapped around him, and said his hellos. Then I spotted *her*! What was her name? Oh yeah, *Chris*! Jesus, she was even more stunning out of uniform, and she stared.

Suddenly, I was happy to be in his arms—very, very happy. *Good kitty!*

He started to release me, and I clung to him. His smile deepened, and then he crouched forward for a passionate kiss and attacked my neck. I began squealing and giggling as he lifted me back up, giving me a big arm-wrapping hug. Then he patted my butt to ask if I wanted to get down.

God, I love you, mister.

"Yes, please."

He released me. I looked over to where Chris was, and she disappeared. *Fist pump!*

He took a hold of my left hand and tucked me under his arm. Then people approached with smiles of joy. Questions were flying, and beers were being handed to us. Robert took one but took mine out of my hand and asked someone to get me a glass of white wine. It was presented to me quicker than a wink.

My platform heels had me a few inches taller. So my shoulder was just snug in his armpit, and his arm was wrapped around me. He had me at an angle, and it showed everyone my great ass. There were a few lookers, mostly women sizing me up.

I took a swig of my wine and looked up into my super awesome boyfriend's face. He looked down and kissed me. *Yes!*

Everyone was talking to me at once. It was overwhelming. Robert kept me tucked into him, and I remembered he told me that we held all the cards. We could go whenever we wanted. And I knew if I said *go* to him, he would scoop me back up, and we would be gone. That was a big insurance policy, and I could count on him.

Louise approached us through the crowd. "Let me through, let me through. Oh, you poor child. Let me see her." She was coming at me with open arms, and I wrapped mine tighter around Tiger.

He immediately took in the scene about to be played out, and he shifted me so she was coming at him.

"Oh, Robert! How are you, love? I'm so glad the pair of you were not hurt. Let me see the girl."

I peeked around his chest, patting it to let him know I was OK. I took another swig of wine, and he straightened while shifting me in front of him then wrapping his arms around me and hunching over, giving me the Robert cage.

There, she could see me.

She touched my face. "Oh, you poor dear. You must be beside yourself going through all that. Well, it's no wonder with what you were wearing and all."

I wanted to say "fuck you," but I was too shocked, and the next conversation with everyone was about my outfit from last night.

I turned in his arms. "I'm going to get drunk tonight."

Robert laughed and kissed me for—I lost count at ten seconds, and then I needed to come down from my high.

"I was hoping to give you a surprise tonight," he said. "But if you get drunk, you might not appreciate it as much."

"Surprise? What surprise?"

"A welcome-to-your-new-home surprise."

"I love surprises. Can I get a little drunk?"

"Yes." Then he kissed me again in front of everyone.

"Get a room!" I heard several times.

Robert just announced that we had a whole house, and it was their sorry asses who insisted on us leaving it for this lame party. That got the music thumping and the food flowing and the drinks a-coming. We were in a crowd most of the evening.

After my first glass of wine, I was feeling pretty good. I loosened right up and played the model girlfriend by my tiger's side. Robert also relaxed enough, so I was standing at his side with his arm around my back and his hand in my back pocket, with his thumb hooked into the waist of my jeans. If anyone questioned if I was not with him, they were just plain stupid.

I had gotten to know some of the girls and had really good conversations with them. Whenever a male approached to talk to me, Robert pulled me a little closer, and the hand usually left my pocket and wrapped around the front of my waist.

I took notice. He was so damn cute—possessive, but cute!

Then I had to pee. Laura and Maggie were the two I spent most of my night talking to. They were both a little older than me (maybe Roberts's age), and they were still hanging around. I asked them where the bathroom was, and they offered to bring me.

I turned to Robert's ear and told him I needed to use the ladies' room and that the girls were going to take me. He growled. I had my hand on his chest, telling him I would only be a minute, and he slowly released me. I leaned in to kiss him, and he made it a full-contact, not-polite-for-the-general-public kiss. Then he smacked my ass before he let me go.

"Five minutes," he warned. "Then I'm coming to get you."

I turned back to him and gave him the gentle peck I was going to give him in the first place. I whispered "I love you" in his ear, and that seemed to settle him down. He—along with all the guys he was talking to—watched me walk away.

Laura and Maggie where extremely chatty, telling me all the dirt! I loved my new friends.

I turned to look at Robert before I went into the house and blew him a kiss. He smiled. Then I saw Chris make a beeline for him. *Whatever,* I thought.

Maggie went on and on about how no one could land Robert, and here I was, and I had moved in with him. She had heard he was holding out for some girl named Kate, and here I was in flesh and blood. Also, that Robert was head over heels for me and how lucky I was because there was a line of women a mile long wanting to be in my position.

We reached the bathroom, and they said they would wait. I did the deed as quickly as I could; I didn't want to miss out on any Robert gossip.

I finally got up the courage to ask about the Chris chick. They went silent.

"So who is she?" I asked.

"An old girlfriend."

"Oh, so why didn't she make the cut? She's beautiful."

"He had his marks set on you. They seemed to date and all, but she wanted more, and he kept her at arm's length. But boy did she try."

"So what's her deal with me?"

"She wants to be you. It's that simple. Don't even know why she's here tonight really."

"She stopped by his house today."

"Did she now! Probably to check out what all the fuss was about."

"Exactly."

I started to make my way back to Robert when Louise stopped me and had a hand on my shoulder. "How are you holding up, love?"

Is she bipolar?

"We're just taking it day by day."

"Good girl. You take care of yourself. You look very pretty tonight and more like your age."

"Thanks."

I turned in to a white chest. It was Tiger. He was breathing a little heavily. "Hi, honey. I'm trying to get back, but I keep getting stopped."

He put his arm back around my shoulders and kissed my forehead. "Six minutes. I came to rescue you."

"Thank you, Rambo."

That made him smile.

"Can I have another glass of wine?"

He leaned into my ear. "Here or back home?"

"I have a surprise waiting for me at home, don't I?"

"Yes, you do, baby."

"Home."

"Good choice."

He scooped me over his shoulder and carried me out and down the stairs like a caveman. When we got to the last step, I opened my legs to slide around his waist. That he actually let happen.

I told him to wait. "If you're going to carry me away, can I have a piggyback ride?"

He grinned and released me. Then he turned for me to hop on. At least we would both be facing the same direction saying good-bye to everyone. I wrapped myself tight, and his hands were reaching back, cradling my butt. It made him happy, so I let it go.

Over to the car, he let me down and turned to me, caressing my face with one of his hands. He was in no rush to get me in, and then he started kissing me. He was making out with me.

Oh man, this is hot. Really hot. I was making out with my man in the front of someone's house while a party was going on in the back. A good five minutes we were at it.

"Come on, baby, let's go home."

I wanted to ask him about his past girlfriend and relationships, but I didn't want to ruin our night, so I tucked it in the back of my mind to be brought up at a more appropriate time. I wanted to know everything about this man.

"So what's my surprise?" I asked.

"Patience, my love." He kissed the inside palm of my hand.

"Oh jeez, don't do the finger-sucking thing. I'll come."

He gave me the wicked grin. "I will have to remember that."

"Don't worry, I'll remind you."

He clamped his teeth down on my palm.

We arrived "home," and I got the full effects of the "skidding into the garage" entry.

"Man you're a good driver. Those marks are right on the money for control."

"Baby, I have full control over everything I do right up until the time I shoot my load inside you, and that's when I am at my weakest."

"So you actually are human?"

"Every inch a man, baby. Come on, let's get you inside."

He took my hand, and we walked to the door. When he unlocked it, he scooped me up and carried me over the threshold then kissed me. "Welcome home, baby."

He carried me up the stairs then deposited me on the overstuffed chair in the living room. "Stay right here!" he commanded.

Walking into the kitchen, I heard him open a wine bottle, and my heart began to race. He came out with two glasses and the bottle. He poured mine first and then a glass for himself. Moving in front of me, he sat himself down on the coffee table and raised his glass. "To us, and to your new home, kitten. I hope you have many happy memories here."

We clinked our glasses, and I took a sip. Man, my mouth was dry and I was nervous.

He reached in his back pocket—*Oh shit! Oh shit! Oh shit!*—and pulled out a key.

What? A key? It's a key! I came down from my high.

"This is yours now," he said. "I will put it on your ring later."

"Thank you." I gave him a little deflated smile.

He put his glass down and told me to wait right there. I did, sipping my wine and sitting back in the chair. I relaxed, closed my eyes even.

He was gone about ten minutes. I heard him coming down the hall, but he stopped in the kitchen and then came back to the living room. The cabinets to the entertainment center opened, and he fiddled with the stereo a bit. Then classical music came on.

My eyes were still shut, and I could feel him leaning down to kiss me softly. *Ah, this is so nice.*

He took the glass out of my hand, and I heard him place it on the table. Then my chair jerked to the left, and my eyes flew open when he came at me with another soft kiss.

I noticed he had his uniform hat on. *What the heck?* And then I took in the whole picture: cop hat, flak jacket, uniform pants, big boots, no shirt underneath, and handcuffs. He pressed the stereo remote. Flo Rida's "Right Round" came on, and he started gyrating. Holy shit, he was stripping for me!

Man, could he move! He was perfect to every beat, swinging and turning, body pumping, and I was clapping with glee, smiling with carnal appreciation.

Oh my god! His flak jacket came off, and he threw it in front of me. There was bare chest, hat, and pants left. He was working his hands over his pants where his cock was, and I was so heated I thought I was going to faint. *Not now, body! Don't faint now. No no no. You must watch! You must watch!*

His pants came off next, all in one quick-jerk motion; and he was in this black G-string, swinging those luscious hips from side to side and body-pumping his arms.

Oh my god! Oh my god! I don't know when I started squealing, but it was making him smile.

The whole time, he was blazing into my eyes, and I was trying to look at *everything*! He then did these little tricks with the hat that just sent me spiraling. Man, could he move it!

Next thing I knew, he was back in front of me, and he placed his hat on my head and took my hands and rubbed them all over his body. Man, every woman must have wanted to fuck him.

Then I briefly thought about past women and quickly barred them from my brain. He was mine! He wanted me! The song was ending, and his crotch was in my face. I just wanted to bite him.

He tilted my chin up and was very pleased by my reaction. "Don't move, baby, I have one more for you."

I couldn't speak. I was enthralled!

He handed me back my wineglass, and it just sat there in my grasp. He gave me a quick kiss and disappeared back into the kitchen. I was beaming, and then I got my own idea. I quickly stripped down to my underwear and strapped my shoes back on.

He called out to me, "Baby, hit the PLAY button again on the remote."

I grabbed it and scanned for PLAY and pressed "I Can Transform Ya" by Chris Brown.

He stood at the far end of the room and fell into a push-up position. So fucking hot! Then he started doing an alligator-crawl push-up thing. I thought my panties were going to combust. As he was coming toward me, he took in the fact I was only in my sexy undergarments and high heels. His sexual energy slammed me! I was panting.

This time, he had on a street dancer outfit, and was he fucking sexy! A few feet from me, he stood up and again was street dancing, using all those fantastic muscles. Oh my god, can he dance! Shirt came off, pants came off, and I sat back and touched myself the way he did in the car earlier. His step faltered as he was watching me, and his eyes began to smolder.

This was a turn-on for him. I will have to remember that.

Then all of a sudden, my panties were ripped, and my vagina was in his mouth. The music was still going. Well, I hope that wasn't part of his act on stage. He licked and sucked and assaulted me until I was just on the edge. Then the music stopped, and it was quiet.

He pulled me off the chair and into his lap, both of us trying to catch our breath. His erection was still filling and topping his G-string, which my vagina was now up against.

His eyes locked with mine. "Katherine Quinn. I promise to love and protect you for the rest of my life. Will you marry me?"

Oh god, I wanted that cock inside me now! Right now!

"Yes, Robert Beckham, I will marry you."

Anything, I will do anything for you.

I thought he was going to take me hard. That's what I wanted right here, right now! Instead, he kissed me tenderly on my lips, forehead, nose, and chin. He wrapped his arms around me and moved me to the floor beneath him and proceeded to make sweet, tender love to me as if I were fragile and cherished. Wow. Right answer!

Chapter 7

I woke up tucked up against my fiancé with his arm securely around me. I moved slightly, and his lips were instantly sealed to mine. "You are beautiful this morning, soon-to-be wife."

Beaming—I was beaming. "You're insane. You know that, right?"

"No, baby. I just know what I want, and I don't want to waste another moment waiting." He kissed my breasts. "These are quite lovely this morning too." And he started licking and sucking.

Oh my god! Oh my god!

And that's how our morning started.

After we showered and dressed, he gave me a little tour of "our" house on the way to the kitchen. It was bigger than I thought. There was the office with a half bath I hadn't realized was there. Then there was another full-sized bathroom down the hall, two smaller bedrooms, and a storage closet/laundry room with a pocket door. Then the kitchen and great room. *Nice house. Score!*

I smiled as I looked over to the pile of stripper outfits my fiancé preformed in last night. *Fiancé!* I am getting married to this big, beautiful, sexy, strong, authoritative, master shooter, judo, jujitsu, grappler of a man. What the fuck did I do right in my life to win him? Oh, and did I mention he was financially secure? And drove around in a sexy hot car?

Mine! He was all *mine*!

"Baby, you make the coffee. I'll start cooking."

I threw my arms around him and jumped up with my legs wrapping around his waist. He crushed me to him and just hugged me.

"I feel like this is a dream and that I am going to wake up any minute, and I will be back at my parents', waking up five days ago with a hangover."

"Baby, it's real. No dream, and we're going to get you a ring to prove it."

"Oh, you're not going to pick one out yourself?"

He kissed my nose. "No, you're going to be wearing this the rest of your life. I want your input as well."

There I go again beaming.

My new fiancé wanted me to be a part of the decision making. *He does exist . . . he does exist. He is real.* I touched him to make sure.

"I want to ask your father for your hand because he looks like a traditional guy. But just so you know, his blessing means nothing to me. I am going to marry you regardless."

Oh, I hadn't thought about that. I relaxed my legs to slide down him, but he just kept them in place. "When were you thinking of asking him?"

"Today when we see him."

"While getting a restraining order for someone who threatened my life?"

"Yes."

"Do you think we ought to hold off a bit until this whole mess settles down?"

"No! Like I told you before, you're lucky I'm not dragging you to Vegas."

That made me laugh.

"Come on, woman, we have a busy day. Station, courthouse, client's house, and ring shopping. I want that ring on you as soon as possible."

"What about the wedding?"

"Ditto, baby. I want you as my wife. The sooner that happens, the happier I will be."

"All right, let's get over telling my folks and go from there." I kissed him.

He smacked my butt and let me down. "Coffee, wife. Now."

"Yes, master." That got me another playful slap and a smile.

Did I mention he is a very good cook? He made us the most delicious omelets that I had ever had. The man was flawless—well, maybe that scary dark side he had could count as a flaw. But my dad had that too. It just comes with people in authority. So yes, he was flawless.

Oh my gosh! I had to tell Pepper I was getting married. She's going to be so mad I withheld information from her. *Maybe I'll text her. No, that's just tacky. Maybe I can scoot over there tonight for a bit. I'll talk to my fiancé (hee hee hee) about it.*

"Baby, I'm going to go change into a suit for the courthouse."

"Should I change too?" I was wearing a casual navy sundress and still barefoot.

"You're perfect the way you are."

"Are you sure? I could put on something more businesslike."

"No. Hopefully, your only business is going to be deciding what ring you like."

OK, I was beaming again! "I'll clean up. You go change, stud."

He kissed my forehead and headed down the hall. When I was finished wiping the counters, he walked back into the kitchen.

"Holy fuck!"

"What? What is it?"

"You!" *Drool!*

He relaxed his stance. "Like what you see?"

"I don't know if I can handle what I see."

He swaggered over to me and caged me against the counter.

"Oh god, I'm going to come."

His hand reached under my dress and played with my clitoris, and I exploded into an orgasm.

"There, baby, that should hold you for a little while," he said.

I was breathing so heavily. He should have fucked me hard last night. Now I have to look at his yumminess all day. I don't care how many times he masturbates me. It won't fix my desire right now.

"No, you're gonna have to fuck me. I'm sorry. I can't look at you like that all day without climbing the walls."

He grinned wickedly. "Your wish is my command, my queen."

There went my shredded panties on the floor, and his pants were around his knees as he spun me around. I grabbed on to the counter, and he rammed that big glorious cock right into the place that was aching for him. He was fucking me like he should have last night—hard and with purpose.

Just as I started to build, he slowed down. He repeated this agonizing torture several times, and just as I was about to protest, he reached around and massaged my clitoris while pushing deep inside me. We both exploded. I heard him bite out that he fucking loved me and then roared my full name. I couldn't speak. I just gasped for air.

Jeez I'm going to have to double up on my birth control with all the sperm inside me. My body had never seen this kind of action. *Maybe I should call my doctor and check that out. I don't want to have a litter right now. And with what Tiger was packing, that's exactly what it would be.* I was wiped.

"How was that, baby?" he asked, grinning at me while I was panting and trying to get myself back under control.

"The suit can come with us now."

A low velvety laugh came from Tiger as he slapped my butt.

He put himself back together, and I stepped away from my destroyed panties on the floor. "One more errand to the list today."

"What's that, love?"

"Underwear shopping. I'm running low."

He pulled me into him and kissed me. "Hurry up, we gotta go." He turned me in the direction of "our" bedroom.

I came back down the hall after cleaning up and sporting new panties. He was on the phone with someone, and his brogue was back. I was so glad he just took care of me. I could not handle that too.

"Yes, yes, I'll tell her, Mum. All right, bye." He looked up at me. "Me Mum is pleased she's going to have a new daughter-in-law added to her life."

I smiled. "So you told your mother?"

"I'm gonna be telling everyone who will listen."

"You're over the top."

"Come on, baby, let's get this shite over with so I can buy you something sparkly." He handed me my bag and took my hand.

When we walked out the door, I look around to see my car then stopped him.

"Hey, can we take my car?"

"Why?"

"This suit of yours and your car are a wet dream. I can get through the suit today, but I don't know if I could handle this suit being in that car." I pointed to the garage. "It's a disaster waiting to happen. It's not for me but for every fucking girl I see 'mind-fucking you,' as you would put it."

He laughed. "OK, kitten, your car. I'm driving."

"Here you go, future husband."

He pulled the door closed, and I handed him my keys. I was scooped up in front of him, and my legs wrapped around his waist in this friggin' awesome outfit.

We headed to the station. It took just under half an hour. He parked out in front, and he stuck his badge on the dashboard. "They don't know your car yet" he explained and took my hand and headed toward the door.

Cahill was coming out and stopped Robert. "Hey, you two. This must be the lovely Kate. Sorry, I didn't get to talk with you last night. You guys left early."

Oh no. Robert was preening as he introduced us. "Kate Quinn, meet John Cahill, a colleague of mine. John, I would like to introduce Kate Quinn, my fiancée."

"Whoa! Wow! Congratulations!" He was shaking Robert's hand. "That's fantastic news. Oh, Kate, let me tell you, you could not have picked a better man. And look at you, my dear. Robert, you certainly are a lucky son of a bitch. Have you set a date? I'll make sure I'm off. This is going to be a hell of a party."

He was shaking Robert's hand the entire time. Then Robert moved between us to prevent John from having contact with me. I just wrapped my arm around Mr. Muscle's right bicep and put my hand in his.

Everyone who stopped, he told. It would be all over the papers by noon! *Shit, maybe I should just text Pepper.*

We finally arrived at the chief's office and walked right in. Chief Conway looked up and then stood up right away. He extended his hand to Robert. "Robert, how are you?"

It was like the chief was really concerned about him. Overly concerned? *That not how it's supposed to go.*

"And who is the lovely lady?" The chief had a brogue. Faint, but I could still hear it.

Robert just blurted it out. "This is my fiancée, Kate."

"Fiancée? When did this all come about?"

"Last night." He was all puffed up. "She said yes."

"Well, I'll be a monkey's uncle. Do you know how many women will be crying in their pillows when this gets out?"

My jealous side was battling with control over my mouth. *No, how many? Why don't you tell me just so I have an idea? Asshole!* But I kept quiet.

And then he continued, "Hearts will be breaking all over the city today. Well, congratulations, Kate."

Fuck you, Chief! I smiled sharply.

Robert was preening. He was a very happy kitty. He pulled me to him and kissed me!

Argh! I'll have to make a rule about no kissing in the courthouse. I don't care how much he pouts!

"Let me know when the big day is, and I will reserve it on my calendar," the chief said. "Not to get off this wonderful news, but back to the reason why you're here. I have some paperwork for you to fill out, and I have the report along with your and your bride's statements."

He handed Robert a sealed folder. "And of course, you'll need to get cleared by a shrink. I have a list of them in the back again along with numbers and locations."

Again? Why did he say that?

"I have a private matter I need to discuss with you, Rob. We can do it now or soon. Either way, it won't take more than twenty minutes." He was giving Robert an option.

Robert turned to me. "I'm a firm believer about facing things head-on. You must have figured that out by now." He caressed my cheek and grinned. "Will you be OK sitting here for a little while so I can wrap this up right now and not have to come back? There's a comfortable sitting area right there"—he pointed—"and I can keep my eyes on you, and you will be able to see me right here."

"Of course. It will give me a chance to call Pepper and let her know what has been happening since she left." I narrowed my eyes at him. "And before she reads about our engagement in the paper."

He let out his velvety laugh. Then he kissed me and turned me around, leading me to the seating area. *What, no ass smack?*

He kissed me again. "I'll be right out, baby."

I smiled to him. "I will be fine. Pepper will keep me occupied."

He kissed my temple and strutted back to the chief's office, keeping eye contact with me until he settled himself in the chair. He glanced around me, and when he was satisfied with the way things were, he looked at the chief.

I pulled out my phone and called my best friend.

"Details! I want details! What have you been doing the last twenty-four hours?" Pepper asked.

I told her about moving my stuff and then about the party. Just kept that one light. Then about my "welcome to the neighborhood" present.

She screamed in the phone, "Jesus! Describe everything!"

Before I did, I asked her if she could choreograph a number for me because his birthday was coming up, and that's what I wanted to give him. She immediately said yes and that we should use one of his songs that he danced to for me. I thought that was a really good idea.

From my smile, Robert was getting curious. I peeked up at him watching me from the office and blew him a kiss. That got me a grin. Then I dropped the bomb on Pepper. I told her he proposed to me after his second number.

Crickets on the other end.

"Pepper?"

"Oh my god! Oh my god! You're getting married—to hunky stripper, cop, Terminator!"

I liked *Terminator* much better than *Rambo*. "Yes!"

"Have you told your parents?"

"Only a matter of about an hour."

"When? When will the wedding be?"

"Soon."

"Well, I'd ask you if you were pregnant, but for fuck's sakes, you didn't have enough time to get pregnant yet. You sure about this?"

"As the sun is yellow."

"Interesting metaphor. The sun burns you."

"But it also nurtures you and gives you vitamins to help you grow."

"Yes, but in small quantities. I don't think you will get Robert in small quantities."

"God, I hope not. He is wearing a suit right now, and it's unbelievably sexy on him. I made him have sex with me before we left just so I could stand being with him in it for the next six hours."

"You made him have sex with you?"

"I know, right? He's just so . . . yum!"

"Wow, you've got it bad."

"That's putting it mildly, my friend."

"So when am I going to see you?"

"Soon, very soon. I have a doctor's appointment—with my shrink—tomorrow, and I know Robert is hell-bent on getting a ring on my finger ASAP. So let me get those two things out of the way, and we will go from there."

"This is really happening, isn't it?"

"Yup."

"At least I will be able to dance with someone now who is worthy."

"I'll let you borrow him on occasion."

Then we giggled.

Robert was coming toward me when I hung up, and I beamed at him. He scooped me up and started carrying me down the hall—one arm around me and his forearm supporting my butt.

Whatever . . . this is what he is going to do anyways. I just hope "Chris" is here.

And there she was, across the hall.

Liam came rushing up to us, shouting his congratulations on the engagement. I think she was going to burst into flames. He patted Robert on the back and then he touched my shoulder.

I was waiting for a reaction, but Robert seemed to be OK with it. Liam asked if he broke the news to his mother. He confirmed that he had. Tiger released me and took his blazer off. I offered to hold it for him as he folded it over my arm and tucked me into him.

Oh man—shirt, tie, and dress pants with a gun.

Visions of him last night were coming back, and I was really trying to hold back the smile. Robert squeezed his arm around me a little. I looked up.

"Are you OK, baby?" he asked.

I scanned my surroundings, and it was just the two of us. Where did Liam go?

I grinned. "My mind is in the gutter."

He turned me to him and backed me up against the wall, pinning me with his hip. "I think I will have to wear a suit all this week."

"Are you trying to test my method of birth control?"

"Every day, baby. Every damn day."

I was not having this conversation in the hallway at the police station, so I reminded him of the next task. "I think you have a very important question to ask my father. And I think you had better do it soon before he finds out on his own."

He purred, "You are so right." Then he freed the pressure from his hip. Tipping my chin up, he kissed me softly then took my hand, heading toward the doors.

"Do you still train in your martial arts?" I asked.

"Yes."

"How often?"

"Usually five days a week for about three hours."

"What? That's a lot."

"Again, had to do something while I was waiting for you, baby."

He opened my door, and I settled in. It was strange being in my passenger seat. He glided in behind the wheel and called my father; then we headed for the courthouse.

My father was waiting, and he had everything in order. Robert and I followed him to a small room, where they conferred. It was time to hear the message. Robert excused both of us from the room momentarily, and my dad seemed impressed by Robert's concerns.

Oh, he was a shoo-in. The restraining order was issued. The message was erased, and Robert talked to my father alone. Of course, they left me in the secured room all by myself. I had butterflies in my stomach. At least I hope those were butterflies.

My father entered the room again. "So, Kate, I have been informed that a very important question has been asked to you."

"Yes, Daddy."

"What was your answer?"

"My answer was yes."

What else would it have been? He was withholding a very talented body part from me that I needed desperately.

"Do you think you can love this man and raise a family with him? Can he make you happy for the rest of your life?"

"Yes, Daddy, and he is already making me very happy and safe."

Oh, good one, Kate. Throw in "safe"—Daddy will cave. He just wants me safe and then happy.

"You have our blessing then. He is a fine man. I did a background check on him, and it is quite impressive. You have a good man, Kate. I am proud to include him in our family. Good choice, baby."

Oh, that was a little creepy! Hearing Daddy call me baby after Robert had been calling me that all weekend.

Dad opened the door and shook Robert's hand. "Welcome to the family, Robert. It looks like we will be celebrating Thursday."

"Thank you, sir. I will love, honor, and protect your daughter until the day I die."

A little dramatic there, Tiger, but Dad was smiling. Two errands down, two to go. He did not carry me out of the courthouse, but he did kiss me.

OK, I can live with that. Now I was real eager to go ring shopping, and we still had one more stop. Do I blow off to Jess? Though he does look real good in his suit. I could really show him off.

"Hey, honey, here's the thing. I need your advice."

He stopped us walking and turned to me with his hands going to my waist. "What is it, kitten?"

"I want to blow off Jess"—he grinned—"and get my ring."

He closed the distance. "We can see her tomorrow, and then you will have something else to show off."

"And that's why I asked you. You think of everything."

OK, I technically jumped up onto him. So he did not initiate it, but I was carried out of the courthouse in his arms. And neither of us cared.

After rescheduling with Jess, he drove to a very nice jeweler downtown. Oh my god! The rings were beautiful in the window display. I had no idea what his budget was, but when we walked in the door, a middle-aged woman nearly tackled Robert. And yes, she was his aunt.

I didn't see her last night. I came to find out she was his father's sister. She was classy, well-mannered, maybe not so much on the greeting. She was also very happy to meet me, finally. I think that's going to be my new nickname: "finally Kate." Maybe I can get a tattoo. I'll have to ask hubby.

She was thrilled to hear the news and brought us over to the counter, asking what shape I was interested in. I was in awe. I really liked the princess cut, but I decided I was a traditional round solitaire girl.

Then she asked what size. I had no idea what to say, and I looked at him, shrugging my shoulders. He made a fist, stacked them on top of one another, and then made a half. I was wondering what the hell he was doing. Then he said to Jane while looking right at me, "I think about two and a half."

I gasped in a breath and blushed. He just smiled like the damn Cheshire Cat. He remembered I was measuring his penis, and that's what he was basing my ring on. *Bastard!*

Jane was very pleased and started pulling all the styles I liked with a two-and-a-half-carat stone. They were amazing. I narrowed it down to three. She took my finger size, and all three rings fit.

He asked me again if I could decide.

I shrugged as I said, "You asked for my input, and now it's time for you to make the final decision. Surprise me, Robert. The choice is up to you."

He leaned in and kissed me. Then he asked me to sit over in the sitting area.

I was so excited; I just prayed I would not trip getting there. I wanted to jump up and down. He made his choice, and she smiled over to me. She took his credit card and finalized the transaction.

He came over and sat next to me, very calm and controlled. I wanted to scream. *Where is it?*

Jane motioned him over, and he tucked the box in his pants pocket.

What? You're putting it away? No! There's no putting my ring away! I want it! Now! Give me my ring!

He strolled over to me with a ghost of a smile touching the corners of his mouth and held out his hand. "Come on, baby. Time to go."

I took his hand and stood up. I think I was shaking a little. Jane congratulated us and said something about a dinner blah, blah, blah. Then we left, and Mr. I'm Always in Control suggested we go have lunch.

I want my ring!

I played it casually. "Where do you suggest?"

"How about the Saint James?"

"Sure, that sounds perfect."

And he drove me to lunch. The anxiety was killing me. He ordered a bottle of champagne. Then we ordered lunch. I didn't want to eat. Hell, I just wanted my ring.

When the champagne arrived, the waiter poured our glasses and excused himself. Robert didn't say anything, just searched my eyes while twirling his glass. I went to take a sip, and he stopped me. "Not yet"

I needed the drink. This was torture.

He said, "I'm trying to find the words to let you know how happy you are making me. How complete I am now feeling in my life."

Holy shit!

He rose from his seat and kneeled in front of me. I was frozen. I could not move to save my life.

"I won't ask you to marry me again because, quite frankly, I liked your first answer. I fell in love the first moment I laid my eyes on you. Your beauty, your personality, your joy and sweetness all planted a seed in my soul that grew and wanted to claim you. I knew you were meant to be by my side. I had a lot to accomplish to show you I was worthy enough to take care of you, to cherish you, and fulfill your every need. I set goals and accomplished my career, my strength, and my control to grant your every desire and to keep you safe. Katherine Quinn, will you wear this ring as a token of my constant love and strength to you and only you? Because with you by my side, I am now complete."

Jesus, he was deep!

"Yes, Robert. I will wear your ring with pride and be by your side for eternity."

Now give me my damn ring!

He pulled it out of his pocket and opened the lid, presenting it to me. I gasped! It was the one in the high antique setting. The one I really, really loved. He pulled it out and claimed his love for me, slipping it on my finger.

The tears started coming. Then he scooped me up and planted a very, very long kiss on me. I think we were making out in the middle of a classy restaurant on a Monday afternoon with my legs wrapped around his waist and tears running down my cheeks.

Everyone was staring and whispering from the other tables. Then Robert just simply announced, "She said yes." We got a huge round of applause.

I couldn't stop staring at the beautiful ring on my finger. I barely touched my food although I downed the champagne no problem.

"Are you ready there, Mrs.?"

I beamed at him. "Yes."

"Good, because I want to see what you look like wearing only that ring."

"Absolutely, Mr. Beckham."

We couldn't get out of that restaurant quick enough. He was speeding all the way home. My new life was hitting me with a force I never expected. This man, this beautiful man, set me as his goal. Loved me and wanted me so badly to wait and build himself to be worthy in his own eyes.

He was always very attractive; but I was loyal, and I think I buried away any outside attention because I didn't know how to deal with it. So I ignored him. Looking at him right now, I had to wonder: how the fuck did I manage to do that? He was a god! In a suit that was everything he claimed to have accomplished. Smart, strong, sexy, respected, and honorable. And I was wearing his ring! Vegas sounded real good to me right about now. We held all the cards, right? I made a mental note to bring it up later.

Right now, he wanted to know what I looked like with only this ring on, and by golly, that was what he was going to get.

He pulled in front of "our" house and carried me up the walkway like his bride. *Yeah!* He opened the door with my keys and headed for our bedroom.

He let me down, and I stopped any further action he was going to take. "I want to undress you, if that's all right?"

A smile spread across his lips as he stood still. I took a step back and admired my man one more time. This was all for me and only me.

I started to unwrap my favorite gift in the whole wide world, taking my time while he caressed and kissed me softly every so often. I got to the point of sliding his shirt off, and he reminded me about his cuff links.

I took one hand and brought it to my mouth, inserting his index finger just as he had done to me.

A silky purr blew out in a breath. He liked that too. His sexual energy wrapped around me like a satin blanket.

I knew he was hard and ready for me. I played with his finger against my tongue and sucked it gently. I then removed his first cuff link. Then I switched hands, and he had to adjust his stance, letting out a low groan.

His shirt now easily fell off his body. I turned so he could unzip my dress, which he did immediately. I stopped his hands from doing anything further, and a low growl came out in protest.

"I'm not through yet, my husband-to-be. This is my turn. You will have yours in a moment."

He stopped advancing and took a controlling breath in.

Man, that was a sexy sound. I slipped the dress off myself and stood in front of him with just my bra and panties. I proceeded with his belt then unhooked my bra and let it fall off my shoulders to the ground.

He adjusted his stance again. I released his button and unzipped his fly then bent down to remove his shoe. I felt another one of his guns.

Oh boy, I'm going to have to get used to that.

He cleared his throat, and I looked up. "There's a snap on the side."

I lifted his pant leg and found the snap and removed the whole thing.

Jeez, it was a big gun. *How do you not notice it under there?*

I just placed it on top of the discarded clothing, slipped his shoes off, and lifted back up to drop his pants down. He stepped out of them gracefully then pushed them back to the pile. There he stood, waiting for my directions.

I proceeded with his last piece of garment that was struggling to hold in the massive bulge. I felt around the material for a moment, taking him in my hands. I gazed at my ring, and the way my fingers were working him set sparkles everywhere. He was watching me as well and took that hand. Lifting it to his mouth, he kissed it.

I lifted the material over his hardness and pulled down while he stepped out. I stepped back, lowering my panties as well. He took his cock in his hand and stroked the length until I was safely removed from all garments.

I held my hand against my stomach. "Well, how does it look?"

He closed the distance between us and lowered himself to place his raging hard-on between my legs. "Perfect."

And then we were on the bed.

He manipulated me with an orgasm before he entered me. Then he proceeded with a carnal assault I think would have been painful if he hadn't prepared me so well. He was strong, commanding, masculine, and he was marking me as his. The moans were erotic coming from him, and just then, I was building another orgasm.

He stopped and pulled out then flipped me over with my ass in the air. And he attacked me from behind with his mouth. I tried to understand how he had me positioned, but I could not get my mind to function. This new sensation was just making my brain cells misfire. I felt his tongue lapping me from my clitoris to my opening, but his nose and his hot breath were against my anal entrance. And it was confusing. Not to mention how he was holding me in this grip that I could not move from.

Then his licks became longer and longer. He moved all the way from front to back, going over my anal area.

Oh no! My sudden climax ripped through my body, but I was locked in his arms, and he was still licking those long slow strokes. I was screaming, pleading, and begging then screaming again from the uncontrollable desire that was ripping through me.

He stopped the licking and inserted two fingers into my vagina and slowly pumped me. When I was done, he dragged my legs to the side of the bed and stood up. Then he flipped me back over and inserted his cock again then continued to pump me at his controlled pace. He slowed down to feel every inch of me then, with two forceful pumps, he emptied himself, milking the last of his orgasm deep inside me.

His look was commanding and radiated pure triumph His goal attained. I think I passed out or fell asleep. I'm not sure, but he was still in me when I did come to.

I woke up tightly tucked up against my favorite man with his arm securely around me. I smiled, and he pulled me tighter against him. It was still light out.

"That was . . ." I could feel his smile. "Holy moly, I don't even have the words."

"I'm going to claim all of you. So you have been warned, baby."

Oh jeez, does that mean he wants anal sex? "Well, consider me your virgin because I have never experienced or felt anything like you before. So I am yours to sacrifice."

"Yes, you are."

I turned and wrapped my arm and leg around him then kissed him. "I was wondering about our wedding."

That gave me his full attention, and he lifted us more onto the pillows and separated us so we could look at each other and talk.

He took my hand and brought it to his mouth, kissing all around the ring. "What about it?"

"I want to start the conversation about it. What do you want for a wedding and when?"

"I told you, Vegas and now."

"Robert! Is that really reasonable? We have family and friends."

"This is about us, no one else."

"Well, I have to admit Vegas does sound tempting."

His eyes lit up. "What do you want?"

"You, first of all, but I don't really know about the rest. I always thought that I would get married someday in a church with all the trimmings and such. But right now, I don't know what I want as far as how the deed gets done."

He laughed. "It's still just a piece of paper, no matter how you get it."

"I guess it's the memory of the whole day that I am trying to wrap my head around."

"How about this, baby? We fly down to Vegas this weekend with your parents and friend. Get this legalized and behind us. Then we can throw a smashing reception here, say next month. Get you an amazing dress and do all the tradition stuff. That way, you get your memory, and I get you right now as Kate Beckham, my wife."

The ridiculous grin was back again.

"You've got a deal, mister."

His eyes widened in disbelief. Then he was rolling me around the bed in delight, and he pounced on me.

An hour later, it was still light out. Robert bounced off the bed, too restless. I checked the clock, and it was five thirty.

"Baby, I'll be in the office making all the reservations." He kissed me then kissed me again.

Tiger pulled out a pair of loose pajama bottoms and a tight T-shirt. Thank God I was wrecked and he was just relieved, because he just looked yummy.

Leaning in for another kiss, he asked, "Babe, do you have any requests with this weekend?"

"Yes, you as my husband."

"Your wish is my command, my queen."

Another kiss, and he headed for his office.

I turned in my pillow and inhaled his scent, smiling, as I too was starting to get restless. I got up and started dinner and did the laundry. I made him a vegetarian dish that he really liked, and then he went right back to the computer while I cleaned up and went back to bed.

I was exhausted, and he finally climbed in around ten, whispering endearments and proclaiming his love for me while I drifted off to sleep.

I woke up tucked under my fiancé with his arm securely around me, and I was wearing his ring. He kissed my shoulder and told me he was going to put the coffee on.

I must've fallen back asleep because I could smell the coffee in the room, and he was beside me, clothed and trailing kisses down my arm.

"Wake up, baby, we have a busy day. Coffee is on the table. I'll go start breakfast."

I turned and he kissed my lips then left for the kitchen. I read the clock: 6:38. *Uugh!* I leaned over to pick up the coffee and took a welcoming sip. Then I held out my hand to check out my ring. Two and a half carats. I giggled. *It's perfect.*

I put my coffee down and slipped on one of his T-shirts, smiling at mine next to his, then tiptoed down the hall, peeking around the doorframe. He was making pancakes again.

I came more into view. "Do I have time for a shower?"

"After breakfast, babe, with me."

"I'll go grab my coffee then."

I headed back to the bedroom as I grabbed my coffee to return to Robert.

The smell was comforting, and I went straight to him. He turned to kiss me, and I squeezed his butt for a bonus. He smiled, pleased by my gesture. I moved to the chair and asked him about our reservations.

He verbally gave me the run-down—what hotel and airline, what we needed for our documents. He mentioned a few wedding chapels and to get the numbers on exact people flying. I thought of my parents, my sister, Pepper, and maybe Mark. He agreed with Mark coming and to call Pepper this morning to confirm.

This was so exciting. I was hungry but could barely eat. We finished, and it was just seven.

"I can call Pepper now and get the numbers," I said.

"Good, I'll clean up."

"Hey, you cooked. I should clean."

"You make the call, gorgeous, so I can book our plane."

"OK. Is the house phone plugged back in?"

He walked over to it. "Is now." And he handed me the phone.

Pepper answered on the second ring. She didn't recognize the number, so she sounded a little irritated.

"Hey, it's Kate. I'm on Robert's landline. As a matter of fact, you may want to note this number under our contacts. Anyways, the reason I am calling is to tell you we've set a date." I was smiling at him.

"And?"

"This weekend."

"What? Are you insane? Is there something you're not telling me?"

"No, everything is good. No, that's the wrong word. Everything is perfect, fantastic, amazing—but we are going to do a big party next month with all the traditional wedding stuff. Cake, dress, big meal, dance."

"Can I choreograph your first dance?"

"Hang on, let me ask. Hey, babe? Can Pepper choreograph our first dance?"

He was leaning against the counter. "We'll have to see it first."

"Maybe. Robert wants to see it first."

"He'll love it. I promise."

"So getting back to the wedding, we would love it if you and Mark could come to Vegas and be a part of this celebration."

"Dallas is flying in Friday."

"Hold on a second, Pep."

"Her little sister, Dallas, is flying in on Friday."

Robert asked, "What time?"

"What time is her flight?"

"Six in the morning."

"Six in the morning," I relayed to Robert.

"Do you know her well?"

"Yes, very well. I would love it if she would come too."

"OK, baby, she's on board then. There is a two p.m. I can book all of us on, and we can fly out together on Friday."

"Pepper, she can come with us as well. We can all fly out on Friday afternoon at two p.m."

"Holy shit! Is this really happening? Damn party in Vegas. I will make sure we are all there."

"Excellent!" I gave him the thumbs-up. "I'll call you later. I have another call to make."

"Okeydoke, Kate. I'll secure my end."

I hung up, jumping up and down, clapping my hands. I ran at him, and he stepped away from the counter so I could jump up on him. He scooped me up and then leaned all the way over so my hair was touching the ground, and he attacked my neck with kisses. I was squealing and giggling once again. When he straightened up, he walked us into the bathroom to shower.

He ran through our schedule for the day, and I reminded him I needed more underwear. And now we had to stop so I could buy something sexy for our first night being married. Then that got me thinking of a honeymoon.

"Honey, I know we are all over the map here with this wedding and delayed reception, but what about a honeymoon?"

"Would you object to us going to Ireland and then over to England? I know my parents are going to want to show you off over there. And this way, we could kill two birds with one stone."

"Object? Are you kidding me? That is way more than I was hoping for."

"We'll do two and a half weeks." And there was a sarcastic smile turning up the corners of his mouth.

"Two and a half you say? Aren't I lucky for that extra half."

"You certainly are, Mrs., you certainly are."

Then I showed him how much I loved that extra half in the shower again.

Not bad. By eight o'clock, we were heading out the door. My stud wore black dress pants and a crisp gray short-sleeved shirt, top three buttons undone. *Yum.* I wore gray dress pants that made my butt look superb again with a black silk shirt that hugged the curves of my breasts. I strapped on my black-heeled Mary Janes. I fixed my hair in a high ponytail just to give it a little edge. Robert approved, and he couldn't keep his hands off me.

My appointment with the psychologist wasn't until ten and not far from my mother's, so we went to show Mom the ring and tell her about Vegas in person.

I was a little nervous. We took his car this time and headed to Mom's. I called her to let her know we were on our way. It took a half an hour while Robert held my hand and played with the ring. I looked over at him. Even his sunglasses were sexy.

Jess is going to faint when she gets an eyeful of my man, and I can't wait to see her reaction.

Robert pulled into my parents' driveway then came around to open my door and took my hand, placing it around his waist. He tilted my chin up for a passionate kiss, cupping my butt with both his hands and pulling me against him.

My mother opened the door. "Kate, Robert!" she called over, so excited.

He pulled back and grinned then gave me a quick eyebrow raise. I winked at him, and we turned toward my mother.

She met us halfway and gasped. "Is that the ring? Oh my goodness, it's beautiful."

She picked up my hand and examined it. Robert had his arm down my back with his hand rubbing my butt—in front of my mother! But she didn't notice because she was too busy looking at the ring.

"Two and a half carats," I told her with a little chuckle.

"Oh, Robert, Kate, you two come here." She put an arm around both of us and took us in for a group hug.

I think she enjoyed hugging Robert much more than me. She seemed to have lost her train of thought momentarily and cleared her throat when she straightened.

"Congratulations, the both of you. I couldn't be happier. I just want you two to be happy."

"Well, we have some more news, Mom."

"What is it?"

"We are flying to Vegas this weekend to get married."

"What? Why so soon?"

Robert stayed quiet, looking for a signal from me to take over. I didn't give it to him.

"We talked about it last night, and we just want to be married. Now. There really is no reason to wait."

"What about a wedding and all your friends?"

"This is how we want it. Then in a month, we are going to throw a big party with all the traditional wedding hoopla—dress, cake, dance, etc." Then I threw her a bone. "And if you could help us with that, I would appreciate it. It's going to be a lot of work in a short amount of time."

Robert squeezed my butt again, this time a little harder.

"But! Getting back to this weekend. We would love it if you and Dad and Stacey could come with us. Pepper, Mark, and Dallas are coming as well."

She smiled. "Of course, I'll do whatever I can to help. Will you let your father and I pay for the reception?"

I looked up at Robert and said, "As long as we have the final say in all the decisions."

Robert went back to rubbing my butt. He approved of that idea.

"Of course, dear," my mother said. "Well, looks like we are going to Vegas, and your sister should be here any minute."

Right then, Stacey pulled into the driveway.

"So is this my new brother-in-law?" she asked.

Robert just stood there making no move for us to go and greet her.

"Damn, sis! He's a catch!"

Robert studied her and pulled me in tighter. He brought his hand around my waist. She came right up to us and started to move in on Robert, and his cop mode kicked into high gear. His stance altered and became cold and commanding like he was confronting a hostile offender.

She stopped in her tracks, feeling his dangerous energy, and just gawked at him. My mother was oblivious to it and picked up my ring to show her and proceeded to tell her about our weekend nuptials.

I put my free hand around him and rubbed his back. He leaned down to kiss me. My sister just stared at us, mouth open, catching flies. When he was satisfied with his kiss, he straightened and stuck out his hand. "Robert Beckham."

She shook it. "Stacey Quinn, Kate's sister."

My mother then announced for us to come in for a cup of coffee and some pastry. Robert took this moment to do as he had been doing all along by scooping me up and carrying me into the kitchen. My sister was horrified by his public display of affection.

Finally, someone who does not approve. Hey, wait. That would be my tacky, unfiltered sister. Fuck her! You go, kitty. Good, good kitty.

Mom just smiled. "Lovebirds."

I touched my forehead to his and my elbows were on his shoulders and my hand cupped the back of his head. He kissed me again then let me down but tucked me under his arm. I put my arm around him and my thumb in his waistline. He went back to rubbing my butt.

My sister started right in. "Why the sudden need to get married?"

I answered, "We just want to do it now instead of later."

"Are you pregnant? Oh, hang on. You just started dating like four days ago, so you can't be pregnant."

Robert took over the conversation. "I've known Kate for six years."

"She's only had one boyfriend for the past seven years and had just broken up with him. You know, the guy you shot."

Crickets . . .

I looked up at Robert. He was calm but dangerous.

He said, "First off, Stacey, he had a gun pointed at her with his finger on the trigger. She is alive today simply because I got to him first."

He was soothing my back with his hand. I had no reaction to their conversation and just laid my head against him to show that I was completely relaxed.

My mother broke the tension. "I will be grateful to you, Robert, for the rest of my life."

Robert still focused on Stacey. "Another thing, Stacey. Kate is the woman I want. I have declared that to her, and she is wearing my ring now to show everyone that she has done the same with me. She is the only woman I will take care of, the only one that I will protect, and the only one I want to share my bed with."

See? Fuck you, sis. Take that!

"So if you can't be happy and respectful for her this weekend, then I suggest you not be a part of this. I assure you, I will not let anyone interfere with her happiness in our union this weekend."

Crickets again . . .

Mom to the rescue. "And neither would any of us. This is all about the two of you. Stacey will be on her best behavior, I assure the both of you, or I will bring her back myself. I am looking forward to my new son-in-law legally bound to our family. This is going to be a glorious weekend."

Stacey took a bite of her pastry. "And congratulations to the both of you."

He turned me to him and dipped me into a kiss. *My kitty, mine, mine, mine.* He put his coffee mug down. "Come on, baby. Your next appointment awaits."

"Dr. Greene," I answered my mother's unasked question.

"Oh, go on. You don't want to be late."

Then Robert did something I hadn't known he was capable of. He walked over to my mother and kissed her cheek then said good-bye. It was very tender to watch, although I could see she was trying hard not to collapse. He took my hand and walked right by Stacey with no further acknowledgment. I waved good-bye to both of them and told my mother I would call her. Then Tiger scooped me up again and carried me down the stairs.

"These pants look and feel really good on you, baby."

"Don't tell me they have to go in the restricted section after today?"

"No, but I plan on being around every time you wear them."

"Oh, you think so?" *Hee hee hee you go, Grammy.*

He put me in the car, and we were off to see the wizard.

"Do you know anything about what your appointment will entail?"

"A little. We did a semester on PTSD in college."

"Do you want me to run through it with you?"

"And why do you know so much about it, dear?"

"I have been through them several times."

"How many is several and why?"

"Seven—and because I shot the bad guys."

"Seven? Shot? As in shoot to kill or shoot to injure?"

"It is always shoot to kill. If I get at them, they won't be getting back up."

"Wow, so you really are the Terminator."

He grinned at me. "Terminator? Aye!"

"That's what Pepper called you."

And there was that low, velvety laugh.

We pulled into Dr. Greene's fifteen minutes early.

Robert walked me through a basic session and told me to just relax and that he would be right outside the door. All I had to do was call out his name, and he would be in there in a heartbeat. He kissed my forehead, and we entered the building hand in hand.

In the elevators, he twirled me into him so my butt was against his crotch. Then he caged me, rocking me back and forth. A few people got on the elevator, and he just continued to bask in the attention.

I snickered as one woman looked on with sheer jealousy.

Yeah, he's hot, and he loves me in front of everyone.

Our floor was next, and he straightened up and said, "Come on, beautiful." He then slapped my butt toward the door.

Dr. Greene's door was the fourth one on the left. It was crowded in there, and they all stopped what they were doing when Hot Cop entered the room.

Every female was staring at *my fiancé*. Right on cue, he kissed me in front of all of them then led me over to the reception desk and checked me in. He handed the girl some paperwork.

What paperwork? Where did that come from?

She just held it for a second as she froze, looking up at him.

I broke her trance. "We're a few minutes early. Do you have a bathroom I could use?"

She pointed and then cleared her throat and told me, "Right around the corner."

Robert walked me, of course. I held him back from following me in, shaking my finger at him. He wanted me again, but this time, he would have to wait.

When we came back around the corner, there was one chair available. I told him we could stand, but he led me right to it and sat down, pulling me onto his lap.

OK, now I was getting a little self-conscious. I could feel the women fantasizing that they were me.

Dr. Greene was standing at the edge of the waiting room, looking curiously at Robert and me.

"Ms. Quinn," he called.

I stood up as Robert followed.

He looked over at Robert. Dr. Greene held out his hand. "Hello, Ms. Quinn. May I call you Katherine?"

"Kate will be fine, Doctor."

"Excellent, Kate. And who is this?"

"This is my fiancé, Mr. Beckham."

Dr. Greene held out his hand to Robert, and they exchanged pleasantries. "Mr. Beckham, why don't you have a seat? We will be about an hour."

"I don't think so, Dr. Greene. I will wait outside her door."

That was an order. *Uh-oh.*

I intervened. "Dr. Greene, I would feel much better if Mr. Beckham was close. I understand he will not be able to come in with me, but it would make me feel secure knowing he is on the other side of the door. He has been my security blanket in this whole ordeal, and I am not quite ready to give him up."

And then my tiger was preening. He leaned in and kissed me in front of the good doctor.

Dr. Greene cleared his throat and allowed it. How could he not? So we went in and took our seats with Robert in a Secret Service stance outside my door.

Robert had coached me on sticking to the incident and not to give him any facts outside of that. It was none of the good doctor's business what we did in our own time. I was there just to deal with what happened that afternoon along with the few times I regressed and what triggered my reaction.

That part went beautifully. He explained why I reacted that way and that it was very normal, and I should be fine. Then he started asking me about my tiger. At first, I reiterated that he made me feel secure; and then a red flag went up. He was fishing.

I told the good doctor that there were no triggers between my fiancé and myself. I then added that I was glad he was there to protect me; and finally, I asked if we could just stick to the reason I was there in the first place.

Dr. Greene wrote some stuff down on his pad and replied, "Of course."

At the end of the hour, he told me he would like to see me one more time and to schedule an appointment for next week. I stood up and shook his hand. I told him that he was highly recommended and that I was glad to be going through this process with him.

He smiled kindly, but there was a weary look in his eyes. "Until next week, Kate."

"Thank you, Doctor."

I opened the door, and there was my tiger.

"Mr. Beckham, she's all yours."

"You got that right, Doc."

He put his arm around me and walked me down the hall. Dr. Greene watched and then slipped back in his office.

I told Robert I needed to make one more appointment, and we headed to the reception desk. Robert made the appointment for me. I let him do it because he was my control freak. He took my hand, and we left the building.

As soon as we were in the car, he started with the questions.

Jeez, his were better than the doctor's. I had to answer them head-on. He was disappointed that the doctor kept prying into my personal life but liked the way I handled it. It got me a twelve-second kiss.

Next, we were on our way to see Jess.

Chapter 8

I called Jess to tell her we were on our way. Forty minutes later, I'm sure she heard Tiger's car pull in. We had arrived. Robert opened my door, and her front door flew open. Jess and Beth were in the doorway.

"Oh god, I just came." Jess gulped.

Beth just looked frozen as we approached them.

With Robert's hand linked with mine, we walked right up to the entrance. Both women watched as we approached them in silence.

I started to make the introductions, and Jess snapped out of it. Robert moved me across his body to hold me in his other arm and extended his hand to greet them. Then he released this dazzling smile that made both women blush.

Come on, girls, get it together.

I then held out my ring and informed them I was engaged.

They looked at each other and screamed. Jess herded us all into the kitchen. I told Robert to follow them and that I just wanted to say hello to Frank. He reluctantly let me go and followed the women, who became very attentive to my man.

Robert could see me with Frank and he relaxed. I was only in there a few minutes; then I came right back to him. He put me on his lap again. This time, the girls were sighing with delight. They thought that was so sweet.

Jess checked out my ring and asked how big it was. Robert answered with a shit-eating grin. Then Beth asked if we had set a date.

He dropped the bomb. "This weekend, we are flying to Vegas."

Crickets . . . followed by screaming, gasping, and squealing with delight. Apparently, they didn't think I should wait either.

We visited for another half hour then Robert smacked my thigh to make tracks. The women followed us to the door. As I turned back to say something, Jess gave me the thumbs-up and mouthed, "You lucky shit." I grinned and told her I would be in touch when we returned from Vegas. They both wished us their congratulations, and off we went.

"Mall?" I asked him.

He looked at me, unknowing.

"Panties," I explained.

Then he smiled. "All right, baby. Mall it is. Do I get to pick some out as well?"

"Absolutely, stud, since you're the one who will be looking at them and destroying them."

He purred, "Damn right, baby."

He put his foot down on the accelerator.

Robert parked in a no-parking zone right out front.

Of course.

We walked hand in hand through the mall, and I had him wait outside a few shops so I could look at dresses. I suddenly came across the perfect sexy, short white satin Vegas-style dress that would drive him wild. I gave it to the clerk and told her I wanted to try it on, but I just had to tell the person I was with to wait. She smiled and said she would put it in the second dressing room. I shot out the door, running up to him giddily.

"What is it, baby?"

"I think I found the perfect dress. I'm just going to try it on. Wait here!" I pointed my finger at him. "You don't get to see."

He let out a low growl. "Here, take my wallet, I'm paying."

He handed me his wallet.

Oh, I could get used to this.

I took it and reached up and kissed him. He wrapped his arms around me and half-dipped me into the kiss. When he lifted me back up, I had to steady myself a moment before he let go.

I backed away from him and pointed again, with the ridiculous smile back on my face. "Stay!" And I bolted back into the shop.

I tried on the dress. It fit perfectly! *Yeah!*

I stepped out of the dressing room and peeked around to the clerk. "Hey, can I get your opinion?"

"Sure." And she came around the corner. "Wow! Whom are you trying to impress?" I pointed toward the door, and she spotted Robert. "Holy shit!"

"Yup, we're getting married this weekend."

"You lucky bitch. Oh sorry. Sorry, that just slipped."

"You, my dear, are completely correct. No offense taken."

"The dress is smoking hot on you. You will have him eating out of the palm of your hand."

I bought the dress. She wrapped it up so much that he would need a blowtorch to get to it.

"You can hold it, but you can't look," I told him.

He took the dress and folded it over his arm. "I wouldn't dream of it, baby."

"This from a man who censored my clothes."

"Well, I assure you that I will not be leaving your side this weekend, so you may wear what you like."

I turned to him and planted a big kiss on his lips. I gave him a ridiculous smile and dragged him toward the lingerie store.

He had much more fun than I expected. He was like a kid in a candy store. He examined everything, chose colors, and mixed up the different styles. I followed behind him, picking out a few matching bras. Then I brought him over to the sexy nightgowns.

I picked out a white baby-doll nightie that looked very honeymoonish. He shook his head. Then I looked around and noticed all the women staring at my tiger open-mouthed and practically drooling.

I am going to have to get used to this.

Then I asked him, "OK, stud, what do you like?"

He went over to the bustiers and picked out a powder-blue one with a thick white lace ribbon up the front that looked like a bow on a present. I smiled and looked for my size. In the drawer, I also found a matching micro-miniskirt and garter. I grabbed those as well.

We put them in the full basket and headed for the register. It came to just under five hundred dollars, and I gasped.

He bent down and kissed me, handing his credit card over to the cashier. "You now have a month of underwear. I can choose to shred them if I like."

The clerk told him if he opened up a store credit card, it would save him 10 percent of his purchase along with double bonus points. She explained the program in detail. He said yes and made it a joint account with my soon-to-be married name on it.

This freaked me out a little. I was going to be married to him. Now I have my first credit card in our name. This was so surreal. I had the ring, the man, the dress, and the lingerie, the date, and the soon-to-be last name. I was high.

I was floating by his side with another package in his hand, and I was tucked under his arm. I never wanted this ride to end.

Two cops were coming toward us. Robert was grinning.

"Rumor has it you popped the question to this little lady," one of them said.

Robert swung his arm around to shake Neil's hand.

"Congratulations there, Sergeant."

Sergeant? Who's Sergeant?

"Thanks, Neil."

I held up my ring.

"Wow, that's a beauty, miss. You are a lucky lady to land this guy."

"So I've been told."

Robert made the introductions. "Baby, this is Neil and Craig."

"Hi."

"Gentlemen, this is my Kate."

"*Theee Kate?*"

"The one any only." He was preening again.

"Well, now I see why you put a ring on her finger."

Craig offered his congratulations. Robert had his arm back around me. Neil asked if we had set a date and that he would make sure to take the day off. Robert dropped the bomb.

"This weekend. We're going to Vegas."

They were stunned. "You're getting married this weekend?"

"Yes!"

I felt the need to do some damage control. "But it's just the first step to our plan. We are going to have a huge party with all the traditional wedding festivities in a month. You won't miss anything except sitting in a church."

Neil laughed. "And I look forward to that celebration. It will be the party everyone will be wishing for an invite to. I had better make the list now that I know your secret."

I smiled.

And then he turned to Tiger, who was still basking in his pride. "You lucky son of a bitch. She's a catch and well worth the wait."

Does everyone know he has been pining for me for six years? Hey, hold on, that's a good thing. I was the prize. He worked and waited to set himself up for me. I'm the one that should be preening. Yes, Robert, you may have me now.

Robert added, "That's why I am making sure she's not getting away."

I beamed up at him. He kissed me.

"Do I keep this hush-hush around the station, or is it public information?"

"Spread the word, Neil. I could not be a happier man."

"Congratulations, Sarge, and you too, Miss Kate."

Craig was very polite and Neil was just sucking up. They said their good-byes, and we headed to the car.

There was a crowd of young men ogling the Shelby when we reached it.

One spoke out, "Nice car, mister."

Robert tucked me in it, and I heard him say, "Get an education so I won't have to arrest your ass!" He started the beast and peeled out for them.

He took my hand to his mouth and kissed. "Anywhere else you want to go?"

Then the idea hit me. "Pepper's studio. I want to show her my ring." I gave him the address, and we were off. We were unexpected, but I always knew I could just drop in.

She was fine-tuning the high school dance routine for the finals. We watched her for a bit, and Robert noticed the bulge in her waistline under her skirt. He smiled. It was a gun.

She stopped mid-routine and screamed with delight and ran to us. She grabbed my hand. "Holy fuck! It's beautiful. Well done, Hot Cop." She didn't hold back. I think the iceberg was starting to melt between them. He let her hug me. "So while you're here, I want to know if you picked out a song yet?"

"Song?" I asked her.

"For your dance at the reception?"

"Oh, we haven't gotten that far yet."

"Yes, I understand. Dating, engagement, marriage have taken priority over the past few days." Robert actually laughed. "But I just want to show *him* what I am capable of, so here is a random song and just watch."

She put on Savage Garden.

"By the way, I'm doing your part, Rob, so take this in."

He studied her. With each flowing movement, he saw her talent. How she glided and how beautiful the dance was. With a gun stuck under her skirt.

He leaned into me. "I admit I didn't give her enough credit."

I turned to him. "Honey, it was you just fighting for custody of me. You both can share. She is a gun-totin' American just like you. She dances supreme just like you. And she is my only friend who loves and protects me just like you."

He kissed me passionately. "I don't share."

"Well, it's either I can hang out with Pepper, or I can pout around all day."

He growled. "Fine, I trust her with you."

"Good choice. It will make me a very happy wife to know you trust my safety and well-being with my only friend. I want her to feel welcome at our home. So get to know her."

I jumped up and wrapped my legs around him, and he leaned forward, attacking my neck again.

"Are you two paying attention!" she protested.

"Not anymore," Robert remarked. "And you're hired," he added and then assaulted my neck again.

We left ten minutes later, both of us hot and bothered. His house—our house—was twenty minutes from her studio, and he floored it. There were two packages out by the door, and he ignored them. With my purchases in his hands, he dragged me to the house, hung up the dress on the railing at the stairs, and carried me to the bedroom.

It was a welcome sensation. I wanted him in me now. He was training me to crave sex. This round was just straightforward, plunging-into-me sex. It was the sex that was normal for me, and it was slightly disappointing from his taking me with his savage urges. I wanted to be fucked. I wanted his intensity.

I took his face in my hands. "Baby, if you want me, show me just how much."

That was it. He was fucking me into next week. I felt the danger from him on the edge, and he commanded for me to wrap my arms around him. He lifted the both of us up, and his bent legs were folded under him, and he was pumping my body with the length of his cock in a steady rhythm.

And then I came—loud, primal, and wanting. He found his release and laid me back on the bed and pulled out. He trailed kisses across my jawline.

"That's how much I wanted you baby."

Did I mention I loved this man? I felt so relaxed, and he curved along the length of my body and caressed me. We lay there silent for about ten minutes, just enjoying our afterglow, and then my curiosity kicked in.

"Hey, honey?"

He hummed an acknowledgment.

"Why did Neil and Craig call you Sarge?"

He popped up onto his elbow and trailed kisses around my shoulder. "That's my rank in the department. I am a sergeant."

I turned to him. "So you have status." I smiled big.

"You bet, baby. I'm the best they got."

"You are a force of nature, stud. Is there anything that can stop you?"

"Not now, kitten." His lips were sealed to mine. When he let me up for air, I could feel his erection on my hip.

"I'm going to need to get into better shape to keep up with you."

"I like your shape now, and I would fear for your safety if you could keep up with me."

"What does that mean, fear for my safety?"

"It means we would fuck each other to death."

I laughed, and he placed his lips over my nipple, making me squirm and laugh harder. Then Tiger pounced, and we were in round 2.

I woke up to him reading the paper beside me, drinking from a bottle of water. I rolled and cuddled up against him. He pulled me up and secured his arm around me while he kissed my forehead.

"Are you hungry, baby?" he asked, and my stomach responded with a growl.

I giggled. "It would appear so."

"Come on and let me feed you. Have to keep up your strength. Don't want you fading away on me."

"You start lunch. I'll put in a load of laundry."

I don't know what I said, but he was in his glory. He rolled over on top of me and professed his love verbally and with a lot of kissing. This was him cherishing my being there, saying yes, and never leaving his side. My simple task was so domestic, so part of everyday life—his life that wanted to include me. And there I was, and I was staying.

"I hope you remember this moment when I shrink your uniform."

He nuzzled me. "Impossible. They go to the dry cleaners. You can claim anything in the basket. If you shrink it, you will wear it."

"I think you just gave me an incentive."

He grinned. "I love you, baby." Then a kiss, followed by a smack on the ass. And he was lifting both of us off the bed and saying, "You get the laundry, and I will get us something to eat."

I kissed his chin. "OK, Sarge."

And he smacked me again.

I went to the bathroom and grabbed the basket. I threw my stuff in there as well and hauled it down to the laundry room. I smelled something really good. I peeked my head around the kitchen door.

"What are you cooking, honey?"

"Grilled cheese and tomato with a side salad."

I ran to him, and he was ready. I leaped into his waiting arms and kissed him. "You're the best!"

"You know it, baby."

He let me down to flip our sandwiches. I ran back to the laundry room, sorted the clothes, and started our first load. I strolled back to the kitchen and felt a little pride in myself. This was my second task as the little woman.

Robert had everything set up when I entered, and he scooped me up in his arms and spun me. I clung around his neck.

"Your food awaits, my dearest."

"You know, you're setting the standards pretty high here, Mr. Beckham. I might even say you are spoiling me. I might have to expect this treatment forever."

"So that will be my new goal, my love."

He put me on the stool, and we dug in.

After we cleaned the kitchen together, I looked around. "So do you keep this house clean?"

"No, I pay Maggie, my cousin you met at the party. She comes in once a week and cleans it for me."

"Really?"

"Yes."

"What's downstairs?"

"Spare bedroom, bathroom, gym, and storage. Come on, I'll show you."

He took my hand and led me down the stairs. It ran the whole length of the house. The back part was the storage. Then there was a full bathroom and a large bedroom that had a metal four-post bed in it, a nightstand, a lamp, and recessed lighting in the ceiling. It was basic, but I could see it as a private room for when company stayed with us. Then there was an open-floor plan mimicking the top floor, and Robert had it set up as a home gym. Weight bench, all the weights, free weights, heavy bag, speedball, treadmill, pull-up bar, yoga ball, and this half yoga ball and some other funky stuff I didn't know the names of or how to use. I'm sure those would not be kept from me long.

"Robert, your house is pretty big."

"Our house, kitten. And I plan on filling it soon."

I gave him the look. "Can I at least have you for a year? Before I'm barefoot and pregnant?"

He grinned. "That depends on how good your birth control works."

"Well then, let the battle begin. I personally think we should practice often. Just to give you an edge."

"Keep tempting me like that, baby, and see what happens."

"I think we have another bed down here we need to christen."

He looked over at the room. "Not here, you belong upstairs in my bed."

"What's wrong with this one?"

"It's been previously occupied."

OK, I got it. He brought other women down here. "This is a perfect segue that I wanted to ask you about. I won't get mad. I promise." And I gave him a kiss with tongue just to reassure him.

He looked at me warily. "What do you want to know?"

"What you have been doing for the past six years without me?"

"You mean sexually?"

"Yes, you know my dating history. Did you date?"

He sighed and brought me over to the weight bench. "Sit. Let's get this over with."

Uh-oh, this doesn't sound good.

"First of all, I didn't really date. You know I was a stripper. That was a huge opportunity for me to make money, and I seized it. And I did make a lot of money. Women where throwing themselves at me. At first, I was just fucking. They paid me a lot of money. Then in my last year, I met you. I became so focused. I took that opening to build my technique for pleasuring you, someday. You were always my goal. I wanted to be the best lover, provider, and protector for you that would keep you safe and satisfied for the rest of your life."

"So you practiced on other women to perfect your skills for me?"

"Yes, I always used a condom. I have never entered a woman skin on skin. And in college, I never let another woman touch me while having intercourse."

"What? What do you mean by that? How could they not touch you?"

"I restrained their hands—with rope or handcuffs—to the bedposts. And since I've bought this house, it's only been down here. I never brought a woman upstairs."

I kept my breathing calm and controlled. "Was that Chris chick one of them?"

"Yes. I know she was hoping for more, but I just couldn't give it to her. She came on to me strong, and I wanted to try some new techniques, and she was willing."

"Oh."

"It was just sex, baby, never anything else."

I wanted that bed gone right now. He only knew how many women were on it, and I wanted to erase every single one of them. My idea hit me like a slap.

"I want you to fuck me on that bed. I want to be the last girl that ever enters it."

He caressed my cheek. "Baby, you belong in my bed with me, not down here."

"Is this my house too?"

"Yes."

"Then I'm marking my territory."

There was a trace of a smile. Then he stood, taking my hand and leading me to the bedroom.

"I want you to cuff me to the post," I said.

He protested. "Your hands belong on me!"

"I want to feel your learning process. I want to experience you experimenting."

He sighed and ran his hand over his short hair. "You have already, but I will give you something I have yet to perfect."

"Deal!"

And he proceeded to handcuff me. Then he caressed me gently with the most erotic strokes of his hands, fingers, and tongue. He was experimenting with making love—something that was foreign to him. This was mine. The one thing no other woman got, and I wanted to put my arms around him.

"Honey, take the cuffs off. I get it."

He removed them right away and held me to him. I couldn't let go either. He was mine, no matter what happened in the past. He was my future, and he proceeded to erase every memory that happened on this bed. Chris was my only connection to his past that reminded me of before I arrived, and I would not let her cloud our future.

I planned on stepping up my boundaries to accessibility on my future husband. God, I wanted to marry him tomorrow. The weekend could not come soon enough. Now I shared the intensity of how he felt, and I turned up the heat. I wanted to take him, and how I wanted to and take control of this memory. I was going to be triumphant and then burn the bed!

There was a new task for tomorrow. Furniture shopping. This room was my new project. It would be a guest room on my design. And he would let me pay. That would be the next topic, but I would save that for tomorrow. Finances. I had a big savings account too. I felt so empowered. My man. My house. My future. And it was only Tuesday afternoon.

I was lying beside him on our bed, caressing his chest, and thinking. "Hey, honey? What did you do other than the deed before I arrived on the scene?"

He studied my expression. "What do you mean, kitten?"

"Like what else occupied you. Besides women."

"I work out a lot."

"Where? Downstairs?"

"No, baby. I have a membership to a gym. And I belong to a dojo and I have a personal trainer."

"Can I work out with you some time or watch?"

His grin spread across his face. "Absolutely, baby. But I don't know how much of a workout I'll get watching you."

"Well then, let's find out. Want to go to the gym, stud?"

Right then, I realized I had challenged Tiger. He wore a purely masculine smile.

"Absolutely." He lifted me off him and smacked my butt. "This should be good."

Hey, I was up for the challenge. I was far from being skilled in strength and agility. Hell, I ranked in the top two in archery up until I graduated college. I was on the equestrian team in college and scored in the top five. I was not without skills coming into this family, and by golly I would prove that to him.

We packed for the gym. I wore my spandex shorts and a sports bra with a tank top over.

His step faltered when I came out of the bathroom. I smiled and admired my own view. He sported a sleeveless-style tee with black shorts that stopped mid-thigh.

I beat him to the punch. "You look delicious."

"You look like I might get into a fight."

"Well then, may the best man win."

"He already has!" And he smacked my ass.

He grabbed two smaller towels and a change of clothes, and he told me to grab a change of clothes as well. He pulled out a backpack and put my things in it with a towel and liquid soap for me to shower and change after. I obliged with every request he stated, and we were out the door, headed to the east side of town.

He tucked me under his arm upon entering the facility then proceeded to sign me up as a member under my soon-to-be married name.

The girl at the counter seemed saddened. He had quite the following. I would have to rise above the influence. I am his bride, and he only wanted me. *Cry in your pillows, girls. He's taken.* And then I took this opportunity to rub my hand over his ass.

When he finished the paperwork, I got a wide grin from my fiancé, and he took my hand and kissed each finger then sucked my index finger into his mouth. *Oh shit.* No matter how many times he was in me, this was an aphrodisiac for me. Was that payback for feeling his butt at the counter?

I knew he was drawing attention, and I had to make him stop. "If you keep this up, I will be forced to relieve myself in the stall, and you will be stuck waiting for me, knowing what I am doing."

He stopped, and then he growled low in his throat. "Don't be long," he threatened.

I stored my stuff and did a quick restroom break, and I was out in the hall between our locker rooms, waiting for my Terminator.

I received a few admiring looks from the gentlemen going in, and then there he was, pulling me to him with a kiss.

"Come on, baby, let me show you what I do."

He brought me over to the treadmill first, and we ran for a full forty minutes. When we finished, there were a few classes starting up that I took notice of: an RPM class (that was spinning) and a body-pump class (that was group weightlifting).

I pulled him toward that class. "Can we try?"

He answered, "I've never done the group classes before."

"So this would be something new to both of us."

"Come on, woman, let's go try."

We entered the class, and he asked some poor female who was all too willing to help us set up. Then two instructors came in and welcomed us all and asked if anyone new was in the class. I raised my hand, and they welcomed me. They explained everything and explained the different weights we should use for warm-up. Robert set himself up, and then he checked on me. We were side by side, and he winked at me.

I looked behind us. A very excited female was behind him, and another female was behind me. I began to think this was a chick class and that I would owe him big-time.

Then they started. The warm-up was just a precursor to the overall dynamics, and I knew it was not a chick class. When the warm-up was over, we started the squat track.

Oh my god! They told us this would be the heaviest weight of the class. Robert loaded up. I was a little more reserved, not knowing what to expect. Six minutes of squats and my legs were jelly. The woman behind my tiger was drooling. *Been there, done that, honey. And you should see him in a suit!*

The instructors guided us step by step, telling us which muscle group we were working and when to add weight and when to decrease weight. I really liked the class, and I think Tiger liked it too. The girls around him definitely liked it.

When we were done, he brought us out to do abs. His routine was brutal. I couldn't do even half. He crawled over on top of me when I gave up and hovered for what seemed like a long time.

"How you doing, baby?"

"I'm going to be sore tomorrow, you know."

"Muscle sore I can fix, baby. I'm going to still have you."

I smiled. "I think that part might be the only thing accommodating you."

"That's good enough for me. I can take care of the rest of you then."

"Oh yeah? How so, stud?"

"Two words. Jacuzzi bath."

My smile widened. "You say the sweetest things, my love." And he caged me at the gym with a lot of people staring. *Argh!*

We arrived home at around four o'clock, and he wanted to take me to a pub in the south end. I fell back on the bed and let him pick out my outfit. I wanted to see what he liked me dressed in. He picked out jeans and a sexy blouse. *Wow!* He matched them up really well. *I should let him do this more often.*

I picked my shoes and a light jacket. My soon-to-be husband actually coordinated to complement my outfit.

We didn't match, but we went together.

Looking me over and liking what he saw, he lifted me up and threw me on the bed. Then he tackled me. I was laughing while gasping for air from the shock. He began to kiss me from ankle to temple with featherweight kisses. He ended with his tongue in my mouth, and after a few passionate moments, he just held me. I wrapped my whole being around him; then he reciprocated, and we entwined our bodies.

The moment was sheer bliss. His hard, strong body tangled with mine. We lay there for one more minute. Then he kissed my forehead. "Come on, baby, I need to feed you."

I kissed him two more times. "OK, let's go."

I checked myself in the mirror and pulled my hair up into a ponytail.

As we walked down the hall, he grasped my ponytail and pulled me back. He sealed a kiss on my lips and then smacked my butt. I guess he liked my hair.

We arrived at the pub hand in hand.

"Ah, and there's himself!" the bartender shouted. "And who have we got here, lad?"

Everyone turned toward us. Robert got a lot of nods from fellow patrons.

I turned my head up to him. "Cousins?" I whispered.

He shook his head slightly. "Cops, baby."

I looked around as he pulled me closer, and there in the corner, looking all leggy, was Chris, the super bitch. *Great!*

I brought my hand up to his elbow, and it gave off a clear view of my new ring. *Take that, Chrissie. Sorry, he wanted me!*

"Mack, this is my fiancée, Kate."

"Your what? Did you say fiancée? My god, son! When did this come about? Only last week you were in here breaking hearts, and now you're getting married?"

Oh boy, he's preening. And then he moved me in front of him, and I was in the Robert cage.

His grin was infectious. Everyone (except Chrissie) was smiling.

"Hang on a second, lad, is this theee Kate?"

Oh shit, he's going to fuck me on that table.

He turned me to him and half-dipped me and kissed. "Yes, my Kate." He looked into my eyes.

"For the love of Christ!" said Mack in astonishment when he walked around the bar. He came over to us as the patrons were cheering.

I was upright and embarrassed as all hell. Mack slapped Robert on the shoulder and shook his hand. He turned to me and checked me over good. *Ugh!* Then he lifted my left hand to look at the ring.

"I wouldn't have believed it if I hadn't seen it with me own eyes. Ah, she's as beautiful as you described, and her ring is lovely. So this is the fair maiden, Kate."

He bowed and kissed my hand. "It is a pleasure to meet you, my dear. You have a fine suitor here, oh lovely Kate. You could not have chosen any better."

The question was, was I blushing or was I going to throw up? I took a steady breath. Nope, definitely blushing.

I leaned on Robert as he kissed my hair. There was a second of silence. Was I supposed to respond to all that crap? I replayed the last bit over in my head.

"I feel very blessed, thank you," I said.

Chris was talking to another girl, shaking her head, and everyone seemed to go back to their own business.

"Tell me, does your mum know?" Mack asked Robert.

"Yes, and my father. They can't wait to meet her."

"So have you nailed down a day?"

"This weekend," Robert announced. "We're going to Vegas. I don't want to waste another minute waiting for her to be my wife."

Chrissie heard that! Her chair went flying back as it hit the ground. She glared and stormed toward the door. Her friend picked up the chair and threw some money on the table then went after her.

Mack smiled. "I suspect you're gonna have to get used to that, my dearest Kate. Hearts are breaking all over the city tonight."

Robert paid no attention and was snuggling me again. I think I looked a little mortified.

Then Robert continued, "We are having a proper reception in about a month with all the traditional festivities."

"Well then, I will keep my eyes open for my invite." Mack winked at me.

OK, I needed to sit now with a big bottle of wine in front of me.

"Are ya staying for a bite, lad?" Mack asked.

"Yes, I want Kate to meet who else has had an influence in teaching me to cook."

Mack clapped his hands together. "Come, sit over here. I'll go get the Mrs." He led us over to the table at the side of the bar.

Robert pulled out my seat and walked behind the bar to fetch a bottle of wine, four glasses, and a corkscrew. He obviously knew them very well and must have worked here at some point being this comfortable.

Mrs. Fitz came barreling out from the kitchen. "Where is he? Where's that child!"

She spotted him with his Cheshire grin coming from behind the bar. She beelined right to him and opened her arms. He swung her around, hugging her.

She took his head in her hands. "You got her! You finally got her! Where is she, child?"

And he put Mrs. Fitz back down then led her over to me.

I stood up. Still in shock of how he greeted her. She had a face-splitting grin and approached me like I was made of fine porcelain.

"There you are, love. Oh, you are such a fine sight to see. My Robert has been setting his sights on you for some time, and he has been working so hard. He has such excellent taste. You two are going to make fine-looking children. Mr. Fitz has told me you both are flying off this weekend to seal the deal. Quite frankly, I'm surprised he is waiting that long."

She winked at Robert, who was now opening the bottle. She hugged me to her and welcomed me to the family. I still wasn't sure about the connection.

"And this ring, it's just beautiful. Did you buy it down at Jane's?"

"Yes," he answered and handed the three of us a glass.

Then Mack came back from behind the bar and raised a toast. "To the future Mrs. Beckham. May you and Robert be blessed with a long, happy life together."

I clinked and downed my glass.

Mrs. Fitz chuckled. "Ah, ya poor dear. Been quite a few days for you, I can imagine?"

"That's putting it mildly. But I couldn't be happier about Robert. I meant what I told Mr. Fitz."

He corrected me. "Call me Mack, love."

"Right! I do feel blessed that I have Robert. He is everything I ever wanted with lots of bonuses."

She smiled. "I taught him how to cook."

"Then I am very grateful to you."

Robert poured me another glass of wine and moved his chair next to mine.

Mrs. Fitz said, "I'm going to cook for you two. Kate, do you like pot roast?"

"Yes, thank you."

"It's our special tonight. Let me jazz up your plates a little. I'll be right back, dear."

I turned to Robert. "Who is she?"

He laughed. "Consider her my other mother. I grew up with the Fitzes. Mary is my mother's best friend over here. They were the first couple my parents met and became very close with. I grew up in their house as much as in my own."

"Did you ever work here?"

"Yes, for a few years. Then I moved when I went to college, and you know my employment then." He kissed my hand.

"Like I said, you come with a lot of bonuses." I turned to kiss him.

He pulled me onto his lap. "She is right. Saturday can't come soon enough."

"Three more days, stud, and you will own me for a lifetime."

"Damn right, woman." He dipped me back and attacked my neck.

When I was upright again, there were a few guys standing around our table, watching opened-mouthed. Their look was one of disbelief, just staring at Robert.

"Hey, Robert, congratulations! This must be the beautiful Kate?"

He wrapped his arms around me. "Thanks, John. Baby, meet the finest tactical team on the East Coast. This is John Murphy, Bill Wiswell, and Kevin James."

"SWAT?"

"Yes."

"Wow, it's nice to meet you."

"Well, you're only as good as your team members. We are lucky to have your man serving with us."

I turned my head to him. "You're SWAT?"

He nodded his head.

They all broke out in low chuckles. It was obvious I didn't know. I stopped with my fifty questions that I wanted to ask, kind of embarrassed that I didn't know this. But what the hell? We have only been dating for, what, five days?

I leaned into him. "Lucky me," I whispered.

He kissed me, and I tried to recover from this missing fact.

"I hope you gentlemen keep my man safe. He's becoming very important to me very quickly."

"You can count on us, Kate, even though he is the fastest gun we have. Although I still say that qualifying round was fixed."

"You're just a sore loser, John. I beat you by a full two seconds."

"We'll see at the next match."

"How was the percussion gun training?"

"We all passed, so you can get off our asses about it now."

Robert laughed.

"But it looks like we can't leave you alone for a long weekend without making national headlines."

"That's a story for another day."

So Hot Cop was actually the Terminator. I felt my groin react to that thought.

"Well, we just wanted to wish you the best on your nuptials. Kate, you will be seeing us quite a bit, so welcome to the family. We are looking forward to that party as well."

I gave them all a little wave. Robert shook each of their hands, and then they left.

"Holy crap, you're on the SWAT team?"

"Yup—actually, top guy. It's my SWAT team. Are you OK with that?"

"You just keep getting better and better. You know how I reacted to seeing you in that suit?"

There was his wicked grin forming on his face. "Mmm-hmm," he purred.

"You just upped the ante. You may have to take me in the bathroom."

I felt his instant reaction with his erection growing beneath me. Just then, Mrs. Fitz came out with two plates.

I went to get up, but he pinned me to him. "Oh, I don't think so, baby. The only reason my dick is not in you right now is because I picked these damn pants for you to wear."

Mrs. Fitz just smiled at the two of us. Robert, full of lust, and me not being allowed to get up. She placed both plates in front of me. Then she sat down across from us.

Oh crap! You have got to be kidding!

Robert spun me so I was straddling him, and both of us were facing the table. His hands were on my thighs. He was slowly rocking himself against my ass.

Jeez! I picked up my glass and drank in half my drink.

"Here, honey, you want to wet your whistle?"

Oh shit! Did I just say that?

"Absolutely, baby." And he ground into me harder.

I handed him his glass. Mrs. Fitz was watching me, waiting for me to try the meal. *Fuck!*

Robert took the glass and put his arm around my waist. I leaned forward and cut some roast with a little potato on to my fork. *Wow!* I nodded as I chewed and swallowed.

"This is delicious!"

I cut off another bite and added a bit of potato again to feed my tiger. He seductively used his mouth and took it off the fork, locking his eyes with mine. And this was how we finished the first plate.

Mrs. Fitz was satisfied with our—well, mostly my—reaction and retreated to the kitchen again.

Robert leaned forward, pulled my ponytail down, and groaned in my ear, "I need you. Right here, right now. So don't start that other plate."

My pulse started to speed up. *Oh jeez! Not here. This place is crawling with people he worked with.*

"Lift up, baby, but stay close in front of me. Otherwise, everyone is going to know exactly what I am going to do to you."

I think I started panting. My body wanted him. That tone, that command—he was taking me no matter what I said, and I was at his mercy. He was making me want him just as bad right here, right now. He was controlling my body.

I lifted slowly, and he stood up behind me, taking my hand. He guided me to the restrooms. There were three: men's, women's, and a family. He pushed me into the family one and locked the door behind us. He gripped the button and zipper of my pants and nearly shredded them. He pulled my pants down past my knees, and then he did the same to his.

He was sealed to my mouth and had his hands cupping around my ass and pulling me to him. It was the same passion and intensity we had in front of the diner that night.

He growled, "Baby, I'm sorry. I am going to take you hard. I have to have you right here, right now."

I looked right into those beautiful, dangerous eyes. "Take me!"

He spun me around and leaned me over so my hands were grabbing the sink, and he slipped two fingers inside, feeling how wet I was. He took a second to smear that wetness around my entrance. He lowered himself behind and shoved his cock right in. I gasped. He rammed me right to the end of his thick length.

There were seven more just like that. It hurt, or maybe it was just because he filled me so deeply. I couldn't separate the feeling right then. I was on my tiptoes, whimpering as he reached around and rubbed my clit.

Oh shit, he made me come!

He pumped me again and rumbled deep in his throat that he loved me (or I think it was he fucking loved me) as he emptied himself. Well, we fucked in our first bathroom at his "second parents'" pub. *Great! All morality gone. Have I lost all self-respect?*

Apparently, the answer was yes. He brought me to levels I could not comprehend, and I wanted this with him. He massaged my breasts and pulled my hair back then kissed my neck and ear.

"Thank you, baby. I love you. Are you all right?"

"I'm fine. That was really sexy. I think I liked that."

"Oh, don't be telling me that, love, or we will never leave this bathroom."

"I need to sit."

He bent down, wiping me with a tissue, and pulled my pants up. Leaning in, he kissed me. Then he fixed my zipper and buttoned me up. When I was taken care of, he fixed himself up and faced us to the mirror.

I looked into his gaze. "I can't wait to marry you. This is like waiting for Santa at Christmas, and it's the four-day countdown."

"Baby, I know exactly how you feel."

I turned and faced him, giving him a soft feathery kiss. He deepened it.

"Come on, my soon-to-be wife. Let me show you off some more."

He turned me and smacked my ass toward the door. Thank God no one was around, but I started trying to figure out how long we were gone. Then I knew exactly when I got a big fat smile from Mack. *Oh crap! Busted!*

Robert stretched out in his chair all tigerlike. I wanted to crawl under a rock. He was turning me into his slut.

The food still had a hint of warmth to it, and I started feeding Tiger again. Liam and Sean walked in and headed right toward us.

"Murphy said you two were in here." Liam put his hand on my shoulder.

I think Tiger was still purring. I fed him another bite as they sat in the empty chairs.

"So, going to Vegas, huh?"

"Yup," Robert answered.

"Mom wanted to make sure that you know you can use the restaurant for the party. She will close for the day."

I looked at Robert. He was too busy preening.

"Tell her 'thank you,' but we haven't gotten that far. As soon as we get this weekend behind us, I will be able to see what we are dealing with."

I turned toward kitty with another mouthful for him. I asked, "Just a ballpark, what are we talking your side?"

He smiled and took in my fork offering then kissed me. He chewed and swallowed then took a swig from his wineglass.

"Guesstimate, baby, I would figure about one eighty with spouses or a date."

They all looked at me. "My side about fifty," I said.

Liam piped in, grinning, "It's gonna be a hell of a party."

Robert smiled. "Count on two fifty then. I am pretty sure that number will work."

"This is an event, not a reception."

Robert let out his velvety laugh. "You're not far off, baby."

Liam nodded in agreement. "That crowd won't hold at the restaurant."

I looked at Robert. "We're having dinner with my parents Thursday. We can check out the club's ballroom."

He smiled and leaned in, pulling me to him, putting me back on his lap. He reached around and poured me another glass of wine.

Liam smiled. "Everyone will be fighting over shifts."

Robert leaned into my ear. "My new wife is going to create pure chaos. I think I have a new pet name for you, love."

I just looked at him quizzically.

"Chaos."

Yeah, all right, hot cop, tiger, Terminator, Rambo, strongman, sexy fuck-me-into-next-week stud. "I have a few for you too."

Chapter 9

I opened my eyes. I was tucked up against my man with his arm securely around me. I moved slightly.

"*Oh shit!* Ow, ow, ow, ow!"

He lifted his arm and turned me to him. "What is it, baby?"

"I am so fucking sore! Don't touch that, ow!"

He laughed. "I take it the gym is out today?"

"If you want to be able to touch me on our wedding night, then that is a yes."

"We have to work on your muscle strength."

"You're not affected?" He shook his head, and I let out a disappointed sigh. "Not fair!"

He moved and I protested with a moan. "Ow, ow, ow, ow!"

"Wait right here, baby. I'll fix you up." He got up all gloriously naked, and I couldn't even watch. I heard him start the water in the tub. He came back, and he put a bottle on the nightstand and crawled over to me.

"It's going to be worse before it gets better, just trust me." Then he kissed my lips—the only place I wasn't hurting. He began by spreading my arms apart.

"Fuck!" I screamed.

Then he started rubbing from shoulder to elbow. I was too weak to move, and this really fucking hurt. I clamped my teeth together, and the pain finally lessened with each new stroke. I relaxed a bit, and he moved to my other arm.

"Fuck me!" I screamed again.

He smiled. "Don't tempt me right now. But on the other hand, you might benefit from a good orgasm." After several strokes down my arm, he then got up and went back to the bathroom. I heard him shut the water off. I raised my arms and rubbed them myself.

Damn, they hurt!

He climbed up across my legs and spread them open. *Oh my god! Oh my god!* His mouth went right on my sex. Arm pain was momentarily forgotten until they touched back down against the bed. He was attacking my clitoris with fervent lashes. I think I lasted fifteen seconds. That was it! I was coming.

He clamped his mouth down and pinned me beneath him. I was gasping for air. He stopped licking but kept me right there. I was descending from my orgasm, and he went right back to the attack.

I no longer felt the ache in my arms. The aching was in my vagina. He tongued me, sucked, and the lapping was what brought me to the edge. My body responded as he was building a gentle rhythm that made me rock against his tongue.

Oh jeez, I was building again. He slid two fingers into me, and I was coming again. Pinned beneath him, I screamed and screamed and gasped for air again.

He lifted off me and slid his length deep inside, positioning his knees under my buttocks as he scooped me off the bed, bringing our bodies together. I was straddling his waist. He moved me up and down over himself.

"Come on, baby, give me one more. Show me how much you want me."

I put my shaking arms around his shoulders and my feet on the bed. Then I started to move on my own. His hands were at my waist, guiding me over him. I picked up my pace, and the end of his cock found that spot. Desire exploded in me, and I rode him hard and then harder.

His teeth clenched and he bit out, "Come on, baby. That's it! Give yourself to me."

A few more pumps, and he threw me back down on the bed and let out a roar in the form of my name. He emptied himself into me, and I climaxed again.

I was aware of my surroundings once again. He was kissing me from shoulder to shoulder, pinning me with his hips.

My breathing was calmer as I opened my eyes. He just continued to kiss all the way from one side and then back.

"Well, I can say my arms no longer hurt."

There was a gravely soft chuckle that came from him. "Glad to hear it, kitten. Come on, let's get you in the Jacuzzi." He sprang off me and dragged my body to the end of the bed, scooping me up and carrying me over to the tub.

I rested my head against him and placed my hand on his chest. He turned the water back on and sat down on the side, cradling me and rocking gently.

"I love you, Robert," I spoke softly.

He kissed my hair. "I love you too, baby."

I felt how calm he was, and then I planned my attack. I kept my head against him as we waited for the tub to fill a little more. "Are we doing anything today?"

"Packing—why?"

"I'd like to do a little shopping."

"Oh yeah?"

"Furniture shopping. I want to get rid of the set downstairs and pick out a new guest-room set."

I could feel his smile.

"That can't wait till we get back?"

I looked up at him. "No, and can this be my project?"

"You're not going alone if that's what you're asking. Not with Adam pissed off right now."

"No, I'm not asking to go alone. Hey, wait a minute. I can't go anywhere alone?"

"No, not right now anyways. Things are too unpredictable at the moment, and I didn't wait all this time to take the risk of you being taken away from me so quickly."

Overprotective lug.

"Well, just go take the bastard out. Case closed."

"Believe me, I thought about it. Bottom line is, you're stuck with me."

I grinned. "Could be worse."

"Exactly." And he kissed me.

"Oh, and another thing, lover boy. I am paying for the furniture."

"And how do you figure that, Mrs.?"

"I'm not coming into this relationship empty-handed. I have about eighty thousand saved in the bank myself."

No reaction; then I narrowed my eyes at him. "Or did you already know that?"

He laughed and lifted me then sank me in the tub. "Now that kind of information would be against the law, pet."

He knew! The bastard!

I didn't want to get out of the tub, but the water was getting cold, and my hands were turning into prunes. Robert was already out cooking us breakfast. I could smell the bacon.

I pulled the drain and stepped out, towel-drying myself. I looked around the bathroom. I wanted to add a bit of me to this room as well. I'll have to ask him about that.

I put on a simple skirt and a V-necked T-shirt—plain but sexy. After this morning, my body was feeling sexy. When I turned the corner, he looked up and muttered something. I went to walk by him, and he grabbed my wrist, pulling me back toward him. I was wrapped in his arms, and he was feeling up my ass.

"Jesus, baby, we might have to test a few of those beds today."

"I think I may have lost a few pounds with all this sexercising. I'm starving, stud, and withering right in front of you. Feed me, please."

Kitty growled and slapped my butt then lifted my skirt. "You're trying to get your way about paying, aren't you?"

I smiled at him. "Whyever would you think that, darling?"

He exaggeratedly looked me up and down. "Because of that." He pointed to all of me.

"These old things? I only wear this when I don't care how I look. But since we are on the topic of new furnishings, would you mind if I added some things here and there to make it a part of me as well?"

He held me at arm's length and sighed. "OK, I'll make a deal with you. The money you have will go to the household funds that you control: any repairs that need doing, furniture, redecorating, real estate, taxes, etc. Half will be invested so it keeps growing, and the other half will sit there collecting interest available to us when we need. I have three accounts with about five hundred in them combined that we will keep as our retirement and build for our kids' college funds, etc."

"When you say five hundred, is that hundred thousand?"

"Yes."

"Jesus, Robert!"

"I told you I'm good with money, and this brings me to my next part of the deal."

"What?"

"I want you to quit your job and take care of me and our home."

Crickets . . . I went to speak, but nothing came out. My body wanted to do a fist pump. The dream job: housewife. Take care of your man. But I was battling internally again.

Give up your job—
Become a hermit.
Shop all day—
Hey, that is a plus!
Take care of Tiger—
Another plus.
Become the woman of the house—
Again . . . another plus.

My mother gave up her career as soon as she married my dad, and she has never regretted it. I looked him straight in the eyes. He was holding his ground.

"All right, I'll quit my job on one condition."

He was about to pounce. "Name it."

"We wait two years to have a baby."

This got him. He knew if he knocked me up now, I would have to quit anyways. But if he agreed, I would stop working now instead of "the when" he knocked me up.

"Two years starting last Friday?"

I laughed. "OK, I'll give you that, stud."

"Fine!" he reluctantly agreed. I could see he was going to do everything in his power to test that time line.

I jumped up and down, clapping to my victory. Then my panties were shredded on the ground and I was pinned beneath him.

"Practice makes perfect, stud." And then his dick sunk deep inside me.

He kissed me in my afterglow. I felt so much power.

I had him for two whole years like this. In bathrooms and in his garage—oops, our garage—bed, showers, and wherever else we tried.

"Mine! You're all mine for two years!"

"One year, three hundred sixty days"

"Don't pout, honey. Just think, while you're at work, I'll be home thinking of ways to attack you when you get home."

He growled against my lips.

I gave him a quick kiss. "Breakfast smells good, and I believe this should be one of my jobs now."

"I like to cook."

"I like you cooking, so maybe we should do it together."

That got him smiling again. He lifted me off the floor. He straightened my skirt and shirt. Then he scooped up my panties and put them in his front pocket.

"Are you keeping those?"

He smiled down to me. "Yes."

"Pervert."

"They're going into my tactical bag to remind me that I need to keep safe because you will be waiting to attack me at home."

I giggled. "Damn right, stud."

"Come on, eat. We have beds to test out. I don't want you passing out on me."

Our breakfast was nearly cold, but I gobbled it down just as he requested.

"We still have to pack today as well," he said.

"What about tomorrow?"

"I have my shrink appointment, and I am dropping you off at your father's office while I am away."

"You're dropping me down to Daddy's? What am I, five?"

"It's either your dad's—where I know you will be safe and I don't have to worry—or I can call John, Bill, and Kevin. Your choice, baby. Let me know now so I can call your father."

I stomped my foot. "Fine! Dad's office!"

He scooped me over his shoulder and slapped my ass. "Come on, kitten, let's go pack."

He stopped in our bedroom and took out a new pair of underwear. He turned and dropped me on the bed, and I scrambled away. Tiger was game to play-grabbing my leg, and he leaped up, flipping himself around so his butt was in my face. I gave him a hard slap. He was restraining my legs to put on my panties.

I tried kicking once, and that got me pinned and then tickled. I was thrashing and laughing as he was pulling up my panties. I tried to grab his sides, and he spun on me so fast while still pinning me. Then he grabbed my wrists in one hand. I stopped struggling. I was toast. He licked from my neck to my lips, and I laughed again.

"OK! OK! You win."

"Always, baby." He relaxed his grip then lay down beside me until I caught my breath.

"You're insane mister."

"Only crazy about you."

I turned to him and wrapped myself around him. I fell asleep at some point. Robert stayed right by my side. He gave me an hour of power nap and then kissed my hair to wake me up. I loved being in his strong arms, up against his chest, all nice and warm. I loved the smell of him.

He rolled me on top of him. "Time to get up, sleepyhead, if you still want to go shopping."

"You are wearing me out. I think I need to start drinking protein shakes or something."

He chuckled. "Not a bad idea. I will add them to your diet."

I kissed his chest. "Isn't it my new job to look after you?"

"Mmmm. Sure is, baby." He was stroking my hair. "But it will always be mine to take care of you."

I looked at him and smiled. He caressed my face.

"Tell me again about this weekend."

"I am becoming your husband. To love and obey, in sickness and in health, until death do us part."

I giggled. "I am fully aware of that, my king. What are the details—days, flights, hotel?"

He pulled me to his lips and turned us to our sides. My arms were still sore. I made a mental note to keep rubbing them today and avoid the gym for the rest of the year.

He went over the general plans. We needed to contact my parents with their info along with my crappy sister, and I needed to contact Pepper as well. Then he informed me that we needed to drop off her itinerary. He booked us all first class so we would be together. This must already be up to the bones of fifty grand, and Robert wasn't batting an eyelash. I wondered if he had saved for this as well.

Smart, sexy, strong, dangerous man—and he was all mine. Again, what the hell did I do so right to get him? And he wanted me home, taking care of the house and him. My sister was going to stroke out. I wondered if I should tell her before we got on the plane so she could miss the whole trip or wait until Vegas so she would be stuck in a hospital while we were having fun. *Hmm, decisions, decisions.*

"I know everything is booked, honey, and I know we are going to Europe after the party, but would it be too much to stay an extra day or two in Vegas? Just the two of us?"

"Already a step ahead of you, kitten. We are going to San Diego while they all fly home. I booked us on the beach until Thursday. Then we catch the red-eye back here."

The ridiculous grin was smeared on my face once again. "You so rock, hubby!"

He kissed my nose. "No one around but the two of us." He kissed my chin. "All alone on a private beach." He kissed my lips. "Just a husband and his wife." He kissed me again. "Starting our new life together."

And then we made out.

After five minutes of bliss, the doorbell rang. It was my mother.

We walked hand in hand to the door and opened it together. This made my mother smile. "Well, good morning, you two."

"Hi, Mom, what brings you by?"

"I was wondering if you were all set for this weekend?"

"Yeah, I think so?" I looked up at Tiger.

He smiled. "Yes, everything is arranged, Helen, thank you. Come on up. I'll put some more coffee on. I have your itinerary."

"Thank you, Robert."

I closed the door behind her, and Robert took the stairs two at a time. Mom watched him. *Cougar!*

She turned to me. "I can't believe this is all happening so fast. I am very happy for you, darling. You could not have picked a better man."

"I got lucky, Mom. He picked me."

"He is certainly head over heels with you."

We headed up the stairs. I was beaming.

"Tell me, how did your doctor's appointment go?"

I looked at Robert, who was pulling down some mugs. "Oh, it was OK, I guess. He wants to see me again on Tuesday. Oh crap! Robert, we won't be here."

"Just cancel it, baby. You don't have to reschedule another since you're not going back to work."

My mother sat on the stool. "You're not going back to work, Kate?"

I wanted to smack him. "No, I'm going to be a kept woman."

He let out a velvety laugh and pulled me to him. "I'm keeping you all right, baby." And he kissed me.

Mom smiled and lowered her head. He has no boundaries.

"So you're going to stay home now?" she asked.

"And take care of him and this house."

Tiger was preening again, all relaxed, leaning against the counter with me backed up to him.

"Can you afford to make that move?"

"Yes, my future husband here double-majored in criminal justice and economics in college. He's very good with money."

Her smile widened. "Your father will be very happy to know this. He is already impressed with you, young man, and this will just add another feather in your cap."

Robert wrapped an arm around me and kissed my hair.

The coffee was done, and I made a move toward it. He kissed me again before releasing me and walked over to the fridge to pull the milk out. I set the three cups on the island, and he took the opposite stool from my mother's. She flushed.

I know just how you feel, Mom. He was oozing with sexiness.

I leaned forward on the counter with my mug in my hands, flashing him a little cleavage. I could see his lips turn up slightly. My mother cleared her throat. Oh yeah, she was still here.

"We have a base number on the reception," I said.

"Oh good, you talked about it. How many?"

"Just a ballpark figure now, Mom. We are looking at about two-fifty."

My mother loved events. She lived for them. There was an even bigger smile spreading across her face. "Would you like to look at the country club's ballroom tomorrow when we have dinner?"

"Yes, we can check it out."

I looked at Robert, who was looking at my chest. He turned to her. "That would be fine, Helen."

"There are also several beautiful hotels to choose from as well. And if you have any out-of-town guests, they can stay right there."

I nodded as Robert took a slow, sexy sip from his mug. I straightened up. Two times this morning and he looked like he was ready to go again. Jeez, he would win. I would be knocked up before the end of this weekend.

"Robert has family in Ireland and England," I told my mother.

"Do you now? Who lives over there, Robert?"

He grinned. "My mother is from Ireland and lives just outside Dublin, and my father lives in England. That is where I was born and lived until I was five. Then we moved here."

"You're English?"

Then he let his accent go. "I am at that, love, born and bred, Mrs."

She spit her coffee back into the mug, and she blushed. *Rein it in there, Tiger, or you're going to see Mom all hot and bothered.*

She looked at me. "I know, right?" was all I could say.

"So you will be hearing a lot of brogue that day. And we are going over to visit and honeymoon after the reception"—I locked eyes with him—"*for two and a half weeks.*" He grinned.

"That's wonderful!" Mom was getting herself back under control. "This is going to be a wonderful party. I can guarantee that. What are you two doing the rest of the day? Can I take you out to lunch?"

"Well, we have to pack, and then we are going furniture shopping."

"Really? What are you buying?"

I looked at him, narrowing my eyes. "A new guest bedroom set."

He raised his eyebrows to me. "Kate doesn't like my taste."

My mother looked around. "But it seems like Robert has very good taste."

"I couldn't agree with you more, Helen." He swaggered over to me.

I pointed my finger in his face. "Behave," I bit out through gritted teeth, and he grinned wickedly and caged me. Then he dipped me back for a kiss.

My mother sighed.

About a half hour later, she was ready to leave. Robert came out from his office and walked with us toward the door. He gave her a polite hug and kissed her cheek. She flushed. Then she kissed me and gave me the eye. I smiled.

"We're talking wedding reception at dinner tomorrow night. Have fun shopping."

Robert answered, "Oh, we will."

Dirtbag!

He closed the door and scooped me over his shoulder. "I have something to show you."

"I bet." And that got me a smack on the butt.

He carried me into the office and over to the command central. He showed me our mini honeymoon retreat.

I smiled. "It looks fantastic, honey."

He widened his stance and just sank into me. I put my arms around his waist and my cheek into his chest.

"This is going to be so good."

"I'll guarantee it, baby."

"Call your shrink and cancel the appointment. When do you want to notify your employer?"

I let out a deep breath. "I don't know." I looked up at him. "I'm not even sure what to say to them."

"The sooner the better. They will appreciate as much notice as possible. And since they have already given you a month, they might want that opportunity to hire someone else."

"I know you're right, but I just don't know how to do it."

"We can stop by before we go shopping. Tell them about our wedding and that your new husband wants you home."

"I don't want to tell them the truth. Can't I come up with some strange condition that prevents me from working?"

He chuckled. "No, go right for the truth. It stops people in their tracks. Can't come up with an argument then, and you won't have to worry about what you just said."

I sighed, "You're right. Again!"

He lifted my chin. "It's going to be so good, baby."

I turned up my smile. "At least for the next two years."

"One year, three hundred sixty days."

I pouted. "With the way you've been giving it to me, I won't even have that long."

He grinned. "Exactly," he said and kissed my forehead. "Come on. Now you know where we are going, let's get packed." He felt my ass up and pulled me against him, giving me one more kiss.

He went to the closet, and I followed since I had not seen the inside of it. Of course, there was another gun safe, and he had everything very organized. I felt his uniforms. Right then, everything south of my belly button ignited.

I pictured him from the first night we kissed at the diner. Oh, those poor girls. I giggled.

He looked up at me. "What?"

"You! That night at the diner and frightening away all their patrons."

"Fuck 'em."

I touched along his sleeve that was hanging up. "I was also remembering how you looked in your uniform."

He slowly stood up and came to me with that energy wrapping around like a vise. He caressed my cheek seductively, asking, "Liked what you saw, baby?"

"You know I liked what I saw, and I can't wait to see it again."

"Well, pet, that can be arranged."

He placed his hand between my legs and rubbed me slowly and firmly. Between his kiss and his fingers, I went right to unbuttoning his pants and pulling down his zipper. He moaned in my mouth. I reached my hand inside and massaged his almost full length.

This room was an aphrodisiac to me. It was him. It was my masculine, sexy, powerful gladiator in front of me; and I wanted him inside me right now.

I broke away from his kiss and pulled down his pants, grabbing at his underwear. I took him in my hands and then into my mouth.

"Jesus! Easy, kitten!"

I wanted him. I wanted him so badly.

After a couple of hard sucks, he was groaning and moving to my rhythm. I stopped and removed my mouth off him. He looked down at me with his hands on my head.

I commanded, "Lie down on your back, right now!"

He did what he was told, and I took off my skirt and panties then climbed on top of him. I guided his beautiful full cock into me, and my feet were at his sides, like I was riding. Hell, I was riding. Then I positioned myself to start really moving and taking him root to tip, and then I moved faster.

"Baby, that is so good."

He was watching me with his hands on my waist. I went harder and kept up his punishing rhythm, locking my eyes to his.

"Fuck! Kate! Aaaah!"

And he pumped his orgasm into me. He reached between my legs and rubbed. I collapsed onto him, moaning some version of his name. I came down from my orgasm, and his arms were around me. "Damn, woman, what was that?"

"It's this closet. It's just so full of . . . you. You look really good in your uniform, by the way."

"I'm going to drag your ass in here at least once a day."

"Just wait until you come home after a shift."

He moaned. "Keep mounting me like that, and crime will be up all over the city. I'll be too busy chasing you around."

"You liked that, hubby?"

"Most definitely. I suggest you do that often."

I laughed. "I rode horses in college."

"I bet you were good at it."

"As a matter of fact, I was."

"Am I buying you a horse?"

I lifted my lower body off him. "Is that an option? I mean I always wanted one. But I never thought about owning one."

"Keep riding me like that, and I certainly will. I bet you look smoking hot in those pants and boots."

"I still have them. They're at my parents' house."

"Well then, we have another stop to make. Those are moving over here."

I was smiling down at him. He just offered to buy me a horse. Staying home was going to be awesome. I lifted off him and held out my hand for him to get up. I was empowered once again, standing there in my T-shirt. He grabbed my leg and took me down on top of him, but I somehow landed in his arms and to the side.

He stood up, taking me with him. My strong, strong man. He fixed himself and put my panties back on, then my skirt.

"Come on, woman, let's get to packing again. Looks like our day is filling up." He handed me a suitcase and followed me out.

I looked at my clothes. There was my new dress hanging up, and I went to take it off the rod.

"Baby, I have a separate garment bag for our dress attire."

I grinned. "Of course you do." And I kissed him.

"Oh, and that red dress is coming with us too," he stated.

I walked over and put the two dresses together then proceeded to pull off several skirts and sundresses, shorts, capris, and a few shirts. Then I went over to the T-shirt drawer, pulled out four, and then matched up a bunch of bras and panties. I took double the amount of underwear. I would see who made it back in one piece.

Robert let out a gruff growl as he looked at how everything was piled into my suitcase.

"Don't worry. I know you'll fix it. I'm just getting it all in one spot for you, stud."

"Don't you want to know how to pack properly?"

"No, not really. I've got you now." I planted a kiss on him before he could say another word. "I'll go make us lunch. Carry on, my husband."

I know he wanted to pounce, but hell, I just drained him.

"You, my queen, can be exasperating."

"And you, my king, I look forward to feeding. You must be hungry."

He lightened his frustration. "As you wish, my love. Go be of use." He still slapped my butt.

I took a good look at the kitchen. He was very organized, and I would have to be careful about that since this was the place we were going to share. I vowed to learn from his methods in here. I poked around in the fridge and pulled out the lettuce then found some bread and canned chicken chunks. I threw together chicken-salad sandwiches and found some chips.

My honey eats junk food? He is human!

I put them on the kitchen island and ran down the hall. He was finishing up my suitcase, and I ran at him to jump on his back. He spun and caught me, tossed me on the bed, and then pounced on top. I was laughing, and he was tickling me.

I was screaming and gasping; he was sucking my breast. I got myself under control after he stopped with his attack.

"Lunch is ready."

"Mmm-hmm." He kept sucking; then he moved to licking.

I just smiled at him. He kissed each one three times and then pulled my bra back over them and my shirt down.

"You have magnificent breasts, my love."

"Well, I'm glad you approve because there are no refunds after Saturday."

"They're already mine, and I'm not giving them back." He kissed them once more through my shirt.

"I made us chicken salad, and I found your chips."

He grinned. "Looks like I'll have to hide those better in the future."

"I was beginning to think you were a god, but now I know you are mortal. If you do hide them, I now have my days to fill looking."

"Well, it looks like I've been beaten before I even started. Point to you, my queen."

"Come on, stud. Let me feed you."

He leaned down and kissed me, and I kissed him back. He pulled me up, and I led him to the kitchen.

"What do you want to drink?"

"Bottled water is fine, baby."

I went to the fridge and pulled out two then joined him at the island. I took a bite. Pretty good, if I say so myself. I threw some garlic, cumin, and walnuts in.

Robert moaned with a mouthful. I smiled and leaned in for a kiss.

"What did you put in here, baby? It's delicious."

"See, I'm not without talents."

"Oh, I never said that, kitten. You have many, many talents—and ones I'm discovering each day. I am a very lucky man."

I just grinned at him. "Just you wait, stud. I have much to show you."

He gave me the wicked grin. "As I look forward to seeing."

We cleaned up together. I leaned on the counter, turning to him. "So am I all packed?"

He gave me a hint of a smile. "Almost."

"What's on the agenda next?"

"Pepper's, your mother's, your work, then furniture store. And we need to drop by the station for a moment."

"Do I get to see your office this time?"

"Sure, baby," he swaggered to me.

I couldn't hold back my grin. He was so fucking sexy.

"Do I have time to freshen up?"

"We hold all the cards, babe. Take as long as you like."

"Give me ten minutes."

I reached up to kiss him. *He's all mine, yeah!*

We left about twenty minutes later.

He tucked me into his car, and I wondered if I would ever be able to open the door on my own again. Would his chivalry be something I would just have to get used to, or was it just because this relationship was so new? Either way, it was sweet yet becoming annoying at the same time.

He slid into his side. And another question popped into my brain: would I ever get to drive this car? He must've known I was thinking hard.

"What's up, baby?"

I grinned at him. "I was just thinking."

He took my hand and kissed the back of it. "Of what?" He continued to kiss lightly.

"Will I get to drive this car someday?"

His grin spread across his face. "Absolutely, baby, just not right now." He sucked my finger into his mouth.

Oh crap! Groin ache.

He released my finger right outside his mouth. "I would have to fuck you again, seeing you behind the wheel, and I don't think you could handle that right now."

"Keep this up, and I could."

He released my finger and let out a low purr. "Soon, baby, soon."

He started the engine and gave me a wicked smile and then tore off down the road. I squealed and giggled.

He pulled up to Pepper's studio. She was working with a few of the girls on the dance squad.

"Everyone, take ten," she ordered and bounced up to us. The girls got one look at Tiger and froze then huddled in a tight formation, giggling and drooling.

Robert handed her a folder, and she smiled. "So you two are really going to do this."

"Yes!" I answered, putting my arms around his rib cage. *I just love my tiger.*

The girls were still staring.

Pepper said, "Robert, I need you to step outside the door for a moment. I have to show your bride something. You can't look, and you can't come back in until we let you."

He looked from her to me and back at her. "Why!" It was not a question; he was challenging her.

"Because it's a surprise for you. And if you stay in here, you won't get it!"

Well, Tiger, meet Tigress.

He growled at her. She pointed to the door.

He kissed me twice. Ten seconds each.

She tapped her foot.

I reassured him. He softened and released me. Then he gave me one more kiss and opened the door, scanning the room one more time before shutting it. His back was facing the door.

I could see through the frosted glass.

Pepper closed the curtain tight. "OK, come on. I have been putting together your strip number."

I squealed and jumped up and down.

She grabbed my arm and led me to the back dance room. There were only the two studio rooms, but this one you could close the door to.

"Since you didn't give me the songs, I used 'Sexy Back' by JT."

She sat me in a chair just as Robert might be and turned on the music. Then she started to move. *Holy moly!* I was excited, scared, and horny all at the same time. She moved around me and swung those hips, placed those hands, worked the hat she was wearing, and moved that body. I was panting when she finished.

"Well? What do you think?"

"Hell, I want you right now!"

She laughed and went to turn off the music.

"I think you have your work cut out for you to teach me"—and I pointed to her—"*that!*"

"You can handle it. You just have to get away from him long enough to learn it."

"Yeah, that's the biggie, isn't it?"

"He can come. He will just have to wait outside."

"I'll have to think about this one. Wait a sec. We have an open-floor plan downstairs. It's a big gym but has at least this much open space. And there is a mirrored wall."

"Perfect! I'll go there. He still has to stay away."

"We have about three weeks."

"I can work with that."

"Shit! Scratch that. We're going on a mini honeymoon after Vegas and won't be back until Friday."

"Where're you going?"

"Robert booked us a place on a private beach in San Diego."

"You know, Robert is a catch. He's got the looks, the job—"

I interrupted her, "I completely forgot to tell you. Did you know he was SWAT?"

"He's on the SWAT team?"

"Top guy! It's his SWAT team!"

"OK, like I said, looks, job, money—I assume with how he lives, we're in for a treat for Vegas."

"He double majored in criminal justice and economics in college. He is really good with money and investing. Already has a full retirement fund set up for both of us."

"You're starting to depress me."

"I'll drop the last one on you to get it over with."

"What, there's more?"

"I'm quitting my job. He wants me home taking care of the house and him."

"Fuck me! You hit the jackpot!"

I smiled and nodded. "Tell me about it. Which reminds me, he is probably ready to bust through your door. I bet he is pacing right now."

"Go let him in then."

I gave her a big hug. "Hey, how are you and Mark doing?"

"I slept with him."

I stopped in my tracks and turned to her. "And?"

"I really like him. I hope it works out between us."

I ran back and hugged her again. "Me too."

I ran to the door and pulled it open. Robert was on the phone, and he came at me, scooping me up to him with one arm. I wrapped my legs around him and clung. He ended the call abruptly and pinned me against the wall and sealed his lips to mine.

Pepper walked out. "Oh Jesus, you two get a room!"

He ignored her and continued kissing me.

She tapped her foot. "I haven't got all day, you know."

He broke off our kiss. We were panting, and our foreheads were touching.

I smiled. "Pepper's coming over tomorrow night. We have something to work on."

He looked at me then looked suspiciously at her.

"Oh, trust me, buddy. It will be worth it in the end."

He pulled me off the wall and took a few steps back, making no move to free me from him.

"I didn't think we had plans tomorrow night."

"We do, dinner with your parents."

"Shit! Six o'clock, right?"

He nodded.

"What time tomorrow?" I looked at her.

She was mentally assessing her calendar. "I can do four or eight."

Robert answered four, and I picked the later time. I giggled; he smiled and kissed me again.

I gave in. "You win, four it is."

He tucked his arm under my skirt and bent over, attacking my neck. I screamed and released my legs, but he had me pinned.

"I'll see you at four!" Pepper yelled, and then I heard the door close.

I begged him to stop, and he finally did.

"What are you up to, Mrs.?" he asked.

"Don't worry, you will see soon enough."

He carried me all the way down to the car and tucked me in.

Our next stop was my mother's. She smiled when we came in. I grabbed my riding stuff.

She asked Robert, "Do you ride, Robert?"

"Yes, Helen, I am very fond of a good ride."

I choked on air. Robert patted my back.

"That's wonderful. Kate was very good in college. I bet she will give you a run for your money."

Just kill me now!

"That's a bet I look forward to challenging."

"It's very good to have a common interest. Makes for a strong relationship. Your father and I like golfing and boating. Kate grew up sailing. Did she tell you that?"

He looked at me quizzically. "We are learning about each other more and more each day." He leaned in and kissed me.

I blushed again. *What the hell?*

"Sorry we just popped in, Mom, but we have to go. I have to tell my employers that I won't be returning."

"I understand, sweetie, and then you're going furniture shopping? Go on, you two have a busy schedule the next few days."

Robert leaned in and kissed her cheek. *Yeah, she was going to like having him around. Cougar!*

He took my gear from me and then took my hand and led us out. Next stop: work. I gave him the address, but somehow I knew he already had it. He kissed my hand and pulled out front.

"I have butterflies in my stomach."

"It's OK, baby. I'll be right with you."

"If you are right with me, they won't hear a single thing I say, and I will have to do this all over again."

He looked disappointed.

"You can come in, but you have to stay in the reception area. I'm sure Michelle will be thanking me later."

"Why can't I go in with you?"

"Because of this!" I gave him that same look as he gave me this morning. "Don't worry, I will introduce you to everyone, and it shouldn't take more than fifteen minutes."

"You have ten from the moment the door closes."

"Fine! Ten! Michelle probably won't be able to handle more than that anyways."

He lifted my hand to his mouth and sucked in my finger. Instant reaction. *Oh shit.* I gotta work on self-control.

"The quicker we are in there, the quicker we can test out those beds." He put his teeth down gently on that finger then slowly released it from his mouth, sucking as he withdrew.

Argh! Now I'm going in all flustered.

He came around and opened my door.

"Behave, mister," I threatened him.

He just smiled. "Of course, my queen."

I led us to the door. He held it open for me and then the other. He stopped me and went ahead, checking out the waiting room. I heard Michelle gasp at the sight of him. He reached back for my hand, and I stepped forward. Overprotective lug!

I went to Michelle. It took her a few seconds to tear her eyes off Tiger. She still hadn't registered who I was until I said her name. Twice. She focused more.

"Kate!" And up she jumped, and her arms came around my shoulders.

Robert tugged me back to his side, and around came his arm. She abruptly stiffened and pulled back.

"Michelle," I said, like nothing just happened. "I'd like you to meet my fiancé. This is Robert Beckham."

"Fiancé?"

"Yes, we are actually getting married this weekend." Hell, get it over with at once.

"Oh my god! Oh my god! You're getting married! This weekend! To him!"

"Yes. This is the one. My one and only."

She looked at me. "What else would you need?"

Robert was in protective mode. I started rubbing his back. *Shit*! It might turn difficult going in there alone. He relaxed a bit and bent down and kissed me open-mouthed. *In front of Michelle!* She had to sit down. It was too much for her.

Elizabeth turned the corner. "What's all the . . . oh my!" She too got an eyeful of my Terminator. She stopped in her tracks and inhaled sharply.

"Hi, Elizabeth, I'd like you to meet my fiancé, Robert."

She slowly approached us. With a widening smile. She extended her hand, and Robert shook it. I think she felt his aura because she flushed.

"Robert, this is Elizabeth Jenkins. She runs the show here. Elizabeth, this is Robert Beckham."

"It's very good to meet you, Mr. Beckham. I take it you were the one to save our beautiful Kate in that unfortunate incident."

"Please call me Robert, and my motives were purely selfish."

"I am glad you both survived it. Kate is an asset to our organization."

Oh crap! This is going to be worse than I thought.

"Elizabeth, could I talk to you a moment?" Robert looked at me and then her.

Oh no. Oh no you don't, buddy!

Then he gave her that look! *I'm coming too whether you like it or not.*

"Sure, we can all talk back in my office," Elizabeth replied. "Come on, you two."

He looked smug. I narrowed my eyes at him. He just leaned in to kiss my forehead. *Bastard!* I wanted to kick him again!

She led the way, and Robert followed behind me. I took the seat directly in front of her so some of her attention might stay on me. Robert sprawled out in his chair next to me, caressing his fingers up and down my arm.

I jerked my head toward him and bit out "behave" under my breath while she collected herself and sat down. I had to give her credit. She really tried to focus on me, but he was a force of nature, very hard to ignore.

"So, Robert and I are getting married this weekend," I began.

"Oh my! Congratulations to both of you."

"Which brings me to the reason why I am here."

She was still looking at Tiger.

"Robert and I talked about our future together. Some goals ahead for us, and we have decided . . . I have decided that I will not be returning to work."

She shifted all her attention to me. "I'm sorry, dear, what was that?"

"I am giving my notice. Robert and I feel it would be best if I gave up my employment altogether."

Her mouth fell open. She collected herself. "I . . . I . . . I . . ." She cleared her throat. "Well, I didn't see this coming."

"I'm sorry, Elizabeth, but I wanted to tell you as soon as possible. Give you the time you will need to replace me."

"I understand, Kate. Believe me, I understand. And you are lucky that the two of you are in that position to make such a choice. I'm sorry. I didn't mean that to come out negatively. We love you so much here, and if you should ever change your mind, you will always have a job with us."

There was a hint of a smile on Tiger's face. I knew he was holding back.

"Thank you, Elizabeth. I know this is all so sudden, but it's what is best for us right now."

"Thank you for telling me so quickly. You will be greatly missed, my dear. How are you doing, by the way?"

"I'm fine. Very busy at the moment."

Robert reached for my hand and just entwined both of his around it.

She cleared her throat. "I wish you both the very best, and please stop in. Don't be a stranger. We just adore you, Kate."

That was Robert's cue, and he stood up, taking me with him. He wrapped his arm around me.

"I will, Elizabeth. Maybe we can do lunch some time?"

"I would really like that, Kate." She held her hand out to me and then to Robert. She flushed as he held it a second longer.

"Thank you for taking care of my Kate."

There, he claimed me in front of her.

"She's all yours now, Mr. Beckham."

"Yes, she is." And he kissed me.

Michelle stood up when we entered the reception area again. "Are you guys off?"

Elizabeth broke the news to her. She just looked Robert up and down. "Lucky!"

I smiled and waved as we walked out the door. He pulled me in front of him and held my head still then sealed a kiss on me. I knew the girls were still watching.

"You're all mine now."

"Yeah, so you better not lose your job, or it's back to work I go."

"Not a chance, baby. Come, I'll show you my office."

"OK!" I brightened right up.

He pulled up right out front. I was beginning to figure out how he was getting away with so much. He was their super cop.

He helped me out of his car and kissed me against it. It brought back the instant memory of me around his shoulders leaning on the roof. He purred in my mouth. "I can feel the charge in you, baby."

"Sorry, flashback."

"Don't ever be sorry for thinking about us." He pinned his hips to mine.

"If you have sex with me right here, I will be really mad!"

He purred again. "Well, we can't have that now, can we?" And he backed off but kissed me again. "Come on, kitten. Let me show you off again."

Turning, he tucked me under his arm. I put my arm around his back, and this was how we entered the station. This time, I heard a lot of people refer to him as Sergeant, and several addressed me by name. Robert introduced me to seven more guys and two older women. They were behind their desks but scurried up to meet me. He handed one of them a folder, and she just beamed at the both of us.

Someone boomed from down the hall, "I should have figured what all the commotion was about. Jesus, it's like a celebrity sighting in here!"

Robert didn't even turn, just leaned over and kissed my hair.

John made his way toward us and stopped at my side. "Good afternoon, Kate. So you're still with him? You know you do have time to run. You haven't signed anything yet."

Robert laughed. "Not a chance. I'd catch her."

"He is really fast," I added.

"I will be more than happy to show you a few tricks to keep him at bay."

"I'm all set at the moment, but I'll keep that in mind."

"Shouldn't you be somewhere, Murphy?" Robert made it sound like that was an order.

John laughed. "Oh, I wouldn't miss seeing your beautiful bride for anything." He turned his attention back to me. "So, Kate, has he got you all packed?"

"Yes, we finished this morning."

"Well, I don't know if I will see you both again before the big day, so good luck and our best wishes to you."

"Thanks, John," I answered.

He slapped Robert on the shoulder. "Congratulations, brother."

Robert nodded to him. "Thanks, Murphy."

"Call me when you get back. The wife is itching to meet the fair Kate."

"Will do!"

Great, I was going to be on display for a while. Get used to it, sista.

We stayed for only a minute, and Robert took me down to his office. I was amazed; it was bigger than the chief's. He had file cabinets, a whoopin' gun safe, and a full desk with everything nice and all neatly arranged. I looked on in wonder. He was a very organized man.

"So how do I say this, hon?" I looked around some more.

He read my expression and turned, concerned. He closed the door behind me and came right over, wrapping his arms around me and kissing the top of my head. "What's the matter, baby? Tell me what's going on."

"I'm nowhere near your organizing level." I wanted to burst into tears. *What the fuck!*

He laughed. "Is that it, kitten? You're worried about something that insignificant? I don't give a crap about your organization skills. That's just the way I am. I had to be. It's what got me through the past six years while waiting for you, baby. I had to have a system. I had to have order in my life. Otherwise, I would have gone mad. I love you. Make all the mess you like because you're the one who has to live in it now."

I chuckled, wiping my tears in his shirt.

"Shh, baby." He bent down to my eye level and took a hold of my shoulders. "You are everything I want, everything I need. Just as you are. Don't change a thing."

I smiled, embarrassed.

"And if you think you need to change, I have only one request."

I looked anxiously into his eyes.

"Change my 'one year, three hundred sixty days' deal."

I burst out laughing, and so did he as he pulled me to him.

"Baby, it's going to be so good. I promise."

I cleared my throat and sniffled in once. The tears were gone. I was in the arms of the man who cherished me, who accepted me just as I was. I think I will have to fuck him in public at the furniture store.

Chapter 10

He held me until I released him. Then he kissed me on the lips softly but passionately. I was back under control. All the failing thoughts had been exorcised from my soul.

I looked around his office. "Why is your office nicer than the police chief's?"

"My job is more important."

"How can that be?"

"Trust me, you will find out soon enough."

"God, you're powerful, sexy, Mr. Beckham."

"You're the only one I care to impress, my bride."

"Come on, stud. Let's go check out some new beds."

"Music to my ears, baby." He half-dipped me and gave me a quick kiss.

Someone knocked on his door. He lifted me and kissed me one more time. Reaching for the door, he pulled it open, and there was a huge gift basket held by Sean with Liam at his side.

"We were about to leave and drop this by the house, then John called and said you were here."

I gasped in amusement. It hit me right there, right then. I was a bride! I loved presents! Robert chuckled at my reaction and let the boys come in.

"We wanted you guys to have this before the wedding. Everyone pitched in a couple of bucks. This is your engagement gift from the department."

"Who organized all this?" I was peeking through it.

"Chief and Robert's secretary."

I turned to him. "You have a secretary?"

"We share."

I gave him that smug look. His lips turned up slightly in the corners.

"Mary arranged everything. Made a list and sent us all in different directions."

Right then, it must have been Mary bombing through the door. "You got it! Thank the Lord! I sent these morons out and who knows what will happen?"

Liam and Sean frowned at her.

"Oh, don't look at me like that, you two. The department is crawling with them. If you didn't have Robert here, this place would be a circus." She gasped! "This must be the lovely Katherine! You beautiful woman, you! Our Robert has finally won your heart."

She looked at Robert. "She is just beautiful, Robert. I wish the both of you many, many happy years to come!"

"Thank you, Mary."

Oh my gosh! There is a soft spot in my future husband. First to Mom and now to Mary. I'll have to congratulate her later.

He gave her a hug. Thank God she was like in her fifties.

She turned to me. "Come here, Katherine. You're part of the family now." She held out her arms, and I went into them, smiling over her shoulder at my tiger. She started to tear up. "I really could not be happier for you two." And she sniffed.

I just smiled and tried to lighten the mood. "This is amazing, Mary." I pointed at the basket. "This has all happened so fast. Besides Robert proposing and putting his ring on my finger, this lovely basket has really hit home with me. This is making me feel even more like a bride."

Robert smiled and came over to me. Kissing me—guess what?—in front of everyone! I know, total shocker! There was a tear running down Mary's cheek. She was so proud.

The basket was enormous! Robert made Liam carry it to the car just so he could tuck me under him as we walked out. We received a round of applause as we made our way down the hall. I personally couldn't wait to rip that plastic open and see what we got! Liam placed it in the backseat, and it took up the whole space.

Tiger secured me in the car, and I peeked in the back. I managed to turn as Robert was sliding in and thanking Liam. I yelled a thank-you as well, and that got me a big, shy grin. Oh, I didn't see that coming.

Robert turned to me, placing both hands around the sides of my face. "I love you, baby, and I can't wait until you are legally mine."

"I can't wait to be your wife."

He kissed me. "Just say the word and I will have us on a plane in mere hours."

"I think we can wait two days. Besides, I want my parents and my friends there to witness our union."

He let out a breath I hadn't known he was holding. "OK, two days. I can live with that."

"If it's any consolation, stud, I do have to admit there are cracks in the two-year plan."

Thank God I was difficult to get to. Otherwise, we would have been fucking in front of the police station on this main road. There, right there was his dangerous "I'm going to take you and fuck the shit out of you" look. I guess it was his dangerous/lustful/sexual heedless emotion. I would have to start characterizing his emotions and come up with a system of my own. *Again! Not without skills here.* I would break my husband down to his different moods and learn how to dance with each of them. I was going to be the best wife ever!

He panted on my lips.

"Maybe they have a bathroom at the furniture store," I suggested.

He turned the key, and Elvis left the building!

Not two miles down the road was a huge furniture store. He immediately asked the girl who greeted us where the restrooms were. She gawked at my man and pointed.

He tugged me along behind him. There were the three choices again. Except when we entered the "family" facility, it was set up like a multiple restroom. No lock!

I looked at him, horrified. He pulled something off his keychain, shoved it under the door, and came at me.

I panicked. "What if someone comes in?"

"No one will get in," he growled. I could see his erection stretching his pants.

Before I changed my mind, before I let my rational side grab hold, I jumped him, wrapping my legs around and sealing my mouth to his.

He moved us over to the sink and put me down on top of it. He unhooked his belt, unbuttoned and zipped down his fly in that two-second mark, and pulled down his pants. He reached between my legs and ripped my panties off me. Sliding me down to the edge, he plunged his cock into me. I bit my lip, not wanting to scream.

Moving inside me, he distributed my wetness, and it felt much more welcoming. Then he started with full-length blows. I knew this should have been a warning—him just wanting to take me right here, right now. No one was going to stop him from his desire for me, but it was really hot. I wanted to claw at him.

I began to meet him thrust for thrust.

"Jesus, Kate, just like that, baby. Oh, that feels like heaven on my dick. Give yourself to me, baby."

I was building, and with my last hard thrust, we both came together. He held one hand around me as he was pumping out his orgasm while the other covered my mouth, muffling my screams. I just melted to the back of the mirror, breathing deeply, catching my breath. It couldn't have been more than three minutes. He leaned into me and scooped my body to him.

"I fucking love you, baby!" he growled.

I caressed his face. "I fucking love you too, stud."

I bit it out so he would know I meant every word. He kissed me first and then picked up my destroyed panties and tucked them in his front pocket.

I just looked at him. "So where are those ones going?"

"Top desk drawer in my work office."

"Pervert!"

"I want you everywhere I am, kitten."

Aww! That was kinda cute—not perverted at all.

"Honey, what if someone has to go in your desk to find something and they come across my underwear?"

"It will never happen, baby. These are to strictly remind me what I have waiting to jump me at home."

Hey, I couldn't argue there; he was right.

I wiped between my legs and straightened myself out minus one pair of panties. He watched me, and I think he was getting aroused again. I looked in the mirror, and I thought I could see my pubic hair protruding through my skirt.

Oh man! Our salesman is going to be a jumbled wreck.

"Look, you. I have to tell you, shredding panties is not always the right thing to do, stud."

He looked at me, confused.

"Look! You can just see my crotch hairs through this now!"

He laughed. "Well, that's one way to keep you close. Stay behind me, baby, and keep your knees together." He kissed me again in triumph. He got to mark me in yet another public facility. He removed whatever he jammed under the door and took my hand, placing me behind him.

A man descended upon us right away. "And how are the both of you this fine afternoon?"

Tiger got right to the point, throwing the man off guard. "We need a new guestroom set."

"Oh yes, sir! We can help you with that. Right this way. Now were you looking king- or queen-size?"

Robert looked at me; I shrugged.

He answered, "We haven't decided the size yet."

The salesman led us to this huge wing filled with matching sets. "Here is the guestroom suite. Please look around and explore. I'll be right over there"—he pointed—"to answer any questions." Then he walked away.

Robert tucked me into him. We walked up and down each display; nothing popped.

The salesman came back to us. "Maybe you would like to glance at the main bedroom units?"

I looked up at Tiger, and he shrugged. "OK," I answered.

Then this old English/contemporary set hit me square in the gut. It was farmhouse meets 2012. I jumped on the bed with my hubby crawling over me. He looked around at the setup and studied the headboard. Then he planted a kiss on my lips.

"You want this one, baby?"

I nodded, grinning like a fool.

He looked into my eyes. "Do you want this one for our room and move what is there downstairs?"

I was shocked by his suggestion. "You already have our set upstairs?"

"If this blows the 'one year, three hundred sixty days' plan even weaker apart, then we will put this in our bedroom, and guests can stay in our old bed."

"It does," I simply answered.

We bought a new master bedroom set with a dream mattress. I was so excited. Robert took care of the delivery and moving project. It was going to be set up and finished before we left on Friday. He ordered a blanket chest, two chests of drawers, and two nightstands. After we left, he suggested dinner.

I insisted on a mall run to get a new pair of panties. He cooperated, and we went back to the same shop with the same girl waiting on us. She clearly gave us a funny look. Hell, I don't blame her.

I let my king pick them out. He went right to a specific display and took a pair. I followed and grabbed a few more in different colors. I think he was getting aroused again!

I whispered in his ear, "You must share with your student what you prefer. I will make sure to accommodate your needs, sir."

He purred. "I will keep you informed as to what pleases me from now on, my queen."

"As I would only come to accept, my king. My body, my soul are only for you and your pleasures, my lord. I look forward to granting your every desire."

His step faltered as we approached the checkout counter. I handed over our stuff, and he pulled out a credit card.

"Mr. and Mrs. Beckham, welcome back. I will just process these for you." The girl took the panties out of my hands.

Robert just gazed at me with lust mixed with the "I'm ready to go again, just say the word" look. He was a fucking machine, and I was in training!

He signed his name, took the bag, and tucked me under his arm. And of course, a kiss. I smiled as we walked out then noticed all the people staring. *Oh shit! I don't have any panties on.*

There was a fast-food restaurant with a bathroom.

"Honey, hand me a pair of those. I want to put them on. I'm feeling like everyone is staring at my crotch."

"Oh, trust me, with or without underwear, they will still stare, baby. You look edible."

Down, boy!

He pulled out a pair and kissed me then followed toward the bathroom.

I turned abruptly. "Stay!" And I pointed my finger at him to reinforce my command. He growled low in his throat and stood outside the door.

I used the bathroom this time and freshened up. *Aahh, that felt better.* Then I slipped on my new panties, checked myself in the mirror, and opened the door. He kissed my hair and tucked me under his arm then rubbed my butt, kissing my hair again.

We made our way to his car, which was illegally parked out front, and there were the usual admirers stopping to look at it. Robert opened my door and settled me in. He then went around to his side with the bag still in his hand. He stuck it in the back with the huge basket. I grinned. He leaned in and kissed me then started the engine and pulled away with much more control.

"Baby, I want to bring you back to a dark place, and I want you to overcome it so we can put this behind us."

I was completely confused by what he just said.

He took my hand. "I want to take you to my cousin's restaurant where the shooting took place. I want to bury any demons that may still linger."

I think I was flushed. I had no way to prepare myself for this. I took in a deep breath. "OK, let's get this over with." He didn't smile this time; he did kiss the back of my hand, and he reassured me with soft, soothing words.

We pulled up to just about the same spot as we did that day. There were a lot of cars in the lot. I looked over to the entrance and took a steadying breath. He still had my hand.

"It's going to be OK, baby. We will put this behind us. I don't want him to have one scrap of memory being able to control you. They all belong to me now. I will love and protect you for the rest of my life."

I tore my gaze away from the scene of the crime and looked into his hard stare. "You are so strong, Robert, mentally and physically. You are my anchor. I feel grounded and completely loved being with you. You make me feel so safe. I'm ready, let's go in."

He kissed the back of my hand one more time then got out and came around to my door. He pulled me right into him, kissing me against his car. He scooped me up just as before and carried me to the entrance. I clung to him. This was where it all happened, and the memory faded.

He pinned me to the side of the building, kissing me with fervor. When he broke our kiss, he touched his forehead to mine. We were panting.

"I love you, baby. Let's bury this now."

"It already is, Robert. There's only you, my knight in shining armor."

Another couple came through the door and looked at us. They quickly walked to the parking lot. Tiger kissed me again then pulled me off the wall, and we went in.

Louise clapped her hands together. "Here they are, here they are! The bride and groom! My, my, my, you didn't waste any time getting that ring on this child's finger. Let me see it, love." She reached for my hand. "It's stunning!"

She turned to Robert. "You better treat her right, or you'll be dealing with me!" She turned to me. "And the same goes for you, young lady."

I moved closer to him, and he tucked me under his arm.

I turned to him and put my hand on his chest. "I promise" was all I said.

"Are you staying for supper?"

Robert answered, "Yes, is our booth available?"

"You mean the one you were in the first time? Let me go check, love. I'll be right back." She went off to check the booth. It was cleared. "Come on, you two, your table awaits."

I sat beside him as he put his arm around me then sprawled out in the corner of the booth.

"Shall I get you a whiskey, Kate?"

"Oh no, thank you."

Robert ordered a bottle of wine for us. Louise nodded and left. He pulled me up against him. "How are you doing, baby?"

"I'm . . . good. I am really fine, thank you."

He kissed my hair. "That's my girl. You're so beautiful. I can't wait to sign that damn paper and put another ring on your finger."

"Hey, I hadn't thought about that, honey. What about the wedding rings?"

"Two options. First is to go back to my aunt Jane's, second is to pick them out in Vegas. What do you want, kitten?"

"Do we have time tomorrow to stop by your aunt's shop?"

"Absolutely, but if you don't see something you love there, then don't feel you have to get it. I'm sure Vegas has a worldly collection to choose from. You'll be wearing it the rest of your life, so make sure it's the one."

He was right. We were going to wedding city, and they were bound to have loads of rings.

"Are you sure I have to go to my dad's office? What if you dropped me off at your aunt's shop instead?"

He growled with his teeth clenched. He took a deep breath and let it out slowly. "Baby, I'm not dumping you at your father's office to be difficult. If I could drag you to my shrink's appointment, I would in a heartbeat. Except he may think I have . . . issues. So to make me feel confident to know you are safe and in capable hands, this is the simple cure. I know you don't see it that way, but just give me this for my peace of mind, please."

"You have issues, all right. But fine, if it eases you to know I'm stuck in the ivory tower, then so it is. Can we stop at a bookstore so I can read while you're getting your head examined?"

He kissed me. "Thank you, and yes, we'll stop on the way home. I only suggest one book though."

"And why is that?"

"You won't get much reading done after I rescue you from the ivory tower."

I grinned up at him.

We had the wine delivered by—who else?—Nathalie.

"Hi, Rob!" She turned to me. "Well, hey there." She looked back to Tiger, who had me wrapped and tucked into him. "How are you guys? Jeez, that was awful the other day."

I felt a need to mark my territory. "It was. Thank you for your concern. It's all over now, though, and we are moving on. As a matter of fact, celebrations are in order."

"Oh? What are you celebrating?"

"Robert proposed!" I shoved the ring right in her face.

She gasped.

"And we are getting married this weekend!"

Double whammy! *Take that, Nat!* I thought she was going to faint.

Robert just looked as proud as can be. *Good kitty!*

I kissed him full on the lips. This got his attention, and he hovered into me, deepening the kiss. *Good, good, good kitty! Nat didn't exist.*

When he let me up, there were two menus on the table and no Nathalie. *Good! See ya, bitch!*

Robert leaned over and grabbed the wine and glasses. He poured some for both of us. I looked at the menu and then put it down.

"You order, honey. You know what I like, and you know this restaurant. I'll eat whatever you want."

Of course, that didn't come out right. His grin turned wicked. There was a slight purr coming from deep in his throat.

I put the menu down and leaned in to kiss him. He pulled back. "I would put you under the table if you let me," he growled.

"Don't abuse your new privilege. You have to feed me before I fall asleep."

"I'll feed you all right, baby. I'll give you mouthfuls."

Oh crap, that turned me on. How the fuck can he make me so ready after multiple sessions of intercourse just in one day?

I can play at that game. "If I swallow you now, there will be less chance of knocking me up later."

He froze. *Uh-oh, what's he going to do?* He was slightly panting. I think he was getting control of himself. His mouth closed.

"I need you now. Right now, baby. I just want my cock to feel your tight hot vagina. We can either go downstairs or you can sit on my lap. Make the choice before I make it for you."

Oh fuck! That's what happens when you play with fire! Or a fucking gladiator. Stupid, stupid Kate!

I looked him up and down and did a quick assessment of the patrons and lighting and space.

No one around us . . . good! Lighting low . . . good. Space . . . shit, that's what the problem was. How was I going to sit on his lap and make it look like his dick wasn't shoved up in me?

"Turn to the side a bit more. Unzip, cowboy."

He did exactly that. I quickly pulled my panties to the side and turned to the side as well and sat on him. He moaned into my shoulder as I slid over him. I quickly looked down for damage control. We looked normal. Just a girl sitting on her boyfriend's lap and acting like a ho!

His eyes were closed, and he was savoring the feeling. I leaned into him; he groaned lowly again. "Looks like I'm ordering for us," I said.

He wrapped his arms around my waist and thrust up in me, grinding in back-and-forth motions.

Nathalie came back. Disgusted, obviously.

"We'll need another minute." I picked up the menu, and she turned and sulked off. "Honey, baby, come back to me. We are in your cousin's restaurant. We have to order. What should I get?"

He moved back and forth below me ever so slightly. "Order the shepherd's pie, baby . . . two . . ." He was thrusting lightly. I leaned slightly away from him, and he took up the extra space with a couple of quick thrusts.

Oh jeez! Why did I agree to this? I peeked around the booth and spotted Nathalie.

"Nathalie?"

She looked over to me.

"I think we de . . . cided . . . two shepherd's p-pies plea . . . se thank . . . you."

I forced myself back down on top of him so he had no more room. "You have two minutes then I'm getting off you."

He went to reach around to my clitoris. I grabbed his hand. "No! Not here."

He panted into my shoulder and rested his hand on my thigh. He made no further gyrations into me. He worked on steadying his breathing. I took a sip from my wine and scanned the area.

Nat came back with rolls and butter. Robert had his forehead against my back. She dropped them and left.

"Bread's here, honey." I buttered up one and leaned back into him. "First bite, honey."

He took it in his mouth, and I could feel his erection fading. I took the second. When I gave him the third one, he took it in one whole bite.

"I'm pulling off you now," I whispered to him.

He nodded. I sat up and lifted off him. He straightened himself and slid a little under the table to tuck himself back in. He zipped and buttoned his jeans.

"Thank you, kitten. I needed to feel you on me."

Should I move to the other side now? Hell no. It couldn't' get any more intimate than that right there, and I persevered from his greedy possessive need for me. Yes, I would survive my tiger. I just had to learn to take control. Now where exactly did I leave that whip and chair?

I handed him his wine and snuggled back into him. He was still feeling the effects of being inside me right there and pulled me close to his side and kissed my hair. "I love you, baby."

I cranked my head to him. "I love you more."

A grin widened across his face. "Impossible." And he kissed me.

Natalie took that moment to set up our food. She put the pot down in front of Robert first and then mine in front of me. "Be careful, they are hot." And she left.

He straightened up and said with a low lusty voice, "I'm dragging you into the closet when we get home."

I laughed. "Well, now I have props."

He thought about that and downed his wine "Damn, woman, you're making me insane."

"But I would suggest we spend it in your bed since the furniture is being moved around. When are they coming?"

"Friday morning. We have the first delivery eight thirty a.m."

"So how are we doing this?"

"Murphy is coming over to help me later tomorrow. I'm giving him the set downstairs. And we'll move the one upstairs down there."

"So where will we sleep tomorrow night?"

"Choices, baby. Upstairs in the bed across the hall. It's a full size, but we will manage. Or we can sleep downstairs. Or if you really want to get freaky, we can sleep on the couch."

"Your bed downstairs will be fine. That way, you can leave me there when they come to deliver everything."

He chuckled. "Oh no you don't, baby. You're the woman of the house now. This is your deal. I expect you right by my side answering the door."

I pouted, but he was right. I claimed and argued that I wanted control, and yet at the first inconvenience, I was bailing out.

"Sorry, momentary loss of brain function there, sweetie. I'll be by your side. No worries." And I kissed him.

We finished our meal, which was delicious, and Robert stretched out in the booth as Nathalie cleaned our plates away. "Hey, there are a few friends at the bar. They want you to go over after you're done."

He looked at me, and I shrugged. "Come on, baby, let's go show you off." He grabbed the bottle and told me to get his wallet out from his back pocket.

I grinned. "You're so bad." And I pulled it out.

"Take out a fifty and put it on the table."

I did as he asked and put his wallet back. With a glass in one hand, he motioned for me to take it. I held a glass in each hand, and his arm was around me with the bottle in the other. He kissed my hair, and we made our way to the bar.

I was pleased to see Maggie and her husband with several others from the party all sitting around two big tables. "There they are!" her husband shouted, and everyone looked up at us and cheered.

"Rumor has it you're marrying this bloke." He was speaking to me.

I angled my left hand to show off my ring.

"Jesus, Mary, and the donkey! Put that thing away, it's blinding."

Maggie smacked his shoulder and shot up to come inspect the jewel. "I wouldn't have believed it if I hadn't seen it for me self."

Robert put the bottle down and took a glass from me. I think he took mine, but who cares?

She held my hand and then went in for a hug. "Oh, congratulations, Kate! And you, Robert! You're full of surprises. Introduce her to the family, sneak off, and drop on one knee. Now you're running off to Vegas? Did I hear this right?"

"Yes. In three more days, she'll be Mrs. Kate Beckham. My wife." He pulled me to his chest and kissed me in front of everyone.

There was a round of applause. I blushed. He grinned, and someone pulled two more chairs over for us. Robert reintroduced me to everyone. *Fuck me!* I wasn't going to remember their names. I just nodded politely and continued to drain my glass.

Robert filled it again with a smile. Leaning into me, he said, "Drink up, baby. I'm going to start working on growing that tummy of yours."

I narrowed my eyes at him. "I still haven't given you the green light."

"But you're not stopping me either."

Fuck, I was right! Damnit! He was testing my birth control. *I will* be *calling my doctor when I go to my father's office tomorrow.*

I grabbed the glass and took a big swig. He leaned back and grinned. *Bastard!*

The questions were coming at us all at once. Robert fielded most of them, but the women were narrowing in on me. Maggie couldn't take it anymore and moved her chair next to mine. Robert laughed and took his arm out from behind me and leaned into the table to give us some privacy.

"Oh, Kate, I'm so happy for the both of you. I know Robert has been sweet on you since the day he met you. Whenever he would come to a function, he'd be alone. Hell, we even thought he was gay for a while."

I laughed out loud. He turned and smiled then went back to his conversations.

"He never brought a date?"

"I wouldn't say that, but they were few and far between. Never showed any . . . emotion when there was one."

"Emotion?"

"Yeah, you know—holding hands, touching? Nothing like the way he displayed when he brought you in the other day. I think we all were in shock. Him carrying you like that and his little show with dipping you. That's not the Robert we know."

I smiled. "What was he like with that Chris chick?"

"Reserved. She was always trying to snuggle up to him. He would step away. It was agony to watch the poor girl. She wanted him so bad."

I had an instant reaction of putting my hand on his thigh. He covered my hand with his and stroked it soothingly. He glanced over to me, leaning in to kiss me. I did the same, and I turned back to Maggie.

"He loves you, no doubt about that, and I can see you were meant for each other. He's a good man, Kate, and I know this is happening very quick, but you couldn't find a better man. Besides, I am pleased you are becoming family. I like you a lot."

"I like you too, Maggie. So Robert says you clean for him?"

"Yes, although you see how he lives. Not much to do besides get rid of the dust."

We laughed.

"He made me quit my job."

"Did he now? Well, you are going to be his bride, and I would think with his ego, that would be expected."

I laughed again. "Proud, isn't he?"

She nodded. "Very!"

I clinked glasses with her. I really liked my new cousin.

"You'll have to call me when you get back. Maybe we can go out on a girls' lunch. Introduce you properly instead of meeting in bars like this."

"I would really like that. But I may have to host you over our house a few times first."

"Overprotective?" She nudged her head in his direction.

"Good reason for that at the moment. Scott's friend threatened my life."

"Did he now? I hadn't heard any of this."

"Yup, we got a restraining order on him, but Robert feels the need to keep me safe. Really safe."

"I see. He's got good reason for that, love, but good luck to that git. He won't get past him. I'm surprised the ass hasn't disappeared yet."

I laughed at first then saw she was completely serious. "Oh."

She raised her eyebrows and motioned to him. "Wouldn't put it past him. Especially how he's been crazy about you."

"Not to get off the subject, but his parents—what are they like?"

She leaned back in her chair. "His father is a serious man. Let me see . . . how should I word this . . . he has a dark side to him. Very businesslike. A successful man. But you feel his energy, and it's unnerving at times. Richard loves his son. He is very proud of Robert. Then there is Emma, his mother. She is a confident woman. She carries a bold and very outgoing personality. She is Louise's sister, if that helps you out. Robert is her only child, and she is very close with him. They both will love you. You need not to worry. Emma is single. His father is remarried to a horrible girl my age with two more children. The bitch fancies Robert, I think, more than her own husband. So watch out there."

"Can't blame her. Look at him, he's a god. Does he let her flirt with him?"

"No, of course not, but she gushes every time they are in town. He used to let them stay at his house, but after the last visit, they now stay at Jane's."

"Do you think she tried something?"

"Yes. That is exactly what I think, and Robert was having none of it."

"Does his father notice?"

"No, she keeps him well . . . how can I say this? Well fucked. How's that?"

"Got it." I took another sip.

Robert had turned my palm over and was running his fingers along the inside of my soft pad. I put my glass down on the table. He filled it up some more, bringing my hand up to his lips.

I leaned into him. "I love you."

He kissed me softly, and he looked into my eyes. "We can stop at the bookstore in the morning before I drop you off."

I smiled. "OK."

He kissed me again, and I knew we were staying a while longer.

Maggie gave me so much history that I was feeling like I was beginning to know the man I was about to marry. I picked up my glass again and told Maggie all our plans for the wedding and my surprise honeymoon.

She looked appreciatively at Robert. "You got a good one there. Don't let him go."

"Not planning on it, believe me."

She shouted down to her husband, "Jimmy, you could take some tips from Robert here. He knows how to treat a woman right!"

"And how so, love? You weren't complaining last night when I was on top of ya?"

"Romance, Jimmy! For crying out loud! Romance, you've forgotten the romance."

"He hasn't sealed the deal yet. Just give him a few years, and then we'll see how the romance is goin'."

Everyone laughed.

Maggie turned to me. "Don't you be listening to that fool. He's a different breed than Robert here."

Robert stretched out and put his arm around my chair. "That's right, baby. I will worship the ground you walk on until the day I die."

I smiled at him.

"Don't be breaking our man laws there, Beckham. They'll all expect that stuff."

"Aaah, Jaysis, why do I put up with him?" Maggie sighed.

"Because I give it to you right there, Mrs. I'm hung like a small pony."

I spit the wine that I just sipped and laughed with Robert.

Maggie was getting irritated. "Arra, be whist! Keep it up, fool, and you'll be in the stable tonight."

"She couldn't live without me, by golly."

Tiger turned my chin. "Small pony, hun? Does two and a half qualify?"

"I do believe it does, my king. You may even have him beat."

He grinned with pride. "That's my girl." He squeezed me into him, kissing my hair.

Maggie looked on affectionately. When he let me up, she leaned over. "You are one lucky girl."

"I know!" I wanted to pinch myself.

Everyone ordered appetizers. I ordered cake! He smiled at me.

"Hey, I'll be burning it off. Don't worry."

"I'm not worried in the least bit, baby. I just like watching you eat something you enjoy so much."

I grinned. "I'll share."

And he kissed me. Eight, nine, ten . . . oh man, those ten-second kisses . . . *wow!* He left me feeling lightheaded.

I got back under control and excused myself to use the bathroom. Maggie stood up with me as I said, "Be right back, honey. Just need to use the bathroom."

It looked like he was about to stand up, but Maggie cut him to the chase. "I've gotta go too, Robert. I'll show her where it is."

Patty stood up as well. "Me too." And she looked down at Toni.

"I'm going with you as well." And she also stood up.

Three women and me. I hope there were enough stalls because I really had to go.

Robert rested back in his chair; he was beat. No way could he make a reason to escort me. *Poor, poor kitty.* I sat across his lap. *Heck, I am his bride!* I kissed him softly on the lips. This bumped him right up to his no-boundaries, take-me-when-he-wanted-me man, and he highly approved of my sudden indiscretion. He pulled me to him and kissed me long and not politely in front of company. When he released me, I was breathless. I think everyone was breathless. His sexual energy began its slow climb into my body.

"I'll be right back, lover."

"You have six minutes." He glanced down at his watch.

"I'm with the girls, and you are"—I turned to the stairs—"fifty feet away? Guard my cake, and no dipping in while I'm gone."

He smacked my ass. "Will do, Mrs. Hurry back, your man is counting the moments away from you."

He picked up his glass and leaned on the table to hear the boys' conversation.

I scurried down the steps. "We have six minutes, ladies, until he busts through that door. Let's cut to the chase and tell me things I don't know about my stud."

They all looked at each other and shrugged.

"Sorry, Kate, he was kinda to himself. Outside of that Chris girl that he kept at arm's length." Tony piped in.

"Yeah, we thought he might be gay—and oh, what a shame for womankind. Thank you, Kate. We secretly worship you as well."

I laughed. "He's so not gay. I have trouble getting him off me."

Patty laughed. "Just pour the salt in the wound, why don't ya?"

I thought about that expression, and I giggled.

We all came out after washing our hands. Patty and Tony just admired me.

"You are one lucky girl, Kate."

I beamed. "Believe me, I feel the same way."

And we all laughed. We barreled up the stairs to check the time. I fist-pumped as I had one minute left. There sat the cake at my space. Oh, it looked so delicious. The girls stared too.

Maggie asked Patty, "What the hell did we order?"

"Not cake" was her answer.

Karen, the bar waitress, walked by. I stopped her. "Could you please bring us three more pieces of that?" I pointed at it as if it were the serpent's apple.

She smiled. "I just friggin' scoffed down a piece as I put yours on the plate. I feel your pain because it's so good. Coming right up, ladies."

We all smiled.

Robert was just watching us, trying to figure out the female chromosome. *Good luck to that, buddy!* We approached the table, all taking our chairs. I didn't dare touch that luscious piece of heaven waiting for me. Robert still studied me, and Karen came through the door with three more plates, setting them in front of my home girls. Robert was the only one watching what was happening. We all winked at one another and took the first bite. Heaven!

Robert pulled me into him. "Forget the romance and flowers. Just find a good bakery and all is forgiven? This is the way to your heart? I'll get what I want?"

"Damn! We are that obvious! This is paving the path with gold, stud. Yes to all your scenarios. So put a good baker on speed dial, and I will forgive you every time. Or simply say yes to your request."

He picked up a fork. "May I, my queen?"

"You may, my king."

And he took a bite. Not quite enjoying the mouth orgasm I was, but heck, this was dessert. How was he going to compare that to my hot vagina? I'd forgive him for his ignorance, but I could also see he was thinking of every bakery in town. *Smart, smart kitty!* I savored the last bite. Hell, all us girls did. We were united by cake.

Robert ordered me another glass of wine. He switched over to water. I don't know why. He only had one glass from the bottle. I was the lush. I asked him to order me a glass of water as well.

The girls all gathered around me, and I informed them of our big basket in the backseat. They squealed in delight, and I could see Maggie thinking hard. It looked like another surprise was in the making. My wine was in front of me along with a tall glass of water. I took a deep drink from my water first before moving back to the vino.

I looked over at my stud and started to remember his dance. Boy, I'd like it if he did that again. Maybe if I was just in my panties and riding boots, I could coax him into a number. He was looking so luscious. *Hey, I think I am getting tipsy.*

He leaned into me. "Penny for your thoughts?"

I put my hand around his ear. "Just thinking about sitting in the living room in just my panties and riding boots while you do one of your numbers for me.

He pulled out his wallet with lightning speed, threw a twenty on the table, informed everyone we would see them after the honeymoon, and scooped me up as I was laughing on to his front while he held me tight.

Everyone stopped talking and just watched him carry me away, giggling into his shoulder. I gave a little wave to the girls, and smiles spread across their faces as they smacked their men and pointed.

He pinned me up against his car and moved his body up and down me. "Let's make it count for your bed being upstairs one more night."

He buckled me in and in no time was in his seat and speeding toward home. He kept with the long strokes up to my sex and down to my knee, fingers gripping and then releasing.

I put my seat back, enjoying his motion. He groaned deep down and stepped on the pedal some more. I knew we were breaking the speed limit, but who would dare pull Hot Cop over? They knew the car, and he obviously ran things over there.

Ten minutes later and I was feeling his energy, and I wanted to jump him. He parked the hot car, grabbed my boots from the backseat, and ran to my side, scooping me up. He kissed me all the way to the door, grinding me to his pelvis. He carried me up to the living room and placed me on the seat, thrusting my boots in my lap.

"Underwear and boots, now! I'll be right back," he commanded.

He walked with purpose, and I proceeded to giggle and strip down to only my panties and riding boots. Shit, they were difficult to put on without my silky socks, but I managed.

There I sat and waited for Robert. He came back but fully dressed and holding his outfit in his arm. He didn't even look at me but fixed the stereo to a new disk. He handed me the remote and dodged into the kitchen. He changed. I could hear the clothes give way to his body, and I pinned my knees together with my feet far apart. He told me to hit PLAY, and Muse's "Uprising" came on.

He rounded the corner. My god, he was hot! He danced and made his way to me. Drinking in what I had to offer, he pulled me out of the seat and began dancing with me, move to move, putting me exactly where he wanted me. He was so hot. I was surprised I didn't climax as he ground me around his groin area.

God, this is how he made so much money. *Shit! I would be shoving twenties down his pants at this point and demanding to be fucked. Don't go there, Kate, don't go there! Just enjoy the man who is trying his damnedest to knock you up.* I was so sexual by his guidance, I felt I could conquer the world—at least the Robert world.

I had him in a nutshell, and it was time for me to prove it. I let him take me around until the music started to fade; then I took over, grinding into him and straddling my riding boots to each side of him.

He was toast and obeyed my every command. All I had to do was push him in the direction with my hipbone, and he heeded with willingness.

I had him on the floor, and I was standing over him in my boots. His eyes were dark and dangerous with that sexual aura wrapped around me tight. I lowered slightly. He ripped my panties from me and grabbed my hips to him.

So OK, I wasn't completely in control. He lifted his hard sex to me, and I lowered myself on top of him. Slowly and deliberately, he moaned out loudly. I had him. We were at the point of two and a half hours since he demanded sliding into me at the restaurant, and I grinned at the irony. My two-and-a-half man. Yes, that summed him up. He was twice the regular man and then some.

I began to move with what I displayed in his fuckable closet, and I rode him hard all the way to the finish line in just my riding boots.

Chapter 11

I opened my eyes. I was in bed, tucked up against my stripper, with his arm securely around me. How did I not know this? When did we move to the bed? Crap, I hated those unaccountable moments.

I closed my eyes again and tried to remember my last thought. Robert was coming and thrusting into me. I collapsed on his chest, breathing hard. Then after a few seconds, he lifted me and brought me down the hall, pulling off my boots and taking a cloth and washing me between my legs.

Yes, my last memory: my future husband cleaning me after sex. Oh man, I loved him, and I felt humiliated at the same time. How could I get through the day? He felt me move and turned me instantly, sealing his mouth over mine. I could feel his erection growing on the side of my leg.

"Baby, I love you so much. I can't get enough of you. Those boots sent me over the edge, and I'm sorry I was rough with you."

What? When were you rough with me? I thought I was riding you?

I blushed. How was I going to explain I didn't get the roughness?

"I'm sorry I was a little tipsy last night."

"Don't apologize. I'll stock the fridge with wine if you do that again."

Oh fuck me! What the hell did I do?

I thought of the most logical answer. "I told you I was a good rider."

"You've proven that to me twice. Let me know when you want a horse."

I smiled. "You're adorable!"

"Baby, your wish is my command. Anything you want, I'll give it to you."

Well, well, well! I must have been really good then. And I perked right up.

"Breed quality to quality and you get a champion."

He stopped his lips within a centimeter of mine. "That has been my intention all along." And then he sealed them over mine.

Should I talk to him about my phone call I wanted to make for my doctor's appointment?

Guilt won. We needed to have this conversation more. I looked into his eyes. "Hey, hon. I need to talk to you."

He pulled up on one elbow. My arms were still sore from the other day, so I stayed on the pillow.

"What is it, love?" He caressed my cheek.

"It's about getting me pregnant."

His lips turned up into a smile, and he kissed my shoulder. "And?"

"You have been mounting me and filling me . . . what, four times a day?"

He held his laugh back. "And?"

"And! We made a little compromise, that to tell you the truth, I am beginning to see your wants and needs."

He just couldn't hold back that megawatt smile. *Damn him and his talented masculinity!*

"And?"

"And I was going to call my doctor this morning to find out what the risks are if you knock me up while I'm on the pill and how much time do we wait if I go off the pill."

He encased me in his arms, rolling me from side to side, telling me how much he loved me and how much I made him happy. His lips were all over me, and I suddenly realized I had a hangover! *Crap!*

"I'm going to throw up if you keep rolling me."

He stopped and grabbed a bottle of water and pulled me up.

Not fair! Oh yeah, he stopped at one glass of wine. Me? Four . . . I so had this coming. But Tiger was happy . . . he practically bounced around the house this morning. Ugh! Stop being so damn cute! He made me breakfast. His infamous pancakes with bacon! OK, I totally loved him again.

As soon as I finished, he refilled my coffee. And he cleared the plates, putting them in the dishwasher and wiping down the counters. He made this look sexy. How could that be possible?

Shit, this man could make breathing sexy! Why wasn't he a model? I just watched him move about. When he was done, he came to me and scooped me up bride style. I put my arms around his neck, and we had a shower.

I chose dress pants and a light sweater with a low V-neck to show a little bit of my assets. Robert sported black dress pants, a crisp green short-sleeved shirt (showing off those muscles and his eyes!), and a big gun on his hip. I laughed.

"And what is so amusing, my dearest?" He made his way over to me.

"So if the doctor doesn't tell you what you want to hear, you're going to shoot him?"

He purred low in his throat. "No, kitten, I like my guns. I am allowed to carry them anywhere, and I will do exactly that. It's only your lovely ass I am interested in defending."

Get your breathing under control, woman. So what if that just hit you square in the crotch? He's sexy, he's seductive, and he would be all too willing to bend you over right here, right now. Mmmmmmhh. I couldn't speak with it coming out all heady.

He leaned into me, widening his stance and anchoring himself firmly on the floor.

"Bookstore?" I had to remind him.

He put both hands under my hair, wrapping them against my neck, and gently pulled my lips to his.

Oh no! I started to count. Fifteen, six . . . teen, se . . . ven . . . teen . . . I was toast.

He broke off the kiss and leaned his head against mine.

"I can't get enough of you, baby. I know we have to go." His hand went to cup around my butt, and he pulled me against him, grinding his erection into me. Do I let him leave like this or get a quickie in right now? It would be in some bathroom once we left the house, and the thought of my father's office had sudden panic brewing in me.

I put my hands on his chest and looked into those piercing lusty eyes. "Here, take me here, right now."

He spun around me so fast, and I could hear his belt coming undone. I worked at my pants and yanked them down, stepping one foot out so I could spread my legs apart wider. He felt up into my sex. I was wet, but who wouldn't be with Tiger?

He moaned and smeared my juices around; then he guided his hard cock up into me. He let out a teeth-grinding growl and then set a rhythm that was building inside me. He grabbed my hips and forced himself deeper and slammed me to his end. After three quick thrusts deep inside and hitting against that deep spot, he reached around and rubbed my clit. The floodgates opened. I moaned and screamed through my teeth. He gave a forceful thrust one more time, and he spilled himself into me. I pumped back against him, rubbing out the last of the orgasm.

"Jesus, baby, stop. We'll never get out of here."

I smiled as I learned another small detail about him.

He reached over to the tissue box and took several out. "Thank you, baby." He gently felt over my butt.

I straightened and smiled at him. "Just fulfilling my wifely duties." I stretched up on my tiptoes and kissed my tiger.

"Damn good wife you're going to be, woman." The caress became a slap.

"Ow! Stop that." I swatted at his hand.

He pulled me to him and growled then kissed me. "Come on, woman, we're going to be late."

"How does my hair look?"

"Perfect."

I checked the mirror real quick just to make sure it wasn't just-fucked hair. I smoothed it out and grabbed an elastic. I decided to go with a ponytail. He adjusted his belt and gun and picked up his wallet on the dresser; he tucked it into his back pocket.

Grabbing his badge and clipping it next to his gun and then his keys, he asked, "Ready, baby?"

"Ready, stud."

And he pulled me to him, tugging down on my ponytail to lift my mouth to his. I smiled and kissed back.

He grabbed my butt again. "You have such a beautiful ass."

"And just think. In two more days, you own it."

He gave a low moan and headed us toward the door.

He grabbed my pocketbook and handed it to me. "Got everything, baby?"

I scanned through it. Phone, wallet, lip gloss. "All set."

We headed out and to the bookstore. When we entered, there were a lot of curious looks from people. Robert held my hand, and I stopped in my tracks.

He looked at me. "What?"

I pulled my hand free from his, and he stepped to my side immediately. There was the stack of newspapers, and on the front page was the announcement of Scott's funeral today with a picture of Scott, Robert, and me!

It was kind of like one of those outer-body experiences. I knew I was there, but I could see everything that was happening. Robert froze at my reaction. He looked around the room to see exactly what was about to happen. He slowly put his arm around me and pulled me to him very gently. I shook my head and took a breath, coming back into my consciousness.

"It's OK, baby, this is the last of it. It's OK. It's all over. He can't hurt you anymore." He just kept talking. I wanted to tell him to just shut the fuck up.

"Robert. Robert! I'm all right. I'm just pissed they fucking put our pictures on the front page!"

I think everyone heard that. *Shit!*

"Shh. Calm down, baby."

I took two big breaths and let them out slowly. I got myself under control until this fucking idiot woman came over and said how sorry she was, and would I sign her paper. "Fuck no! Get away from me, you lunatic."

Robert had me a step behind him. "If you will respect our privacy and just step away."

She saw the badge and gun on his side. "I didn't mean anything by it." And she backed up.

He scanned the room and took my hand then walked us back out the door. "I'll stop at the drugstore and pick you up some magazines."

I huffed out a breath. "Don't bother, just drop me off at Dad's office." I picked up my phone. There were eleven text messages, all warning me about the paper. "Why the fuck didn't someone call the house?"

Robert's phone vibrated. "Yeah!" he answered, "we fucking know already." And he hung up.

Two more people called, and my phone started going off as well.

"I need some coffee. Can you stop at a drive-through?"

"Sure thing, baby."

It was only eight thirty. Everyone was probably waiting for a respectful time to let us know. But there are some things that should not wait. This was one of them.

I answered my phone. "Yeah, Mom, we just found out. We're on our way to Dad's office. Why didn't you call the house?"

She told me she had been trying for an hour. She must have just called when we left.

"Well, this is a clusterfuck!"

Robert just grunted. He made no attempt to soothe me, and it was a damn good choice on his part. I was pissed.

Robert ordered us each a coffee. He put them in the drink holders, and we headed to my father's office. He called someone at the police station and told them where we were headed and to make sure to clear out all camera crews if there were any.

Twenty minutes later, we were in front of my father's office building. There sat two squad cars out front, and Robert parked between them. I didn't wait for him to open my door. I jumped out with my coffee in my hand.

Robert shouted at me, "Kate! Wait right there!"

I did and he pulled me to him, aggravated. He looked at one of the guys.

"All clear!" the cop shouted to him.

Robert led us to the entrance of the building. My father was waiting in the lobby.

"Sorry, Kate, this will all blow over." My father's words were not soothing—just angry like I was. "We tried to get word to you."

"I know, Dad. We found out at the bookstore on our way here."

Robert still kept a strong grip on my hand. He was not letting me go.

"Some woman even asked if I would sign her friggin' paper!"

"People have no consideration nowadays. Robert, I am really looking forward to getting her out of town this weekend. Good choice on getting her down the aisle."

That shifted Tiger's mood. *Hey, was that a smile? Oh crap! There's no smiling right now. I'm mad as hell. Stop that! No! Oh man, here it comes across my face too.*

Before I knew it, he had tugged me into his arms and kissed my cheek. "Very happy to oblige, sir."

No! No! No! No happiness. Must be angry, must be angry! I melt. Oh crap . . .

He scooped me up in his arms and kissed my lips. I wanted to pout, but he was so damn cute.

My father led the way.

"You can put me down now," I requested.

He just kissed me again to shut me up. Everyone was staring.

Then my little force of nature barreled through the door. "Put her down, I want to hug her!" Pepper demanded. Mark was standing next to her.

Robert just tightened his arms around me and let out a little growl.

"It's OK, honey, I'm good. You're going to have to learn to share with her."

"I don't share!" He kissed me again then put me on my feet.

She came at me and hugged around his arm that was still around my shoulders. "Are you OK? I've been trying to contact you since seven. By the way, I need the landline number again because you don't pick up your fucking cell!"

I laughed.

She didn't care about respectable times; she wanted me to know first thing. I love my friend.

She gave Robert the narrow eyes. "I've been taking care of her longer than you, so just get used to me. I'm going to be around a lot."

He tucked me closer to him, and she let me go. He didn't answer, just pinned me to his side. "I'll make sure you have that number before you leave."

"I'm not leaving until he gets back from the shrink."

He glanced down at his watch.

Great, Robert and Pepper for a half hour together.

My father had us all go into a conference room. He had breakfast Danish and coffee set up in there.

My mother burst through the doors. "Thank God you're here! Your father called and said you made it. I had to wait for the nurse to help with Olive."

"You hired a nurse?"

"Yes, your old agency to be specific. With the wedding and the planning for the reception next month, we decided I could use some help with Olive. Letting me be more available to you."

"Good for you, Mom. That's a big step for you."

"Hey, I admit when it's time. You on the other hand—oh, and, Robert, you may want to take a note. Kate takes everything on herself. It's my genetic flaw."

Pepper nodded in agreement. "I say an amen to that."

I narrowed my eyes at her. "Whose side are you on?"

"Yours, buddy, but you do kinda take on too much."

"She'll have me now. I'll help her with anything she needs."

Pepper rolled her eyes, and my mother smiled.

Mark whispered something to Pepper.

"OK, go get 'em, big boy. Do me proud."

He touched her backside, and she smiled. He excused himself with my father in his wake.

"Mark's due in court at eleven," Pepper explained.

Robert looked down at his watch again. He too would also have to leave soon. I could see the apprehension on his face.

I leaned into him. "I will be fine. Look who is here to keep me company."

He looked at my mother and Pepper then pulled me into his lap. "I know, baby, and a few hours ago, it would have been fine. I have strong instincts to protect you, and this isn't going to be easy for me."

I smoothed my hand around his head and neck. "What will put your mind at ease?"

"Nothing. I can't take you with me. I know your father is right here, and you have two women who would give their lives for you. I just have to let go."

"Hang on." I stood up off his lap and motioned for him to follow. He stood up and obeyed. "We'll be right back," I told Pepper and my mother.

I led him to the ladies' room. I looked around and pulled him inside with me.

He let out a low growl. "Baby, we don't have enough time—"

"Shh. Stop talking!" I commanded and undid my belt and my pants as he watched in a possessive manner. I removed my pants and shimmied down my panties. Then I put my pants back on and fastened my belt.

He was stunned.

"Here, honey." I put my panties in his front pocket. "When you are worried about me, think of me without these on. Just rub them between your fingers and know you will be back with me soon."

He smiled a dark seductive smile—almost devious. He pulled me against him and felt my butt up, knowing there was nothing else under the material.

"You are driving me crazy. I'll probably have a hard-on through the whole session."

"Is that allowed?"

"I don't know, and I don't give a fuck at this point."

"I'll see you in two hours, lover. Close this chapter so we can move on."

"One hour forty minutes. Then I'm taking you back home and locking the door, and I'm going to make you come over and over again."

"What about our wedding rings?"

He growled. Ah, Tiger forgot about that. He got his breathing under control, taking slow deep breaths to push back the lust. "All right, baby, wedding rings it is."

I threw another one at him. "And what time is Murphy coming over?"

He forgot about him as well.

"And don't forget Pepper is coming at four."

He leaned his head against mine. "After the rings, before Murphy, is when I'm going to plant myself inside you."

"I'm glad you reminded me. I have to call my doctor."

He pinned me against him. "You maddening woman. You're toying with me, aren't you?"

"Panties, front pocket. Feel the silk, feel me with you, and come back as soon as you can." I kissed him and jumped up, wrapping my legs around him. "I love you, Robert."

"I love you, baby."

I insisted he put me down before leaving the ladies' room, and he complied. He was not very happy about it, but he did as I requested.

He had his arm around me as all of Dad's female coworkers looked on with admiration at my tiger. He had his hand in his other pocket, feeling the softness of my panties under his fingertips. He saw me to the conference room door and opened it then kissed me with gusto in front of Mom and Pepper.

"Get a room!" Pepper scolded.

My mother let out a little laugh.

He drew back with his kiss and ran his knuckles down my cheek. "I won't be long." He turned to Pepper. "What are you concealing?"

She gave him a genuine smile. "Right now, a .40 caliber."

He thought about that for a second. "Good girl. Take care of my woman." He kissed me again more softly. "Stay close to Pepper. I love you!" He kissed my forehead and walked away.

I went and sat next to my guard.

"Overprotective bastard, isn't he?"

"What does that make you?" I accused her.

She laughed. "Overprotective bitch."

And we giggled. My mother was trying to figure out what just went on.

Dad brought in three daily papers. "Look them over. It's better to know what you're dealing with than to be ignorant about it."

Shit, he wanted me to read them.

Pepper grabbed the first one and started to read it to us out loud. I sat back and grabbed a pastry and listened. I looked at the clock. It was only a half an hour since Robert left. One hour ten more minutes, I thought.

My mother studied me. She interrupted Pepper. "Are you all right, Kate?"

"It just occurred to me I haven't been separated from Robert since last Friday. It just feels a little strange."

"You mean you have been by his side every moment?"

I blushed. "Yes."

"I can attest to that. They came to the studio yesterday, and he freaked out being told to wait in the hall. Hell, I wanted him to go for a drive, but he was having none of that, so he guarded my door."

"And a very good guard he was," I replied, smiling.

"Don't even try to rationalize it, Helen. They are like two teenagers with stars in their eyes."

"I know the feeling all too well, my dear. When I first met your father . . ."

Oh no! Not another Mom and Dad's dating story.

"He was all I could think about. I couldn't eat. I couldn't sleep. I just wanted to be with him."

"Well, see, it's in my genetic makeup. It's your fault, Mom."

"It pleases me, darling, that you are head over heels with the man you are going to marry in, what, forty-eight hours? And that he is just as crazy for you."

Pepper piped in. "He's crazy all right, and you're stuck with him as a son-in-law."

"Oh, Pepper, he is a lovely young man. I couldn't ask for a more attentive and loving husband for my daughter. Just wait until you have kids."

Kids! *Shit, I gotta call my doctor.*

"Hey, I gotta make a phone call. You guys mind giving me a few moments alone?"

They both looked at me, surprised.

"I'll just be a few minutes, work related."

Pepper rose up. "I'll just be outside the door. God forbid if something happened to you, and then I would have to deal with your fiancé!"

My mother kissed my forehead. "I'll go see your father. Be back in a bit."

I scrolled through my numbers, found Dr. Peters's, and hit SEND. I talked to the front-desk girl. I gave her my name, and she gasped and told me to hold on.

What the hell?

I was put right through to my doctor. "Kate, I can't say how sorry I am that you are in the thick of it right now. How are you holding up?"

"I'm OK, but this isn't why I'm calling."

"What do you need? Do you need me to prescribe something to help with your nerves?"

I thought about that. "Aaah, no, I'm pretty good. Look, the reason I called you isn't about this circus. It's about . . . my birth control."

Crickets . . .

"Oh." She cleared her throat. "What's going on? Did you miss a day or two?"

"No. I haven't missed any. But I am getting married this weekend, and my fiancé is—how shall I say this—very sexually active. We're having sex sometimes four times a day, and I am not used to that, so I was wondering if the pill I'm on is potent enough?"

I'm not sure, but I think I heard her smiling over the phone.

"Yes, Kate, I think you're safe from pregnancy."

I let out a sigh. "Here's the second part of my question. If I wanted to get pregnant, how soon after stopping the pill should I wait?"

"I would give your body three months just to adjust to your new cycles, and start keeping track when you ovulate. Listen, why don't you set up an appointment and we can go over everything."

"OK, sounds good. Can I bring my fiancé with me?"

"Yes, of course. I'll transfer you back to reception. I'm glad you're OK, and I'm here for you should you need me."

"Thank you, Dr. Peters."

She transferred me, and I made the appointment in two weeks.

I texted Robert: "I love you. We have a doctor's appt with my doc to talk about family planning in two weeks. Xoxo, wife." Sent. I smiled and wanted to hug myself.

He replied immediately: "I love you, wife. Xoxo, husband."

I snickered. *Oh crap! He was in with his shrink. I hope I didn't get him in trouble.* I stood up and went to open the door.

Pepper came back in. "What was that all about?"

"Had to call my doctor to make sure my birth control was going to hold up."

She laughed. "Is he testing the limits?"

"Definitely. He wants to have kids right away."

"And what do you want?"

"I thought I wanted to wait a few years—you know, just the two of us. But I gotta tell you, the idea of carrying our baby is appealing to me."

"Well, shit, girl, aren't you all the little housewife."

I grinned. "I know, right? It just seems like everything is coming as it should be with him. I want to stay home. I want to raise a family. I want to be by his side. I miss him right now. It's been, what, less than an hour, and I can't wait to have his arms around me again, breathing in his scent. I know I'm whacked."

"You're just a girl in love. That is how it should be. Shit, did you ever experience romance? I can't say your first pick was that versed in it. Now you're dealing with this freak force of nature, and he's slamming you with romance. By the way, if it's a baby you want, then that dance number will send him over the edge to knock you up. Am I still coming over at four?"

"Yes! You want to stay for supper? Oh crap! I'm supposed to be having dinner tonight with Mom and Dad!"

"Can't anyways. I'm working the dance team to the ground after."

"When we get back then. You and Mark?"

"Looking forward to it."

My mother knocked on the door and poked her head in.

"Come on in, Mom. And by the way, I'm canceling tonight."

"I understand, dear."

We talked about Dallas's arrival and the weekend nuptials. My phone vibrated. I looked down.

It was Robert: "On my way, baby."

I grinned and replied: "It's about time, stud! :D xoxo." And sent.

Pepper knew it was from him. "You sending him a dirty text? Don't forget he's driving."

I giggled. "He's on his way."

"And let the show begin. Ah, Helen, you might want to cover your eyes when he arrives."

She gave Pepper a smile. "Oh, I've been there, sweetie. No matter what my child has done, I did it first and probably better."

Crickets . . .

Eww—a sex declaration coming from my mother! Eww . . .

Pepper just laughed. "Well, lucky Mr. Quinn then."

"Oh god! Don't encourage the woman, Pepper."

"I'm just saying, Kate. We can see how much he loves you, and it doesn't bother me one bit. As a matter of fact, if he were reserved, I think I would be suspicious of him."

Change the subject quick. I don't need her giving my tiger permission for public groping.

"He wants to buy me a horse."

There, that should do it.

"Really? You're getting back into riding? Isn't he enough?"

I narrowed my eyes at Pepper.

"Just saying."

My mother bragged, "Robert rides as well and apparently is a very good mount."

Oh, Jesus, just take me now!

Pepper grinned. "No doubt about that, Helen. Can't argue a single bit."

"Kate is a lucky girl to have such a well-rounded man," she added.

I brought the conversation back to Dallas and what we were going to do with her the next month.

I felt him before the door flew open, and I stood up. He took five long strides and scooped me up, wrapping my legs around him. He pinned me to him and sealed my mouth to his. Yup, French kissing in front of Mom and Pepper.

Pepper grimaced. "Yuck, let's give them a few minutes, Helen. Come on."

Then we were alone.

He pulled back, breathing very heavily. "That was torture. I hate being away from you."

"Me too, honey, me too."

And he kissed me again. It took ten minutes for him to release me, and when he finally did, he inspected what shape I was in.

I smiled at him. "So how did the panty trick work?"

"Made me think of fucking you the whole time."

"Ah, so were you able to talk about the incident with the good doc?"

"He was more curious about what was happening today."

"I bet."

"I'm sure he was also wondering why I had my hand in my pants pocket the whole time."

I laughed, and he pulled me to him. "Do I get them back now that you have me?"

"I kind of like the idea of knowing there is nothing to stop me under these pants." He felt around my butt and then moved to my front.

I pressed myself against him. "Oh no you don't, stud. Wedding ring, remember?"

He let out his low growl and squeezed my behind with both hands. "Wedding rings. Right, baby. Come on then. Let's go find your da and get out of here."

My parents were around the corner with Pepper. Robert had me tucked under his arm to his side. He went right to my dad. "Thank you for giving me peace of mind." He turned to my mother, letting me go. He kissed her on the cheek. "Thank you for being here with us." Then he turned to Pepper.

She just looked at him. "You're welcome, Robert."

"Thank you, Pepper."

"See you tonight, big guy."

"See you later."

I went over to hug her before he could tuck me back into him. I told her I would see her later and that we were going ring shopping. Robert was itching to pull me back under his arm, but he resisted. Huh? That was new.

Pepper went to hug me again, and that got his hand around my wrist, tugging gently. I gave her a quick squeeze and released.

My mother hugged me as well. He let my wrist go, and then Dad gave me a kiss on the forehead. I went back to my overprotective lug into his side, and he held me tight.

We made it to the elevators, and he leaned against the back in his wide stance and pulled me in front. "Wedding rings?"

"Yes."

"OK." And he kissed me.

The elevator stopped, and a few people came aboard. He made no move to change his stance or let me move to his side. We got more than a few smiles and curious looks. The elevator stopped several more times, and soon there were people that had to get close, and I could feel how uncomfortable we were making them.

"Maybe you should let me turn around?"

"No. Fuck 'em. I don't want anyone getting a good look at you in case they recognize you from the paper this morning."

Oh shit! He was right.

I buried my face into his shoulder and put my arms around his waist. Ground floor. Everyone got off the elevator as quickly as they could. When it was cleared, he took my hand, and he stopped us next to the bathrooms.

"Oh no you don't, not here!"

He grinned at me and pulled out his phone. "We're leaving the building now. Good. Thanks, Cahill."

"Why, Mrs. Your mind seems to be in the gutter."

"I thought . . . I thought . . ." I looked down, blushing.

He grinned and slapped my butt. "Come on, baby. Let's go look at wedding rings."

He had his arm around me as we were leaving the building. People stared. I think they recognized us. Hell, two squad cars out front with his mean machine in between them. Yeah, we were not drawing attention to ourselves. *Riiight!*

He opened my door, and I slid in. He leaned in to kiss me. I buckled up. Then he was at his side, and we were escorted by the squad cars for about a half mile. Then they broke off in different directions.

Jane's shop was a few miles away. Robert pulled out his cell and called her, putting her on speaker. Then he handed me the phone. She sounded delighted, and he let her know we would be there shortly. I hung up and handed him his phone.

"Hold on to it for a bit, love." His brogue just automatically responded to Jane's conversation with us. I beamed at him.

"What?" he asked.

"That's so damn hot."

"What is, baby?"

"That sexy, hot little accent that just falls out of your mouth when you're talking to someone in your family."

"Ah, lass, if that's all it would be takin' to get back in your knickers, then I'll be havin' me way with ya' all afternoon."

I was toast and couldn't stow that ridiculous grin smeared to my face. He picked up my hand and sucked in my index finger.

Oh crap!

"I'm going to have to deal with your aunt all hot and bothered."

"I could just take you to a hotel right now."

"I don't want the publicity, honey."

Well, that was a mood killer.

He released my finger and kissed the back of my hand. "Let's go look at rings, baby."

"OK, stud."

We pulled out front, and Jane was waiting with the door open. She locked it and turned the sign over when we stood a few feet away from her. She held out her arms. "Robert, dear, how are you two holding up?"

He kissed her cheek. “Outside of a public spectacle right now, we’re fine.”

“And our darling Kate? Can I get you anything, my dear? Coffee, tea, champagne, whiskey?”

I snorted. “I’m good, but thanks for the offer.”

She put her arms around me too. “Welcome to the family, love. I just talked to Richard and Sylvia this morning. They are shocked this is happening so quickly. I told them what a beautiful girl you are, and you are a jewel for our future lineage.”

Robert puffed up and pulled me to him. “That you are, baby. That you are.” He kissed me tenderly and looked over to Jane. “Let’s see what you have. I want to get her back home as soon as possible.”

A little blunt there, buddy! I smacked him and pointed my finger.

He laughed and lunged at me, dipping me in a kiss.

Jane looked back and smiled.

“You’re impossible,” I muttered against his lips.

“Ah, but I am your impossible.” He gave me a quick kiss, and I was standing again.

Jane was behind the counter, pulling out trays for us. Robert picked out an all-diamond band for me, but I didn’t like the way it felt on my finger. Too uncomfortable.

Then I spotted a beautiful gold band with small diamonds set into the gold and an open circle swirl between the diamonds. It was simple but really caught my eye. Robert smiled, examining it. He counted the diamonds. His grin spread wider.

“Can I try it on?”

Jane was smiling as well. “It will make your mum happy as a pig in shite.”

It fit perfectly. I looked up at them.

“What? What did I miss?”

“Nothing, baby. Do you like it?”

“Yes!” I felt so giddy.

She pulled out the matching one, but his had white gold in the center wrapped with yellow gold, and the circle things were in yellow gold. No diamond inlays. His was a little tight, but Jane assured him she could have it ready in the morning.

He looked at me. “Well, baby, what do you think? Are these the ones, or do you want to look at some others?”

I gave a quick scan. Nothing popped like this one. “I really like these.”

He took my hand and looked down at my ring. “It’s Irish, the design. The spirals are a sign linked to the goddess, the womb, fertility, feminine serpent force, continual change, and evolution of the universe. There are six diamonds as well. Is that a coincidence that I have been waiting for you for six years?”

“This is my ring, Robert.”

“It certainly is, baby, and it found you here in my aunt’s shop.”

Jane was amazed at the references. “I’m not a superstitious person, so to speak, Kate, but I think this is your ring as well.”

I stared at it, amazed.

Oh man, looks like he won. We’re going to work on having a family of our own.

Robert handed his to her.

“I’ll have it ready first thing in the morning,” Jane said.

I reluctantly took my ring off and handed it back to her as well.

“Kate, would you like me to have it blessed for you?”

I looked at Robert. He just smiled. “Who would do that?”

“I know a few Irish priests in town. Robert’s mother is a cousin to one of them.”

“Sure, but don’t go out of your way. I believe I already am blessed.”

He pulled me to him. “I love you, baby.”

“I love you too, Robert.”

He kissed me then scooped me up in his arms. Jane followed us out and unlocked the door, turning her Open sign over again.

“Now I’m taking you home and having me way with you, love.”

He carried me to his car. I was giggling and intoxicated with love. I couldn’t believe I had found the perfect ring. Two days was going to be agony waiting for it. Robert, no doubt, was going to have them under lock and key until he slipped it on my finger forever.

He slid in on his side. “Are you happy kitten?”

“Extremely!”

“Good, let me get you home, and we can lounge around a bit. Pepper’s not due for several more hours.”

“And how would you like to fill that time?”

“I have a few ideas.”

“Do any of those ideas include me in my riding boots?”

He grinned over to me. “Yes please.”

“You’re in luck. I’m taking requests today, stud.”

“You’re gonna need a nap after, Mrs.”

“Should we stop and grab a burger through a drive-through?”

"Not very nourishing, love."

"Quick, easy protein. Will keep me going."

"I'll cook you something healthier later. I'm not big on fast food. It's all junk."

"Got it! No fast food. What else is out since we are in this conversation?"

"I'm not a fan of ice cream."

I sucked in a large breath. "What? That's sacrilegious! No ice cream?"

"Baby, you can have all you want. I'm just saying I don't like it."

"Anything else?"

"Usually, the only sweet thing—besides you—that I am fond of is pie."

"Any kind of pie?"

"Yes, any—but especially apple. Apple pie with whipped cream. Make me that and smear it all over you, and you can have anything you want."

"Good to know. I can work with that."

"What about you? What do you like and dislike?"

"I dislike any real fishy-tasting seafood. I've a mild seafood palate. I love steak and potatoes, never met a veggie I didn't like. Chicken and pork are a close second. I love breakfast. I could eat that any time of day. Dessert: second favorite meal."

He laughed. "Somehow I think I already knew that."

I smirked. "And you are definitely my favorite snack."

"Good to know, love." And he kissed my hand.

It took us half an hour to get home, and there were news trucks parked down the street with squad cars lined between them.

Robert picked up his phone and dialed, noticing several missed calls. "What the hell is going on?"

"Just snoops looking for a reaction from you two. We have your house secured, and they can't come within a quarter mile."

"Good! We are coming up to the news teams."

"Hang back a minute, Sarge. Let me get Michael in front and Dennis behind you."

"OK." He slowed down and stopped.

I looked over at him.

"They just want a statement from us."

"I don't want to give them a statement."

"We're not going to."

"Should I call my father?"

"That's not a bad idea. Do you mind if I talk to him?"

"No, not at all"

He pulled out his phone. "James, it's Robert. Kate and I seem to be the center of attention at the moment, and the television stations are very hungry for a statement. We are almost home, and my boys have secured the house."

There was silence for a few minutes, and then Robert gave a few hmm-hmm's and then said, "Thank you, James. You want to talk to Kate? Here she is."

He handed me the phone.

"Hey, Daddy,"

"Well, seems you're very popular, baby."

"Appears to be so, Dad."

"Robert has filled me in, and I'll be making a public statement on both of your behalves. Don't worry, Kate, I'll take care of them. You two just get inside and lock the door. I'm sure Mom will be calling you later."

"All right, Daddy, and thanks."

"See you tomorrow, baby, on the plane."

Yup! It was definitely weird hearing Dad call me baby now. That was Robert's endearment to me now.

The squad cars pulled up: one behind and one in front. And we moved. Robert told me to put my head down to my knees so they couldn't get pictures, and I obliged. Even though his windows were pretty well tinted. Think happy thoughts, think happy thoughts.

There was another call coming in for him. "Yeah? No, I'll take her in myself. Can you pull the car in the garage and come in with the keys? Thanks, Kevin."

"Who was that?"

"Kevin James, you met him the other night. He's on my tactical team."

"Oh, I remember."

"He's at the house, securing the grounds."

"Jeez, it's good to be king."

"That's right, baby, don't forget it." He rubbed my back, and we were past the news line.

The guy in front pulled to the left, and Robert accelerated forward. Both squad cars were side by side, blocking the street so no one could get through.

"Get your keys out, baby."

I fished through my bag. "Got 'em."

"Don't open your door. I'll come around to get you."

When we pulled out front, there were three cops. One was in full tactical gear, helmet—the works—with a shotgun standing locked and loaded. There's no way we were that important.

Robert shot out of the car, and Kevin stood at his door, not entering yet. Handing his gun to the cop next to him, Robert came around to my side and pulled me out with his arm around me, not casually like all the rest of the times. This was way different. This was like he was ready to throw me to the ground and shield me.

I know I should have been scared, but this was exciting. He was oozing danger, and it was sexy hot. *I am sure putting on those riding boots immediately.*

We were in, and I know I was giving off some erotic vibes.

Kevin knocked once.

"I'm going upstairs to change." And he just watched me go.

He opened the door, and Kevin came in, filling Robert in with everything that had happened in the hour and what they were going to do the rest of the day.

Robert told him we contacted my father, who was preparing a statement on our behalf for the five o'clock news. I was scrambling to put on a sexy pair of panties that I would only have to say good-bye to shortly. And I zipped up my boots, secured my ponytail, and let my fiancé find me. Should I lie on the bed propped up on my elbows with one knee bent up or sit on the side of the bed or just stand? I heard the front door close, and I jumped on the bed, going for the bent knee.

He rounded the corner and froze. He stared and took in all of me.

"I think there were ideas in the making and promises made. I'm keeping my end of the bargain, stud. What about you?"

He leaned against the doorframe. "Well, well, well, Mrs. I do seem to remember our conversation, as a matter of fact."

He lifted himself off the frame and walked to the closet, undoing his belt with a hint of a smile in the corners of his mouth. He released his gun and put it on a shelf. I watched him untuck his shirt, and he slowly unbuttoned each one. He was whipping me into a frenzy; I figured it out. Two can play at that game.

"Looking mighty fine there, Mr. Beckham."

"As are you, my pet."

He slowly pulled his shirt off one shoulder then the other, letting it fall to the floor at the end of his hand.

"I love the curve of your body there, Mr. Beckham."
"Do you now, love?"

I extended my leg straight up, reaching the top of my boot and slowly wrapping my hands around the top of my calf. I glided them toward my sex. Oh yeah, he was watching.

He had to clear his throat, and he was hard and ready. He slowly undid his pants button as I crossed my knee over my extended leg and twisted, giving him full view of my buttocks and stretching my hands above my head in a flirty manner.

He unzipped his fly and eased his pants down until they fell to the ground. He was topping his underwear as he was so hard. I smiled, quite pleased, and turned over so I was on all fours.

"So any ideas surfacing, stud?"

"I have a few, Mrs."

I turned my head in his direction. "I think we should get some practice in for our wedding night." I sank my legs and hips to the bed. "And this is the last time we will be in your bed up here. I think we should give it a proper send-off, wouldn't you agree?"

"I couldn't agree with you more, love. As a matter of fact, I think you have a brilliant plan, but the question that remains is how much practice and how much of a send-off. One is clearly stronger that the other."

"I see your point, Mr. Beckham, and I think we should give a proper send-off to the downstairs guest room. Outside of tonight when we sleep in its new location and everyone else gets to sleep our sins."

"Our sins? What a playful use of words, my lover." He was behind me, rubbing over the material of my panties.

"Yes, my king, we have yet to join in marriage." I was panting at his closeness.

"Oh, my queen, the deal is practically sealed, and you shall reign by my side forevermore." He was kissing the line of my panties, and his hand was rubbing against my sex.

I lifted back up to my knees so he would have unrestricted access; he pulled my underwear to the side and felt my naked wanting skin. I pulsed back against him slowly. He growled and moaned, feeling me with deliberate slow strokes.

I felt him leave my sex, and I gasped in protest. He stood up from the bed and removed his briefs. He put his hand around my waist and angled me to the side of the bed. He slowly pulled my underwear off, lifting one boot at a time. He didn't shred them, just leaned into my ear. "These are my favorite," he said and took them off carefully.

I so wanted him. He stroked his hand over my buttocks several times and then dipped his fingers over my sex like a caress, but with a mission. I was so hot for him. I wanted him inside me right now. He was being very calm, very precise with each stroke. He was thinking and waiting, wanting and controlling. I was coming unglued. Each time he ran his fingers, he escalated my sexual tension.

I started to command my own satisfactions. I moved against his fingers to get a better rubbing. He moaned and let out a controlled breath. I began to back up and slid my boot off the bed to the floor and pulled the hand that was on my waist up to my breast as I backed into him with my butt and my chest out. He kissed at my neck, groaning at the temptation dangling before him.

I guided his hand, squeezing my full breast and then to the next. He took over, not needing to be asked twice. Both his hands were in front of me, playing with my two most erotic assets. His cock was so full and pressed behind me.

I turned my head slightly. "Now, Mr. Beckham" was all I said.

He drove his beautiful length into me. I came immediately; he was so overwhelming. He bent me over and started a merciful amount of thrusts into me, making me build my next orgasm. He felt me and slammed into me.

"Baby, I have to take you deep and hard."

I let out a soft cry.

"I can feel you give to me, baby. Come for me again. Squeeze my cock inside you, baby."

And I did. He moaned down deep and shot his load inside, grabbing my hips, pumping into me still. I didn't want it to end. I pulled off him as soon as he released my hips, and I sucked him into my mouth.

"Jaysis, Kate. Aaahh! Oh fuck, yes! Just like that, baby!"

I was building him up.

"Ahh, that's it, baby. You do this so fucking good!"

He took over fucking my mouth. I gave him two and a half minutes; then I released him from my mouth and pulled him down on the bed and mounted him.

"You think taking me from behind is good? Just see how I do riding you to the finish line, Mr. Beckham."

I began to pump him. He held on to my waist, helping me up and down on him.

After a few minutes, I moved up to my feet like I was in the stirrups. I took both his hands into my weak grip and put them above his head. "Don't help. I want to make you explode all on my own."

He just looked into my eyes and surrendered himself to me. I started pumping him hard then harder. He raised his ass off the bed to meet me thrust for thrust. I could feel how hard he was. Taking him was a commitment. I rode him all the way into the OK Corral. He was coming hard, gritting his teeth, cursing out my name.

Breaking the ties of my hands, he gripped my hips while pumping into me. I collapsed onto his chest, finding my own release from pure muscle fatigue. He pulled me against him, flattening my body to his, kissing anything he could get his lips on.

"For fuck's sakes, baby, you drain me so good."

I was panting. "You're so intense. I need to get in better shape. Help me off with these damn boots."

He rolled me to the side. "Don't ever curse at my new favorite footwear." And he took my boots off one at a time. "I'm going to polish them later."

I laughed. "You're insane!" Then I flopped on the bed, sliding my body between the sheets and comforter. "Come join me, future husband, your future wife needs a rest."

He tucked me tightly against him, and it was exactly where I belonged. With his arm securely around me, I fell into a deep sleep.

I woke up to the smell of . . . burgers! He was making hamburgers!

I leapt out of bed naked, backed up to our pile of discarded clothing, and grabbed my panties and his shirt. I buttoned only a few in the middle, and I ran down the hall and stopped myself at the doorframe. He was at the stove in his totally hot pajama bottoms.

I gave him a heads-up of me leaping onto him. He turned, ready to accept me, and I went for it. He cradled me to him and kissed my hair.

"Did you get enough rest, kitten?"

"Yes." I kissed him.

Chapter 12

Pepper arrived to the same circus we went through. Except I warned her, and the police were notified of her coming, so she received a full escort as well.

Dad stepped up to a podium with a full statement on our behalf. It was very legal and very threatening. He didn't get many questions after. The news crews all went home.

Pepper banned my tiger to the top step. He couldn't even answer the door, so he barricaded himself in the office, miffed at his nemesis.

I excused myself briefly and bolted up to him on the three-minute reprieve Pepper allowed. I kissed and kissed and kissed him. Then I kissed him some more, topping it all off by telling him I loved him. He was satisfied when I left him for the dungeon. Then we got down to business.

She broke down every step to an eight count. I perfected the first forty counts. She was very pleased, but I had another hundred and forty to go for hubby's birthday pressie. Pepper promised to snag me away for a few more eight counts here and there on the weekend, so my goal was another twenty-four counts under my belt before coming home.

We decided to use Dallas as a distraction. *Lord, help me now.* I don't know what this little twenty-two-year-old could do up against Robert's force of nature, but she would have my mother as backup. Mom loved Dallas—always said she had a free spirit, and she admired that about her.

Dallas vs. Robert: Let the rumble begin! I would coach her to just talk firearms, and they would get along just fine. Would he let me out of arm's length? That was another whole can of worms I wasn't sure about.

Before Pepper left, she announced to Robert I was all his again. Smart-ass! He was busy emptying the drawers to move the furniture. I practically hopped into the bedroom and jumped on my future husband to make my mark. He scooped me around and threw me on the bed; that left me giggling and squealing. Then he pinned me with his whole body.

"How long until Murphy gets here?" I asked.

"An hour. Why?"

"I'd like you inside me for at least half that time."

"Baby, you are a dream come true."

And he worked at my jeans and panties. I couldn't get to him, of course. Then he freed himself; but first, he put his mouth on my sex.

He lifted his head up. "I was deprived earlier. I love the taste of you." And he got down to business. I couldn't have lasted more than a few minutes. I was screaming and coming against his mouth.

A flash of panic rose in me. Were the boys still outside? Could they hear me? How could I ask him when he was filling me now with that talented length between his legs?

He slid in so deep that he hit the very end, bypassing that spot that craved him. I tilted my pelvis slightly, *and—oh, fuck me!* There, right there, he was nailing me square on.

I began to build my climax again. He went for it hungry, and I caved all around him, giving off a teeth-clenching groan. He gave two more deep thrusts, and he spilled himself inside me. I felt every pulse from that cock, and I was hungry for him. I stroked myself three times on his full length; then he held my hips still.

"Baby, you're draining me so good."

"Isn't that the plan, Daddy?"

"Quite right, kitten, quite right! You do that so well. I have a new talent to brag to your mum about."

"Don't you dare, buddy, or it will be downstairs in the old bed for you."

"Forgive me, my queen. I meant not to humiliate you but only to glorify you, my love."

"Not to Mom! Every time you show no boundaries with personal affection, she starts to bring up sex between my father and her. I just can't handle it."

"Baby, sex is the most natural experience a person can share."

"Not with your mom, it isn't. And just wait, stud. I hope our first child is a girl. Wait until she is fifteen and wanting to fuck every boy who makes googly eyes at her."

Crickets . . .

"Yeah, I thought so, buddy. It's different when they're your own. My father's brother always said you bring a boy into the world, you had to worry about only one dick. With a daughter, you worry about all the dicks."

"Wise words. Is he coming to the reception? I'd like to meet him."

"I'll invite him. He's damaged from Vietnam. Doesn't like big crowds. I'm his favorite niece, so maybe he'll make an exception."

"So he's older than your dad?"

"Yes, by a couple of years."

"If he doesn't come, I'd like to meet him regardless."

"Oh, don't worry. He probably has a file on you as we speak, and he will most likely just show up one day."

"My kinda guy."

"Definitely your kinda guy."

He pulled out of me.

I flopped back on the bed. "Hey, honey, are the guys still outside?"

"Yes, why?"

"Do you think they heard me?"

He grinned. "I would like to reassure you, baby, but I think the whole neighborhood knows you're a screamer." He let out a low laugh.

I put my arm over my face.

"Baby, it's a big turn-on for me. Makes me even harder."

"How can I look at them ever again?"

"You'll be fine, baby. They will never bring it up."

"But I know they know."

"And they know I am the luckiest man alive."

I smiled under my arms.

"Come on, baby, let's strip the bed. Don't need Murphy scenting you all over them as well."

Argh! I jumped off the bed and ran to the bathroom and turned the shower on. I gave myself a quick body wash and quickly dried off. Then I grabbed my college sweatpants, underwear, bra, and one of his T-shirts. He watched me dress while he folded up the comforter.

"Damn, woman. You're still sexy. Even under all that."

I took the pillows off the bed. "Well, I think you're a bit biased, stud, since you've been stalking me for the past six years."

"Oh no, baby. Trust me, it's not just me. It's going to be a full-time job keeping the admirers at bay."

"Well, they can look, they just can't touch. And same with you, stud. It's going to take a lot of reeling in my jealousy watching your admirers. Especially when you're in uniform. I could make a fortune selling posters."

He laughed and leaned over to kiss me. "As you said, they can look, but they can't touch."

I grinned and remembered the fact that he wouldn't let other women touch him. I was happy and so sad for them all at the same time. He was made for me to possess him. He was mine, and it was only my right to lay my hands on him.

I wondered if this was why Pepper freaked him out so much. She was possessive of me as well. He said he didn't like to share, but surely, that would be all right in friendship. I didn't have any sexual relationship with her. It was a sisterhood more than my own friggin' sister.

I was going to have to figure this one out. To give him what he needed around her and the same with her. I hoped, in time, they could ease up. He had no one that I had to share him with. This must be really hard for him. I would have to be more sensitive to his needs.

The doorbell rang.

He swooped in to kiss me again. "Moving time, pet."

He left and answered the door. I could hear Robert laughing on the landing. His laughter brought a smile to my face.

I quickly scanned the drawers then brought the sheets to the laundry. Murphy was coming up the stairs. He was a handsome guy too. Why hadn't I noticed that before?

"Hi, Kate! Getting ready for the big day?" He had a cat-ate-the-canary grin on his face.

"Yes, I think we are all set. We picked out our wedding rings earlier, so that should do it now."

"Jeez, that was easy. My wife took weeks to find the 'perfect ring,' and it looked no different than a hundred others we looked at before."

"I kind of know the feeling. My ring—when I saw it, I just had to have it. We are picking them up in the morning. Right, honey?"

"You betcha, baby." And he pulled me into him, kissing me possessively on my mouth.

"OK, OK, come on, you two. I'm going to be doing all the work if you keep this up."

Robert released me and slapped my butt. Then he gave me a *grrr*. He clapped his hands and rubbed them back and forth. "You have the U-Haul?"

"Right out front."

"Let's load you up first. Then we can bring everything downstairs."

"Sounds good. The wife is looking forward to the new set."

"Will I have time to give the room a quick vacuuming before you move the set from upstairs to the downstairs?" I asked.

Tiger smiled. "Of course, baby. I have a vacuum cleaner downstairs. It's in the closet of the guest room."

"Cool, I don't have to lug this one then."

"There will be no lugging for my wife."

"I'll just start downstairs." Murphy excused himself.

I shooed my tiger away. "I think we're making him sick. The quicker we do this, the sooner I'm lying down on the couch with you watching TV."

"Ah, another incentive. I shall have you wrapped in my arms soon enough." He kissed me once more.

I started the laundry, and I dragged all our dirty clothes in and tidied up the bathroom. Robert called to me and said the first floor was ready. I grabbed an old cloth from the laundry room and bounded down the stairs.

He caught me at the bottom step and pulled me up against him. "You're so sexy, baby." Then he released me.

Murphy came through the door. "OK, first part done."

"I'll just be a minute, guys" I said. "Oh, and I put some cheese and crackers out in the kitchen if you want a snack."

Robert preened. "That's my woman." And he lunged at me again as I was backing away.

Murphy grinned, and I squealed and squirmed from his embrace.

"Stop, honey, let me get the room cleaned. Remember: couch, TV, cuddle."

He let me go for a kiss. Then he leapt up the stairs to the kitchen. I quickly dusted the baseboards and pulled out the vacuum and went to work. I took ten minutes and shouted up to them that I was done.

Robert answered, and I heard them move to the bedroom. I looked around his gym some more. He had nice stuff in there, all very clean. I remembered what Pepper taught me, and I started to practice before they made their way down. I worked those first forty counts and racked my brain to remember the next sequence.

They were coming with the headboard first, and I watched. *Yum!* Two muscular men doing heavy lifting. *Drool!* Robert grinned as I cleared my throat and shot back up the stairs.

I cleaned up after the boys and changed up the laundry. They had the bed set back up in no time. He put it where the other one was. It filled the space much better than the whores' bed. I grabbed a set of sheets and went back down to make the bed.

Robert and Murphy were carrying the second dresser down. I followed behind, smacking and rubbing my husband's lovely buttocks.

"You'd better run when I put this dresser down."

"I wouldn't dream of running, honey."

He growled at me.

"You'll only end up catching me anyways."

Murphy had to add, "Kate, anytime you want me to show you how to subdue this man, I'll be ready."

I answered before I thought it through. "Oh, I already know how to subdue him."

Oh crap!

Robert gave a wicked grin. I stopped rubbing his butt.

"That's right, baby, and you bring me to my knees every time."

I blushed.

Murphy grinned. Robert preened.

Murphy asked if we got a chance to go through the basket. I had completely forgotten about our presents.

"Tonight we will," Robert answered.

I smiled again. "We've been a little busy."

Oh shit! Did I just say that too?

"I bet you have been," Murphy answered.

They put the dresser down, and Robert turned to grabbed me. "We certainly have been, Mrs."

He locked me in a kiss and threw me onto the bed, with him landing over me and tickling me. I screamed with laughter while Murphy went to grab some of the drawers.

Robert stopped with his assault. "If you keep making any more suggestive comments, he's going to have to jerk off in the bathroom."

I gasped.

"You already look like a hot momma in my T-shirt and these sweatpants."

I grinned. "I'll behave, it just slipped out."

"I'll give you something to slip out and then in again and slip out again." And he resumed with the tickling. I screamed, and he attacked my neck with his tongue.

Murphy put the drawers outside the room. "Come on, Beckham. The quicker I'm home to the wife, the better."

Robert stopped and gave me another quick kiss then jumped off the bed. I just lay there breathless.

He loaded the drawers back into the dressers and dragged me to the end of the bed. I giggled. He bent down and kissed my chest then went up to grab more drawers. I sat up and started making the bed.

Murphy came in. "It's good to see he has another side to him, Kate."

"What do you mean?"

"He has a strong work ethic and keeps everyone at a distance."

"Yeah, I can see that in him. He is driven."

Robert rounded the corner with an armful of dresser drawers. "You flirting with my bride?"

I smiled.

"Wouldn't dream of it," Murphy replied. "I have a beautiful woman waiting for me at home who puts up with me. By the way, she wants to meet Kate real bad. I had to tie her to the chair to come over on my own."

Robert laughed; I looked mortified.

Murphy chuckled. "Just kidding, Kate. It was the bed."

"You're so bad. I'm going to tell her that when I meet her."

"She is fully aware of my sense of humor," mocked Murphy

"I promise we will go out when we get back." Robert put the last drawer in and left to get the comforters and pillows.

"Are Bill and Kevin married as well?" I asked.

"Bill is divorced, Kevin never married. He's our resident slut," smiled Murphy

"Really? A ladies' man?" I tried to ease the name calling

"Slut fits better."

"Oh."

Stud came in and handed me the comforter and put two pillows at the end. "What secrets are you revealing to her now?" he asked Murphy.

"He told me Kevin is a slut."

Robert grinned. "Yeah, that about sums it up."

"You two all set? I gotta go untie the wife."

"Thank you," I said. "And tell her we will be in touch."

"Will do, Kate." He shook Robert's hand and slapped him on the back. "Good choice there, buddy, and congratulations."

"Thanks, Murphy, take care of my unit while I'm gone."

"Will do, Chief."

I followed them up the stairs.

Robert closed the door. "And what do you want to do first, Mrs.? Eat, open presents, or hit the couch?"

I put my arms around his waist and my head to his chest and shoulder. "I have one more chore. I want to vacuum our room."

"OK, baby. You hungry at all?"

"Sure, what do we have?"

"How about pasta with vegetables?"

"Perfect. I'll be right in to help."

He kissed my forehead. "I'll open a bottle of wine."

I followed him up the stairs, groping his butt again gently. He kissed my mouth before disappearing into the kitchen. When I came back in, he was cutting up the veggies. He handed me the knife while he prepared the sauté pan.

"So what where you laughing about when Murphy arrived?"

There was a grin spreading across Robert's face.

I stopped cutting and turned to him. "What?!"

"You seemed to have whipped Kevin from panic to envy in a split second."

I looked at him, not understanding.

He couldn't keep a straight face.

I stomped my foot to let him know I was not amused. "And how did I do that?"

"When you started coming, you started screaming. He heard and thought you were in trouble, and when he was about to kick the door in, he realized that it was not a panic scream but one of pleasure."

Oh my god! Could it get any worse?

"He told Murphy, who relayed the info to me."

Yes. Why, yes. It can always get worse.

I sat on the stool, and he came over to me with a glass of wine. "Like I said, it's the sexiest sound in the world, and it makes me even harder."

"But they now know. The slut out of all of them heard."

"And I'm sure he had to relieve himself just hearing you. I did make you come several times."

"Stop! Stop right there. Too much information."

"I'm just saying I was the lucky one filling you, baby."

I took the glass and drank half of it. How was I going to look that man in the face ever again? And what was he going to be thinking each time he saw me?

Robert tilted my chin up. "Don't ever be ashamed when you are with me. I'm rightfully yours, and you are rightfully mine. In less than two days, we will be married."

I blinked, and the shame started to wash away. Or was it the wine?

"I love you, baby."

"I love you too."

"Good, get back to chopping. I'm sure you're hungry, and your man needs to eat after all that lifting and pleasing his woman."

I kissed him and went back to chopping. He put the pasta in and sautéed the garlic and onions. I brought over the rest of the veggies and stood behind him with my arms around his waist.

The phone rang. "Answer that, baby. I've gotta drain the pasta."

I was shy about answering his phone. "Hello?"

It was my mother. She was checking in on us.

We sat down to eat and, my god, he was such a good cook. Mrs. Fitz taught him well. We cleaned up and made our way to the couch.

Robert grabbed the gift basket and put it on the table in front of us. He went back and retrieved the wine and filled both of our glasses. He hit the remote for soft music in the background.

I lifted my glass. "To us. Thank you for waiting, lover."

"To us. Thank you for saying yes," he countered.

We clinked, kissed, and took a sip.

Robert pulled the bow off and tore the cellophane apart. I smiled as he just said "Go for it, baby." And he leaned back into the couch, rubbing my back.

I grabbed three cards and snuggled back into him with my legs folded in front. I gave him one, and I opened one. Both were gift certificates—one to our lingerie shop and the other to a frilly bath products shop. Both read $50.00.

I gave him the one I had and opened the next one. It was for a couple's massage at the spa downtown.

"Wow! So far, so good."

I grabbed four more cards. I gave Tiger two and the massage certificate. I opened mine first. It was a two-hundred-dollar gift certificate to a kitchen store.

He waited for me to open the next one. It was a fifty-dollar gift card to his favorite coffee shop. He grinned and handed me the two he was holding.

"Don't you want to open them?"

"I'm having too much fun watching you."

I gave him a girlish grin. "This is awesome . . . hey, while we are on the subject of gifts. What do you want for your birthday?"

"You, baby. All I want is you."

"You've got that already. What are your hobbies?"

"You and you and you."

"So you're just going to leave it up to me?"

"I'll be happy with anything from you, or just you with a big bow around yourself."

"Fine, I'll use my imagination."

I was about to ask him what kind of cake, but I will make him an apple pie. A huge grin spread across my face.

"What? What are you up to, Mrs.?"

"No good, stud." And I opened the next envelope. Gift card at Target for $50.00. And then the last one was a card signed by everyone.

I unfolded my legs and rooted in the basket. I pulled out massage oils, bath oils, chocolates, coffee, tea, Irish biscuits, two fluffy bathrobes, and a couple of bridal lingerie sets for me in white and lipstick red.

Robert took that one from my hands. "This one's coming to Vegas." And he tucked it to his side.

I grinned. I pulled out two bottles of wine, one red the other white.

Nuts, oysters in a can, glow-in-the-dark condoms, a bottle of lubrication . . . He took those out of my hand as well, saying, "This too."

"Should I be frightened?"

"Oh no, baby. I'm going to take you to a level of pleasure you have never felt before." And right then, he ignited everything south of my belly button.

I handed him the chocolates. "Here, open these."

"With pleasure, my love."

I took a long swallow of wine. He opened the box and presented it to me. I took one out and fed him then took one myself.

I dug through the basket some more. There was flavored body butter. He laughed. Pink fuzzy handcuffs. I laughed. And a couple of cold compresses. I laughed harder.

I could have used those the first night with him.

There was a long feather, smelling salts, and some aspirin.

He was grinning. "Well, I guess that just about covers it."

I ran the feather over his shoulders. "Should we bring this as well?"

"No, we'll leave that here, but hand me the smelling salts." The wicked grin spread across his face.

"This was very generous of them. I'll write out a thank-you card."

"OK, baby, I'll leave it up to you."

"Just give me back the card. I want to include them all."

"Here you go, Mrs."

I packed everything back into the basket. Robert got up with the little red number, lubrication, and he fished through for the smelling salts.

"You're not serious?"

"Just a precaution. Can't have you passing out on me."

I slapped his butt.

He leaned in for a kiss then took his new treasures down the hall. He returned with his pajama bottoms on and a tight white T-shirt with a bed pillow and blanket. He put it on one end of the couch, grabbed the remote, and climbed in behind me to lie down.

I leaned up against him and put my feet on the coffee table, still drinking my wine.

He massaged my shoulders and flipped through the stations. He stopped on CNN and caught the market update.

"So you understand all that stuff?"

"Yes, kitten. I can teach you if you are interested."

"Eventually. I might be a slow learner, so don't get frustrated with me."

"Baby, I make learning fun. You'll have this stuff figured out in no time. Then I can go over all our investments in detail, and you can watch our money grow. We can set up a small account for you to play with and see how you do."

I put my wine down and lay right next to him on my side, facing him. He pulled me closer into him so my face was right into his chest, and I worked my top leg between both of his. He wrapped me into him, and I fell asleep.

When I opened my eyes, I was turned the opposite way. He still had me tucked into him with his arm securely around me, and we were still on the couch. He had his leg between mine.

I looked at the clock on the stereo. Five minutes past five. Oh my god, I slept nine hours!

He felt my breathing change and began kissing my shoulder. "So you do like to live on the wild side."

I giggled.

He gave the couch the last choice for sleeping arrangements.

I turned into his chest. "I believe this is where it all started."

"Correct, baby, but I moved us."

"Well, I think we should pick up where we left off." I could feel him growing against my stomach. I stretched up and kissed his chin. "Hold that thought. I gotta go pee."

He released me and got up as well. "Good idea."

And we both went to different bathrooms. I brushed my teeth quickly and met him in the hall.

He scooped me up and carried me back into our bathroom and put me on the sink while he brushed his teeth. He gave me a toothpaste kiss, and I smiled while wiping my face. I went to hop down, but his leg and knee pinned me.

"I just wanted to take my sweatpants off."

"I'll do that," he replied with a grin.

He rinsed and put me around his waist again. We headed back to the couch, and he launched me into the middle. He straddled over me and kissed all over my face and neck. He pulled his T-shirt off himself and then pulled mine off, making his way down over to my breasts—licking, sucking, then kissing each one.

He was on the floor, kneeling, and he pulled my sweats down with my panties, kissing all the way down one leg and up the other. I was laughing because he was tickling me. Then he looked up at me with that sensual smile and started rubbing me with his fingers. I immediately stopped with the laughter and started with the erratic breathing.

This man was so good at this. I could only think that it must have been torture not being able to touch him. Those rules didn't apply to me, so I ran the backs of my fingers gently down his face and then my nails through his hair. He moaned at the feeling. Another thing my kitty liked, being scratched at the top of his head. Why didn't I think of that sooner?

I leaned forward, offering my breast to his mouth again. He slid his two fingers into me and sucked and tongued my nipple. I felt this pull right from my nipple to my sex, and he withdrew his fingers. I arched my back and gently held his head to me.

He pulled my hips to the edge of the seat and released my nipple then took my sex into his mouth. He flicked that amazing tongue up and down over my clitoris and pushed the upper part of my body back against the cushions. When I was where he wanted me, he spread my legs farther apart and tucked his hands on each of my buttock cheeks and lifted me off the couch even more into his mouth.

This was so friggin' hot. I was on the edge of an orgasm when one of his fingers brushed the entrance to my ass, and I jumped while he held me with his mouth and hands while slowly feeling around that area. His tongue was relentless with its attacks.

My body was a little confused as to what it was feeling with that finger stroking uncharted areas. He made a slight penetration and sucked my clit hard; then I hit a 7.0 orgasm on the Richter scale. I screamed and moaned and said Robert's name, and I remember the good Lord was thrown in there somewhere and then more screaming.

He removed what he had in the back entrance and pulled me off the couch some more. I could feel him filling my vagina up, and then he started to slowly move. I knew I was conscious, but I also felt exhausted. He built up a stronger rhythm, and he filled me completely, rubbing that spot deep inside me. No, it just wasn't possible to build from that.

Well, Mrs. Impossible, meet Mr. Possible. I was going to come again.

"That's right, baby. I can feel all those squeezes on my dick. Give me another one, baby, and then I will let you rest. Come on, give it up for me."

Oh god. Oh god.

And he started ramming his length in and out so perfectly then one, two, three—we both came.

I felt him pull out. I felt him move me to lie me down on the couch so I was stretched out. I felt the pillow go under my head, and he covered me with a blanket. I felt his kiss, and I heard him say he would love me forever. I just don't remember falling back to sleep.

I smelled the coffee and opened my eyes. Robert was on the floor in front of me, reading the paper, and there were two mugs on the coffee table. I put my hand around his shoulder, and he caressed it and kissed it.

"Good morning, beautiful." He put the paper down and turned to kiss me.

"You're going to kill me."

"Not a chance, baby."

"What time is it?"

"Seven thirty. You have a good hour before the delivery truck gets here."

He saw that I was starting to sit up. I was still naked under the blanket, but hell, I didn't care. He's seen every bit of me, had every bit in his mouth or his hands. Modest I was not right now.

He handed me his T-shirt. I waved it away.

"You might want to reconsider putting this on."

"Why? You have had every inch of this body. You know it like the back of your hand."

"Yes, I agree, but I still want it. Right now, seeing you flaunt it in front of me is going to push me over the edge."

I took the T-shirt and put it on. "Happy?"

"More like less of a distraction." He moved from the floor up next to me on the couch. He handed me my mug.

"I am so wasted. It's like I have a sex hangover."

He laughed. "Best one to have."

"Why are you"—and I waved my hand over him—"fresh as a daisy?"

"Baby, my workout regimen is far more intense than yours."

"Well, this has given me a new incentive to boost my cardio."

He kissed the side of my head. "Glad to hear it, kitten. Because that's nothing to what you're going to experience with me."

"What? There's more?"

"Baby, there's always more."

"Great, I'm going to become super fit and die from an orgasm."

"I promise not to kill you. I need you around for a long time." And he kissed the side of my head again.

I sipped the coffee. "This is really good. Where did you get the coffee? It's not what we had yesterday."

"It was in the basket."

I looked around for our engagement basket. "Did you sort it out and put everything away?"

"Had to do something while my beauty was sleeping."

"OK, that was just corny."

He laughed. "You want breakfast?"

"Yes, do you have steak?"

He laughed again. "You want steak and eggs, kitten?"

"Yes."

"Coming right up." He turned my head and kissed me right on the lips. "I love you, babe."

"Yeah, yeah, yeah. I love you too."

And there was a playful look on him. "We'll pick up our rings after the furniture gets here."

I brightened, and a genuine smile turned up my lips.

He took my coffee out of my hands and pulled me into his lap. "Baby, we're going to Vegas today. And you're going to be my wife tomorrow."

OK, ridiculous grin has crept in, and my sex hangover left me. I was getting married tomorrow to this gladiator whose arms were around me . . . *Yeah!*

"What time are we leaving?"

"Liam is picking us up at eleven."

"That's in four hours."

"Plenty of time, love. We will stop by my aunt's store on our way to the airport. When the delivery guys are done, I'll bring our bags to the hall so we'll just load and go. Everything is done on our end."

I kissed him then my stomach growled.

"Time to feed you, kitten. Gotta keep up your strength." He scooted me off him, gave me another kiss, and went to the kitchen

"Do I have time for a shower?"

"Go ahead, babe."

I leapt up and grabbed my coffee and went into the bathroom. I turned the shower on and just stood under the warm water for a few minutes. *Ahhh! This feels so good!*

I scrubbed up and got out, wrapping a towel around me. I gave a shout to the stud. "How am I doing with time?"

"About five more minutes, baby."

I went to the closet and pulled out a simple miniskirt and a three-quarter-sleeved shirt that fit my upper body like a glove but was not clinging. It had a nice pattern on it.

I walked into the kitchen barefoot. He was putting the steaks and eggs on plates.

He looked at me and grinned. "Is that what you're wearing on the plane?"

"Yeah, you think it's all right?"

"I think we will be joining the mile-high club."

I giggled. "Yeah, somehow I don't think you would get stopped following me in the bathroom. As a matter of fact, there probably would be a line forming for you."

He placed our plates on the island and licked his fingers. Then he pulled me to him. "Only you, baby, only you."

And I squeezed his ass. "That's right, and don't you forget it." I was getting more comfortable claiming him.

He ran his fingertips up my miniskirt, tracing the line of my legs and buttocks. "Come on, let's eat before I eat you."

I kissed him then released him, shaking off his instant desire that I felt deep in me.

Steak, yum! I ate the whole damn thing.

Robert watched with enthusiasm. "I'm so glad you're not one of those chicks who picks at their food."

I laughed. "Can't ever accuse me of that. I like food. And the way you have been working me, I have no reason to count calories."

He pulled me to his mouth. "Good answer." And his lips were on mine with soft kisses.

The delivery guys came and set everything up. I made the bed while Robert filled the drawers with our clothes. Instead of sharing, he put them in alternate so his underwear was on top and mine was on the next drawer down. Then his T-shirts and my T-shirts; we shared the bottom drawer with the sweatshirts. The same with the other chest right next to this one. His pants, my pants, his gym clothes, my gym clothes, and our pajamas shared the bottom along with my negligees.

As we put the last of our clothes away, he led me over to the bed then laid me down with him, wrapping his arms around me.

I reciprocated. "I like what you picked out."

"Thank you, honey. It goes well in this room. I liked the one downstairs as well."

"But this is a fresh start, just like us." I smiled into his chest.

"I'd try to christen it right now, but I know I wore you out this morning, and I'm going to have you tonight, baby. In Vegas."

I thought about that for a second. "Shouldn't I be away from you tonight to build the anticipation of our wedding tomorrow?"

"No, I wouldn't recommend that. You won't be able to handle me, and I don't want to hurt you."

What the hell was he talking about? "Honey, you won't hurt me, and it would only be for a few hours."

"No! I don't want to be away from you, baby. We are sleeping together, and that's final!"

What the fuck?

"Is it because of my safety?"

"It's a lot of things, babe. I just won't handle it very well if we separate."

I knew it! He was insane. He couldn't be that perfect without some flaw surfacing. I could feel his anxiety. Time to calm my tiger. "OK, no big deal, honey. I think I would miss you too." And I nuzzled into his chest.

His breathing relaxed, and he loosened his death grip on me, and right then I felt his arousal.

"Do I get to dress up and get pretty without you seeing?"

He let a low snicker deep in his throat. "I think I can handle that. But Pepper has to be with you as well as your mother."

"I can do even better. Our room with Dallas and my rotten sister as a bonus."

"Then I shall be waiting with baited breath."

His sexual aura was wrapping me now. I think the thought of not being with me was a trigger for him, but he needed to release the tension that was building. I was wiped from our earlier transgression. I had about two minutes to decide how this was going to play out or I was going to be under the assault of that talented mouth of his.

Wait, that's it! I'm not without skill.

I pushed away from him, and he let me up a little. "Trust me, you will like this, and I can kill two birds with one stone."

"What are you up to, Mrs.?"

I went right for his belt and undid his pants. He watched with a dark grin. He lifted his hips to accommodate my pulling. I brought them just past his thighs. Then I took hold of him and pulled his silky briefs down as well. He put his head back on the bed and closed his eyes, and I gave my best blow job thus far. I mimicked what he did to me, and I sucked the very tip of him until his body convulsed. Then I took him as far as I could in my mouth and down to the back of my throat.

He growled out curses and wrapped my hair around his fist without interfering with my movement. "Oh fuck! Kate, baby. Oh that is sooo . . . fu . . . cking good. Get ready, baby . . . I'm going . . . to . . ."

That was all he could get out with the teeth gritting and groaning with a couple of curses and my name again. Of course! I swallowed a mouthful, which was more than I thought he had in him after this morning. But what else would you expect from a gladiator? His body was probably wired for producing sperm constantly.

After I finished licking him up, he pulled me to him. "Baby, if I wasn't marrying you tomorrow, I'd have you chained to this bed until you did."

I giggled into his neck. "Best blow job ever, stud?"

"No comparison, baby. Absolutely best ever."

"I took notes from you, master."

He laughed. "Told you I was a good teacher."

"Proof is in the pudding."

Oh jeez! Why did I just use that expression?

"Sure is, baby. Sure is." And he kissed me.

He made out with me for a good five minutes. My tiger was calm, happy, and drained. I was good to go until tonight, where I knew he was going to return the favor. And knowing my tiger, he would take it up a notch or two.

We lay there for another ten minutes. He finally moved us, and we had about forty-five minutes until Liam was due to pick us up.

"Baby, are you all set with your girly stuff?"

I laughed. Hearing him just say "girly stuff"—it was clearly not in his tough-man vocabulary.

"As a matter of fact, no. And thanks for reminding me." I kissed his cheek and went to get up.

He pulled me back down onto his lap. "I love you, baby."

"I love you too, stud." And I hugged him.

Then he let me go with a slap to my butt. He grabbed my wrist again. I stopped and was getting a little annoyed now. He held me with one hand and lifted my skirt to check out my panties with the other. He smiled and fixed my skirt back to where it was then let me go.

"You approve, stud?"

"Highly, baby." They were the ones he picked out a few days ago.

I gathered all my makeup. "Hey, honey? Do you have a ziplock bag or something? I need to put my make up in it."

"I've got something better, kitten." He came back a few minutes later with a ten-by-twelve-inch bag.

"Perfect! What was this used for?"

"Ammo."

I giggled as I stuffed my things in there. I even fit a brush and hair accessories. When I finished, I gave it to him. "Any room left in my bag?"

"Of course, kitten." And he took it from me. "I'll go bring everything down to the landing."

"Ok. I just want to freshen up."

He kissed me and left, closing the door behind him. When I came out, I straightened the bed and looked at our new bedroom set. I looked around the room, making sure I wasn't missing anything. I played with my ring and smiled.

When I came back into this house, I was going to be Kate Beckham—married to my husband, Robert Beckham.

Robert rounded the doorframe. "All set, love?"

"All set, hubby."

He smiled and held out his hand to mine. I took it.

Liam was prompt and had chilled champagne and glasses in the back of a new Cadillac.

"Wow! Didn't expect this, Liam! Thank you." I leaned in to kiss his cheek. He blushed.

Robert opened the door then led me around. He handed me my pocketbook. I stretched up to kiss him then slid all the way in. He followed, giving me a deep kiss. I was so excited, I snuggled hard into my man, and he wrapped his arm tight around me.

I was a girl totally in love and on her way to pick up her wedding rings and a flight to Vegas to marry the jackpot of men.

My freak of nature, overprotective man. But still a jackpot.

He popped open the bubbly and poured us a glass. "Baby, I'm over the moon. I feel like I have been wishing for the lottery for six years, and I have just hit the jackpot."

I snuggled against his arm and swung my legs over him. He was pleased with my new position.

I held his face in my hands. "I feel exactly the same way."

We had a make-out session with Liam driving. I felt like I was eighteen.

Our chauffeur made our first stop. Robert jumped out of the car, dragging me behind him.

Jane was beaming. She took Robert by the hand (who had me by the hand) and had him see if the ring was a perfect fit.

It was.

She gave me a great big hug and wished she could be with us. Which made me think if he asked her to come. Robert picked her up and swung her around with his joy. He thanked her and kissed her cheek then let her down. She was not used to such excitement.

She blushed and kissed both my cheeks again. "Good luck, darling. I cannot wait for the real party. Do I get to bring a date?"

"Jane, you bring whomever you want. Let me know what the total is."

She kissed both of Robert's cheeks. "She is such an asset, my darling, my only nephew. You have made me proud, and I shall add her to my will as your gift, my child."

Robert went from joyful youth to preening like the great Siberian tiger. Wow, that was intense to see him shift.

We had the rings. Robert tucked them into his pocket as we slowly made our way back to Liam. He waved to Jane.

She smiled as she waved back. Then she murmured, "If only he was twenty years older."

I snorted into Robert's arm.

Robert just said, "Cougar," and she brushed him off.

Off to the airport and I couldn't seem to get close enough to him. He pulled me on his lap. I put my arm around his neck and shoulder. There, that was close enough. I was happy, happy, happy, happy.

Robert poured us another glass of bubbly. I witnessed a soft side—so carefree—of him that I would make my goal to see as often as I could. This beautiful man was beginning to be my life ambition. My center of attention. My goal to conquer and mold. What a sweet deal I had. Robert the man! Center of my universe. Yeah, got that one covered.

We arrived at the airport.

Liam helped with the one bag I would have to carry. He said his good-byes and hugged me. He then shook Robert's hand and cupped his shoulder, telling him he deserved another chance.

What the heck was that all about?

Robert had all three bags under control. So this left me tucked under his arm with nothing to wheel. All my family and friends arrived at the same time. They were in the first-class line, all six of them checking in.

I heard Dallas gasp from there and then vocalize, "Holy fuck! Is that who she is marrying?"

My mother tried to calm her. I saw each of the flight check-in girls look up. Business stopped to a dead halt as they admired my tiger.

Dallas shifted from one foot to the other. I heard her tell Pepper, "He's a freaking *god*!"

Pepper answered, "He's far from being that. Oh, by the way, little sis . . . he can dance. And I mean dance."

She gasped.

I went right for the kill. I pulled her into me. "Dallas! My god! You have grown up, girly! Thank you for being so accommodating on such short notice. I really wanted you to be with us. Hey, by the way, this is my future husband, Robert."

Stud kept his distance but still held on to my hand. I could tell he wanted to reel me in and cage me, so I would have to give him credit for this.

She gave it her best shot to look so casual but failed miserably. She blushed and giggled into her hand. I couldn't help but giggle with her.

"I know, right?" I whispered to her.

Robert stuck out his hand. "Hello, Dallas, nice to meet you. We're happy you're able to join us this weekend and witness our union into marriage."

She pulled herself together. "Thank you for inviting me and paying for all this. It is very generous of you."

"You are very welcome, Dallas. If it makes my Kate happy, then it makes me happy." Right then, he pulled me to him and caged me in front, kissing my cheek.

Everyone thanked Robert as well.

Even my sister, who was acting very respectable, came over to me. "I'm happy for the both of you. I hope you have many joyful years ahead."

"Thanks, Stacey."

Robert corrected her. "A lifetime. We will have a lifetime of joy. I will make sure of that."

She looked at him, and I think there was jealousy in her expression. I couldn't blame her for that. He was the jackpot, and he was mine.

We all checked in and went to the first-class lounge. We had it to ourselves, and Dallas gave all of us an update from the last year. Robert listened and even laughed a few times with me on his lap. He liked Dallas; I could tell. Mark and my father were talking shop, and Pepper was egging on Stacey, telling her now she had to go out and find a man.

"Maybe I'll find him in Vegas" was her answer.

Dallas challenged her. "Let's have a contest of who can get a marriage proposal first."

Pepper and my mother laughed.

"Game on, little girl!"

There it was, our official entertainment outside of the wedding. I laughed and snuggled into my groom. We were the only ones in first class. Our flight attendant was very attentive to Tiger—who was very attentive to me.

When we landed, I had butterflies in my stomach. There was a strong energy around Robert that made him even sexier. As the plane taxied to the gate, he was trailing kisses up my hand all the way up my arm and to my mouth. The kiss was not decent for public viewing. I heard Dallas giggling and Pepper's backhanded comment about it.

He pulled me out of my seat when we got the all clear and into his lap, lifting both of us up. He carried me off the plane this way, and I just buried my head into him, laughing. Halfway down the corridor, he shifted me over his shoulder and patted my ass. I squealed as I looked back at everyone.

"Put me down!" I half laughed and half bit out. "You are not carrying me through this airport!"

My mother had my pocketbook. Robert turned around, walked over to her, and took it from her.

"Robert!" I bit through my clenched teeth.

He turned back and headed for the end.

"Please let me walk."

He stopped and let me down.

I pointed my finger at him. "Bad boy."

And he dipped me into a kiss. I was laughing again. He tucked me under his arm, and we headed to the baggage area.

All our luggage came out first. When we hit the lobby, there were two chauffeurs holding his last name.

"Is there another Beckham on our flight?"

"No, baby. We have our own limo. Everyone else is in the other."

"Oh."

Robert went over to one of the guys and straightened out who was in which car. Our chauffeur took the luggage cart from Tiger, and he tucked me back under him.

"See you at the hotel," he stated to everyone then kissed the side of my head and hugged me to him.

I looked at the world in amazement. Everything was beautiful to me right now.

Our driver opened our door. "Welcome to Las Vegas, folks."

"Thank you," I said through my smile and slid all the way in.

Robert followed and closed the door himself. He pulled me close to him, leaning back and pinning me down. Then he kissed and kissed and kissed me until the driver was behind the wheel.

Robert hit the button for the partition to go up, and then his hands were all over me. "You're so fucking beautiful."

I had no idea how long it was to the hotel, but there was no way I was having sex with him in this car.

I let him feel and then I put the brakes on. "Not here!"

He was holding everything he could get his hands on. "Just let me feel you, baby. Real quick, I promise."

"No, Robert. I'm not getting caught with my pants down . . . so to speak."

"You want me walking around with this?" And he showed me his protruding length against his pants.

Oh fuck!

"Fine, make it quick!"

He was on his knees in front of me in that two-second law, unzipping and pulling himself out. He yanked my panties down this time then just freed one leg from them. He lifted my shirt and pulled up my bra, taking my right breast into his mouth. His fingers explored my sex, and he smiled to see how wet I was.

OK, so I wanted it too.

He brought my hips down to the edge of the seat to meet him, and he slid himself in while watching himself enter me.

Why was that sexy hot to see? He was turning me into a dirtbag.

He moaned and groaned, sliding himself all the way in. "You feel so hot, baby. I think you want this too."

I looked into his eyes. "Go!" I commanded, and he was pumping himself in and out, rubbing my spot that was just for him.

I was building in no time. He took his hand off my hip as he felt me coming and covered my mouth to muffle my cries. He exploded himself, spilling into me.

He removed his hand and lifted me to him. "Thank you, babe. I needed you to do that for me. I love you so much. It makes me crazy sometimes."

"Thank you for not letting the driver hear me."

He smiled and kissed what he could get his lips on.

I motioned. "Oh look, champagne?"

He slid himself out of me and grabbed some tissues, wiping me up.

Jeez, this was just weird. "I'll do that, stud."

He handed me a few more. "You don't like me cleaning you?"

I smiled shyly.

"I could always lick that clean, you know."

Blushing. I was blushing.

"That almost sounded like a threat."

And he spread my legs apart. "Never a threat, baby. Just a promise."

I covered myself with my hand.

"Now, now, now, kitten. Don't make that a challenge. You know I will win."

"Robert! Open the champagne. Please . . . I want to celebrate with you right now and put myself back together."

He purred and backed down. "I'll be having you for dessert later."

"I look forward to my last night send-off as Kate Quinn, Mr. Beckham."

This made him very happy. I quickly put my panties back on and fixed myself.

Robert was still hanging out. I reached over with a few tissues and wiped him up. He had no reservations about me doing this to him. I think he really liked it. He did. This was what he wanted, me taking care of him. I could handle this.

I finished and tucked him back into his underwear.

He grinned and kissed me. "I love you touching me."

"So I'm learning, big boy."

He handed me both our glasses and finished putting himself back together. He sat next to me and put his arm around me. He clinked my glass. "To your last night as an unmarried woman."

"And to your last night as an unmarried man. Hey, what time are we getting married tomorrow?"

"Three."

"Three o'clock?"

"Yeah, are you all right with that?"

"Yes. That's my favorite number."

"Right now, it's mine too. We have dinner reservations for five in a different hotel."

"Why?"

"Top pick in Vegas."

"Then what?"

"Then we have a little time to roam around. And about eight, we are going to a big nightclub, and I'm taking you dancing."

"Everybody going?"

"Yes, I have reservations."

I gave him my megawatt grin. "You're the best!"

"I'm the best for you, my queen."

We arrived outside the beautiful hotel. Our driver came around and opened Robert's door. He hopped out and held out his hand for me. I looked around, stunned to see how much excitement was in the air.

Robert tipped the man, and I floated into the lobby of the hotel. He found the check-in desk then let go of my hand. He checked us in and then everyone else since it was all under his name. He collected all the keys and had them hold off showing us the rooms.

We waited ten minutes. Ten minutes of caresses, strokes, and soft kisses—along with loads of admiring women passing by Tiger. He was such a chick magnet. One group of young women even gave me the thumbs-up as they passed by.

I smiled.

He smiled when he spotted our entourage. He waved them over and signaled to the receptionist that we were all here. Quite frankly, I don't think she ever took her eyes off him. She smiled and gave him a nod then stuck her chest out a little more.

Yeah, good luck, honey. Watch and learn.

I touched his back, and he leaned in to kiss my mouth full-on.

Ha! Take that, you hussy!

Pepper and Mark reached us first.

"Would you two save it for later?" she said.

Robert smiled into my mouth and kissed me again. He handed out the keys—my parents, Pepper and Mark, and my sister and Dallas. I think Pepper was a little shy about the pair-up, but it didn't bother Mark in the least. He gladly took the key from Robert and took hold of her hand. She gave him a shy smile.

Well, hot damn! She really, really liked this guy. He was toast.

Four bellmen came over to show us the way. Three got off on the twenty-fifth floor.

Robert held me back. "See you all in a bit."

The doors closed, and he hit the button for the thirtieth floor.

"We're not on the same floor?"

"No, baby. This is our weekend."

The bellman led the way. It wasn't the penthouse but pretty fucking close. He opened the door and let the bellman in first—who was very nice, talking away about the hotel and what it had to offer, the name of our suite, and other random facts. Robert bent down and cradled me in his arms, carrying me into our mega suite.

The bellman grinned. "Are you two newlyweds?"

Robert answered, "Shortly, mate."

"Well, congratulations! Best wishes to you both. My bride and I are celebrating fifteen years soon."

"That's great," I answered as Tiger put me down.

"Well, let me show you around so I can get the heck out of here and let you two alone."

We walked hand in hand. Robert paid attention; I just followed with my mouth open. There were three huge gift baskets. Todd the bellman left with a fifty palmed to him.

Robert closed the door and stalked his way over to me. Jesus, he was sexy! He kissed me gently, and my excitement exploded as I jumped up on him. He spun me around and dipped me into another kiss. I held on to him then let go because I knew he had me. I put my hands on the sides of his face. He lifted me back up, and I pulled back first.

"This is awesome, honey! Just awesome!" And I went back to kissing him.

He must have held me for ten minutes like that, completely using his own strength because I couldn't squeeze around him any more with my legs. He walked us over to the baskets and put me down on the table with them.

"Where did these come from?"

"One is from the hotel, one is from my credit card company, and this one is from my father."

"Really?" I peeked through that one first.

He opened it for me. There was a bottle of champagne, an envelope with a full day of spa vouchers, eight tickets for the show at the hotel tonight, and an envelope with "casino fun" written on the outside.

Robert opened that one first. There were two thousand dollars, all in hundred-dollar bills. He smiled.

"Holy crap? How much is there?"

"Two grand, baby."

"We'll never spend all that!"

"Wanna bet?"

I laughed. I opened the card. It was a wedding card. He wrote on the inside, "Congratulations, son, and to my new daughter-in-law, Katherine. Treat each other well." It was signed by him.

How did he pull that off?

Robert kissed me. "You'll meet him soon."

"Soon—what is soon?"

"Don't worry. It's not this weekend. He's not that kind of man. You will meet him at the party. As well as his wife and their kids and my mother."

"Can't wait." I looked in the other baskets.

Robert opened the one from the hotel. We went through that one as well: a bottle of wine, two glasses, nuts, a big box of chocolates, fruits, cheese, and assorted crackers.

"That's nice."

Robert pushed that one back and opened the one from the credit card company.

Top-of-the-line champagne, a big box of imported truffles, deluxe assorted nuts, a bag of hard candies, trial-size toiletries, a sewing kit, a travel first-aid kit, fruits, and cheeses with assorted crackers.

"Wow, they really like you."

"Baby, they love me right about now."

I laughed.

He pulled his phone out of his pocket and looked at the text. "There is a Pepper Harris looking for your cell phone number. She claims she is with you this weekend. Can we give it to her?" He laughed.

"What"

"Pepper is looking for us. Wants my number."

I hopped off the table and went to my purse and pulled out my phone. Seven text messages:

"What room R U guys in?"

"What floor R U on?"

"Why R U not with us?"

"Where R U!"

"Call me!"

"They won't give me your room number!"

"Answer me!"

I laughed. "Can I tell her where we are?"

"Sure, baby."

I texted her our room and floor numbers with a "give us twenty minutes" warning.

Robert took our luggage to our room. He started unpacking it. I grabbed the credit card basket and brought it into our room, put the champagne in the small fridge, and kissed my stud's shoulder. That was not good enough, and he kissed me properly.

There was a knock on the door. I smiled at him. He took my hand and led us to the entrance.

He opened the door, and there stood Mark and Pepper. She took no prisoners and gave Robert a hug. I could see the internal battle inside him. He half-hugged her then peeled her off. She latched on to me next. Mark shook Robert's hand.

Pepper released me. "Robert, our suite is amazing, thank you. It is so very generous of you. Thank you for this whole trip, for letting us be a part of the wedding. This really means a lot to me. I will never forget this."

He just smiled at her and caged me. "You are entirely welcome, Pepper. It made Kate happy, so it makes me happy."

There was another knock at the door. Since Pepper was closest, she answered. That way, Tiger didn't have to release me.

It was the rest of the crew. The girls came in first. Dallas was shy. And so was my sister! *What the hell?*

Dallas came forward. "I know I thanked you before, but I have to tell you that our suite is just beautiful. Thank you so much for including me in on your wedding. I couldn't be happier for the two of you, and I look forward to getting to you Robert with our Kate."

He smiled at her.

Stacey said, "Thank you, Robert, this is all extremely generous. I've never been treated better in my life. I wish the two of you many years of happiness."

Robert corrected my sister immediately. "It will be a lifetime of happiness."

"Yes, of course." She blushed.

He released me as my mother walked over to us.

"Yes, Robert, you are very generous to all of us. Thank you."

He gave her a full-on Robert wrap, and I think she actually melted. Mental note to self: he has no problem showing my mother affection. She actually wobbled, walking away from him. He caught her as well as my father.

Pepper looked around. "Is this the penthouse?"

A tone changed in Robert. "No, that one was taken. This is the next room below."

He sounded disappointed. Was he going for the penthouse?

"I like this one better!" I immediately spoke out.

He grinned at me and pulled me back to him.

"You guys want a tour?" I asked, as if I didn't know the answer already.

We brought them around, and they had the same awestruck expression I had. We brought them back to the baskets, and Robert opened his father's bubbly. I found extra glasses, and we shared a toast.

Then Pepper asked what we were all doing for the night.

I jumped up and grabbed the tickets. "Anyone want to go see a show?"

Robert explained the tickets, and they all cheered. Then Tiger suggested we all have dinner before the show, so he made reservations for all eight of us. We had two hours and fifteen minutes. They all scattered within fifteen minutes. Robert handed them their tickets and gave them the name of the restaurant downstairs under his name.

When he closed the door, he picked me up and carried me to the bedroom. He laid us on the bed, and I snuggled right into his chest.

"This is a dream come true. As a matter of fact, this is a dream I never could imagine in my wildest fantasy—and you just topped that."

He caressed my back, and man, did he smell so good.

"I'm happy you are happy, baby," he said. Then he kissed my forehead, and I fell asleep.

Chapter 13

My eyes flew open, and I hit panic mode. I smelled the coffee, and Robert was nowhere around. I jumped out of bed and ran down the hall. There he was. In a crouch position, taking in everything and looking to where the danger might be.

"How could you let me sleep!" My eyes filled with tears, and he understood immediately. "We missed everything."

He straightened up. Then he held his arms out to me, and I went into them. "Shh, baby, we didn't miss anything."

The tears just spilled out of my eyes.

"Babe, you have only slept for twenty-five minutes. I was just about to come down with some coffee and wake you up. Shh, it's OK, baby. We still have an hour and a half to get ready."

He kissed the top of my head.

My brain was starting to accept my surroundings. Suddenly, I felt exhausted. He held me tight as I started to catch up with this new information.

My groom asked, "Do you want to have your coffee in the bedroom or out here?"

I sniffed and wiped my eyes in his shirt. "Out here please. I don't want to be near that bed unless we are done for the night."

"That's a deal, baby. Come on."

He guided me over to the couch and then went back for both our mugs. He sat next to me and tucked me to him.

I rested my head on his shoulder and took a sip. "Wow, this is good coffee. Is it the hotel's?"

"No, ours. I brought it from home. From our engagement basket."
"You're so thoughtful. Thank you."
"I knew you liked it."
He earned a kiss, and I gave it to him.
"Feeling better?"
"Getting there."
"What are you going to wear tonight?" he asked.
"The red dress."

He took in a sharp breath. I was nearly done with my coffee, and he ordered me to finish it up. We were having a shower. I did as he asked and put my mug down.

He moved us off the couch and led me back down the hall to our bathroom. We showered with a very sweet sensual feel about it. No sex. And after he shaved, which was sexy as all hell, he left me to groom myself. He walked in with my dress, shoes that matched perfectly, my red thong, and red bra. OK, I was all set, and he left me alone again.

I finished with my simple makeup then slipped on the goods. I checked myself out in the mirror. *Hell yeah!* I looked smoking hot! I opened the door to see my tiger sitting on the edge of the bed, looking ripped in the same outfit he wore on our first date! Holy heck! That was only a week ago! And here he was—sexy, hot, and mine. *Tomorrow I will be Mrs. Beckham. Married to that!*

He rose from the bed and took a few steps toward me. He swallowed and held out his hand. "Come on, baby. I need to get you away from this bed . . ."

I smiled at him, taking his hand. "There's always a bathroom around," I reminded him from the way he was looking at me.

"Oh no, love. A bathroom will not do tonight."

And there! With his tone, he got me wanting him south of my belly button. He ignited everything.

He handed me my purse and escorted me to the elevators.

I could feel him. I could feel every want and desire he was radiating, and it was intense. The elevator doors opened, and we walked inside. He just held my hand. I wanted to kiss him but felt a sort of danger in that gesture.

As we made our way down, several other guests boarded our space. A man looked me up and down then nodded at Robert, who ended up tucking me behind him. The women got an eyeful of sexy hot-cop/stripper, who was now guarding me. I wanted to wrap my arms around him. *Heck, he was mine.* So I did. His hands covered mine and brought one hand up to his mouth as he kissed my knuckles. Everyone piled out into the main lobby.

Tiger pulled me to him and secured me under his arm. He looked so fucking hot. I would have to coax him to go dancing after. I wanted tonight to top our first night together. Suddenly, it was my secret mission. My arm was tight around his body, and we arrived before everyone else by a matter of five minutes. We were all seated at once, and the menu looked incredible. Tiger leaned into me and asked if I had any preference.

"Meat, I'll take a side of cow at this point."

He purred and ordered for us.

My mother was watching and smiling. She loved her new son-in-law—how he took care of me, how generous he was with my family. She truly loved him. I looked up at her, and she winked at me and smiled. Full acceptance there! I leaned into him, and he put his arm around me.

Pepper started to say something and stopped herself short!

"What?" I asked.

She brushed it off. "I just can't believe you are going to be married tomorrow. And a damn good Mrs. Beckham you will be!"

That got Tiger's approval, and he raised his glass. "To Mrs. Beckham!"

Everyone joined in and clinked glasses. "To Mrs. Beckham!" They all cheered! I had a stupid grin on my face; I was sure of it. Tiger just kissed me. He didn't care.

Our meal was fantastic and then the show. The wine and champagne were flowing on Mark's tab. I was feeling pretty giddy when the show ended.

I asked my stud if we could go check out the local nightclub.

He put his hand between my thighs. "Are you sure?"

I grinned. "Yes!"

He offered an invitation for everyone to join us. My parents graciously declined, but the rest were eager to go.

Dallas strutted out in front, catching many admirers. She just pointed to the club, and they followed. My sister stepped up her game. She was six years older. That had to account for something.

I held on to my tiger in utter bliss. I noticed a few women followed. *Just wait, ladies, until you see him dance.* And my grin stretched from ear to ear.

The techno was pumping. Pepper, Dallas, and Stacey hit the floor, leaving us behind. Mark secured a group of seats, and Robert pulled me to the dance floor. There was a crowd already watching Pepper and Dallas dance. My sister seemed to have snagged a cute guy. No one was attempting to ask the sisters with their dance skills yet.

Then my almost-husband started to move. He cleared a space ten feet wide for us and spun me to and away from him. Women were drooling. *Heck, I was drooling!*

He danced one of his numbers all up against me. I glanced over. Pepper was getting an eyeful; her mouth just hung open. Dallas was pointing and saying something to her.

Tiger turned it up a notch, and I think a few women had to leave to sit before they fainted. He moved all around me, incorporating me in this dance, and I was the one preening for once. Yes, this is what my man could do, and he did it so well.

When the song ended, there was a round of applause from everyone who was watching, and that was nearly the whole club. The DJ came over the speakers, making a comment, calling Robert some name I didn't catch and ending it with "in the house tonight." He then slowed down the music, and Robert pulled me to him, moving both of us. I was the envy of the club. I claimed my man, feeling him and holding him.

He cleared his throat. "Keep that up, baby, and I'll have no choice but to take you in the bathroom. I'm only a thread away from taking you right now."

I smiled. "Let's go. I want to take you to bed."

That was it. Elvis has left the building. I waved to the girls as he grabbed my purse. Pepper gave me the thumbs-up. Mark said good-night, and we made our way to the lobby. I really think Robert just wanted to carry me because I wasn't moving quickly enough in my heels. But this time, he resisted. We entered the elevators, and he had me pinned against the wall, moaning and breathing deeply. He just inhaled my scent. We actually had a solo ride all the way to the thirtieth floor.

Tiger dragged me out, and I was giggling. He scooped me over his shoulder, held me in place by my butt, then opened the door. He told me to drop my purse on the table then he took me down the hall. I couldn't help with the giggling. He was just so damn cute. He put me down at the edge of the bed, walked away for a moment, and put something on the nightstand. Then he pulled out that little red number from the engagement basket.

I laughed some more. He spun me and unzipped my red dress and then let it fall to the floor. He put me back over his shoulder and bent down to scoop up the dress. When he had what he wanted, he put me back down. Then he held me at arm's length to admire my undergarments.

I quickly shimmied off my thong. I liked this one, and it matched my bra perfectly. I didn't want him ripping it off. I stepped out of it and then unclasped my bra. My brain caught up to me. Shouldn't he be doing this? He was just watching with appreciation.

I started to unbutton his shirt then pulled it out from his waist. He kissed me when he could and caressed my arms. I got the shirt off! *Yeah!* Then I went for his belt. He gave me a slight push, and I fell back on the bed as I laughed. He pulled his belt off then his shoes. He dropped his pants, revealing that beautiful full length. I wanted to take him in my mouth.

No such luck. He was calling the shots from here on out. I surrendered to him, giving him full control.

He pulled me up higher on the bed and kissed me from head to toe. Then he got me ready with his mouth on my sex. I have to admit, the alcohol took a bit longer for me to register those feelings. But then the gates opened, and I was screaming.

He filled me immediately, pumping me in a steady rhythm. As I was building up again, he stopped and pulled out, reaching over for that bottle he brought with him.

"Baby, turn over. I'm going to take you from behind."

I flipped over as asked, and I was on all fours. His cock brushed down from my back across my anal entrance and to my vagina. He was big, and he slid himself back into me. He had a hand on each of my buttocks instead of my waist. He pumped me with that same pleasure as always, and I was building again. He moved his hands back around my waist, and with his next couple of hard thrusts, I was coming again.

He stilled himself, and I could feel this warm liquid pour down my buttocks crack, past my anal entrance, and to where he was inside me. I gasped slightly, but he continued to pump me just where he was. His hand moved back to my buttocks. Then his thumb began to play near the entrance, and it played some more. His rhythm was steady in me, and he was just playing. Suddenly, his thumb made a good penetration. I stilled and gasped. He didn't withdraw but leaned into me.

"Am I hurting you, baby?"

I thought about it a quick second. "No."

"Do you want me to stop?"

Oh no. I didn't know what to think, but my body craved him. "I don't know . . . no, don't stop."

"Good girl."

He continued prepping me with his length. After a few moments with his cock doing its thing, he began moving his thumb slowly in and out of me. My head was screaming no, but my body had no morals when it came to him. I started moving against him.

"That's it, baby, feel how good I can make your body feel."

Then he picked up his game, and he twisted his thumb, and his cock was slowing down with full root-to-tip thrusts. I had a constant feeling of confusion. I started to put them both back on track, backing up into the both of them with my own rhythm. He groaned and moaned, and I could feel him getting bigger.

Out of nowhere, I came. Another megawatt orgasm. And Tiger gripped my waist and emptied himself. He twisted his thumb around once more, and a sound I never heard came out from me while I was still coming. Then he pulled out of me suddenly.

I finally stopped. I felt my tiger pulling the blanket over me while kissing me, then telling me how beautiful I looked tonight and how much he loved me. I was out like a light.

When my eyes opened, I was tucked into the man I loved with his arm securely around me in a beautiful bedroom that I never wanted to leave. We were under the blankets between the sheets, and I tried not to move, but I think it was my breathing that gave me away.

He turned me over and kissed me. When he released our kiss, he smiled and said, "I'm marrying you today." He kissed me softly. "In eight hours."

I did the math and smiled. "You know there will be no backing out." And I wanted to kick myself with that expression, knowing what he did to me last night.

"Baby, I wouldn't dream of it. I want you. All of you. I crave you."

Aww! That was sweet. I loved that. "I crave you too, stud. So what are the plans today?"

"We are spending the morning in the spa then having lunch. And at your request, I am leaving you to go to Mark's suite while you girls get ready. You'll have two hours. That's all I can handle. Then I'm coming up to get you, ready or not!"

"Don't worry, I'll be ready."

He kissed the tip of my nose and then sealed his lips on to mine. Then he sank himself into me.

I started my wedding day with my groom between my legs and one hell of an orgasm.

"I wondered how you would sing 'happy wedding day' to me. Would it sound like the birthday song?" I was claiming the tune anyways. I put on my yoga gear.

He stopped in his tracks. "If you wear that to the gym, I have to be with you."

"You'll be with me always. You're my motivation."

He slapped my ass. I jumped ahead, and the chase down the hall was exciting—which ended up with me pinned underneath him on the floor. He had me spread wide, and I couldn't stop laughing as he assaulted my neck. When I screamed for him to stop, he did and picked me up, nuzzling into me.

We made our way downstairs for breakfast. I checked my phone. There was a text from my mom asking what our plans were today. I sent everyone the same information.

We were joined half an hour later by my parents. Robert and I had just finished our breakfast, and my mother was gushing.

"I can't believe my baby is getting married today!"

My father added, "We welcome you to the family, Robert. Kate, you picked the finest man to settle down with. I couldn't be more proud of your choice."

"Sir, I am also proud to become a member of your family. I will take care of Kate until my last breath, and I will cherish and protect her. Thank you for your approval. I will do my best to honor your family."

My mother couldn't help herself. She got up and came over and hugged both of us. With tears in her eyes. Great—I was filling up myself.

Robert pulled my chair over to him and put his arm around me. I got myself quickly under control.

Pepper and Mark found us next.

"Where's the coffee?" She plunked herself down in a chair. "Oh, and by the way, your sister won last night. That guy she first danced with was proposing by the end of the night."

I laughed out loud. "What time did you guys leave?"

Mark gave me a look. "I dragged her out of there by one."

I giggled again. Robert caressed his fingers around my shoulder.

"You guys bailed pretty early," Pepper commented.

"I needed my beauty sleep. Couldn't be waking up on my wedding day with bags under my eyes."

"Good call. Besides, I don't think the women in the club could handle Robert dancing again."

My mother brightened. "Oh, you dance, Robert?"

I blushed.

He looked at me as he answered her, "A little."

Pepper let out, "Ha! I don't think you can say just a little. They applauded when they were done. The whole freaking club applauded."

Mom smiled widely. "Kate, you are very lucky to have a man who can dance. It's a true asset. Your father is a great dancer as well. That was one of the things that first attracted me to him."

Robert just held my gaze, and I was grinning. *If they only knew.*

I turned to my mother. "Yes, I am very lucky he is such a good dancer."

Then Tiger stretched out, preening. He loved it when I complimented him.

Dallas and my sister were the last ones to show. Dallas had sunglasses on as she dragged herself over to us. Grabbing an extra chair, she pulled it over.

"Jesus! It's too bright in here!"

Robert chuckled at her. I giggled.

"What time did you guys leave?" Pepper demanded.

"About a half hour after you. I had to peel this one off the man of her dreams."

Stacey grinned. "He was cute."

My father scowled at her. "Watch yourself here, Stacey."

She pulled herself back together, and she kicked Dallas under the table.

"Ow! What the hell was that for?"

"Big mouth!"

"Your dad's right. Have fun, but leave it on the dance floor. Oh, and speaking of dance floors. Robert, I think you made a few women faint watching you dance. You lucky bitc—" Dallas stopped midword and corrected herself. "You are very lucky, Kate."

I laughed.

Robert looked at his watch. "Sorry, guys, we have a date in the spa. We'll see you upstairs in four hours?"

My mother quickly asked, "What is everyone doing for lunch?"

"We're eating in the spa," Robert replied. "So we will see you about twelve thirty in our room." He stood up and took my hand then led us out and down the lobby.

The spa was on the third floor. We were greeted with mimosas and congratulations on our upcoming nuptials.

We started in a lavender whirlpool bath. Robert rubbed my feet and—oh my gosh!—did that feel good. They took us into a seaweed wrap next. I couldn't help but giggle the whole time to see Tiger wrapped in seaweed. He kept telling me to shush. I kept giggling louder. Then we showered off, and we had side-by-side massages.

His attendant was delighted. A little too delighted. And he let her rub him. *Hmmm, that was curious.* Why would he let a masseuse and not one of his dates touch him? I'll have to ask him about that later. We were done, and they asked me if I would like any waxing. Robert answered immediately with a no, and I grinned.

They served us lunch and led us over to the sofa. We were still in fluffy robes and slippers.

"How do you feel, baby?"

"Like I want to run down the wedding aisle."

He laughed and pulled me into him. "Me too, baby, me too."

"I have a question for you, stud."

"What is it, love?"

"Why are you comfortable with a masseuse touching you all over and not one of your former dates?"

He looked at me curiously. "One is about sex. Sex I imagined us having one day. No other woman had that right to touch me where your hands belonged. No matter what I was doing with them. As far as a massage—well, there is no sexuality involved, and it's benefiting my body to a relaxed state."

"I think your masseuse had a different opinion."

He grinned at me, pulling me on his lap. "Did my kitten get her fur all ruffled?"

I giggled. "Yes!"

"It's OK, baby. I'm only yours, and I will be legally yours in three more hours, as you will be all mine." He kissed me with passion.

We walked hand in hand through the lobby. I could feel his smug expression. He had victory right around the corner. He walked us slowly while I wanted to run.

"I have to give you up for a few hours when we get back. I'm in no rush, baby."

We were in the lobby, but I didn't care. I jumped onto him. He grinned and held me to him. I had my forehead to his, and he was just strolling along. We were getting admiring looks and definitely drawing attention.

He made his way over to the elevators. I pressed the button. He just rocked me slowly back and forth, grinning like he had the best secret in the world. In the elevator, he released me then caged me to him. Several people caught on as we made our way up. They tried not to look—but the way he was holding me, it was kinda hard not to want to look. He softly kissed and gently glided his lips across my forehead.

We arrived at our floor, and he walked me out. We were holding hands. Pepper and the girls were waiting outside the door, champagne in hand, and Dallas held a fruit-and-cheese platter.

He spun me to him and wrapped his arms around me. "You can't have her," he joked to Pepper.

What was that? My playful tiger? I giggled into his chest, and he half-dipped me and we kissed.

"We just want to make her perfect for you, Robert. I promise to give her back."

He grinned at all three of them then opened the door.

"Here, we brought some bubbly. Stay and share a glass with us before you go down to the boys."

He let them all in and carried me into the suite. "Just practicing," he said, and he let me down. He excused himself and went to our bedroom. He had his garment bag over his arm and a pair of dress shoes in one hand.

"Is that what you are wearing?" I asked, trying to peek.

"Yes." He pulled it away from me, securing my hand.

I laughed. "If I can't see what you are wearing, then you can't see what I am wearing." I rubbed my free hand over his chest. "Please? Pretty, pretty please? Just a little peek?"

He kissed the tip of my nose. "No."

Pepper handed us each a glass of champagne. "Here you go, kids." She raised her glass. "To Robert and Kate, may you both have your 'happily ever after' in your union today. Cheers!"

We all clinked glasses; he kissed me then sipped.

My mother knocked at the door. Robert let her in.

"Robert! Darling, what are you still doing here? James and Mark are waiting for you!"

Pepper took the blame. "I invited him to share a drink with us before we kicked him out."

My mother also came in with a bottle of champagne. "Well then, drink up. We only have two hours to get your bride ready." She looked at her watch. "Less than that. Come on, finish up."

He let out a velvety laugh.

She and the girls went flush.

"Come on, stud, no one's gonna get anything done with you here." I took his glass, patted his ass, gave him a kiss, and tried to push him out the door.

He took me with him and shut the door. "Baby, I'll see you in"—he glanced at his watch—"one hour and forty-five minutes." He tilted my chin up and began kissing me with so much passion, I was feeling a dull ache down below.

He parted our kiss, and I was panting. "For fuck's sakes, baby," he moaned because he was panting too. "I want you badly."

"I know the feeling, stud. I'm just as crazy for you. But the bonus is . . . tonight is our wedding night."

"That's right, kitten. I'm going to have all of you."

My sex clenched at his tone. "You have all of me."

"I still want more."

"You've got it. I surrender to you, my king."

He purred.

My mother opened the door. "Come on, Kate! Time to come back in."

"See you soon, baby." He kissed me once more then released me. I took an unsteady step toward the door. He caught me. "Easy in, baby. Don't break anything."

I laughed. "Got it, stud."

My mother closed the door.

"Quick, let me show you a few more steps to your dance." Pepper brought me back to the bedroom.

My mother was taking the plastic wrapping off my dress. "Wow, where did you find this?"

"At the mall. Wait until you see it on. It fits me perfectly."

"So here are the next four sets of eight count." Pepper brought me back to the task at hand.

Now that I saw them again, I remembered. I had a third of the dance down, and Pepper had me record the rest on my phone so I could take it with me to San Diego. She thought of everything.

The girls all started getting ready. My mother and Dallas curled my hair and pinned it up in an updo with some strands hanging down. I did my makeup, and Pepper brought me another glass of champagne.

"Does this seem real to you, Kate?"

"Yes. I feel like I have been with him forever."

"In reality, it's been only eight days."

"I know. Last night, he wore the same outfit he did on our first date just a week ago, Friday. When I came out of the bathroom and there he was sitting on the bed in it, it hit me that it's only been a friggin' week. But it feels like we have been together forever and that this is meant to be. I don't know. Maybe I'm not explaining it right."

"You explained it perfectly. You both belong together. He is crazy about you. It's kind of overwhelming to see at times. I know you are handling him just fine."

"I miss him. Right now, I miss him. I crave the man body and soul."

"That's the way you're supposed to be when you're in love. I'm happy you found it. I'll do better by you to get along with him and not wind him up so much. I promise."

"Thank you, Pepper. I love you, buddy. Thanks for coming with us this weekend."

"Thanks to your generous husband for footing the bill. He didn't skimp on one detail. We are very well taken care of here. Mark is a little overcome by it, so you can expect a smashing-good wedding gift."

We giggled and clinked glasses.

"OK, I'm ready for the dress."

I put my new white satin push-up bra on and a pair of white lace panties in a style he picked out. Then I slipped on my dress. *Fist pump. Boo ya!* It was sexy hot, falling about five inches above my knee in a stretchy satin material that fitted my body but did not cling.

It was a simple A-frame style that had a slight flair to the bottom so when I twirled, it would circle out a bit. I put my red necklace on and my red pumps. I checked myself in the mirror, and I heard the men down the hall. Pepper was telling Robert I would be right out and to let me make my entrance. I walked out of the bathroom. I grabbed my clutch and put my gloss, cell, and tissues in it. Then I headed into the living room, and everyone gasped.

My mother instantly had tears in her eyes. Pepper came over to me, kissed my cheek, and told me I was beautiful. My fiancé was frozen, taking in every inch of me as I was him in his black tux, white dress shirt, and bow tie. Holy crap, he was so handsome! So sexy, so powerful. My new favorite suit! *Drool!*

He made his way over to me and leaned his head toward mine. "You are so beautiful, baby. I feel like I am stealing Helen of Troy away from the world."

I smiled. "Not stealing. Going very willingly. You look very handsome, by the way. This is definitely my new favorite suit."

He kissed me ever so lightly on the lips.

"Can we get some photos?" Dallas interrupted us.

My mother seconded that. Everyone got his or her camera or phone out. Robert handed his phone to Mark to take some pictures.

"You two look like friggin' models," Pepper added. She took about fifty on her camera. She had us in different poses and angles.

Once Robert touched me, he didn't lose contact with me. There was always some part of him touching me. They took photos of Robert and me with each couple, and then we got a group photo with the timer. Tiger gave it five more minutes and then ordered everyone downstairs.

Before joining them, he closed the door and took both my hands. "Baby, you are making me the most fortunate man on this planet. You look exquisite. I love you more than anyone has loved before. You are my life, my love, and I look forward to filling your every need and desire. I will be proud to call you my wife and serve by your side forever."

"Robert, I will be proud to be your wife. I will also be proud that you are my husband. Thank you for not giving up on me. Thank you for all your love. I will return it with equal passion. I will grant your every desire and need. I am so blessed to have you. I love you, Robert."

He kissed me then kissed me and really kissed me. Once again, we were left panting.

"I've gotta get you out of here before I fuck the daylights out of you. I love the dress."

"I love the tux. Do you have all the stuff we need? Rings, paperwork?"

"All set, kitten, let's go get married." He held my hand. He was simply prideful. People came on to the elevator looking at us and gasped. Jeez, we must have looked really good together. Tiger was an eyeful all on his own. He nodded to them.

The woman spoke. "Hey, are you guys models?"

I giggled.

Robert looked at her. "Yes."

"Oh, that's so cool. Where is the show tonight?"

"White Chapel, east side."

She tried to think of where that was. The guy she was with grinned. "They're getting married, Lynn."

"You're getting married?"

I nodded. Robert tucked me into him.

Then she proceeded to tell everyone who got into the elevator. We received all kinds of well-wishes, along with admiring looks. We reached the ground floor. Tiger took a hold of my hand again, and everyone piled out of the elevator and stood on either side of it, clapping and cheering as we went by. This drew the attention to the whole lobby area.

Our group was waiting in the seating area, amused by the ovation we received. All the way to the entrance, people were cheering, whistling, and congratulating us. I was just mortified and exuding joy at the same moment. Joy won out. Again, there were two limos—one for us and one for them.

We made it to the chapel, and it was just charming. Robert called ahead, and we were met by the owners themselves.

He took my hand and brought me to him. "This is it, baby. You're stuck with me now."

"Just like glue, stud."

He gave me another quick kiss, a little squeeze to my buttocks, and a low purr.

They led us in, and went over the ceremony. It would last about ten minutes, and that's it—we would be married. I set myself up in the back. They gave me a lovely bouquet of flowers. I put on some more lip gloss. Pepper came back and took my purse and took a few photos.

"You really do look like a beautiful bride, Kate."

"I feel like I'm in the clouds. How the heck did I deserve him?"

"You were made for him, my friend. Now come on, let's get you a new last name." She air-kissed both my cheeks then took a position as photographer even though there was one there.

My father took his position beside me. The music started, and they cued us to walk. I was beaming. There was my new husband just a few short steps away. My mother had tears in her eyes, and my sister was smiling brightly. Mark and Dallas had big grins on their faces, and my father was next to me, making sure I got there safely.

We arrived at the end, and my father verbally and physically handed me over to my Robert when asked by a justice of the peace, who was standing up for me. Dad kissed my cheek, and Robert then took my hand and kissed it tenderly. We exchanged our vows, and there was another outer-body experience. I saw everything, including myself.

He then slipped my ring on. I slipped his ring on, and we said our "I do's." And then it was time to kiss the bride. He took my face in his hands and kissed me. Then his arms wrapped around me, and he crushed me to him and dipped me into another kiss.

Pepper took all the shots on her camera. Then Robert gave me his megawatt smile, picked me up, and spun me around while holding down my dress at the bottom.

Everyone rushed over to us. It was a huge group hug from the girls, and he only let me go to pick up my mother and spin her too. He kissed her cheek and put her back down next to my father, who shook his hand and clapped him on the back.

I beamed. I was now, officially, Mrs. Katherine Beckham! We signed the paperwork, and Robert took all our documents. Then he dragged me to the limo, where the champagne was chilling.

"Let's go celebrate!" he announced. He kissed me all over and repeatedly said "mine!" after every part of me he kissed. Then he got on the floor in front of me, lifting my dress. "This is especially only mine."

"You bet, stud, bought and paid for. All yours. No returns or exchanges."

"God, I love these knickers."

"Good. Be gentle with them tonight. I'd like to wear them again for you."

"I'm taking all of you tonight."

"You can have all of me because I belong to all of you now."

He slid me onto his lap. "Yes, you certainly do, wife."

He kissed me, and his hands just didn't know where to begin. He put me back on the seat. "Not now, love. We don't have enough time, and if I stick my dick inside you, it's staying there until the morning."

I giggled as he grabbed the champagne.

He handed me a glass. "To my beautiful wife."

"To my handsome husband."

We clinked our glasses and sipped.

He had me hold his glass a moment as he pulled out his phone. He was texting: "It's official! We are married! Meet the new Mrs. Kate Beckham." He pulled up a photo of both of us in the suite, attached it, and hit SEND.

I was plastered with my smile. "Who did you send that to?"

"Everyone!" He took his glass and turned off his phone then tucked it back in.

We made it to the restaurant, and I was still giddy. He held me to him, with the champagne bottle in one hand and me in the other.

Our group was there ahead of us, all clapping and cheering. Other people got an eyeful and joined in. We were seated right away, and there were three bottles of wine already on the table along with hors d'oeuvres.

Robert and I sat in the center. My sister sat next to Robert, and Dallas sat next to me. Pepper, Mark, and my parents sat opposite. He poured from our champagne bottle, for him and me.

His English accent fell out of him. "Isn't she the most grand wife a fella could have?"

My sister was still, as were everyone sitting across from us. He just tilted my head up and kissed me. Pepper smiled. I cleared my throat as my mother explained his heritage.

"Double score there, Kate Beckham! He can dance, and he has a hot accent!" Dallas declared in admiration.

Robert hadn't realized it came out like that. He just grinned and kissed me again.

The food was amazing. Robert ordered for us after asking if there was anything I fancied. I gave him full control. He did me proud again. Our dish was delicious. He ordered me water in between and told me to drink it because he wanted me to remember everything about tonight, so I did as he requested. Then he poured me some wine. He had a special cake brought out to us, and we got to cut it. I fed him; he fed me. We kissed. This was like the mini version of what was to come next month. I was just beaming.

We were at the restaurant for two hours. Pepper took more photos, and I was so grateful she did. Then we all were ready to go clubbing. My parents left us to do some more exploring of the strip. Mom kissed me then Tiger. Dad kissed me then clapped Tiger on the shoulder. Then my mother reminded me that we still needed to get together and start working on the reception, and we still needed to come by the club. We cancelled our last dinner with all the commotion going on.

Robert promised her that would be top priority when we got back. She was satisfied, and they went in the opposite direction as us.

We took our limo to the club, and the other four took theirs. My parents walked around and assured us they would be fine to get back on their own.

"Should we go change?" I asked.

"No I want everyone to see you in this gorgeous frock."

"What's a frock?"

"Dress, baby. This stunning dress."

There was a huge line, and Robert led us right past everyone to the front. He just looked important, and I was just his slut bride hanging off his arm. I was so happy.

The rest of the entourage followed with attitude. Robert gave his name, and the woman checked him up and down then smiled. She opened the rope, and we were in.

We were holding hands, but he was slightly dragging me because I was a step behind, giggling with Pepper. He spun me into him and gave me a kiss. I was laughing. Then he tucked me under him. My song was on! "Sexy Back." Pepper shook her head no to me, but I started to sway slightly.

Robert ordered champagne and water. We sat at a private booth in the VIP section, and I recognized some athletes and a few celebrities. They were checking us out as well. The next song came on, and we were hitting the dance floor. Mark stayed behind, watching our things.

Robert took off his tux coat and undid his tie just to let it hang. Then he rolled up his sleeve and undid a few buttons . . . *Drool!* My arms were around and down, exploring that strong chest. He was all mine! That's what that piece of paper said.

He took my hand and, with that wicked grin, brought me to the dance floor. Then he did a repeat of dazzling the crowd once again. He spun me into him then pinned my body to his, making me mimic him and his moves. Damn, I looked good! Pepper was videotaping it with her phone. After the second dance, I needed a break. He escorted me back, and we got several praising comments from Tiger's new fan club.

We stayed for another half hour, and Robert leaned into me. "Finish your drink. I want to bury myself into you."

I downed that champagne quicker than a lightning strike.

I turned to him. "Ready!" I was beaming.

The girls made their way back with a trail of admirers. We said our good-byes and reminded them they had a limo out front.

Robert handed them a card in case they got in trouble. Sexy had me around the waist as I hugged the girls, and he tucked me under him with his tux jacket over his arm. I was feeling very happy and light. Tiger was radiating sex when we jumped back in the limo, but he remained very controlled.

"Thank you for such a great day, husband. I will never forget this." I kissed his cheek.

"You are most welcome, Mrs. Beckham." He kissed my hand.

There was the presence of danger about him. Hot, sexy danger! But I remembered his warning, and I followed his cues.

We made it back to our hotel in fifteen minutes. Our driver opened our door. Robert palmed him a hundred as a tip. Then he pulled me to him with my clutch bag in my right hand and my left arm around his lower back.

The elevator ride was slow. I leaned on him, and he kissed my hair. We finally made it to our suite. He picked me up in his arms and carried me over the threshold.

He kicked the door closed and took me right to the bedroom. Then he laid me on the bed.

"Hold that thought, stud, I have to use the bathroom."

He stepped aside but said nothing. I bolted into the bathroom and relieved my bladder. I gave myself a quick wash and pulled up my panties, and down went my dress. Then I jumped back on the bed.

"Ready!"

He grinned. He sat on the bed next to me, caressing my face. "I have waited so long for this moment. I just want to savor it a little longer."

I brought my hand to his and cupped it. Looking right into his eyes, I leaned upward and took his handsome face in my hand. Then I kissed him tenderly. He pulled and lifted me around him onto his lap.

Our kiss intensified. I was feeling my hunger for him. His hand explored my dress. Every curve of me was felt by his commanding hands.

He lifted us off the bed and let my feet meet the floor. He released our kiss and took out my earrings; then he took off my necklace. He placed them on the bedside table.

I noticed the lubrication. Uh-oh, he was going in again. My sex pulsed with just the thought. He kissed me again then brought his mouth down my neck to the end of my bare skin on my shoulder.

He bent his knees and took the bottom of my dress, gathering it up as he pulled it off. He held me by my shoulders and admired my body. "You're really mine?"

"I'm really yours." I caressed his face.

He pulled me to him, wrapping me with his arms. His hands were feeling my backside and venturing into my panties. He moaned as he cupped my buttocks. He pulled my panties down and lifted my calf. He slid one side over my heels and then repeated with the other. He buried his mouth into my sex, taking my tender clit into his lips and sucking it with need. I gasped at the intensity, and he released with a long lick; then he kissed his way back up me. I was panting, fighting the urge not to come right away.

He unhooked my bra. I let it fall to the ground between us. There I stood in front of my new husband, in nothing but my heels.

I began with the rest of the buttons on his shirt and pulled it free from his pants. I guided it off his sumptuous frame then went down to his belt. I unfastened it then brought my hand over his chest, unable to control my wanting to feel him under my hands.

He pulled me into another kiss. I unfastened his pants and bent my knees to guide them off. I pulled his shoe off first then his pant leg. Then the other shoe and his other pant leg. I kissed his length through his silk boxers and pulled them over him and down. I wrapped my hands around him and kissed his tip then took him into my mouth. I twirled my tongue around his head then gave a few strong suckles on just the tip. I released the pressure then took more of him into me, moving my tongue all along him.

He commanded for me to stop and pulled me up to him. Picking me up, he then laid me on the bed. He spread my legs apart and just slid right in all the way to the end. Oh my god, I wasn't ready for all of him, and at that last bit, I gasped. But he was in. He released some of his weight and kissed me.

My hands were at his face, feeling him and returning his passion. He moved slowly at a full-length rhythm, nearly pulling all the way out then plunging back in. Oh my god, he was so intense, and he was rubbing all the right places. I was building up, and he growled low. Then he stopped.

No! Don't stop! I tilted my pelvis in protest. He ground his length into me and thrust deep. He kept up with the tiniest of thrusts, grinding himself against my clitoris. *Holy heck, what was this!* I exploded and I was screaming his name incoherently, cursing and gasping for him to stop.

He moaned at my body exploding around him; then he started to move. Really move. He was slamming with his length, and then he stopped again and flipped me over on all fours. He pulled out of me and shot his load against my anus. I could feel the hot liquid against my skin. He inserted himself back into my sex and began pumping me from behind, building his cock back up. With his left hand still at my waist, he spread his orgasm all around in my crack with his right fingers. It was a warm feeling, and he was gentle but testing. I was igniting once again.

He reached over for the lubrication, and now he was back at full length. It rested against his spot in me. I wanted to feel it, so I began pulsing against him.

"That's right, baby. It's all yours. Take what you want."

I felt the lubrication slide though my crack as he dispersed it over the traces of his orgasm. I backed up to him with more confidence now and started to ride him. I was waiting for him to insert his finger into me. I was craving that feeling again.

He put his right hand around my waist this time and began meeting me thrust for thrust. He tilted himself a little higher, and there it was. I was coming again. He stroked me a few more times and pulled out. I was butter—so relaxed and well fucked.

I heard something I wasn't sure of. Then I felt him against my anus. I was still high from my orgasm. He gave a quick thrust and his head penetrated. I gasped and jumped. He held me in place. My orgasm halted, and he just held me tight and didn't go any further.

"Shh, baby it's OK. Am I hurting you?"

I thought quickly, no. No, it didn't hurt, just an intense pressure. "No."

"I have a condom on, baby. Can I keep going?"

Oh my god, he wanted my permission. "Yes."

"That's my girl." And he pulled back slightly then pushed forward some more.

Oh god! It was so intense! He made a moan as he pulled back and pushed deeper in. He poured some more lubrication on to the condom and rubbed it in. He had me around the waist again. He was halfway. I needed him to stop. I was so full.

My mind and body were confused. "Hang on, honey. I need you to stop."

He growled deep and pulled out almost to the end and slid himself further in. He wasn't stopping! *Oh no!* The feeling was scrambling my mind. He did that again, and this time, my body took over and made the choice. I arched my back and pushed up against him, sending him even further into me.

"That's it, baby! Take all of me! I'm so fucking hard for you!"

A few more thrusts and I was coming uncontrollably, but so was he.

I lost my voice only to hear his piercing growl. He gave me a slight final thrust then pulled himself out. I felt tears running down my cheek. I wasn't aware that I was crying.

He kissed the top of my head and went into the bathroom. I fell into a deep sleep. I woke up tucked into my new husband with his arm securely around me, and I had to pee.

I moved away from him slightly. He pulled me back to him.

"I have to pee."

He let me go, and I scrambled out of bed toward the bathroom. I noticed right away that he had cleaned me and that my butt hurt just a little. *Oh man, he was in me. He was all the way in me!*

I wiped myself and tested the area of my opening. It's all right. I'm OK. I let out a sigh of relief.

I brushed my teeth and climbed back in bed with him. He was watching me cautiously. I turned and wrapped my arm around him. He relaxed and kissed my hair.

"Good morning, wife."

"Good morning, husband."

"Are you all right?"

"Yes. I am all right."

"I love you."

"I love you too."

"Thank you, baby. I couldn't help myself last night. I wanted to claim you."

"And you did. I am yours."

"That you are! How do you feel right now?"

"A little sore and a lot confused."

"Don't be confused, baby. It's just another way of me exploring you and pleasuring you."

"Well, can we save that one for birthdays and anniversaries?"

He let out a laugh. "I have to wait that long in between?"

"OK, Christmas too."

He squeezed me to him. "How about holidays, birthdays, and anniversaries?"

"How about I think that one over!"

He laughed again and rolled me on top of him. "You're so beautiful."

He caressed my face. He rolled me over again, and now he was on top of me. He spread my legs and reached between, guiding his head to the entrance of my sex. I lifted slightly, and he pushed in, kissing me. He moved in and out, and I was responding to him immediately. I wanted him. I wanted all of him. I didn't know what I was doing at the moment, but he moaned into my mouth and picked up the pace. I pulled my legs up and around by his waist.

He broke off the kiss and really pumped into me, gritting his teeth. He stopped and rolled onto his back. Now I was on top of him. I ripped the blankets off my shoulders and dug my feet to the bed on the side of him. He lifted my waist to help, but I didn't need him to. Then I took his hands off and pinned them to the side with mine. I picked up my pace, and he was making these sexy noises from his chest, and I was working his length against that area that only he could reach.

"Come on, baby, I'm not going to last. Give it to me."

And there. His words were my undoing. He grabbed my waist and gave himself another few pumps, and then he pulled me down onto him, emptying himself into me. He was muttering curses along with *wife* included in there.

I collapsed on him, and he wrapped me tight. Too tight. He was squishing me to him.

"My legs, honey. I need to move my legs."

He eased up, and I straightened them against him.

He rolled again so we were both on our sides. He just held me, and I fell back asleep.

I woke up tucked into my husband, facing the other way with his hand stroking up and down my body. I smiled. It felt really nice.

He kissed my shoulder then turned me to him, sealing his lips over mine. "Good morning again, wife."

I giggled. "Déjà vu?"

"I certainly hope so, kitten." And he kissed me again.

"You'll have to feed me this time."

He smiled. "If I must, woman."

I giggled again. "What time is it?"

"Eight twenty."

"Jeez, that's it? I thought it was around noon."

"Almost noon our time, if that makes you feel better."

"It does. Thank you very much."

"Baby, do you want to eat here or downstairs?"

"What time does everyone leave?"

"Their flight back is at two, so the limo picks them up at eleven thirty."

"What time are we leaving?"

"We leave the hotel at five. Our flight is at seven, and it's just an hour to get to San Diego."

"Let's eat downstairs. I want to see them all before they go."

"I'll get your phone, kitten, and send everyone a message for brunch in an hour. Then I'll call downstairs and make the reservation."

I kissed him. "You're the best. I'll start the shower."

"Be right in." He kissed me and headed down the hall all gloriously naked.

It felt so good under that water. Robert slipped in behind me—*ugh, wrong expression! Oh shit! No, no . . . deep breath.* Oh my. My husband arrived in the shower. *Gack!* That act was taking over my mind; then the thought of horror came over me. *Oh no!* His birthday was in a couple of weeks, and I would have to do that again!

Find your happy place! Find your happy place! Double whammy for me. My happy place was him . . . . fuck me! I was screwed! Time to just suck it up and take one for the team.

My mind came back to what was happening right now. There was a whole lot of soap everywhere on my body, and hubby's hands were cleaning every crevice.

Time for my distraction technique. I went to my knees and blew the bejesus out of him—or, rather, sucked. It nearly brought him down. He was out of breath. I rinsed off quickly and soaped him up, rinsed him off, and got the heck out of Dodge. He staggered behind me.

I put on a simple gray miniskirt and my black V-necked tee. He was recovering in the bed. I crawled up next to him. "Come on, stud. Let's go get some food."

He pulled me down to him. "You're so fucking good at that, woman."

"Well, like I said, I'm learning from my master."

He laughed. "I should start teaching sex ed. Then I'll make a bloody fortune."

"I'll make the coffee." I kissed him, and he released me.

A few minutes later, he came out wearing dark cargo shorts and a tight white T-shirt and Converse sneakers. Mother of God! He looked delicious! I handed him a mug, still staring at all the muscles that had been perfectly chiseled onto him.

He smiled. "Like what you see?"

"Definitely!" I kissed him then turned.

He grabbed my wrist, and it stopped my momentum. He yanked me back without spilling a drop and kissed me again. "I love you, wife."

"I love you, husband."

Then he smacked my butt, releasing me.

I took my coffee and followed him to the couch. Peeking through the basket, I pulled out the nuts. I proceeded to feed us both and sat back, bringing my legs under me and to the side. Our phones were right there, and I asked him if anyone got back to him with his announcement.

"Check it out, baby. I shut the phone off before anyone could respond."

I picked up the phone and repositioned myself so we could both look at it. I turned it on: ninety-four messages. "Holy moly, honey!"

He just sipped his coffee and put his arm around me, tucking me into him. He kissed the top of my head. "Everyone knows you're my wife now."

I grinned and opened up the first. One after the other, they went "congratulations," "way to go," and "you both look fantastic." I was so happy.

I straddled him. "I guess they all approve."

"Why wouldn't they? You're perfect."

"Perfect for you, stud."

"You were made for me, baby." He finished his last swig. "Come on, wife, get some shoes on and let's go down and eat."

I kissed him on the forehead and hopped off. I put my sandals on. "Do I need my bag?"

"No, just give me your wallet. I can put it in my pocket."

I handed him my wallet.

"Here, take this too."

I gave him my lip gloss after applying some. He took that too. What a trooper. I bet he would carry my tampons if I asked. I grabbed his hand and bounced my way to the door.

He grinned. "I see I'll have to burn off some of that energy later, kitten."

And I jumped up around him. He scooped me up and placed one hand under my butt then closed the door with the other. I kissed him and kissed him with my arms wrapped around his neck. He held me all the way down the elevator this way then let me down in the lobby.

I heard all the slot machines and grinned. "Did you bring down any of the casino fund?"

"Yup! Got it with me."

"Can I try a slot machine real quick?"

"Of course, baby."

We walked past a whole bunch of them, and I went for the roped-off area at $10 a pull. He handed me a hundred, and I picked the third one to the right. I kissed him quickly and pulled. He grinned at my excitement. It showed 7-7-7-7-7 all across the board, and the lights on top started flashing.

He just looked at me. "Baby, you won!"

"I won? How much did I win?"

An attendant came right over to us, and a crowd started to gather.

"Congratulations, miss, you hit our jackpot!"

Robert was reading the machine. I felt faint, and he scooped me up to him. "*Baby, that's fifty grand!*"

"Are you fucking kidding me?"

"No, baby! You just won *fifty grand*!" And he kissed me.

The attendant reset the machine and asked if we would follow her. Now there was a big crowd.

"Honey, there's still the rest of the hundred in there." He stopped an old guy. "Go play that machine. We have a ninety-dollar balance in there. Good luck."

He thanked us and scurried right over. Robert put me down and tucked me into him. We were almost to the office.

"We're going to be late for brunch. I don't have my phone with me."

"I've got it, baby." He pulled out his phone and hit a number. "Hi, Pepper, it's Robert. Kate just won a jackpot on a slot machine we were passing by. See you shortly. Start without us."

I gave him a puzzled look.

"All set, kitten."

"She has your cell phone number now."

He laughed. "It was only a matter of time anyways, right?"

"Right."

I thought for a second. Did I ever give him her number? I wasn't sure. Oh, who cares? I proceeded to fill out the paperwork.

Twenty minutes later, they handed me a check minus all the taxes. It came to just over $35,000.

Robert shook his head; I was beaming. They gave us a basket filled with jackpot-winner paraphernalia: T-shirt, mugs, key chains, towels, etc.

He carried the basket and stuck the check in his wallet. I held on to him and was giggling all the way to the restaurant. We found the others, and they all cheered.

Pepper stood up. "Well, that's two jackpots in two days."

I laughed and gave her a hug.

My father asked, "So how much did you win?"

"Fifty grand!"

My sister gasped.

Dallas laughed. "No fucking way!"

Robert hugged me. "I knew I picked the right one."

My mother just smiled and shook her head. There were two end seats left. Robert put the basket on one and pulled the other one out. Pepper looked around for another seat.

"Don't bother," he simply said and sat down then put me on his lap. I sat down exactly like him, facing everyone, and he secured his arm around my waist. I shifted over slightly, putting my right arm around him and my legs over his right leg.

The waitress came over and asked if we wanted anything to drink. We both ordered more coffee, and she handed us a menu then mentioned we could go for the buffet. Then she asked if we wanted another chair. We both declined. Robert rubbed the side of my butt with one hand and my legs with the other.

He looked at the menu. "Steak and eggs, baby?"

I grinned. "Perfect!" I kissed him quickly on the lips.

He grinned and closed the menus.

Everyone ordered from the menu instead of the buffet. Dallas ordered a round of mimosas and got carded. We laughed, and that was going to be the joke of our trip.

My sister was pea green with envy. Not only did I get the guy, but I also got the jackpot. She was wise to just sit there. Pepper was watching her too.

The waitress came back with the drinks. My mother asked what time our flight was, so Robert gave her all the information. He also mentioned he had a copy of our itinerary back at the suite for them in case they needed to get a hold of us. My father gave him an approving nod.

Yes, Dad, I married a very responsible man—who has a bit of a kinky side to him, by the way!

Dallas asked, "Where are you guys going?"

I smiled at Robert and let him answer.

"I'm taking my wife to the beach for a few days." He looked at me as he said this. I leaned into him, and he put his arm around me.

"Cool! Which beach?"

"San Diego."

Pepper smiled. "You will be back Friday, right?"

"We will be wrecked Friday," I added.

She laughed but held her tongue.

"Is everybody all packed?" I asked.

Dallas, Pepper, and Stacy all answered no. Mark and my parents answered yes.

I looked at Tiger. "See, I'm not the only one."

"Don't worry, baby. I'll be taking over that job from now on."

I grinned and kissed him again in front of everyone. *Hey, this was getting easy.*

He preened and stretched out a little more in his chair.

Dallas asked, "So what are you two going to do for the next seven hours?"

Before I could answer, Robert looked into my eyes. "Oh, I have a few ideas."

I blushed scarlet and kicked his calf. He let out a velvety laugh then crushed me to him. *Argh! He was so . . . so . . . so . . . exasperating at times.* Everyone awkwardly laughed.

The food came, and it was really good. I finally took my own seat next to Tiger so he could eat without spilling anything on me.

They were huge portions. I couldn't finish it, but my tiger could. He pulled my chair closer to him as he finished my steak. I sat back, rubbing his back, and he really liked that. He grinned over his shoulder a few times at me. When he finished, he stretched back and scooped me up onto his lap again, so I resumed where I was. Everyone just kind of stared for a moment. I don't think they really knew how strong he was, and he lifted me with no effort.

My mother smiled; she knew. He wrapped her in his arms the other day.

Dallas couldn't keep it to herself. "Holy crap, Robert! How much do you bench-press?"

He smiled. "Two hundred thirty pounds."

"Holy smokes!" My sister's mouth just hung open.

Pepper smiled and held Mark's hand.

It was 10:40 a.m. by the time we were done, and we all went up together. Tiger and I invited everyone up to our suite when they were packed so Robert could check them out all at once.

They all made it by eleven fifteen. My mother offered to take a bag home for us. Robert had them take our wedding gear and the red dress back in the garment bag. I guess we were not going anywhere fancy on the beach.

He closed their tab out in the rooms, and we waved good-bye at the limo. We walked the strip some, but it was too friggin' hot. So we checked out a lot of the other hotels and found a nice place to have lunch.

When we arrived back in our suite by one thirty, Robert filled the tub for us to have a Jacuzzi bath. He put some lavender oil in, just like at the spa, and we just soaked. It felt so relaxing. When we were done, he carried me to our bed and proceeded to proclaim his love for me.

I packed everything that was worth packing from our baskets. The nuts, chocolates, our travel kits, and lottery trinkets. We ate everything else. Robert did one last sweep, and I followed behind as well. Ready to rock and roll, I gave him one last kiss and told him how amazing our suite was and how special all of this was. My memories I would cherish forever. He took a picture of us leaving with his phone. I kissed him again, and we left our beautiful suite.

He rolled our big bag, stacked with the duffel and our carry-on bag, on top of one as I rolled just the one medium bag. He tucked me under his arm as we headed for the elevator. We were the only ones in it, and I turned to him, wrapping my arms around his waist and looking up at him.

"Thank you for a memorable, most beautiful wedding weekend."

"You are entirely welcome, my magnificent wife."

I kissed him until the doors opened and more patrons piled in. He reluctantly withdrew. I still hugged him tightly.

We checked out, and he smiled—almost laughed.

"What?"

"My father has added an extra wedding gift."

"What is it?"

"Seems he cancelled my charges and paid for our room."

"No way! Score!"

Then he let out that velvety laugh that caught the attention of the girls behind the desk. One of them blushed.

"With the luck we're having, it's too bad we couldn't get married every year," I said.

He pulled me into him. "I could arrange that."

He kissed my forehead, and I grinned.

Our limo was exactly on time. Next destination: San Diego.

CPSIA information can be obtained at www.ICGtesting.com
Printed in the USA
BVOW08s1157010316

438619BV00001B/3/P

9 781483 617213